NEVER COUNT OUT THE DEAD

ALSO BY
BOSTON TERAN

God Is a Bullet

NEVER COUNT OUT THE DEAD

BOSTON TERAN

ST. MARTIN'S MINOTAUR ☙ NEW YORK

Ter

www.minotaurbooks.com

Library of Congress Cataloging-in-Publication Data

Teran, Boston.
    Never count out the dead / Boston Teran.
      p. cm.
    ISBN 0-312-27115-8
    1. Los Angeles County (Calif.)—Fiction. 2. Miss-
ing persons—Fiction. 3. Sheriffs—Fiction 4. Revenge—Fiction. I. Title.
PS3570.E674 N48 2001
813'.54—dc21

                            2001019153

First Edition: May 2001

10 9 8 7 6 5 4 3 2 1

DEDICATED TO

G.O. ———————— Birdhous-gal
One of life's many Landsharks tryin' to make it work.

and

To the local newspapers of America. The smaller dailies,
weeklies, and giveaways that manage to inform, educate, enlighten,
and entertain with underpaid or unpaid personnel and on
budgets no bigger than the head of a pin.

Thanks for the alternatives.

ACKNOWLEDGMENTS

I would like to thank John Cunningham of St. Martin's Minotaur for the opportunity. To Kelley Ragland of St. Martin's Minotaur for her enthusiastic support, editorial discipline, and earnest hard work. To Mari Evans of MacMillan for her thoughtful advice during the obstacle course known as book publishing. To my agent, David Hale Smith of DHS Literary, who is a master of the term "dedication of purpose." To Seth Robertson of DHS Literary: You are diligent, diligent, diligent.

On a personal note; as always, to Deirdre Stephanie and the late, great Brutarian . . . to Mz. El . . . to B. Kuhl, if it wasn't for our conversation that day on L. Blvd., I would never have the title for this book . . . to Harriett Bara, who made what I thought and wrote look like what I thought and wrote, only better . . . to Constanza and Jinx . . . to Barbie, Don, and Baby Jack (Mega) . . . to Iona Harry . . . to G.G. and L.S. . . . to Janet Wade, for her music clearance . . . and finally, to Nadine Cutright for letting me use her incredible photograph "Alia" as one of the emotional motifs of this work.

Every victory contains the germ of future defeat.

—C. G. JUNG,
Psychological Aspects of the Mother Archetype

PART
ONE

———

THE
ULTIMATUM

ONE

Near midnight and no moon. Alicia Alvarez's thick mouth moves faintly as she tries to calm away her fears. San Frasquito Canyon is the last place in the world she wants to be. Especially now.

Lights from the few scattered ranch houses have no effect upon the landscape, and without a moon the winding ten-mile drive up through a stretch of national forest is a black hole the high-beams can barely eat into. She understands too well why this isolated canyon has been a notorious dumping ground for the murdered.

San Frasquito Canyon connects the northern San Fernando Valley with Lake Hughes and the edge of the high desert. It's where the aqueduct pipes make their iron climb across the mountains to water that urban sprawl known as Los Angeles.

She had begged Charlie not to make her come. With his hearing less than ten days away it was too dangerous. He could be under surveillance. It was a risk to her, to Burgess. It put them all in jeopardy if ever a connection was—

Her headlights rake the trees along a curve. A Gothic structure forms out of the darkness behind them, concrete white and two stories high. Appearing as it does through the black silence causes her to lose her breath until she realizes—it's the Department of Water and Power substation Charlie had given her as a landmark.

She starts to slow. Her high-beams float the ground. San Frasquito bends back and the narrow turnoff on the west side of the road is there just as Charlie said.

She pulls in. The stones under her tires crunch as she comes to a stop. She shuts off her lights. She looks back down the pitched canyon as if, somehow, someone could or might be following her.

Certain there is nothing coming on that black chamber of a road, she turns her attention to the tree-lined cul-de-sac. Charlie had said up that small inlet were a handful of homes owned by the DWP and rented to employees who worked the district.

Without headlights she starts up the road. Around the first turn on the right sits a disheveled California bungalow. That must be where one of Charlie's dealers who works the desert is staying. Just past the bungalow, also on the right, a lineup of attached clapboard garages the DWP uses for storage. She pulls alongside the first as she was told.

Alicia slips out of the car, is morbidly afraid to be seen. She watches, listens. Is met with the tinkling of a mobile from the sagging porch and a single bulb that illuminates a doorway like a dying star. Huge pines overhang everything, making the air cool and damp.

A slight whistle spins her around. A figure smokes beneath a shroud of branches, and waves.

"Charlie . . ."

Her high heels move quietly as they can across the asphalt. She and Charlie Foreman kiss. He is stubble-faced and tired, but there's no mistaking the unkempt anger that has divined more than a few destructive scenarios.

As she is led further back into the trees, Alicia asks, "What's wrong?"

He squares up a look that could drain her blood. "I'm getting ready to eat seven years in stir, okay. What's right?"

"Can't your lawyer—?"

"He works as far as the money goes. I got priors for dealing, remember?!" He flicks his cigarette into the dark, takes her by the arms. "I need to know something, honey. I need to know you're with me."

"Jesus, Charlie, how could—"

"No, I mean like when your ex was practically using your pussy for target practice, till I worked him. Like that, okay?"

"What did I say when we first met? One is the body, the other is the wings. It's still like that."

She holds him, but is afraid. He runs his fingers across the dark skin of her face, then down the thick padding around her ribs. "I don't want to have to do this, okay. I don't like putting you in the middle. But I need you to talk to Ridden, okay. You tell him. . . . He's got to get that indictment off my back."

A dense, malignant feeling starts to fill up her insides. "I don't understand. How can Burgess—?"

"You go to him and that Storey cunt who runs his head. She'll understand better than him. They can work with my people. Even if they have to kill that shitass in Baker. I want the indictment snuffed. I can't do more time, okay? I can't make it. I'll fuckin' disintegrate."

His own muscles are heaving. "You tell Ridden and you tell Storey, okay, if they don't help me I'm going to the District Attorney and . . . trade my ass . . . for that scam being worked on 56th Street."

Alicia's lips go dead white at the thought of having to climb into that nightmare. "Where does that leave me?"

His whittled eyes flash red from whatever he's been smoking and drinking. He reminds her, "One is the body, the other is the wings."

She closes her eyes and leans against his chest. Can smell his raw, sour perspiration. "It's Dee," she says; "I'm afraid of her."

"You tell her, okay. They don't help, or they try any shit on you, and I will mix a killer fuckin' cocktail and pour it down all our throats."

THE TRAP

TWO

Shay Storey sits across the kitchen table from her mother. There is midnight about the windows and traces of damp cling to the glass. She watches as her mother cleans the semiautomatic that will be used for the killing. Shay Storey is just thirteen.

The room is lit only by a small worklamp on the table. Shay's whole future seems articulated in the shadowy arcanum of a mother's face and hands bent to the task of lubricating the firing mechanism of the Parabellum she has laid out in pieces on the milky gray formica.

"Are you following what I'm doing here?"

"I'm watching."

Her mother pushes out from the half light. Her eyes are small dark seeds as she stares into the moon-shaped face of her child. "I didn't ask if you were watchin'. The fuckin' mindless watch. I asked if you were following what I'm doing here. You're gonna have to know how to take one of these apart and put 'em back together yourself. Otherwise, you'll always be at the mercy of some cock with a little attitude."

"I'll learn," says Shay defiantly. . . . "I'll learn."

Dee Storey is a woman for whom everything is done in a blood rush. She takes a hit off a cigarette and bears down on her daughter long enough to make it clear she means to have her way.

Shay can feel her mother filling up the space around her. And then slowly she takes over the space inside Shay. She does it with an unvoiced power, with a simple but deadly call to will. All marked by a look, by a breath. By a pose of determined affection.

"I'm followin' you, Mama. Now go on."

Dee goes back to the task at hand. Her fingers work the weapon into shape with taut, sure moves. Shay watches silently. In her mother's hands the blue-black monster seems almost childlike. Not something to be feared, but a benign trinket of certain construction and design. Not a creation of terror, but something that can be tamed and controlled. Something that one could use to hold sway over the tales that feed on them.

The firing mechanism of this weapon is housed in the backstrap. Hammer, strut, and spring, from cocking lever right on through to the ejector. It's the latest advance in selling efficient death. Clean and ready, Dee pieces the semiautomatic back together.

"It's all falling into play," she says. "No more living through one abortion after another, if we do this right. Lake Piru and your goddamn grandmother . . . are history. Having to sneak to Mexico . . . history. Sleeping in the car in Torreon, surviving on watermelon juice and water, packing tortilla chips and whoring wets . . . all history. Stickin' our asses up into the camera for those sleazebags out in North Hollywood . . . history. Sleepin' in this slab of pink squalor . . . history. We can make it all go away with—"

The ground begins to tremor. Walls, glasses, light fixtures, doors, they all rattle with this unearthly Parkinson's that comes with living along faultlines.

"You think it's another earthquake?"

"Probably just an aftershock," says Dee.

There had been a 5.9 banger that morning centered in Whittier, California, birthplace of one of America's more infamous gangster presidents. The quake had filled eight gravesites and shook down dozens of buildings. The shocks had carried up into L.A., stretching as far as Elysian Hills. One had thrown Shay from her bed.

While they wait for the aftershocks to settle out, Dee's confrontation that afternoon with Alicia begins to feed on all that rage she carries around.

Shay hears her mother mumble, "Fuckin' loser."

Shay is not sure if her mother means her and asks, "Who's a loser . . . me?"

"I'm talkin' about the wetback," says Dee. "She's a gutless shit, and Foreman. . . . He gets busted by some needledick sheriff and they hit us with a goddamn ultimatum like we're—"

The earth begins to settle back and Dee turns to Shay. "Go get my speed and the hair clippers."

"What do you want the hair clippers for?"

"I'm going to shave your head."

"But why?"

" 'Cause I don't want anybody to be able to identify you tomorrow, that's why. Now get the clippers . . ." Shay starts down the hall. "And don't forget my speed."

Dee leans around in her chair and looks out the barred kitchen window. That little stucco piece of pink slab they sleep in is partway up Laguna Avenue, on the slope side of the hill. From there they can see out over the roof of the Sir Palmer Apartments to Echo Park Lake.

Dee looks south toward the skyline of the city, then up Glendale Boulevard to the huge white egg-shaped Angelus Temple, with its white rooftop cross-branded onto the night sky. This neighborhood was part of that long-ago L.A., when they were still selling a protean landscape of climate and quality of life. And all you had to do was plop your ass down for a reasonable price.

You have to go a lot farther out to have all that now.

"Here's the clippers, and your speed."

Shay sets the clippers and vial of pills on the formica. Dee palms two 15-mg amps, reaches for a pint of Southern Comfort on the sink counter, and gets the pills down in a couple of lean swallows.

Shay waits beside her. Dee picks up on the nervous gloom that has settled in and pulls her baby close. They can both feel the cool night air coming off the window glass.

Dee points toward the window. "Ain't we a pair, raggedy girl?"

Shay looks into the glass. Their reflections are marred only by the window bars. Their white skin is a powdery contrast to the dark, dark eyes. Their shiny black hair ephemeral, so ephemeral and black. Their heartshaped mouths, their faces translucent enough as to escape capture in the dewy frame of the window light. Dee birthed Shay when she was only fifteen, and even now, at twenty-eight, she looks more like an older sister.

"We're going to kill a man tomorrow night. . . . It won't be easy, I know. I know . . . and I know you're afraid. It's to be expected. It's alright. I'm some afraid myself, but . . . I have to be able to depend on you, Shay. I have to—"

Two worlds, parent and child, they are eye to eye in the glass, with the lake and its lotus plants and pedal boats for rent as a backdrop, and beyond that graffitied bungalows and dilapidated, avant-garde one-story hideaways etched into a hillside that holds up a skyline which didn't exist fifteen years ago.

Dee runs her hand down Shay's hair. "I'm sorry about havin' to clip off your hair, but it'll grow back." She runs her fingers along her daughter's cheek and across the mouth she shares with her child. Shay can smell the lemon perfume her mother wears and the gun solvent on her fingers. Dee rests her head on Shay's shoulder and closes her eyes. Moments pass. Shay's whole being is naked space and time facing horrid darkness. She watches a slow procession of taillights heading out Glendale Boulevard trawl past the imprint of their features on the glass. Echo Park hipsters on their way to Club Lingerie and low riders out for a little stud humpin'. Then there's the lone black-and-white comin' off the boulevard and doin' the lake with a slow, nasty searchlight.

Down by the freeway overpass there's a wall mural of interracial hip-hop types all running through a series of high-hope schemes. Kids makin' it in all walks of life . . . and playin' by the rules. This whole fantasy is bound up in a spray-painted catchphrase: LIFE IS A MASTER-PIECE TO BE PAINTED . . . OR LOST.

Just a little dream cartoon, Shay thinks, to chase the truth away.

Shay notices her mother's other hand resting in her lap and the fingers running out words in sign language for the deaf, a last vestige of Dee's life at Lake Piru growing up with a violent, hearing-impaired mother.

Shay tries to imagine her own mother as the wild streetwise girl of fourteen who climbed out of hatred and suffering. Whenever Dee is stressed, or the speed turns up the heat on those dusky movie memories that come out of the darkness to hunt her psyche, those finger moves kick up. They got to talk it out, get it out, scream it out.

Shay reaches down and takes the hand in hers. Dee's eyes open.

"Was I talkin' away?"

"Yeah, but it's alright."

Dee stretches up a bit, looks her baby over. "You're stronger than I am. You don't know it yet, but you are."

"I don't think so."

"Oh yeah. You could survive without me. But I couldn't survive without you. You're my lifeline. You are—"

Shay sees Dee shrug off some lingering thought. She whispers to Shay, "Ain't we a pair . . ."

"Wherever we're going . . . we'll make it," answers Shay.

Dee nods, then starts to walk through the black moments of what will be tomorrow night. "Killing someone isn't all there is. It isn't even the hardest part. No. The preparation . . . and the cleaning up afterwards. That has to be done right. The details . . . that's what counts most. The cleaning up afterward . . . yes. That's the difference between escape and discovery. Between dyin' and drivin' on. You have to remember that—"

Shay can see her mother's slateblack eyes swim with liquid fire and she knows the speed is kicking in.

"I'll remember."

THREE

Sheriff John Victor Sully sits in his patrol car just outside the Davenport Motel Coffee Shop and does license checks on the road traffic coming off the interstate at the Baker exit.

Baker, California, is one of those atrocious desert landmarks dry-docked on the northern border of the Mojave National Preserve. It is literally a choke line for traffic running through L.A. and Vegas along I-15.

A town of four hundred survives on a grotesquery of all-night gas stations and tow yards, fast food franchises, and motels. It's home to the infamous Bun Boy Restaurant, whose roadside billboard is about five times bigger than that firetrap of a drive-thru eatery. The best Sully can say about Baker is that, "It's in the wrong place, at the wrong time."

Sully is only twenty-five. He has lived most of his life around Baker. He hates the limits providence has sent him and maintains his responsibilities through delicate hesitation and unanswered dreams. He saw a mother meet death here in '85, and a stepfather this past summer. He cared for both through the failings of their health and now lives in the mobile home left to him in their will. He lives there alone. Sully cannot believe that existence would be bitter enough to bear him along from year to year on the back of license plates he has tagged.

"That's the fuckin' corpse," says Dee.

She points with binoculars. She sits behind the wheel of a parked Cherokee about a hundred yards east of the Davenport by the restrooms of a Shell station.

She passes the binoculars to Shay. There's a bedraggled line of date palms along the perimeter of the station's property that Shay has to focus through. She locks onto the police cruiser as a rig carrying slaughterhouse livestock cuts up the dirt lot and chops off her view. She waits.

The rig passes on, and when the curtainy sand the tires sent up settles out, she spots him.

He is soft-featured, with matty brownish hair that hangs over his forehead. She has now seen more of him than she wished she ever had. A bleeding sunlight off the windshield speaks of coming dusk. The killing is only hours away. Inside her stomach are the first sparrings of nausea.

As a woman steps from the Davenport coffee shop, Shay's mother says, "That one. The fake blonde thing carrying the styrofoam cup . . ." The woman makes for the driver's side of the cruiser. "That's the other sheriff's wife. We don't want nothin' to do with either of them. And don't let that cunt get a look at you—"

Karen Englund hands Sully the styrofoam cup. "Hugh just called so stick around. He needs to talk with you."

Sully just manages the steaming cup through the open window. "On his day off, Hugh's coming over here?"

As he places the cup down on the console so the coffee can cool, Karen notices a snapshot of Sully's parents clipped to the dash.

She points, "Recent addition?"

He nods, then seems to just bundle up into silence.

"You want to come over this weekend and hang out with Hugh and me?"

"I'll be in Barstow this weekend. I've got to meet with the prosecutor on the Foreman hearing."

She leans a little to one side to lure Sully into eye contact, but he makes sure the dashboard gets his full attention.

"You stayed in Baker too long, Sully." He won't look at her. "Did you hear me?" He keeps focused on the dashboard, as if within the sleek black panel Promethean answers were to be found.

"First it was the job," she says. "Then your mother's illness. Then the job again. Then your stepdad. You don't even really like it here."

"The queen of good intentions rocks on," he says.

She scoots down low so he is forced to contend with her presence. "You were always afraid . . ." She can see his cheek muscles tighten. "I don't say this to hurt you. I say it 'cause you're my friend, and Hugh's. And we care for you." His cheeks ratch up a little tighter. "You need to find out what it is you are afraid of. What it is that keeps you here.

You have a college degree. *You* can have a life beyond all those license plates. *You* deserve one."

He wants to think of something hardened and sure to spellbind her with, some comment that cuts across the line of everything she has said, but all he is capable of is gathering in the coffee cup and burning his mouth in a series of short sips.

She watches his little drama, and stands. "Death puts a question mark around all our lives, Sully." She points at the snapshot. "Take advantage of it."

As Shay hands the binoculars back to her mother she catches sight of her alter-image in the windshield. Head shaved, filthy oversized white sweater: It's Thunderdome survivor meets Bonnie-Brae dope-a-thon poster child.

The eyes, though, those gem black coals in the moonplate setting. You don't need a jeweler's loop to rate their fear and panic. It's the total soul showing of a child on the edge of cracking out.

A brown beat-up 240Z swings into the Shell lot. It skirts past the Cherokee and slows. Shay can smell its bum muffler. And the driver, he's a gnawed-down character with a ponytail that you'd swear still has to flash ID to make the bars.

He drives past, honks once. Dee turns to Shay, "Everything is set now—"

Shay watches the Z turn onto Baker and into the opaque expanse of fast food row. "Who was that?"

"He's a coke dealer that runs with Foreman." Dee reaches into the back seat. "I told Alvarez to make sure the fuckboys get into that cop's trailer and drop a little stash on him they could find later." Dee comes away with a rumpled purple baseball cap. "Here . . . wear this too."

While Dee is reaching under the front seat for the Parabellum, Shay says, "Do we have to do this?"

Dee sits up, lays the bagged semiautomatic on the console. Staring at her daughter, Dee's features go from numb to grudging, then she says, "No . . . we don't have to do this. We could call Ridden and tell him we're not into it. To keep the money." Her voice is so calm it further unnerves Shay. "We could say, 'Chill out, Burgess, we're sorry that your whole friggin' life will become landfill, but Shay and I decided . . . *we'd* rather sign up for trade school and become fuckin' yuppie wannabes.' "

What follows is a single burst of caged physicality behind a face gone barbed wire. Shay recoils, figuring she's gonna get a dose, but Dee only rips at the passenger door handle. The door swings open. Shay slips backward. Her mother tries to shove her into the parking lot. "Get out, fry girl!"

Shay wrenches down in her seat so as not to fall head first into the pavement. "What do you mean?"

"I mean I'm gonna do this without you. You're on your own now, fry girl!"

Shay goes completely child. Terror sweeps down into the brakes of muscle and bone. Her face becomes a triangle of darkened eyebrows and anguish. There's a landrush of memories her body still carries in the wake of her mother making her spend a week on the street. The punishment of sleeping by the dumpster behind the Pescado Mogado Grill, being cruised by filthy streetmen, hiding under cars when gang-bangers made the neighborhood scouting up young white targets. Christ almighty—

Her fingers grab at the doorframe and dashboard to keep from being flung upon the world. She cries out, but there is no mercy in her mother. Dee is, at this moment, pure gutter outrage.

Shay's whole body is a summoned course of twisted flesh trying to hold out for a precious few inches of self. "Don't," she begs. "I'm just afraid."

"I've always tried," says Hugh, "to keep a good relationship with you because of Karen. But I have to confront you on something, Sully."

Sully and Hugh stand beside the police cruiser, within feet of the Davenport coffee shop windows. Inside Karen works the register, and watches them talk.

"I don't understand what you mean by 'confront.' "

"The Foreman hearing. In your report you said you did a plate check as this 'Foreman' was coming off the interstate. That he was pumping gas at the Pay-Less on Van Ella when you pulled in and tagged him. Then you did a car search and found five ounces of crack cocaine in the glove compartment, and you hadn't spoken a word to him *until* you asked for his registration and license at the pumps."

"That's pretty close to Bible and verse."

Hugh is a big man. Did some time at Redlands College playing Division III football. Was outside backer in a three four defense. At twenty-eight, Hugh still has it around the shoulders. He is giving Sully the arms-folded, studfucker stance and grave warlord face he usually reserves for hard cases, and it is making Sully very anxious.

"Sully, have you ever . . . or are you now dealing in any kind of narcotic sales?"

Sully's eyes flicker. His first instinct is to glance at Karen. She is behind the register making change. She and Sully trade momentary looks.

"Karen can't help you with an answer, Sully."

Sully comes around. His throat feels like it's closing up to any kind of traffic. "I don't see how anyone could come to this."

"Two reporters called the captain. Foreman's lawyer contends Foreman was coming out of the Burger King when he saw you parked on Community Avenue, in that open lot. You were with a couple of Inland dealers he recognized. And that you followed *him* over to the Pay-Less where he had left his car, and you threatened *him* to forget anything he saw, and when he told you to fuck yourself, you went after him. You looked for a reason to get in his car, and you planted that crack in the glove compartment to ruin his credibility and save your ass with those Inland dealers."

Sully is running through any number of poisoned, fugitive thoughts. He feels like he is being shoved off the edge of the world. "I can hold myself up against this kind of bullshit."

"Can you hold up against a witness?"

Hugh can see Sully has a very bad moment.

" 'Cause there is one. A CalTrans worker coming back from Vegas. He's straight. He was at the Pay-Less pumping gas, and he will testify to what Foreman is saying."

Suddenly, Sully is very, very frightened.

THE
MURDER

FOUR

The high desert autumn air chills Sully's back, yet he is sweating. He leans against the cruiser and sips the last of coffee now gone cold. Inside of him are the first stirrings of raw discord. And rancid disbelief. He looks toward the coffee shop window, but Karen has stepped from the register.

Could there have been some hidden meaning when she said, "Sully, you've stayed too long"? Did she know? Had Hugh cut her in on these insinuations? And that belligerent tone of his. Mr. Desert Prince of Cops. Could heaven and earth be sending him some horrible message?

He barely hears the voice behind him. "Excuse me, sir . . ."

He is not sure if it is a boy or a girl standing there with that shaved head and purple baseball cap. "My aunt's car broke down in the desert . . ." It is a girl. "And she's still with the car."

Sully's voice comes out swimmy and stalled. "Where is she?"

"Indian Springs Trail."

"You walked all these miles?"

"Yeah. I was over at the Shell station . . ." Sully finds himself glancing at the register. ". . . But nobody there could help me. Their tow truck's out . . ." Karen is not back. "My aunt's got a broken leg and . . ." Above the register is a television for people eating at the counter. ". . . And it's gettin' dark outside . . ." One of those smiley-faced reporters is doin' his blurb, pointing to a ruined row of storefronts taken out by the Whittier Quake. "Can you help me?"

Sully knows it ain't just the fucking ground that might be coming undone. His head and stomach double up. "Let's go get your aunt," he says.

As they climb into the car he tries to clear his mind. He does not notice Shay has let the oversized sweater cover her hand so when she takes hold of the door handle she leaves no prints.

"Indian Springs Trail?" he asks.

Now it's her voice that stalls and sinks. "Yeah, Indian Springs . . ."

The cruiser heads south on Death Valley Road, which upon crossing
I-15 becomes Kelbaker. Continuing southeast they enter the preserve.
They embark upon a country of horribly disfigured limestone, of cleft-
tailings and slides. A desiccated landscape of cinder cones and coarse
ravines barren of light, barren of man.

Shay now realizes how cunning her mother is. But for a couple of
highway patrol units working the interstate there are only two sheriff's
deputies to cover an area of Eastern California larger than the state of
Connecticut. One of the sheriffs is off-shift, the other. . . . He stares
straight into a matchless dark only minutes from his death.

And she is leading him to it. Child and stranger. Stranger and child.
Down through fired dimensions of lavaed rock and sand. The terrible
country where no scream can be heard.

Shay has a blunt desire to run, fearing the best she can hope for is
that somewhere in the future all this might be nothing more than the
dark breath of some dream she can wake from, to forget.

Everything bad possible has found its voice within Sully's head.
From ear to ear his mind has been slit apart. He knows what Karen
said is true. The queen of good intentions is blessed with sensing the
familiar sorrows.

Yes, Sully knows he is afraid and that he carries the fear around
with him like someone would an old photograph in a wallet. That he
lacks the confidence to move on, his only safety being inside the shell
of that police cruiser. Reality is an open wound that can bleed you to
death.

But this Foreman thing—

It seems there is always a Rubicon to cross, or to drown in. They
reach Indian Springs Road, and Sully brings the cruiser to a stop. That
lake of a desert has become a shoreless plain he looks into. "I don't see
any lights," he says. "How far down is she?"

"My aunt went pretty far."

"You walked a long way . . ."

She hesitates. "It didn't seem so long."

For the first time Sully hears the girl, and the trepidation he picks
up in her voice he mistakes for honest emotion.

Sully clicks on the police radio. He calls headquarters in Barstow. Dee had told Shay this would happen and not to let any wild or headlong thoughts freak her. Shay tries to keep her breaths even as she stares into scars of moonlight along the engine hood.

This far out into the Mojave the radio crackles. He explains where he is, and what he is doing there. What follows is a long interpretive silence, then a voice cautioning him on the state of the road.

He puts the cruiser into gear and works the gas. Indian Springs Trail is nothing more than an alluvial hollow that grinds up gravel and sand under the skirting tires. They snake past dunes the wind has collected and everything is exposed to the cold and dark. Everything.

"What in the world was your aunt doing out this far?"

"She's . . . a nature freak. We were driving in from Arizona to see my grandfather. He just got out of the hospital. My aunt . . . she had to have her desert fix."

Shay has rehearsed this little scenario so many times it sounds almost real, even to her. Sully listens, and believes.

The headlights surge then swamp with the grim contours of the land. As the cruiser bobs and sways Shay can feel the shotgun beside her canted up in the console rack. The heat is on inside the car, yet she is shivering.

To the east the mottled earth climbs toward Devil's Playground, to the west the brecciated ridge teeth of the Providence Mountains stand out against the faint light of the casinos on the Nevada border. But the world around those headlights, that pitched tunnel of night, has taken on the blue-black casement of the semiautomatic that will tear this man's life apart.

To get away from the barrel of that shotgun she presses against the door and keeps close check on her face and eyes under the purple cap. She lives out a silent monologue. Pretend this is just a secret. A petty concealment that won't outlast the night. A private mystery the weight of nothing in the world. Tell yourself how much of this is your mother.

From stark desolation, headlights signal. Ill-shaped against the cavernous dark. They flash on, they flash off. They flash on again.

"There she is," says Sully.

He points. Shay nods. She is passing through the last hours of her youth as evening star headlights guide them toward a manger grave. Toward the moment of skulls.

They drive through a scant relief of rock formations huddled along the roadside like denizens of some scriptured hell about to strike. Huge, girded shapes the cruiser's headlights can hardly fill.

The roadway cuts an angle into a caked wash, and there's the Cherokee. Shay buckles down everything inside her as the cruiser slows, then stops some fifty feet back of the vehicle. Dust off the tires trains skyward across yards of high-beam, and the cruiser door opens. Out steps Sully, and Shay delays and delays and delays, then he calls out, "Ma'am—"

The word clings to the chilly darkness before it dissolves. Shay steps out of the cruiser. As her heartshaped mouth fills with cold, Sully looks the Cherokee over for the woman, and calls out again, "Ma'am—"

The only answer to come back is wind-tilted silence.

Sully turns and looks to Shay. "Where did she . . . ?"

He sees Shay is trembling. He sees her head move from side to side like a candle flame searching the darkness, and she is stepping backward, backward, backward—

Suddenly the voice locks in his jaw around the word . . . *trap*.

Sully's body kickstarts through the moment at a warning in mortal sounds behind him: boots quickly chopping through crusted ground, followed by the metal trigger snap of a semiautomatic.

Sully spins around. He sees a force in the shape of a woman pointing a gun cross through the high-beams. A battery of trained reflexes goes into motion. He tries for his revolv—

The dark is struck apart by a flashfire of orange vapor. Sully is thrown back up into the Cherokee liftgate. The shot crushes through his pelvis. Shay screams and crabs down into the sand alongside the cruiser.

Sully hangs against the tailgate, helpless . . . a thought in panic. . . . What have I done . . . ? His hand spasms at the holster clip. I'm the wrong man. . . . A closer flash of orange nightfire and the tailgate window explodes. . . . It can't be . . .

Shay watches the body fall in a strange slow motion of wrong directions at one time. Through the blackboard night her mother charges in. Shay can hear her breaths grunt. The alpha bitch is gettin' ready to obit Mr. Faceless.

Shay can feel the concussion of shot three all the way down into her ribs. The shot tears through Sully's back, tears a burning metal road dead-on through his right lung. His mouth snaps open as if to spit out the shock of what has hit him. A burst of blood scatters past his teeth and lips as he staggers around the side of the Cherokee.

Shay can't take her eyes off that five feet of ground that will be the kill-zone. She can feel her insides sick-swim with bile.

Dee comes charging around the Cherokee expecting to face the washed-up carcass of a dead man. Of a life going gravebound slack.

But the dying memory of life, that adrenal hot needle to the heart, that fuckin' gut engine that fires up the last of human strength is still at play. Sully climbs upright, using bumper and door handle. He wavers, but turns to face what aims to kill him. To go cougar on what intends to take him out.

And with all that's left, with a mouth full of blood and a head swimming in the broken remains of what's precious, double desperate and doubling down, he bets on one lunge.

Shay sees it first. Sees it before her mother does. She wants to scream. To warn her. But doesn't, can't, won't.

Sully lunges. And Dee charges headlong into it—

The whole desert becomes a deathbed of screaming mouths and eyes gone electrocuted wide. There is a shot that goes wild, and a gun lost when the two bodies collide. They hard tumble to the earth locked in a death grip. Man and woman. Killer and cop. Alpha bitch and Mr. Faceless.

The killing has taken a right turn at the moment of impact. Boots cudgel dust, interknit with flailing arms. Hands rake chests and throats. It is the manifest language of human violence.

Dee screams to her daughter for help. Screams for her to get the gun and kill him. Sully tries to sink his teeth into Dee's throat. To get his teeth into her pale white flesh. To gore apart the main vein.

Shay can hear her mother, but can't move. The fear cuts through the hard earth of her being; still she doesn't move.

It is the reign of hell in faces she is left with. The wrenched and tortured angles of the desperate undertow of her mother trying to claw and crawl, crawl and claw her way clear to a rock she can see at the edge of her grasp.

Dee can feel Sully's hot bloody mouth at her throat. He is dragging up the last of his strength. Uses one fist as a bear knife to stab her into unconsciousness and the other as a vise under her jaw to hold the thread of her neck in place for his teeth.

She thrashes her head from side to side. She screams to her daughter to get the gun and kill him . . . get the fuckin' gun and wipe him out. . . .

Shay wants to, but can't.

It is a shivering wail that tells Shay her mother might be killed. A fierce desperate cry that shocks her back from some abyss. Shay begins to crawl toward the gun, to crawl toward the dust whirl around the volcanic thrashings.

Shay can see the Parabellum lying there in the cold ashy sand. She digs out the inches toward it as Dee feels the teeth lock into her flesh.

There is no time, and Shay can't find that hidden place to give her arm the courage to grab the weapon and fire. Dee can see her child there, frozen, kneeling in the sand, looking face down at the weapon. Dee can feel herself slipping, weakening, weakening—

But the memory of dying life is her own adrenal hot needle to the heart, that fuckin' gut engine firing up the last of human strength, to keep the body in play. And with what she's got left, she gets her fingers around the cold stone.

One swing. One. The scabbard gray bludgeon lands a clean blow to his nose and skull. Everything inside Sully's head lights. Burns. Then goes black.

Dee rolls him over, drags herself from his grip like a caught beast from a trap. She turns to and on her daughter. She grabs Shay and lifts her. "You goddamn fuckin' coward. You goddamn frightened little—"

She throws all her panic into her rage. Shay covers herself up so she won't be hit. "We got to get out of here," she pleads. "We got to move . . . now!!"

Dee tries to compose herself. To kick off the adrenaline and speed. To clear out the black blind rush of killing so she can clear this all up right.

Her face is covered with Sully's blood. She gasps to get oxygen deep into her lungs. Pull it all in, she tells herself. Pull it in. . . . Shit!

She turns to her daughter. "Get the fuckin' shovel." She shoves her, "Go on!"

THE BURIAL

FIVE

They pull him by the legs toward the shallow grave. With arms out-
flung, he is like the tail of some great beast leaving a dragline across
the continent. At the edge of the hole they kneel and shove the body
up a lip of cakey sand they have dug from the earth.

The body rises. They are poisoned with exhaustion and weakening.
Sully's motionless body hangs on the cusp of the hole. They have to
grunt out the last few inches. Dee screams, "Push!!!"

Her voice is a stark-raving naked command to will it done. The
sand gives, and the soft flesh rolls down, taking a landslide of grit with
it, and thuds against the lee side of the hole.

Still gasping, Dee stands. She grabs Shay. "Fill in the hole . . . I got
to . . ." she gasps again, ". . . make sure we didn't leave . . ." she wipes
at the spit that has clotted up in foamy blotches around her mouth,
". . . nothin' in that fight that can . . . they can . . ." she grabs a shovel,
gives it to Shay, ". . . get us with."

Shovel in hand Shay stands alone. Her mother runs back to the
vehicles. Shay's throat feels like leather as she begins to shoulder-throw
in the dirt. The high-beams of the cruiser cast bare slants of light across
her back, across the hole, and before Dee shuts them off, in that lingering timeless instant, through scant motes of ghostly haze, Shay sees
his chest heave.

Her eyes flinch, then tighten to make sure this is not some mad
mirage. She leans down toward the grave and sees blood oozing from
Sully's nose, and the nostrils pluck and pinch for air.

Her eyes, that outpost to the brain, snap shut. They cannot bear to
see. Wild and reckless afraid, she begins to throw the dirt in. Throw it
in. The shovel clicks against the rock like bone shards tossed as dice
would click on stone.

She can't get the hole closed fast enough, on the chance her mother
comes back and sees, and blames her. Comes back and makes her

daughter prove herself by killing the defenseless object that was once a man.

Pretend this is just a secret, Shay tells herself again and again. Like when you posed naked with little yellow flowers, and spread your legs so grown men could photograph your hairless, young pussy. Pretend it's another secret, just like that.

With each toss of earth, a hole inside her opens up as the one beside her closes. The fear in one to become partner with the other. She pants and shovels blind, covering up that shadow poem of butchered life.

THE ESCAPE

SIX

————

The click of shovel on rock grows dimmer. The earth itself is raining down on him. And he is bleeding back into that very earth from which he came. The short voyage of life is almost over. He'll be docking soon at the limits of existence.

The ground itself is a strangling cold through which he can feel—

Yes, in the starless reaches of his skull something unnameable surfaces. Something more than fear. His lungs rack with pain as if a heated metal serpent with razored skin were dragging through the coiled recesses of his soon-to-be-corpse.

That something unnameable comes out of his own darkness, and his parents' faces wrap around his heart. He can hear the breathing of their last days commingle with his own.

How hungry he was to outlive that. To outlive the mobile home and Baker, California. To survive the police cruiser and the simple generosity with which his mother and stepfather warned the world was too vast, too harsh, and too unstable for him.

"Yes, you're better off where you are, son."

He carries the scars of that something unnameable around his throat, and chokes. The dirt his lungs take in gags him and his body shunts as if the very dirt itself were trying to stir him.

Death has no partners and seeks out the slender dares we pitch against it. It means to have the world, and not by halves.

But something incarnate wills his fingers to move. To make them caterpillar out the sand. To burrow through the cindered clay in search of night.

But which way is up? Which way is home? There are no signposts here, nothing that can articulate a horizon except the need to breathe.

He pushes through the pain to outlive what is no premonition, no dream. He pushes through the pain to get the full weight of the earth off him.

In that deep brown feral ocean he sees his mother walking down the Boulevard of Dreams. A desert road leading to where, if you eat right and think right and live right . . . it will be alright.

But it isn't. And there is no mercy for the kind. We are all strapped to the sky as it caves in on the unsuspecting.

I don't want to die—

He hears the words stillborn inside him as his fingers move and curl, tracing out a map of escape through the broken sediment.

They pluck and push. The ground gives and gives, then gives away. The flesh has periscoped through to the chilling desert air. He can feel the cold of it all the way down inside him. It almost burns.

He makes a fist, a weak fist, and begins to arm wrestle with the caked sand. He is cracking holes in the soft ground cover of his grave. He can hear a car engine rev and burn, and the earth near his tomb tremors as the Cherokee races up the wash and away.

His blind hand finds rock. He grapple-hooks it as best he can, and begins to pull. He pulls and pulls. He pulls himself like an ox dragging a wagonload of bloody man through mud.

Grating against his tongue is the agony of sound his wounds have made of him. But he keeps rising. The earth opens like a careless broken egg around his head. His eyes can see blearily past a battered, broken nose.

The car radio—

The moon and unseen creatures watch him use his elbows as picket pins to score out foot after foot.

The car radio—

He claws his way through twenty miles' worth of twenty feet, leaving another dragline of blood in the same tracks he made when they pulled him toward the burial hole.

He is coming back for more.

He reaches the cruiser. The driver door hangs open. He starts to climb from floor to door handle to seat. The leather creaks and his head swoons from the height. Blood from his nose and mouth leaks down his face and chin. He can see it spotting the leather seatcover as he holds on and hits the radio switch.

He is so far out, it crackles. The voice at the other end can hardly be deciphered. He gets his face as close as he can to speak. His words are hung on the barest thread of sound.

"Officer down . . . officer down. . . ."

SEVEN

———

Based on the criteria that L.A. is famous for when it comes to notions of human happiness, Burgess Ridden should be one happy fuck.

He is second-generation Studio City going on twenty-five. Schooled at The Oakes, he was properly pampered in the arts and self-expression while given the lax read on personal responsibility. He's got enough looks to blow past the usual character shortcomings. He owns his own home, and if that Eleventh District mortgage gets a little nasty from time to time, his parents beam Captain Checkbook down from the Starship Iredell, which is where their three-quarter-acre homestead hovers just off Laurel Canyon three blocks from the Gene Autrey estate.

His parents call and invite him to dinner. It's a little pre-celebration, celebration for popping his cherry on a business deal they could be proud of.

They warn it's nothing fancy—the dinner, that is—just a couple of hors d'oeuvres and entrées delivered from La Serre, one of the more elegant bistros in the Valley.

His parents use their smoothest pressure tactics to get him to take that ten-minute fly over Coldwater, but he works a beautifully contrived blowoff. It's all crème de la crème bullshit about how he's got to make sure his Los Angeles Unified School District package for the 56th Street School project is neatly wrapped. That the filings are stet, and then some, so this deal goes down smooth and clean with the city.

After he gets them off the phone he lingers in the hallway outside his den. There are no lights on except for the flash shadows on the wall across from the television, which is spotted up to the news. The sound is off, so the hallway and den are just an eerie mood piece of oddly colored lightning cuts as the news goes from shot to shot.

The truth is Burgess Ridden is in no fucking shape to take that ten-minute fly over Coldwater. He's got all he can handle right there keeping a lockdown on his emotions while he waits for word about the murder.

———

Burgess lives in Franklin Canyon, which backs up to Mulholland Drive on the Beverly Hills P.O. Box side of the city. It's a late eighties stronghold of BMWs, nature trails, and Golden Labs. The only blemish on the place, which was once part of the Doheny Estates, was the occasional corpse the Hillside Strangler quietly trashed in the grass along the dirt and asphalt roadway that led to the reservoir.

Of course, tonight may change all that. Burgess may add a little infamy of his own to L.A. murder folklore.

To try and keep the tension of waiting for Dee from getting too toxic he goes out onto his deck and smokes. The couple one house down from him in the canyon are having a birthday party on their patio.

They're part of cutting-edge television. She's a boutique literary agent and he's a network executive. He's also an Allman Brothers freak and they're doing the whole catalogue of classics tonight.

Burgess leans against the redwood decking, and up through a channelway of trees come those cool Southern slide guitars. All Dickey Betts and Greg Allman: *Pick up your gear and gypsy roam. . . .*

Burgess listens to those burned voices and knows they don't have anything in common with the young successes bullshitting each other under gas jets and golden lamps.

He knows it's all the polite slice and dice down there. A neurotic bout of patio manners working the what's-in-it-for-me. Self-aggrandizement distilled to a new level. To himself, he's no less kind. He knows when he signs as who he is, it will be the classic signature of a selfish willful money worshipper willing to discard a few extra social trappings to close a deal.

Those nerve endings have begun to implode waiting for word when headlights coming up the canyon catch his eye. They flicker then disappear with the trees following the curve of Beverly up toward Desford. The way those headlights are booting it, this could be ground zero. When a kicked around Granada pulls up in front of the house, Burgess knows.

The house's garage and high wooden fence face the street. Dee gets out, takes a gym bag from the trunk, and orders Shay inside. Shay follows her mother's fast half steps through a gate, across a small bricked garden, and into the garage back door.

This is one of those houses built partly against the hillface so the bottom floor serves as a basement of sorts. Off the garage is a small indoor atrium with a stairwell leading to the main floor. Beyond the stairwell is a bedroom and bath.

Dee shoves Shay towards the bedroom. "Go change. Take your clothes and dump them in that plastic bag that's in the gym bag. And shower. Scrub yourself down good!"

Dee turns. Shay is gamy and pale, and calls out, "Mom . . . don't leave me down here—"

Dee blows her off with a hand motion and is halfway up the stairs when she sees Burgess holding in the dark on the top landing.

"Well?"

She doesn't respond. She just keeps on up the stairs. He isn't sure if making him wait for an answer is one of her nasty little throws of power, or if she's just fucking plain burned down.

When she's beside him in the dark he reaches out to her and asks again, "Well?"

"Be careful," she says, "I still might have a little blood on me."

His hand pulls back almost autonomically on the word "blood."

She starts for a small alcove bar beside the den to hunt herself up a drink. She pours a Coke glass worth of Southern Comfort. "I can feel a crash comin' on."

Burgess approaches her. "The Cherokee taken care of?"

"The last I saw it was no bigger than a package of pressed meat."

She drinks. Her swallows are gulped. Burgess is behind her now. As she comes around . . . a distant grimace.

For the first time he has a real look at her thanks to the bounce of light from the television off the hallway wall. His eyes do frenetic jumps from the blood-caked corners of her nose, to the skewered swollen mouth, to the ghastly discolored oval of teeth marks across her neck.

Her jaw tightens slightly at the sight of him staring at her throat. "The son of a bitch didn't die easy."

EIGHT

Shay stands in the shower staring down at her feet. At the water washing the dirt and sand down her legs, down the small lip of pubic hair, down the perch of her nipples. She stands there in the stream on the verge of womanhood possessed by one unwanted vision.

She squats and holds her arms across her knees. The pink tiles are much too bright. She closes her eyes, and she tries to find the silence of some lightless mind alley to hide in. The water beats down on her back. It is so hot it scalds the skin, but she uses the pain to override the sight of that phantom chest as it fought through a breath, as the nostrils pulsed like the heart of some tiny, helpless creature.

Above her voices, above her footsteps. A tiny helpless creature . . . Why that one image? Her fingernails bite into the skin of her thighs as a phone in the bedroom rings.

Burgess grabs the cordless beside the bar. Hearing his father's voice, he leans into the den doorframe, "Dad . . . what's going on?"

"I'm alone upstairs." His father's voice is unusually low, cautious. "The money I gave you to take care of that paperwork. It's taken care of, right?"

Burgess turns away from Dee as if this might keep her from picking up any weakness in his voice. He can only imagine if his father found out quite how far this has all gone. He closes his eyes. "It's taken care of."

"Are you sure, son?"

Dee watches Burgess, framed in the doorway. She reads how he keels a bit under pressure. The television lightning flashes the wall behind him with cobalt blue, then yellow, then back to cobalt blue.

"I'm sure, Dad."

Before he can finish, Burgess' mother invades the background and asks who his father is talking with. While Burgess wades through his father's ploy about "I was just seeing if *your* son wanted a little care package from La Serre sent over . . ." he notices the television screen has become a cobalt blue flashcard that reads: BREAKING NEWS.

As his mother's voice virtually flutters with the idea of having food driven over the hill, the news cuts to a reporter in a windy hospital parking lot beside the flashing red hoodlight on a police cruiser. But the one detail that can open his gut is a sign above the Emergency Room door that reads: BARSTOW COMMUNITY HOSPITAL.

Well, Barstow is an I-15 soulmate of Baker, California. Just one quick beer west of the murder site, so he grabs the remote. He gets the volume up enough to hear the reporter say:

"A sheriff was critically wounded tonight and buried in a shallow grave in the Mojave National Preserve—"

Burgess pivots on his heels in panic. Guards the phone mouthpiece. Snaps his fingers for Dee. Points to the television. All the while Burgess goes through a little family ping-pong chatter about how he's not hungry and waits while his father passes on to his mother he's not hungry and his mother makes sure his father reminds him one more time how proud they are of their son's achievement. Then Burgess hangs the fuck up.

Silent in the doorway, side by side, Dee and Burgess listen as a senior officer is questioned on early reports the attempted murder had all the makings of an Inland Empire drug war hit. A pure-execution type takedown against one of their own. The senior officer works his way around any real comment on the facts.

Burgess stares at Dee. His features are carried on a wave of bone chilling reality that the sheriff isn't dead. Hers are a cold loathing that this could even have happened.

Burgess screams at her, "You left that fuck alive!"

As her mother's boots stalk across the bedroom ceiling after Burgess, Shay looks up. She can hear the white upheaval of voices that rise to mouthfuls of anger. Still wet, she slips on a T-shirt and starts like some slight, frightened bird toward the hall.

Her damp feet leave marks on the carpet through to the atrium. She slides under the slat stairwell to hide and listen as the fighting swills down through the open black skylight of the living room.

"If he survives, we're totally done."

"If he survives," Dee kicks back, "they'll find out he was nothing but a desert shit drug peddler comin' on like Mister Decent. He's finished either way. Right. . . . Right?!"

Burgess drops down on the couch. In the dark the whole room is like some dead gray street that starts nowhere and proceeds on to even less. "Of all the men in Los Angeles Alvarez could have hooked up with, she had to pick Foreman."

Dee kneels in front of Burgess. "Don't go clit on me."

"Of all the people I needed to hook up with to make all this work, it had to be Alvarez."

"Burgess, don't-go-fucking-clit-on-me!"

He isn't hearing. He sits there like some toked out flatliner whose mouth is a white constant sea of clenched teeth.

"Burgess, I'm not gonna let you sit there like one of your Jew clit friends who can only rant or coma out when things get ugly."

"Shut up with that!" His arm and fist take up the pure bare hitting pose. "You like to stick me with that 'cause my mother's Jewish and you think I'm some wimp-ass." He pushes himself up and knees her in the chest.

"Clit."

"Fuck you." He starts back for the den. "You wanted to handle this yourself. For the money, remember. It's your fault he's alive. And if he makes it he might be able to identify you . . . or *Shay*. Think what that means. How are we . . . *you* . . . gonna handle that?"

Under a lightless stairwell Shay can feel the body climbing from the crypt inside her mother's eyes, small and black and deadly, blaming her. Blaming her for not getting that gun. Blaming her for not having what it takes to kill.

Her mother will know. Even in the perfect silence of a lie, she will know. She will be able to read the least flickering emotion, the least substanceless shadow of movement to a question. It will be a useless ballet to try to beat her at the game. Mother is lioness, child is lamb. And how could any helpless creature be forgiven when their weaknesses are too numerous to name.

———

Burgess is back in the den doorway, braced there, trying to bear through the tail end of the news:

> *The Barstow sheriff's office reports Deputy Sully had called in shortly before the attempted murder and was in the process of taking a female hitchhiker back to a family member waiting with a vehicle that had broken down somewhere in the preserve. But . . . at this point there is no confirmation, other than the report, and so far . . . no witnesses!*

"By morning they'll know exactly who he is," says Dee.

Burgess turns to her. She is exhausted and on a speed burnout, but there is a contemptible sting about the eyes. She gets a little more Southern Comfort in her and waits for his reply. When she doesn't get one, she kicks in with, "Right. . . . Right?!"

Inside his head Burgess manages what approximates a note of confidence, but then just blurts, "If my father finds out how I lied to him. How far things went. How I fucked up—"

She slams her glass down and grabs him around the shoulders. "A drug-peddling cop has been taken in a hit. For real. And that's what they're gonna get around to come morning. That's the lean, freethinkin' truth of how it was fuckin' done."

Burgess hacks loose from her grip. "Yeah, but he's still alive, and *until* he's dead, we could be."

Her mother is gonna make her pay. Shay knows. It'll start with those mad locomotive hand movements, and then watch out, who knows.

She might end up like one of the fuckers her mother is always talkin' about who are working their way through eternity as lampshades 'cause someone had it in for them.

Dee watches Burgess slide down to the floor, his back against the doorjamb. He hits the television remote, blows off the sound. From Hollywood central, one house down, the Allman Brothers are going at it. *I'm no angel . . . I'm no stranger to—*

Burgess crams his head between a set of fists. Dee can see he's startin' to freak. Takin' the thought road down through the terrible country of helplessness, guilt and fear. There's no white line there, either. Not one to guide you, not one to snort. It's all just gray shadows and a cell door that sounds like a gunshot as it slams shut across the heartland of your skull.

Dee gets down, gets in his face. Gets in close enough she can inhale his panic. "Look at me, Burgess. See me. See my face. Look! See those marks." She holds him so he can't escape a hard close-up of her wounds. She holds him like some street guru trying to heal an alkie loser, and says, "This is what killing demands. I'm sorry, but it's fuckin' real. So don't go white-bread citizen on me now. We're still in control here. You and me."

"I'm just slightly fuckin' freaked, okay?"

He pulls loose again. He is breathing heavily.

"Remember," she says, "when I was bartendin' down at the Blue Flame and the Pistol Dawn and you were sittin' in the Nu-Art every night like some fuck zombie 'cause your life was nowhere? And you'd come into the bars and get loaded and complain to me how all your yuppie friends were scoring? Who got you on track, Burgess? Who?"

"You did."

"And when you were plotting out this deal it was in my bedroom and my kitchen, and who was there all the way to help you?"

"You."

"Who took care of Tills?"

He closes his eyes on that one. "You."

"When Alvarez proved to be a screw-up who went and got Foreman his lawyer? Who got it together to try and clean this mess? Who carried all that forged paperwork for you?"

"You."

"Fuckin' ass right. I been more family to you than—"

"I just didn't expect to turn on the news and find out he was still alive. How could it happen?"

She is rheumy-eyed and tired and needs another little Black Beauty to light a burn in her, 'cause there's still a lot of little messes around the edges of this "attempted" murder that have to be dealt with. She still has a pretty good idea on why the sheriff's still alive, but she's wily enough not to let on to Burgess.

"He wasn't breathing," she answers, "when I shoveled him under."
She stands.

"What if he can identify you?"

"We made a promise when we started. I take the heat, you take care of Shay. They could open me up like a goddamn piñata and I will protect you as long as you protect her. You fail that—"

"Of course I'll take care of Shay. What are we talking about here? And I don't want anything to happen to you either. Jesus, it'll be alright." But then, "What if he can identify her?"

Dee takes one last drink of Southern Comfort. She puts the glass down. Her fingers twitch through a thought.

"No one will be able to find her. Not where she's goin'."

NINE

———

Dee is down the stairwell so fast she catches Shay trying to steal across the atrium. Her eyes ride Shay hard, "Be in the car in two minutes. And don't forget the plastic bag with your clothes in it."

"Where are we going?"

"Don't ask questions, Shay. Not tonight. I got a head full of bad ideas, girl, so don't push me!"

Shay runs back to the bedroom. Dee waits on the stairs for Burgess. Once beside her, she turns. He's doing his best to work up a real gut check.

"Where are you taking her?"

"Better you don't know."

Worried suddenly, he asks, "Dee?"

She won't be questioned or cornered, and says only, "Better you don't know, Burgess. So don't ask."

He tries to read into that settled razorous stare, but can't. She stretches out and kisses him before she goes, working her swollen sore mouth against his own with a coarse sexuality.

In a show of tenderness she leans back and wipes gently at his mouth with the length of a finger: "You got a little of my blood on you."

Burgess is sitting at the bottom of the stairs when Shay crosses back through the atrium. She moves like a heart-dragging castaway; gym bag in one hand, pulling the plastic bag with the other.

She stops, then asks, "Am I gonna be alright?"

The grave begging behind that question and all he can manage to whisper is, "It'll be alright."

"Yeah . . . alright." Her voice sounds like it's fighting its way up through thorns. She stands there slumping.

Burgess gets up and holds her. He tries to imagine having to face his own father as he runs his hands softly down her back and whispers again, "It'll be alright, honey."

Dee takes Sunset Boulevard to the 405, then starts burning oil south. The drive is black ugly silence with the windows cranked open and the cold blowing in 'cause Dee is already starting to sweat-pump from the speed she popped back up there in Yuppieville Canyon.

From LAX to Long Beach the silence is compounded by her mother's hot-skillet breathing, and Shay's brain begins to boil with visions of a murder replayed by nightmares shaped as humans.

Her mind kicks back into the conversation she overheard. What if the policeman lives? What if he *can* identify her? What if they find her? What if they try and turn her against her own mother?

Things start jamming up inside Shay's head. A cross riff of panic and paranoia as that funky Granada is humping out a wall of smoke signals from its chewed up muffler down toward Orange County. Why didn't her mother tell Burgess where she was taking her? Why didn't she tell her? What if she lied to Burgess? What if she means to kill her?

With her neck shivering from the cold wind across the dashboard she tries to steel through this freak session of feelings by watching the nightworld along the freeway scrim past. It's all demon slogan billboards selling tacos and Toyotas. And neon insult advertisements that call out from discount warehouses and RV lots and Motel 6s, the vile insane colors of a country that means to hang you by the purse strings.

That world seems so anchored, so right there and tied down tight, yet one night ago it was shaken to its roots by the Whittier Quake. But still . . . it's there. In all its gaudy patchquilt electric promise. And it hasn't been vomited back into the face of creation. If *that* can survive, why can't she?

In Long Beach Dee gets off the freeway at Cherry Avenue and pulls into a blind alley behind a 7-Eleven. She makes Shay wait while she goes to buy cigarettes. The whole ride, her mother has been totally queered out, and for the first time in her life Shay considers running away.

She rolls up the windows and turns on the heater. The hiss of the blowing vents sends her back into that police cruiser as it rides toward the black etched rocks. She's suddenly all disoriented nausea. She tries to meet the horror that her mother might do her harm with an intractable belief that her mother would be inescapably empty without her. That she is her mother's lifeline. Even at those moments when they are tied together by nothing more than her venomous abuse.

Shay jumps when the rear door snaps open. Dee climbs in back. She begins to undress. She stuffs her clothes into the plastic bag. Naked, she leans forward and uses the rearview mirror to look over the rake marks the sheriff's teeth have left along her throat. The wound resembles some unsettling tattoo that she responds to with a vented bitter grin.

Dee sits back, slips on a T-shirt and jeans. When she is certain there are no witnesses she slides out of the car and buries that plastic bag deep in a trash-filled dumpster.

Dee gets back in the driver's seat and sits there staring straight ahead. Shay, too, stares straight ahead, waiting. Down that long blind alley, beyond a chain-link fence, is a maze of huge silver refinery drums connected by a lattice of piping.

Dee lights a cigarette. Her hands are jittery from the speed, but in a quiet menacing tone, she says, "You overheard our conversation back at the house, so you know the cop is alive."

Like face cards their images resemble, flat and stoic on that black gaming table of a windshield. Two queens, baby. One there, and one on the come. If she lives long enough.

Dee inhales, then blows the smoke out through the penny-sized hole of her mouth. "But you knew that, anyway." She watches Shay in the glass, "Fuckin' right." Her voice is hardly audible, "Yeah, back in the desert you knew. You just didn't speak 'cause ... I'd have made you shoot him. And you knew that too."

Shay's look stays on that long dark blind where the steam from the concrete refinery stacks hovers above the blue lamplight like liquid windshorn spirits. In a moment of selfhood, or maybe just self-preservation, knowing how useless lying would be against the trip-wire stare, Shay says, "Yeah, Mama, I knew ..." She takes a breath ... "So you can hurt me now if you want."

Dee sets the cigarette between her lips and flips the ignition. The Granada stutters, then turns over. Dee looks Shay right in the eye. "Well, raggedy girl, this is gonna be an interesting ride."

TEN

———

Burgess lies in the dark with the unwilling wish Dee and Shay would die. He is caught by a reflexive disbelief he has been attacked by such a thought. His insides scar with obscenities because he is such a coward his feelings for them could be poisoned like that.

He tries to kill the thought with a drink, then with a joint. But as the pot starts to morph the corners of his mind, the lantern and the gas lamps from his neighbor's party turn the sleepy trees outside his window into a fugue of restless shapes.

It's as if nature itself has begun to play havoc with his head. To finger-fuck its way into his consciousness. He is afraid to look away, and afraid not to. Once he even flinches when he's sure he's seen a face in the wild, moving branches that scratch at the glass above his head.

He wants this kind of fear away. Let them die. Let them all die. And by all, he even means his father, who he believes has frightened him into being a failure.

Shay watches the exits bleed by for the next two hours as they rip down the left coast. Her mother silently excoriates Burgess for not listening to her about that fat spic bitch and her boyfriend. She never trusted Alvarez, she never trusted Foreman. And she said so. The cunt was willing to let those forged papers slip through for too little, and . . . Dee thought they'd both do the fold if it got ugly. And look where they are now. Foreman is willing to burn them all down, including his plump brown hump, just to keep his ass out of stir.

By the time they reach Palm City, just past San Diego, Shay pretty much has tagged their destination, and she starts to freak.

———

Behind a building of sootblack brick just off the freeway, Dee makes Shay get out of the car.

"We're going to Mexico, aren't we?"

Dee pops the trunk lid.

"I won't go."

"Get in—"

The child is shockwaved. The dip of that trunk causes her to seize up. A junkyard grave if ever there was one, rent with clothes and trash, tire and jack. She is blind fear, bitter, barely able to . . . her head donkey shakes violently, "I won't—"

"And I won't get us fragged crossing the border 'cause that cop might have been able to identify you and they're—"

Shay screams again, "I won't!" and the force of her voice carries up through a forsaken emptiness of warehouses.

The two of them are a mongrel free-for-all watched over by a wall of barred and boarded up windows. No white flag to this fight. It's the cobra versus the mongoose. But in the end that cold metal trunk slams shut on a cowering, defiant girl.

Shay keeps screaming so her mother bangs a fist down on the trunk lid. "We won't get through the border station with you yelling like that."

Shay answers her mother's blow with one of her own. Dee retaliates by punching the same spot. "If you don't stop I'll drive into the ocean and drown us both."

Inside that speeding coffin, that depression of drained light, the world starts to bend out of shape behind Shay's eyes. The bad shocks and the smell of gas, the tire rammed against her back and the morass of junk that clips her in the face as the Granada does a curve in the road make hell of that vault.

She can hear her mother trashing Burgess through the thin metal reef that separates her from the back seat. It's a verbal rip at him being freaked 'cause his father might find out he lied to him. Shit . . . that old ass reamer would shiv you at the dinner table with the family cutlery if it meant an extra ten percent on his taxes.

The space around Shay feels as if it is being sucked out by some invisible vacuum till she is cocooned by a violet blackness.

Under huge fluorescents, about a quarter mile ahead, the border becomes a hazy orange line of stalls against the shroud of Mexico.

The Granada slows. Dee yells towards the back, "We're there. Not a sound now."

There is no sensation in Shay's fingers, none in her toes. A rivery panic begins to drown her lungs.

At this hour the border station has more guards than cars. Unfortunately, an unhealthy number have gathered around the few open stalls on the Mexican side, and are chatting away.

Shay is nothing left but nostrils gasping for air and a chest in upheaval against the gravity of a confined death.

Death, the black sacrament, is moving through her brain, leaving little soft spots that visions of graveside slaughter can sneak into.

Dee reaches into the glove compartment for a bandanna. She ties it around her neck knowing some guard might get close enough to see those romantic teeth marks. As for her swollen mouth, well—

Shay can't close her mind tight enough against visions of graveside slaughter playing out on the black heaven movie screen guts of the trunk. Something inside Shay fuses with that dying policeman. Some haunted narrative of victimhood she can sense only as image and sound.

She wants out of that trunk. Wants out bad. She isn't ready for the cool down under. Not ready to be permanently boxed or bellied. Her fingers have started to claw at the trunk lid when the Granada comes to a sudden halt.

Those guards around the booth, their bored faces in the apricot light. It's an all-male pack and they give Dee a collective going over with their eyes. One makes her answer a few perfunctory questions, if only so his cronies can get close enough to see what kind of tits and legs chickie is wearing inside that smog trap. They check her insurance tag to make sure it is up-to-date.

Dee fronts them with a smile. Doesn't even bother with any half-assed hand jive to cover up her swollen, battered mouth. Between puffs she manages a little repartee. She is a master of the ice-cold calm until some fat boy starts taking a turn around the Granada. That's when she knows you can't go clit if you mean to survive.

Shay can hear feet scuffing at the pavement cut through the soft voices up front. Can hear fingers begin patting the side panel with their nails till they drum past the gas tank to become a tactile and malevolent tapping along the trunk lid.

"Hey, your bumper's hanging off here."

Shay's throat closes around her heart. She squeezes into a fetal fist to try and fight back the fear. To try and outwait the worst it has to hell you with.

Dee leans a little out the window, "That's why I'm going to Tijuana. A girlfriend of mine got a brother-in-law there who owns a body shop. He's gonna clean this car up."

One of the other guards cuts in with, "The only kind of body shops open this late are chop shops. This Granada wouldn't be stolen, would it?"

Dee doesn't need to look into the sullen tracery of those faces to know they're fucking with her. She's seen this kind of gutless head prowling before. The bullshit late-night butt jockeys trying to make a freak show out of a simple crossing. "Well," Dee says, "I guess I should have driven the Mercedes I stole last night instead of this. I'd probably be in Tijuana by now."

A minute passes while other cars at other stalls are just waved through by other guards after their insurance is checked, and Shay lies there like some rank piece of fallout just inches from the sonar of a single fingernail going through a deliberate tap, tap, tap on the trunk lid.

"Yeah," says the guard, "this bumper looks like it might fall right off." And with that, he labors a boot right onto the metal and begins to rock it hard to see if it's gonna give.

Oh, Christ, thinks Dee.

Shay locks her breath down to hold in a gasp at the sudden jerking of the ass end as it jams down on the bed shocks, squeaking hard, and the loose jack claws along the trunk floor to clip her in the chin.

Hold on, baby . . . Dee tries to reach her daughter telepathically and tell her not to lose it. Not to flip while fatboy goes right on trying to fuck that bumper up regal.

Dee calls out to him, "You got to quit rockin' the car 'cause I'm gettin' seasick."

"Is that right?"

Shay keeps holding her breathing so no one will know she's there. Keeps holding that breath in till her whole body white-knuckles from the stress. She'll seal herself up till she's stone cold out.

Dee knows she has to act. She's in a mortal race with some black luck. That raw instinct for deliverance kicks in. She's gonna will her and Shay across the border.

Before Dee has even killed the engine and pulled the keys she is half out of the car. She starts toward the trunk, trying to keep the tempest of all that speed and anger in check.

"You got trouble with me?" she says to the guard with his boot humping the bumper. "Okay. Let's deal with it. 'Cause I'm real exhausted tonight.

"I had a boyfriend who ripped me off and left me with only this piece of crap you're wrecking . . ." She jams a hand up toward her battered mouth. "And this nice landmark I'm sure you've all noticed."

She gives fatboy and the others a cold blast from her eyes as if any one of them might be the type who'd honor some chickie with a little pounding.

"I got a daughter back in L.A. I need a car that runs for work. And I got a loose tooth from a beating." She holds the keys out for any one of them to take. "You want to search my car, okay. You want my license and shit, okay. Otherwise, please . . ." Her voice drops to a pitch of perfectly roused grief. "Let me go. I want to get back to my girl."

A woman friend of Dee's from the day she and Shay lived near Torreon is now holed up in San Luis Rio Colorado. She works as a short-order cook for a bar kitchen and lives with her two small children in a motel across the way that rents to day labor for the farms and factories near Bataques.

Shay waits in the car while her mother makes the arrangements for her to stay. She is dragged-down wasted and sits with the passenger door open and her feet scuffing at the dusty ground. The earth is still profiled in darkness as she looks out over a skid row of bungalows that will be her home.

It is a place of hopeless faith. Of stucco shell boxes with flat roofs and vegas all encrusted with tractor smoke and Sonoran dust. The poor of this world have begun to stir. Shay can see them in the raw lamplit windows preparing for the day.

She glares back to the open doorway where her mother and Honora talk. The woman gracefully rocks a small baby in her arms as she listens, and it isn't long before Dee returns to the car.

"It's all settled now, so listen."

Shay voices her disapproval by looking away.

Dee squats down and leans against her daughter's legs. "This isn't easy for me either, leaving you here like this. But—"

"Then take me with you. Take me back home."

"I can't!"

"That's a lie."

"Jesus. You have to stay here. If that cop is dead or he can't identify you, that's one thing. But until I know something you have to stay, at least when your hair grows out and no one—"

"But you're going back!"

She doesn't want to tell Shay any more. Certainly not that someone has to be in L.A. who Foreman and Alvarez are afraid of. And that if they can't ride this out they could have their throats cut by the holidays.

Instead, she tells her, "I got things to watch over."

Shay hits the car door with her fist. She stares past her mother and focuses on a mutt that's tied to the rotted shell of an ambulance up on blocks. And just beyond that, along a bungalow wall, an old field woman is asleep on a broken-backed couch bundled against the cold air.

Home sweet home, girl. You can toast that with a little agua de sandía and rat poison.

"Honora will take care of you."

Shay does not respond.

"I'm doing this to keep you alive. That's why I didn't even tell Burgess where I was taking you, on the chance. . . . Honey, no one will find you. I promise that."

"I should be happy you're going. That way I can't fuck things up. And you can't look at me like I fuck things up. It's all about you anyway, right? That's all it ever is."

Shay swims in unworthiness, she swims in anger. She covers her face. She wants to cry. From Silverlake to Sonora all in the space of one murder. She wants to beg her mother not to leave her, but she won't ask again.

"I know what I am, girl. I don't dance around it. And don't you forget it. I'm speedfreak nasty. And don't you forget it. I have killed, and you are my daughter. And don't forget it. That . . . that is the truest thing there is. And if they cut me open and look for my heart, you know what they'll find there? An empty shelf . . . with only your picture on it."

She reaches out and holds Shay tightly. Shay tries to fight loose, but her mother won't have it. This lifetime of a night and the speed have left Dee so brittle that her teeth feel like they could crack in half under the stress of almost crying.

She kisses her daughter once, then stands. "You can't call me. I'll call Honora at the bar to talk to you." She pulls Shay out of the car, closes the door, goes around to the driver's side, gets in. All this is done in one long, fluid, hard motion. But once behind the wheel, Dee hesitates.

Shay stands beside the white vapor of the headlights, arms folded. Dee leans into the steering wheel and crosses her arms stiffly.

The two of them at that moment are the hard parable of drama. They are the hard line between the origin and the end. Inside Shay is the power of freedom and hate at being left behind. For a moment her eyes are her mother's eyes completely.

In a tone chinked apart by emotion, Dee calls, "Hey, raggedy girl," and using sign language, tells her baby, "I love you. . . . And this is blood talking."

Shay chases a blast of headlights as they rush down that dusty road and turn. She stands in the street near the bar and watches those flaring beams bleed into the blue deeps of an impoverished landscape.

She is alone now, a ghost figure on the moonlike asphalt crying vengefully. As she screams her mother's name, the red morning creeps to life behind her. She wishes she could crawl back into some womb and come forth again, exempt and pure, but she can't escape the feeling she will be torn apart endless times.

A mourning desert wind, that mutt barking since their car raced past, and Honora rocking a baby in the doorway—they are the greeting card she faces as she turns away from the road.

DEATH
BY
LIVING

ELEVEN

———

John Victor Sully does not die, but a moral disease has been put into play that will destroy what's left of all he is.

No calm fixed mind can help him. No parade of strength, no skill can see him through. He's at the boundary of the shaken world where men get mangled by the facts.

While he undergoes two bouts of surgery to shore up the ravaged pathways each bullet has left, members of the highway patrol and sheriff's department meet at the site of the attempted murder. They begin like numb spectators to try and piece together the crime. Behind flashlights their unreal shapes come to grips with details that don't add up.

The ground from the grave to Sully's cruiser has been curried over with brush, leaving neither boot nor shoe tracks in the sand. The only prints inside the police car belong to Sully and Hugh Englund, which puts into question Sully's radio report that he'd been approached at the Davenport by a young girl and was driving her into the preserve to pick up a family member stranded with a broken-down vehicle. And why was the shotgun ripped from the console rack and stolen?

By daylight Hugh Englund and the other officers had worked through a long act of many hours. No one at the Davenport, including Karen Englund, had seen either a girl or young woman approach Sully. Within a quarter mile of the Baker exit not one gas station attendant remembers a female of any age requesting a tow truck to go out into the preserve. Add the peculiar aura of all this to the obscene imagery of that shallow holesite Sully had clawed his way out of, and the officers were left with the derelict feeling this mimicked a couple of hits last summer that Inland Empire drug dealers had used to serve notice on one of their own.

Hugh eyes his car radio. Hangs on a chest full of nervous profanity before he makes the call. The crime scene so far is a nest of contradictions. Sunlight off that saline playa pierces his eyes. Exhausted, he gets his captain on the line. Begins to lay out the details of his conversation with Sully about the Foreman hearings just hours before the hit.

It wasn't the substance of what Sully said, but rather his tone, his lack of anger at the insinuation he trafficked in narcotics that sated the wound Hugh felt at even having to confront a friend and fellow officer about such a thing. Then he asks the captain, "If what Foreman's attorney says is true, well, that could have an impact on the crime."

Since it's only a matter of time before they find out, Hugh wants authorization from the captain to tell investigators at the scene. He finishes by reminding the captain, it may look like they were covering up for Sully if they don't.

One call to the DA confirms that a CalTrans worker named Jon Pettyjohn has been deposed, and his story matched in principal Foreman's, including one stunning fact. He'd overheard Sully requesting to search Foreman's car, and Foreman told him no. Hunkered down around the hood of a car it doesn't take investigators long to build up a scaffold of premises they could hang Sully from.

What if Hugh Englund's conversation with Sully had freaked him? What if he called these traffickers to warn them or enlist their aid in keeping Foreman quiet? What if they set a time and place to meet? What if it was a setup to lure him out into the preserve and kill him? They might have feared Sully could be rolled by the DA and would deep-six them to beat a possible indictment.

Maybe his radio call was just so much bullshit cover because a quick meeting had been called. Or maybe they knew he wouldn't chance going that far out into the preserve so they sent one of their doper girlfriends with a trumped-up story about a broken down car to bait him out, and end it.

While a news chopper rides the rough winds overhead, Hugh watches the investigators start hard wolfing the case. After arguing amongst themselves for the better part of an hour they come to a stark consensus and request a search warrant for Sully's trailer on the suspicion he might actually be dealing.

So, while Sully is taken for a second run under the knife, police cruisers speed through the wrinkled heat waves of late afternoon toward a mobile home out on Mesquite Road.

When Karen pulls up there's a crowd of Sully's neighbors around the double-wide. His place has become a burning zone for the investigators. Every cupboard, closet, and drawer is under attack by these unshaven and edgy men.

They're getting nowhere, and Karen wants them to crash and burn on the idea that Sully might be—

Inside, heads turn toward an unseen voice. Outside, neighbors watch through the windows as investigators herd down a back hallway towards the bedrooms. Enough time passes so there are whispers of shaken confidence, and a friend of Sully's folks murmurs desolately, "Good thing they're both gone. They couldn't handle this. Not the way they were."

A flashlight sets the stage on a furrow of pried-apart closet floorboards. A hand wearing surgical gloves reaches toward a shiny surface wedged down in the subflooring.

Two flashlights back up the first. A coffee tin is lifted to the light, the top is pulled loose. Exposed is a convex surface of clear dimpled plastic.

Silence. A nonfiction of tragic stares at the bundled wad of snowy white powder, then a vindictive pronouncement by an investigator, "One grave opens while another is dug."

While a river of tubes is run down his nose and throat to drain the wounds, Sully's prints are found on the coffee can, though not on the plastic the coke was wrapped in. By the time he regains consciousness and stares up into the swimmy dark of intensive care, a gnawed-looking young CalTrans worker with a ponytail has reconfirmed his stark testimony about what he saw at that gas station in Baker. While Sully faces the tragedy of aloneness, of having no family by his side, the assistant DA drops the case against Foreman as a matter of sensible practicality at ever getting beyond reasonable doubt with a jury.

The staggering weight of just being alive, of having lost the lower part of his right lung to a bullet, of having been tossed like so much trash into an outcast hole collides head-on with officers who show up one morning around his bed and begin the slow arc of an interrogation.

His mind can barely fathom a tide of pointed questions reserved usually for potential suspects. But with each rise and drift towards some kind of clarity he begins to recognize what is said on the detectives' features. He is now just a human forgery of the man he once was.

He feels an onslaught of shock that his survival has led to this. He tries to get a few scarred words in defense of his honesty past the tubes and pipes passed down his throat. He fights each gagging reflex to make a stand at innocence. The interrogation has to be stopped when a slough of blood forms across his chest where the wound seams have ripped open with rage at the events manipulated against him.

In the moments thereafter, while Sully lies there listening to the doctors and nurses go about the business of shoring up his flesh, he begins to feel the full measure of his world being torn from its moorings. He is now more frightened than he ever was in that short minute when he was shot, because he does not fathom how to fight *this*, to survive *this*. There is no road map he knows of through the anarchy of suspicion and lies and planted evidence.

TWELVE

―――――

Dee and Burgess hunker down while the system begins its blood waltz across reality. The local stations can't play enough helicopter shots of that open grave and ransacked police cruiser. Bookending a full-throttle investigation by homicide detectives to find suspects in the attempted murder, the case against Foreman is officially dropped while an administrative probe is launched against John Victor Sully.

The Daily News, the San Fernando Valley's leading newspaper, coups *The L.A. Times* by publishing the first complete composite sketch of the alleged accomplice that led Sully into the desert. It's a nothing likeness of Shay straight from Officer Sully's memory bank, and capped off by his description of the girl, "Could have been seventeen or so, and possibly Chicana." As for the shooter, Sully has no recall of what she looked like.

By November Burgess and Dee are just starting to get a deep breath of what it's like after you clear the first big hurdles in an attempted killing. At a ground-breaking ceremony on 56th Street in South Central, Burgess' parents play the proud backdrop at their pride and joy's first big success. But having to pose for the camera over a few ceremonial shovels of dirt being dug up from the empty lot sends a poisonous little reminder up Burgess' spine about the fetid origins of this whole fuckin' deal.

After the ceremony, Harold Ridden hosts a celebration for about a hundred underofficials of the Los Angeles Unified School District in the Le Petite Trianon room of the Beverly Wilshire Hotel. Between bouts of boasting about his son, Harold manages at least one quiet backhanded aside to Burgess about his choice of bed partners: "Even when you dress her up, she still looks like a street whore."

At the party, Alicia Alvarez is politely fielding praise from fellow Department of Education workers for all those months of hard work it took to birth the 56th Street Middle School when Dee slips among

Alicia's admirers to ask if she can steal the center of attention for a few minutes.

Dee leads Alicia up the cobblestone driveway between the front and rear sections of the hotel. It's a windy fall day that's playing hell with workers trying to put up Christmas lights. When they reach Rodeo Drive and Dee keeps walking, Alicia nervously asks where Dee is taking her.

Dee keeps on till they come to the service alley behind the hotel. When it's just the two of them, and enough away from the street traffic to talk, Dee turns. Looking over this slight frump of a hustler, she is tossed back into the memory kingdom of her own egregious, cunt mother, and she says to Alicia in gutter Spanish, "Garage rocker and Neiman Marcus on Rodeo Drive. Talk about your upwardly mobile melting pot, heh." Then her tone darkens. "I guess a little blood makes us almost family now, doesn't it, cholla?"

Frightened, Alicia says, "I don't need any more trouble."

Dee's tone could slap her quiet as she keeps on in Spanish, "You know why I took that policeman's shotgun?"

Alicia doesn't want any part of this, and tries to walk away, but Dee won't have it. "Because if you or Foreman ever again get close enough to do anything that could fuck us all up, I am gonna spike that shotgun up your couch-cushion ass and do you. And him. Then I'll go home and fuckin' masturbate with the barrel. Get it, cholla?"

THIRTEEN

———

The new year seems intent on ushering in another ruined man as the world of Los Angeles invades "Down Below." "Down Below" is a nickname for areas of the California desert east of San Bernardino.

When Sully hobbles out of the San Bernardino Community Hospital it is straight into a vampyric onslaught of reporter questions and photographs. He must now watch himself be turned into a civics lesson on the symbols of unresolved conflicts. He watches himself become no longer a man, but a piece of space used to fill space. He will be the meat of two warring tribes. Those who see the policeman as protector of the wrongfully condemned and those who see the policeman as purveyor of our darkest guilts. As to the legal tender of his own humanity, that has no value whatsoever.

The arbitration hearing takes a hard run at indicting Sully, and it looks like he's going straight into the teeth of a grand jury when his defense attorney, Joseph Stinson, himself a former homicide investigator, discovers one piece of exculpating evidence "overlooked" by investigators. A small window in Sully's second bedroom showed signs of possible . . . *possible* . . . forced entry.

This one detail is not enough to save the man, but it is enough to stave off the system.

Sully is sitting alone in his living room like some dispossessed creature when the call comes. His attorney tells him the arbitration hearing has decided he is to be IOD'd. Permanent disability. Thirty-percent pay for life. Sully's attorney asks him to consider this a small victory, a slight opening for the rest of his life to come through.

Sully tells him he sees it for what it is: The quiet and efficient re-

moval of him from their consciousness. It is their polite way of exe-
cuting him because they cannot, or will not, bring themselves to
honestly exonerate him. His attorney warns against this kind of destructive thinking, and Sully screams into the phone, "I'm the one who
crawled out of a fuckin' grave to face a firing squad because of planted
evidence, not you! Not you!"

He bitterly slams down the phone. Thirty percent. He lost that
much lung. How much is thirty percent of his salary? Maybe seven
hundred dollars a month. Just enough to qualify as trailer trash if you
never work again.

In and around Baker, Sully becomes a ghostly figure more talked about
than talked to. Even Hugh and Karen Englund feel forced to maintain
a polite distance. Sully now walks with a hitch from the wound to his
pelvis. His breathing grows harsh and raspy because of that missing
piece of lung.

The investigation into his attempted murder reaches a phase of
purposeless mechanical procedures, so Sully begins to use his disability
money to fund the clockless hours of a private investigation. As he
pushes himself past the limits of his recuperation, he takes to surviving
on Percodan and Scotch. He begins a clandestine surveillance of both
Charles Foreman and Jon Pettyjohn, trying to prove some connection
between the two men. Then, one night, while he is following Pettyjohn,
Sully is pulled off the Hollywood freeway by the LAPD.

Once his ID is checked and his identity established, his notoriety
quickly comes into play. The cops walk the car with flashlights. While
Sully waits by the side of the road with waves of Saturday night traffic
slowing to watch, he is back at that day in Baker with Charles Foreman,
only this time he's playing Foreman.

A flashlight catches the tip of an open pint of Scotch hidden under
the front seat. This leads to a full search of the car, where an unregis-
tered .38 is discovered tucked up in the glove compartment.

It's the full court press of bad news. An arrest for carrying a concealed
weapon and a DUI. More reporters. More legal fees.

He now hates the country of his birth. Charles Springer, the radio
evangelist whom his parents followed into the desert outside Baker,

used to say, "Every tragedy hides some blessing that will heal you with time."

Time he does not have. To meet his legal fees Sully borrows against his mobile home. He is maxed out by medical bills and liquor bills and all those months working to prove he was no liar. He not only hates the country of his birth, he hates his parents. He hates them for poisoning his thoughts with the idea that he was ill-equipped for the world outside of Baker.

He is moving blindly through some imposed dream. He finds he cannot make the day without a handful of Percodan. He cannot find the self-confidence to hold himself through these times. Not a spiritual self-confidence, not a self-confidence of any kind. He falls into a devolving panic when he gets notice of his foreclosure. Rage eats through the shadows to have at his heart. He wants someone to die, and that someone does not have to be guilty of a crime. He is a piece of raped manhood sinking, and so the panic grows worse. He suffers heart palpitations and nightmares about two faceless figures who attack him from the terrible channels of a molten deathscape. He drinks endlessly till there are garbage bags of scotch bottles beside his service porch door. When he is only weeks from being homeless he considers one final cocktail of Percodan and scotch to kill off all those skin and bone delusions.

He sits through days staring at the walls, at the sunlight off the metal roofs around him, at the dust trailing past his screen door in the summer heat. Aimless, pointless, feelingless stares where there is nothing but a silence that speaks louder than any words. Where there is no consolation and only a kind of desultory dusk about his eyes and soul. He is becoming stone and he knows it.

He fills a scotch glass and readies the pills that will turn the river of his life to salt. But when the moment comes to swallow truth he spits the concoction back into the sink, then hoards up the Percodan for another assault against his will to stay alive.

The terrible claws of himself are leaving their signature in both the desire to obliterate and the drive to exist. So, caught within the intangible walls of a living grave, he decides to run.

He packs two small suitcases and loads them into his Ranchero. Everything else in the house he leaves as is, a world in mid-step for sheriffs and movers to find. Clothes, furniture, family photos, wash in the dryer, an air conditioner blowing out cold air, dirty dishes in the sink. And while Mesquite Road lies in sleeping darkness, he slips away.

It will be almost eleven years to the night of October twenty-seventh before Sully returns to the birthplace of his destruction. He will have changed his name by then, and be known only as Victor Trey. Almost eleven years to that night, he will be sitting in the lobby of the Sunshine Hotel just off Texas Street remembering how he came to be. He will be looking through the rainy darkness, past the switching yards of El Paso, towards a black and glassy Rio Grande, when the night manager tells him there is a call.

It will be from an agoraphobic columnist he's never spoken to, never met. A columnist who calls himself Landshark, who claims to have information that a conspiracy was in play the night of October 27, 1987, in the Mojave Preserve.

PART
TWO

THE
ULTIMATUM

FOURTEEN

"He fucked us, Charlie. Burgess seriously fucked us."

From their hillside patio, Charles Foreman rolls another joint and looks out over the town of his youth.

"His company gets half a million dollars from the MTA for drawing up an ethics report for its employees and contractors, and how do I find out?"

"Burgess Ridden doing an ethics report . . . for the subway . . . what a rip."

Foreman's offhanded tone only angers Alicia all the more. "The rip is this went down weeks ago. But I hear about it in a press release. It's a slap in *our* face."

Foreman licks the rolling paper, then smooths it closed.

"I called him after I saw this. There's a head consulting job as part of the deal. Sixty thousand dollars. I could have the report done in five weeks. Five weeks, sixty thousand dollars. The whole ethics report is nothing but a kickback anyway. It probably won't even get done."

"What did he say when you asked for the job?"

"He said he'd call me back. Then, two hours later, it's Lady Macbeth on the line with, 'Sorry, but we had to take care of so and so's son.' "

"That yuppie fuck." Foreman takes a long hit off the joint, then desserts by snorting in a little extra smoke. He may have slowed some over the years, but there's no mistaking that cell-block attitude around the eyes and jaw. "With all the shit Storey's pulled, and not one hour in stir. Talk about your double fuckin' standard." Those grizzled eyes redden at the obscenity of all that money doing a little detour around their lives.

"The 56th Street School . . . Belmont . . . none of it was possible without me. And that Tills. If I hadn't cleared out his reports none of— Now Burgess is living up in Los Feliz in some landmark, and where are we? Where are we, Charlie!?"

There's that desperate, vicious bleat to her voice he'd like to back-hand down the hill even though he hurts for her when he hears it.

"He fucked *us*, Charlie. And it's only gonna get worse, if you don't do something."

He lets the smoke have at his head as he stares down Santa Susanna Pass Road toward Stoney Point. At dusk, with a few tokes in him, all he really sees is the Chatsworth that once was. The Chatsworth before they put in the 118 Freeway and turned what was once the largest back lot in America, known as the Iverson Movie Ranch and Corriganville, into a grid of tract homes and rundown strip malls. He used to pony his pickup on dirt roads that cut through long hillsides of huge sand and taupe boulders heaped atop each other in a wild geometry that defined the art of delicate balance. It was ground that once was part of the canon of movies like *Stagecoach* and *Fort Apache*. It was where *The Lone Ranger* and *Rin Tin Tin* and *Zorro* made black and white history. Now it is a purgatorial township of motels and Christian memorabilia shops, of palm readers and Thai take-out storefronts . . . and smog. A smog so thick it fired a sunset into the red of some darker curse. With everything they'd done, this is as far as their money had gotten them.

"Are you just gonna sit there and get fucked up?"

The first inklings of a discarded fury. "Okay."

"One of us is the wings, the other is the body." Her voice hurts when she says it. "Remember that night up in San Frasquito Canyon when you were facing down an indictment?" Her heavy frame muscles with the patio chair. "Remember when you asked if I was with you?"

"I remember, okay."

She can see he's starting to feel besieged, and when he's like that she can have at him, "One is the body, the other is the wings. Burgess made a lot of money."

Charlie peers down at the 118, stonejawed. Rush hour is one long blanketing hiss. "It could get ugly."

Her exasperated whisper, "Is this another excuse for doing nothing?"

THE TRAP

FIFTEEN

Jon Pettyjohn is lying in the dark, in the bedroom of his small yellow house on Toluca Street. He's grooved into an all male hole-banging video shot by one of his partyboys. The phone rings and he drags himself up to answer it.

"Charlie . . . what am I doing?" He watches the screen as some puffed-up piece of manhood gets body slammed. "Just puttin' a little of that bad religion in my head."

Pettyjohn listens for a few moments then cuts Charlie off. "What is this, 'how am I doin' for money' shit? You know how I'm doin'."

He grows angry as Charlie continues to talk. He shags the remote, shuts off the video and sits up. "I fucked up by not selling this place to the developers, alright." Pettyjohn's long, ringed fingers feel their way through the morass of clothes and fast food boxes that have collected on the bedstand until they score a cigarette.

"Did you call to rub my dick in it again? Is that what this is about?"

Pettyjohn stands on his front porch smoking. He considers Charlie's plan for sticking it to Burgess Ridden from all its different angles.

Burgess is a mama's boy. A mule they've all ridden, so to speak. As for Dee Storey, she worries him less than she does the others. Even with her all dick posturing, he can see how she has to come around.

Standing in the light cast from his open front door, Jon Pettyjohn has no idea he is, at that moment, being photographed.

SIXTEEN

Shay Storey is cranking out a battle line of hard cocktails and bottled beer when one of the waitresses leans through the crowd and tries to outyell a chainsaw guitar to let her know there's an emergency call. Shay does a one-arm turn for the phone beside the register and gets it tucked up under her chin so she can keep right on racking a nasty set of double gimlets.

Over the band and a blender full of ice she can barely pick out that well-known Burgess whine. He's slightly panicked . . . so what else is new. Needs to find Dee . . . right. Has no idea where she is . . . nothing original there. Has left a dozen calls at the house and on her cellular . . . all is status quo in Burgessville.

Before she can put together even one half-assed sentence about not having a clue or a care as to where her mother is, Burgess has swung into a full parable about responsibility and business and screw-ups and the strained turn of their relationship so . . . by the time his little rant has skidmarked to a close, Shay answers him by just plain hanging up the fucking phone and getting straight back into a groove of nicely poured martinis.

Dee Storey is at home on the bathroom floor clocking some bang with a pool cue she picked up at the Club Reggae Soul. During cleanup, when the manchild starts in with his slanted version of, "Maybe we should get together and blah, blah, blah . . ." Dee tosses him a handbill with Mr. Hamilton's face on it for the cab ride home.

Then, and only then, does she turn her attention to all those phone calls.

There's a fog across Los Feliz. The hills above Ferndell Park are a night-shade of ill-shaped lights from the homes behind walls and gates. Roadside trees are dipped with a grainy mist. All is silent save for a lone set of tires speeding up through the damp slender streets.

Against the wet gray quiet, Lloyd Wright's sleek white concrete monument stands out from the hillside like some modern template of Mayan artistry. The only light within comes from the stark white video room beside the pool where Burgess watches a laser disc of *Blade Runner* on his Hi-D home theater, and waits. His guts turn over as if they were on a spit. And when he hears the blue-green garage door electronically lift, all that tangled jealousy mines a few new pockets of pain.

Dee shoulders up in the doorway of the video room. Burgess won't look at her, so she waits. They remain the dead center of silence, with only the projected images of a rain-smoked cyber Los Angeles bleeding blue electric out over the white walls and through the patio doors onto the shimmering pool surface.

"Are we gonna talk about this extortion meeting or watch the movie?" she asks.

A look that's wrapped in starveling anger and need. "Where were you?"

She won't indulge that, and goes on, "I asked you to give her the consulting money even if you didn't want to hand her the gig. I said it made good sense. And what did you tell me?"

"You were probably out with some vibrator you picked up at a bar."

"Don't knock the bars, darlin'." She smiles. "Remember, that's how we hooked up."

A slave chain of reactions rattles his insides. He wants to fuck her and hurt her, to hold her and throw her out. He goes back to the film.

She glances at the screen, watches as the huge blond android turns against the father figure who cannot, or will not, extend his life.

"How many times have you seen this movie?" Silence. "I remember every time they'd play this at the Nu-Art and you'd come into the Blue Flame afterward and rant on about what you really thought 'Daddy' deserved for being so down on your ass. Well, if you're trying to work some symbolism here on me, not happenin'. Now, we got things to deal with, so—"

"I know I'm the hopeless cause in this relationship, if that's what this is. I'm just a fuckin' drop of water in your bucket. But I'd like to make one small point." His face nasties up. "Pretend I'm you and you're Shay. Feel how I can't get inside you like you can't get inside her, and how much it . . . shall I dare use the word . . . hurts."

A short series of visual reactions and he knows the wound has been exposed. Yeah, he thinks, then he goes back to the film. Dee comes over and sits at the far end of the couch. They both lose themselves in the screen as the blond replicant kisses the man who made him and then goes about the business of crushing his skull.

In a singsong whisper, Dee starts, "Some need to use you, some need to be used by you . . ." She slides her leg up on the couch so the calf comes to rest against his cock.

Another short series of visual reactions . . . his. And all those other little wounds that poison and plague and ply your head with demands are exposed. Yeah, but he knows something else, too. He knows that it's his very weakness that keeps her locked into him. So who's using who . . . who's using who?

SEVENTEEN

Foreman has Pettyjohn call Dee to set the meeting. Pettyjohn picks a downtown bar for fags. It's an inconspicuous little slum that caters to the deep-choke crowd and where Burgess Ridden isn't likely to run into any of his nearest and dearest.

But Dee also knows this is about who is setting the agenda. It's how the boys like to prove to each other who is carrying the heaviest cock. It says Foreman and his can demand where and when and Burgess better be there.

The Scorecard is a doorway nooked into a brick wall due west of a tenement hotel called the Barclay. The bar door is always open so the street can throw in just enough light to give you a sense of the chrome barstools and the scarred-to-pieces parquet floor.

Burgess looks at a small handpainted sign above the door done in that "ye olde English" lettering: THE SCORECARD—A DOWNTOWN CLUB FOR GENTLEMEN. Talk about a complete juxtapoz' of the ridiculous.

Dee watches from the car as Burgess takes that first nervous step in. He doesn't know she's watching him. He wanted to play stud and go it alone, so she got there early and parked in a lot on the southeast corner of Fourth and Main in case any life support was necessary.

She shaves a little speed into her coffee. Finds she can't get her mind off Burgess' comment about Shay. The idea of her daughter being lost to her lays her bare. Strips her of the only connection she really has with womanhood. She suddenly finds her fingers coming to her defense with all the familiar sorrows.

The bar is a black hole with a sound system and a couple of small booths in the back. Even the rats need fucking miners' lights to get from the bar to the men's room.

Burgess is the first to arrive. Is faced with ordering a drink at the bar, alone. Avoids eye contact with a heavy blinker who seems to have some kind of hypoplastic swelling around the cheeks.

Burgess takes his beer and finds the blackest corner he can hide in to wait it out.

Main Street is running heavy with traffic. One block over, Broadway is nothing but street construction and south on Fifth a movie crew is prepping a stunt jumper for a rooftop dive into a wall of Panaflex cameras.

Dee tries to kill off her black mood by taking in the crowded absurdities of all that street life when she notices a young Chicana with a camera on the southwest corner of Fourth and Main. Probably some idiot chickie, she guesses, trying to nab a few celeb shots for an ego boost.

That dreaming evil thought that Shay hates her comes back hard. It's a vivid business that burns up the minutes. Dee is lighting one cigarette with the butt of another when Pettyjohn frames up in the sunlight just outside the Barclay lobby that fronts Main.

Jon's gone totally freak with the years. Sports a nose ring and dresses like some ass waver for Mother Fist. Pettyjohn turns to talk with someone stepping through the lobby doors. When Hugh Englund enters the equation, Dee knows things are gonna get toxic. The full court press for cash.

They swing onto Fourth, talking and breathing as one shape. Dee knows Englund divorced his wife a few years ago after he quit riding for the blue leather out in Baker. She wonders if that bleached blonde ever found out he was a coke-dealing phony who preferred rubbing his cock on the inside of some stud boy's asshole.

As they pass, bursts of sunlight off the filthy Barclay lobby windows force her to look away. And in that momentary pause, her eyes panning through a landscape of inconspicuous details suddenly shunt—

The chickie with the camera. She's creased back in the doorway of a closed-down bank. The doors are all glass and Dee can see through the panes enough to eyeline the target of that single lens reflex.

It can't fuckin' be—

A heartbeat later the fuckboys disappear into the Scorecard.

The booth is black, the small talk strained. The sound system speakers are just behind them and loud enough so the men have to lean into each other to talk privately.

Dee is out of the car and pressing toward the parking lot fence. Through a stream of trucks and buses she watches the girl reload her camera.

"Alvarez is angry, so Foreman is angry. Foreman is angry, so Alvarez is angry. I've been here before," says Burgess. "What do you want? And where do you all fit in this? Are you both . . . angry? Is this some genetic thing, when one of you is angry the rest—"

Pettyjohn jumps right in with, "You don't want to see us angry. So you better clean up that look and clean up that tone or—"

Hugh cuts Pettyjohn off before he goes one octave too high for that little gathering at the bar. Then to Burgess, "You made a lot of money the last couple of years."

"And so did you. And you both could have made a lot more if you weren't so fucking greedy. Right? The house on Toluca. Have you forgotten? I pass you inside information they want to raze the block for condos. I took care of you. I help you get the loan to buy a place. There was a fast two-hundred-thousand-dollar profit and who tries to stiff the developers for more. So now where are you? You're sitting on a white elephant they're gonna build around. Let that be a lesson here."

Maybe I'm wrong, thinks Dee. Maybe the chickie was just getting some art shots of the building or the light off the lobby glass. Maybe she's a people shooter. Maybe the freak and his ex-jock boyfriend made a grab portrait she had to have. Maybe . . . but why is she just hanging in that alcove waiting?

"Listen, Hugh, I don't want to sit in this dickhole all morning."

"Don't start," warns Pettyjohn.

"Shut up, Jonny," says Hugh.

"What does Foreman want? What does Alvarez want? What do any of you want? If it's the ethics report gig, I can't do it. If she thinks, he thinks, you think, you all got ripped—"

"Two million dollars," is Hugh's matter-of-fact answer.

The speed has Dee's head engines cranking through possibilities. You throw out all the art photography bullshit. You dump the celeb shot idea since the Chicana's not showing any interest in the action a block away. She ain't people shooting. Not now. And you're left with answering two basic questions. Two. What is the reason chickie might be copping pictures of Hugh and Pettyjohn and . . . who is behind that reason?

Too stunned to talk, Burgess just sits. And with the sound system pumping some old Meatloaf tune off *Bat Out of Hell* into the base of his skull and a sot at the bar troweling up a smoker's laugh, he can barely get his head to make a connection between what they're asking and . . . what they're asking.

"Alicia," whispers Hugh, "has kept all the documents you forged on the 56th Street School. All the EPA paperwork. The same with the Metrorail parking lot. And the Belmont School complex. The LAUSD documents you used as backup."

She looks too young to be LAPD. Too funky to pass Fed agency bullshit look requirements. Could Hugh and Pettyjohn be back in the trade? Could the DEA have turned this Chicana out after some possession rap and are using her? Could it be a sub-rosa insurance investigation or some attorney working up discovery? Shit . . . the possibilities are on the ugly side of endless. And Burgess. What if he walks out with them?

Gets himself innocently framed up in some criminal go down. Thanks
to all that adrenaline, Dee gets a savage flash. What if this is somehow
connected to—

"Alicia doesn't want to go there, Hugh. She opens all that up what am
I, stone? I'd wrap her in every indictment that they throw at me."

"She comes forward innocently, acts like she didn't know. Says she
started doing some checking 'cause she had some reservations now that
Belmont is getting all that bad press. She can make a pretty good case
for herself."

"You'd have the most to lose," warns Pettyjohn.

Burgess looks from one to the other, "Are you forgetting about
Baker, California? Foreman's little problem."

Incriminating silence. The nothing light the street throws in makes
the men's faces like the wreckage of some other time, some other place.

Burgess keeps on it. "I'd like to see you explaining your relationship back then when it gets out that the sheriff and lead witness in a
criminal investigation were a couple of—"

"Don't say it," warns Pettyjohn.

Hugh leans forward. "All the more reason to pay her."

"Pay her, pay him. What are you, my legal counsel? Where do you
both fit in?"

"We fit in very nicely, thank you," says Pettyjohn.

Burgess would like to shove a fistful of high-voltage wire right down
Jonny-boy's throat. Get Burgess on the cellular, Dee thinks. Just have
him cruise right out of there alone. Burgess stands. He is angry because
he is frightened. He is frightened because he knows he is being worked,
because he knows he's weak enough to be worked. He puts on his best
game face. "Why don't you fags go tell . . ." He really mauls the word,
'Alicia' . . . "We'll see who puts their ass up in the sky."

Pettyjohn would have at Burgess right there for the "fag" comment
except Hugh gridlocks him halfway across the table. Dee grabs her
cellular from the glove compartment and is one finger click short of a
speed dial when Burgess steps into a scythe of daylight across the front
of the building.

Dee spots him. He's alone, then he's not. The three men become a

brackish verbal assault, a spectacle of faces and chests. Very fuckin'
nice, when dicks get together for a little dialogue.

As soon as the Chicana spots those two low-rent predators she rack-
focuses right on them. That little bundle of discord in front of the Scorecard doesn't last long, just long enough for Dee to see past the buses
and cars, past their stuttering exhaust, through the wavering bank window glass, what chickie's lens is hot for.

THE
MURDER

EIGHTEEN

———

As he paces out his living room, Burgess is a man going in two different directions at the same time. Freaked at the thought he might fumble everything he has because of Foreman or Alvarez, and firm that he holds the "fuck you" card.

Dee sits there taking in his flyweight prattle, but her whole presence is on that shooter with the camera she has yet to mention to him.

Burgess comes to a taut stop, notices the twisted language Dee's fingers are going through. He kneels down in front of her. "I know you see things I don't." He takes her hand. "You've been really quiet. What's going on inside that head of yours?"

"They're playing a high-pressure game of chicken. You handled it right . . . today."

"Alicia isn't crazy enough to go to the authorities."

"You forged the papers. You gave her false documents. She could try and come across as the concerned Latina, I could see her talking it up behind that fat-assed doe look, who sensed something was wrong after all these reports on the site and did a little investigating back into the paperwork to see if anything was there."

"She buried Tills' original report on the land."

The old man's name carries a few seconds of blood-stained silence with it.

"Lucky for us," says Dee, "he passed away when he did."

Burgess folds his hands across his forehead. "We did some terrible things."

"Yes . . . *we*."

Her tone sets him straight. "I only meant—"

"Alvarez and Foreman. They are exactly who I knew they were."

"Would Alicia take that kind of gamble? Would Foreman let her go to the district attorney? I could indict them."

"Sure. And look what that door opens up. Next thing you know we're back in the desert."

"That's just what I mean. They can't take that chance either. Let's tell them to go get fucked."

"Burgess." Dee shakes her head in disgust, in anger and frustration. "We've been here before. What if something happens to Foreman? He gets busted and they find the papers in his house. What if he's facing hard time and turns state's evidence to cop a lesser plea to save his ass. Christ, he was willing to turn us and his old lady over if we didn't clean up his shit mess the last time. We . . . you and me . . . we got to have those papers, and he knows it."

Burgess screams out, *"Fuck!"*

The familiar patterns of his body language start to act out. She pulls him toward her. Tries to finger roll some relaxation into those shoulders. He lets his head dip into her lap.

He is suddenly paralyzed by the facts, and when that happens he lets everything fall away but her. He goes to that spot inside her wanton strength where he can hide. Where he can exist unconditionally within its essence.

The next few minutes are an entanglement of quiet breathing. As Dee tries to get the knot of him under control, she picks up on their image in an urn made of antimony glass that exclusively owns one wall. Talk about an album cover for the abandoned life blues.

Dee starts to feel something in the sleepless part of her heart. An incorrigible need. She closes her eyes. She does not want to know its name. She wants to focus, instead, on the dangerous symmetry of events around her. And that girl with the camera. That disturbing sidewalk reality is going to have to be dealt with.

In these moments Dee can sense the brutal architecture of her mother. The slash and burn mute who practically invented misery. Who—

Dee needs a drink. She needs . . . Shay. She needs her child back in the circle of her own life. She needs from her own daughter what Burgess needs from—

Another head flash. Another little black turn in how the cards could run. "I know we've talked about this," she says. "Your father knows there were payoffs on the 56th Street School. But you never told him it was Alvarez, right?"

"He didn't want to know the details."

"What about . . . the rest of it?" Burgess doesn't answer, but his neck creases uncomfortably. "Burgess?" The muscles in his back become a panel of tortured physicality. "Honey . . . ?"

"I'd rather die than they ever know."

Yeah, she's got the view now. How the crackdown could work. What it would be like not just for him, but if that *People* magazine image his parents had so proudly paraded all these years was suddenly exposed.

His head rises tentatively. "Why are we talking about this?"

"Can't you hear Foreman say, 'Man, what if I go and rub your folks' face in it?' That would totally fuck you up with them."

Staring into the face of that scenario spreads a little more character panic through Burgess' system.

"I should never have gotten into any of this. I should have done it straight."

"No one does it straight. Your father is the king of payoffs. He took your mother's inheritance and bribed his way to the top. Yeah . . . and who did he have carry his money for him like a proper servant. Who made some of those late-night deposits but his obedient little college boy."

"Alright, you've said enough."

"You wanted to step out instead of staying Daddy's little shadow."

"Bribery is one thing. But if I had known where all this would lead—"

"Sometimes you are just like your father. And he was always at his best when he had someone else doing the dirty work."

Burgess is up fast, "Go fuck yourself."

"I do all the time."

He turns hard at her, "No, really."

"Don't get nostalgic over someone you never were." She stands. "All this will clean up." She starts for the door. "Get sixty thousand dollars together, then I'll go see Foreman and Alvarez and make a pitch of my own."

The marquee above the Nightland parking lot reads: IT'S HIP-HOP TIME FOR ANGRY HEARTS. Inside the bar, a wave of faces is looking for their after-hours dream. Dee hangs back in the crowd where she can watch her daughter without being seen.

Dee notices Shay's hair has been cut short, except for a slender braid that hangs Indian style from her temple past the shoulder. The hair is slicked back, and the upper part of her face and eyes have been done in a black mask that makes her look like some ritualistic cat burglar. She is feeding beer to a row of bar dogs when she spots Dee through a surge of living shadows.

The blue light from the bar underscores the secret pain around her mouth and cheeks. Lends sorrow and haunting to eyes hidden within a black façade.

Crack Emcee is hard charging the sound system, doing a riff on social ills. His street epiphany is all linked together with samplers from *The Manchurian Candidate* and *American Pie*, with bits of newscasts and confessions from a crying street whore. It's a freakish human moment, the perfect snatch of rant to backscore her mother's entrance.

Dee doesn't come toward Shay. With a moving world of footlit voices and laughter between them, Dee signs to her daughter: "I need to talk to you."

Shay won't have it.

Again Dee signs: "Don't you know how much I love you? And need you?"

When Dee uses all that resignation and despair Shay can feel the coiling around her heart. With long, slender fingers, Shay answers in sign: "I love you too, Mama. But please, love me from there. I am susceptible to your hurt, so please, love me from there."

Dee swings onto the Silverlake entrance of the Hollywood Freeway and into a running line of taillights. She's making for Hollywood proper. For Sunset Boulevard. For a transient motel known as "The Garden of Allah" she followed the Chicana to from downtown that afternoon.

Dee reaches into the glove compartment for a vial of amphetamines. She's not shaving one either. It's gonna be the full tank of body flex with a little Southern Comfort chaser.

The last twenty-four hours she's been nothing but sideswiped by surprises. Time to get the body armor out of cold storage. To give that gun grip a little exercise. Wipe the dust off those shotgun eyes. Time to know what camera girl is all about.

NINETEEN

———

The Temple-Beaudry district is just west of downtown L.A. At the turn of the century it was a succession of low dusty hills marked by oil rigs and shacks. Over the next sixty years it followed the racial trail of the city toward an unenviable conclusion. Temple-Beaudry became an ethnic firetrap of bleak and abandoned buildings. Strings of homes were razed. Sections of hillside were nothing but stairways leading up to cratered foundations. Streets ended in a short tide of debris and plowed down palm trees. Burned car chassis and hulking broken mounds of concrete. It remained a blasted reminder of the sweep of poverty and disinterest.

The late eighties money rush changed all that. Speculators saw in the twenty-five-acre steal the centerpiece for one faulted land scheme after another. But when the early nineties recession hit, Temple-Beaudry sat as it was, an eyesore west of a revitalized downtown. Until the Belmont Learning Project was launched.

The neighborhood on the northwest side of Belmont Project construction site is a strained mass of lives in collision. Rundown apartments and barred homes, shabby turn-of-the-century monstrosities on their last clapboard legs, are giving way to condos on the come.

The south side of Court Street is two hundred yards of ascending chain-link fence that guards the construction site. On the north side, all the homes have been razed for apartment construction, except one.

Magale Huapaya walks past the small yellow house, trying to be as inconspicuous as a single woman could, out alone in this neighborhood at night.

The house sits on a short incline back from the sidewalk by maybe twenty feet. There are a few lights on inside. But she can't see much beyond the barred and curtained windows. She keeps walking till she's past the house, then turns. The backyard continues on to a block of condos that are half framed up. She scans the yard. It is fenced and topped with barbed wire protecting a series of small connected sheds. No lights on there, not tonight. She is considering a sneaky little look-see when her cellular rings.

She paws through her shoulder bag for the phone. Flips it open. "Yeah?"

"How are we?" asks Landshark.

"I'm at the house on Toluca and Court."

"Any sign of Pettyjohn or Englund?"

"A few lights on inside. Nothing else. If I knew they weren't home I'd sneak up there and—"

"Don't do that. No. Not after this morning."

"Those pictures I took outside the bar, did you get them yet?"

"A runner just brought them up from the lab."

"Did you call him?"

"No. I haven't quite figured how to tell a total stranger I want to drag him back into the horror of his life."

Somewhere nearby an incorporeal noise. Gravel maybe . . . or the chain fence tattling on some slithering cat. Magale scans the street. Her red Chevette is the only car parked by the Belmont School construction site fence. The street otherwise is deserted.

Suddenly uncomfortable, "I think I'll go back to the motel."

"Good idea. Take a bath, pamper yourself. I'll talk to you after I call El Paso. Oh, Magale . . ."

"What?"

"You're doing such a fine job, I . . ." His voice takes a sudden humble, even sad, turn, ". . . I find myself envious."

For a moment she flirts with pride. "Street newsie makes good. How 'bout an honorable mention in your column?"

"Just an honorable mention? No byline? No book deal?"

Tempered youthfulness: "That will come later."

She flips the cellular closed. Slips it back into her shoulder bag. Crosses the deserted street to her Chevette. She should be watchful of shadows, careful about pockets of silence. This is not the place, nor the time, for your head to go lazy.

But for a few seconds, hunting her coat pocket for the car keys, Magale drifts into the weightless world of yet-to-be achievements. She's walking the altitude of a byline and book cover with her name on it when forced scuffs come on fast behind her. Startled, she turns too late.

A gloved hand hard into the side of her face. Her jaw rams into the hood. A gun barrel and a woman's voice behind her. "Don't scream." A second hand takes a clump of coat between the back of Magale's shoulders. The woman's voice again, "Don't fight me now."

Dee pulls Magale away from the car. "Don't fight me." She pulls her back up on the curb. "Stoop down." Magale stoops down. Dee leads her back through a torn mouth of chain-link fence. Magale's coat gets caught in the wire.

"I'm stuck. Please."

"Shut your mouth." Dee pulls hard on the girl's coat. The chain link rattles as the body thugs its way through. Magale's face is gouged by the severed link.

"Stand." Magale stands. Her arms outstretched. She is led back into the vast, dark construction site. Back . . . her breathing fearful and erratic. The shadowland of the street slipping further and further away. The ground begins to give. There is a razorous pain down the right side of her face. Back . . . a slippery incline. Magale slops against Dee, against the gun. They almost tumble and fall, but Dee holds. Back . . . the sand is porous. And leaky. A horizon of window-colored light and an overcast sky, of barren streets, receding further and further.

On both sides of them now are acres of open ground covered with plastic tarps to keep the dust down, to keep the earth from eroding with the rains. Any thought of help is falling helplessly away, and all the headlines that ever frightened Magale feed the nausea inside her belly. She begs, "If you want money . . . just, please don't hurt me."

"Fuckin' close your mouth."

More horrific images. For a moment the moon slips the clouds, but it is nothing more than a small clock in a large, black room.

Dee keeps leading her back. Back through a corridor of earthmovers and water trucks, through a double row of backhoes and bulldozers. Machines huge. Silent. Lifeless.

Again the ground gives way like wrecked stairs. Thoughts of coming death Magale tries to close her mind to. Dee is breathing fast, very fast. Her heart a black pulse against the girl's back. They slide down another short drop. Magale finds herself in an excavation hole. She finds herself being taken around a thirty-foot-tall pyre of loose rock. Finds herself forced to her knees under the shadowy gallows of a conveyor truck.

Dee makes the girl endure moments of her violent presence before she takes her by the hair and demands, "Look out there. Look!"

She twists Magale's head around. Magale stares through the darkness toward the vast rigging of the city, where highrises, remote and polished, look like doorways into a wall of charcoal sky. Where headlights burn, then dissolve down through rows of buildings, and leave nothing but the fluted echo of far traffic. Life is going about its alchemical business as Dee says, "That's the last you'll see of it, if you fuck with me.

"Now lie flat." She pulls the girl's hair downward. "Lie flat!" Magale obeys. Dee kneels into the prone figure. Magale can feel the cold sand on her scored, burning cheek. She can hear in the earth the low fugue of the Harbor and Hollywood Freeways just blocks east. A night traffic of lives speeding into the flueblack distance. If only there was someone who knew. Someone who could—

"I feel how frightened you are," Dee whispers.

Magale is shivering uncontrollably. "Don't hurt me, please."

Dee worms the gun barrel into the soft crease between neck and skull. "You were taking pictures of some men downtown. Why?"

Magale's eyes empty of all hope this was just some kind of robbery or ... She quickly tries to stumble through an ill-thought-out lie. "I wasn't photographing any men. I was—"

Dee stabs the gun handle into Magale's spine. A violent grunt, then Magale begins to cry up her insides. "You were cruising the house. I watched you. You were taking pictures this morning. I saw you. Why!?!"

All the courage Magale ever imagined of herself is ravaged, and the words begin to leak out of her mouth. "I was hired to follow them. I mean, it was him at first. Pettyjohn. But then—"

Years of safety are rocked with each phrase, and now Dee's questions come spitfire fast. "By who—? Who wanted these pictures? Why ... was somebody ... Why should somebody wa—want—"

On Toluca Street sudden shouting, and everything else just stops. A couple of young street turks are cruising up the block, giving that fence a working over as they spit obscenities out into an unsuspecting world. Dee holds back till they clear. Magale's eyes are held tightly shut, her hands remain where they have cored up the sand, but she can hear them. Over Dee's rushing breath. And if she can hear them, they could hear her. One scream. They could hear one scream. She knows she is going to die. Her head might lie up some different end, but the reeking hole of her stomach knows. If only she could just scream and hurl herself upward in one lunge, maybe—

Just do it. Do it while the woman waits those street boys out. Don't become the next unsolved poster face 'cause you're too goddamn frightened to act. Just—

She screams. She screams and flings herself upward into Dee's chest. It's adrenaline-fueled desperation. A thrashing hitch-kick and scrabbling—

Her voice carries shrill for acres. Dee is thrown back, but she doesn't panic. She doesn't fire. The scream carries like locked-up brakes as Dee whipsaws her arm downward. One blow. One ferocious thud to the temple, and that bellpeal shriek is stunned into silence by the underbelly of the gun.

Dee knows the instant the girl defecates, she is dead. Dee pulls back behind the front tires of the conveyor truck to wait those rippers out as they work their way through shadowland. She can make them out against the vaporous ground light of the city. There's three, maybe four.

They slow and stare down into the construction site, and one yells, "We see you down there, motherfucker!"

Sit it out. Don't go clit.

Another brazenly yells, "You got some pussy down there, you ought to share it."

Your future is being discounted in minutes, so work through the head fever.

"Maybe we'll just invite ourselves down."

It ain't the murder. It's like you told Shay, afterward . . . that's where your survival is defined.

One climbs up on the fence and yells, "*You* hear us!"

And there's a few little facts you got to goddamn know yet, like who is this dead thing . . . who hired her. Why . . . why . . . what does it have to do with Pettyjohn. . . . The cellular. She was talking to someone and staring at that house.

Another of the street boys starts riffing something iron against the chain-link fence, then works up a mock on some rap number, "Do what you gotta do to maintain . . ."

Dee slithers out from the truck to the corpse. Lightly pulls at the shoulder bag. Slow. The ropey arm won't give. Keep on slow. Keep on. Now the coat pockets. Now—

Another joins in, "Do what you gotta do to that pussy . . ."

The stench from the girl's bowels is overpowering. Dee rolls the girl face up. The body thuds lifelessly. She gets a hand down the girl's jeans pocket. They are soaked with urine.

Another turk climbs the fence and hovers like some wraith shriek-
ing.

Dee slides back behind the front tires. Wait it out. Wait it out 'cause
you need time. You got to get into her car, you got to get into her motel
room. You got things to know, and you got to deal with that body.
And time is all you can buy with that. But what if those fuckers jump
the fence and come hunting up trouble? What if—

But they don't. Whatever they saw or didn't see. Whatever they
heard or didn't hear. Whatever they know, or don't. Whether that
scream to them was some love movement or clean-assed rape the picture is don't get too fucking close. Case shut. 'Cause a couple of loose
homeboys get too close, they might eat some blame, and they know it.
They're not interested in their asses becoming a flesh canvas for some
of Rodney King's oppressors to skin surf an indictment on.

Dee holds on till there's only the hollow of speeding car tires back
down on Beverly. She stands. Collects all those loose threads inside her
head.

You got to deal with the body. You got to. You can't drag it out of
here. You can't bury it 'cause tomorrow they might be digging anywhere in this pit. Whoever hired the girl knows why she was here, so
you have to—

Something is obscenely remembered. That night in the desert when
she and Shay dragged and rolled the sheriff into that grave. She doesn't
recall the stench. He would have shit if he were dead. She should have
known that. She didn't think. She blamed Shay. Always put it down
as just Shay's failure, but now she knows. She hadn't thought it
through.

The wind kicks up, and those acres of plastic tarp begin to ripple
as if something had awoken, as if some nightbeast had come alive and
begun to move.

She closes her eyes a moment. All those murders were years behind
you. Now you have to start all over again. Only this time someone
might be out there watching. Someone who might know more about
you than you know about them.

No mistakes here. None. You have to try and derail. . . . No, you
have to derail any thought this murder might be connected to those
photographs. To— But how?

Make matter-of-fact out of brutal work. This is about survival. Otherwise you might as well go clit and crawl next to that slack murdered
thing while you wait for morning.

Some answer's got to be hammered home. Even if you got to tear the inside of your head to shreds. She makes herself hover over the body. Makes herself stare it down. Then . . . moving through manic impossibilities like some nova, she sees it.

Straight off the rack. Thank you, homeboys, for the thought. Yeah she remembers lying in that Chicana's position once. In the lecherous dark, fighting off some poisoned muscle.

She kneels over the girl. Clenches her teeth against the foul odor. She starts with the shoes. Then the jeans. They have to be dragged off. They come slow as the molting skin of some snake. Next is the girl's white filthed underwear. Dee almost retches.

She stands. Begins to scour the darkness. Hunched over, she moves across the excavation pit. There's ghastly work to do as she searches for something, anything that will alter a murder with rape.

Landshark sits at his desk staring at two photos. One Magale took of Jon Pettyjohn walking into that little yellow house on Toluca. And the other, also at that little yellow house, was taken almost eleven years earlier. But in this photo Charlie Foreman was wielding a crowbar and trying to smash a car windshield that separated him from the unseen photographer.

Landshark puts the photos down. He looks at the phone, and before he dials tells himself, "I can't let myself fail this time . . . Not this time."

THE BURIAL

TWENTY

Vic watches the rain against the hotel lobby window. Beyond that, a switcher makes slow time through a freightyard of gray mist.

He listens to the long-termers at a card table. The usual blow and roll of losers and loners staked out to a night of poker, and beer in paper cups. On the windowsill a half-assed ghetto blaster, bootlegged from the trash and repaired, plays a worn down Seger cassette.

"Hey, Vic."

He comes around in his chair. The night manager points to the house phone on the sideboard, "Call for you."

"Who is it?"

The night manager shrugs, goes back to his badly thumbed magazines. Vic guesses it's one of the bartenders at Bliss seeing if he wants to grab a few extra bucks keeping the biker crowd in line.

"Hello."

"Victor Trey?"

A voice he doesn't recognize. "Yeah."

"Victor Trey, who once went by the name John Victor Sully?"

Somebody has been digging. Vic nervously fingers his hair away from a shirt pocket so he can hunt up a cigarette.

"I worked very hard to find you, Victor."

The voice sounds well manicured. Vic lights up, "I guess I should roll over in my grave at being found, hunh?"

"I can understand—"

"You think so." Vic realizes his voice has taken off when the night manager looks up over the rim of his magazine. Vic turns toward the wall, lowers his voice. "Why are you calling?"

"I do a column for *The New Weekly*. Local politics . . . gossip . . . exposés . . . commentary . . . investig—"

He has a quick recollection *The New Weekly* was some throwaway piece of shit with its left-wing head up its ass and an overdose of ads. "What's your name?"

"I go by the name of 'Landshark.' "

Jesus Christ, he thinks, What is that, a joke? He whispers now. "Did you call to dig up the corpse? To open up wounds for a couple of catchy phrases? That 'Where are they now' stuff? Obviously, if you found me you know where I am and what I am."

"I am not," says Landshark, "dishonest enough to say I wouldn't go back into your personal wounds for a few good quotes, but that is not why I'm calling."

"Right. Now, what do I have to bribe you with to leave me quietly unknown here?"

The voice at the other end starts politely, calmly, "I have information I believe lays a foundation that the murder attempt against your life could have been, and here I frame the phrase 'could have been' . . . a conspiracy. Which I have always believed it was."

Vic can feel all those locked doors and the cataclysm they will let loose if opened. He starts to tremble. "Go on."

"I need you to come back to Los Angeles. Review what I have. If it holds up, and I think it will, let's work together on this to—"

"What do you really want?"

"I? I want what you want."

A sound that could never pass for human. "You have no idea what I want. Or what I feel."

"Victor, I can imagine what an innocent man wants after years of suffering. And about how you feel. As foolish and trivial as it may come to seem when . . . if . . . you get to know me, you will find I have very much in common with you. I have my own grave—"

Vic's whole body goes into one involuntary spasm, and he hangs up. Inside him, things were perfectly numb, except for that seething coffin corner which he held in check with a special disregard for himself.

He walks over to the window. Picks up on that raspy Seger voice: *Your thoughts will soon be wandering the way they always do. . . .*

He should not have hung up. In the window, a reflection to remind him who he is. No off-key chance of youth left there. Just another toppled human being covered in rain.

He should not have hung up. But who was this man asking him to throw aside all the years of tragic clarity to return to Los Angeles and make the flesh thirst for another chance at what . . .

He should not have hung up. A blunt saxophone and Bob Seger

singing, *Here I am on the road again*. . . . Uphill dreams from a city that has his ghost by the throat. . . . *There I go, turn the page.*

— 25 SEPTEMBER 1998, 994 ANDALUSIA AVENUE, MOUNT WASHINGTON, CALIFORNIA —

William Worth is not a coward, in any sense. He is just deathly afraid. Fear *is* him. It drives the engine of everything he does, or should it be said, everything he does not do. It is the unknown protagonist that controls his emotions. That has left him feeling—no, believing—the world is a harbor of dangers, and he is unsafe anywhere except within the walls of his house. This fear has so come to dominate his public and private life that in the last ten years there have been barely a dozen times when he has been off those two acres of fenced and hidden property, and then only when medicated. In your basic Psych 101 parlance, William Worth, otherwise known to his reading public as "Landshark," is a housebound agoraphobic.

His four-story Mount Washington retreat is built into the hillface of an isolated ridgeback at the end of Andalusia Avenue. His office completely takes up one of the lower floors. Through a 270-degree battlement of windows, he looks out over the city where he made his name. From Glendale south to the downtown skyline, then east to Boyle Heights and Monterey Park. This is not the chic angle most monied Angelenos prize. The "I" in Mount Washington is not big enough for most egos. But for him, that living island of lights he looks out upon serves up the limited and illusory promise that somehow he is at the center of everything that is going on without him.

He sits quietly staring at the phone as if sharing secret minutes with another of Saturn's children. He can understand why Victor hung up on him so abruptly. Some stranger calls with a two-minute sound bite on your stolen life and asks you to bundle up all that frustrated rage and head back into the land of ilk and money for another possible beating, another possible betrayal.

He is trying to mentally articulate his next call to Victor when he notices two helicopters moving fast across a mural of downtown highrises. He gets up, takes binoculars from the top of a filing cabinet, steps out onto a deck that runs the full length of the house. They're police helicopters. Just southwest of Elysian Hills and Dodger Stadium. Their searchlights are strafing a small circle of blocks. By his estimate they would be in the vicinity of Temple-Beaudry.

This gives him pause. It should be him out there working this, not some enthusiastic twenty-year-old. He should be confronting the risk, but he can't even control the panic that stalks his insides.

He goes to his desk and sits. It seems that envy and anguish are his personal passwords for the day.

Enough with self-pity. He swallows a shot of half-cold espresso, then abruptly grabs the phone and redials El Paso.

TWENTY
ONE

———

Shay is doing the Nightland closeout alone, which is how she prefers it. Just her and the kitchen workers in the back, hosing the place clean. She makes herself a bourbon and rocas, then checks out the CD to find something that qualifies as a mood tranquilizer.

She's behind the bar, tallying up and sipping, when she hears a woman's voice in the kitchen hustling an entrance in Spanish. She closes her eyes, and wishes for invisibility.

"You and I have to talk, Shay."

Shay's eyes open. They shift from the tally sheet to the bar mirror. Inside that black mask of makeup, there's a matter-of-fact anger Dee has no trouble reading.

"I thought we had talked." Without waiting, Shay collects the receipts and heads for the office. Dee is left to wait, or leave. The minutes stretch on till they feel longer than the Great Wall of China. Shay returns, sullen and silent. Dee's lips and nose pinch as her daughter will not even acknowledge her with a look, and instead begins to put down the lights till all that's left are the fluorescents under the bar.

"You and I are gonna fuckin' talk tonight. It ain't a matter you don't want to. I need you to hear—"

Shay slices into her speech, "You need?!" She turns, shuts the sound system down with quick, sterile snaps. Comes back around. "The more I stay away the more you try and weasel back into my life. I get a good month, sometimes two, then there you are." Shay starts to mimic Dee. " 'Shay, I'm down' . . . 'Shay, I'm sick' . . . 'Shay, I'm drugged out.' " Shay walks away, stops, comes back. "You don't get it. I'm trying to survive here, okay. I'm trying my best to hold it together. Fuck! Doesn't that mean anything to you?"

"It means everything to me. And little do you know—"

"How little? How little do I know? I got enough shit in my head to fill a friggin' minivan with psych patients, but I . . . hold it together . . ." She closes her eyes, opens them. "Hold it together." It's as if she's talking to herself. "Just hold it together." Now, to her mother, "You are not gonna skullcase me anymore. I did things for you. . . ." She grabs her glass and gets down as much bourbon as she can swallow. She is on the verge of tears, "You know, Mama, for the Chinese and the Eskimos, when food was in short supply—"

"You're not gonna lay some of your book bullshit on me. Not now. Not—"

"When food was in short supply the Chinese and the Eskimos would kill their newborn daughters." Shay leans toward the bar, her face so close to her mother's to be almost an alter-image. "You should have killed me, or aborted me. It would have made both our lives easier."

Dee's whole body takes a hard turn into pain. She clenches up at Shay saying such a thing.

Then, she slams her open hands down on the bar so brutally Shay jerks back. There will be no discrimination tonight on who gets flacked.

"I'm trying to save our lives, you ungrateful—" Under siege or not, Dee gets a hold of herself. Looks toward the kitchen to make sure none of those filthy wetbacks can hear. "We could be in serious trouble. Me . . . and you. Worse than jail time. Get it now?" Fevered breathing, quick trembles. "Read me, Shay. Look!"

The painted mask around Shay's eyes rings tightly. She wants to run, but she is afraid. As afraid as she is, she better find out what hole her life may be tumbling down into without her knowing. She crosses her arms. "Talk."

Dee glances at the kitchen again to make sure she will not be overheard. She begins by slinging a rip at "the Spic and Foreman," hits the ethics report hard, takes a few inches out of Burgess' ass for "not paying Alicia up front." Her hands rise and fall in fevered gestures as she lays out the ultimatum "those two fags" hit them with. But it's when Dee spots up that girl with the camera the piping around Shay's eyes tightens and her mouth goes flat against her teeth.

Dee is now sheer instinct on legs staring into a mere of nickel-colored lights as she describes the argument on the street and that the Chicana was getting a lens full, then following her through hot traffic to the Garden of Allah Motel up on Sunset, tracking her to Toluca Street later that night.

There are threads of sweat along Dee's jawbone. Words and phrases piled up on each other, thanks to all the speed she's eaten. . . ."Fuckin' Pettyjohn . . . the girl cruising the house . . . Pettyjohn's house . . . making a cellular call." Dee's fingers nub the barwood, make a squeaking, almost silly noise Shay wishes would stop. Then Dee jump cuts to, "She was hired to follow Englund and Pettyjohn. I got that much out of her." Fingers still nubbing barwood. "And you know what that could mean for us."

The silence makes the room seem darker, emptier. Wading through all this, Shay looks down at her mother's hands, notes for the first time gash marks along the knuckles, grime under the fingernails, dirt curried up her jacket sleeve.

"The way your hands are trembling, someone might think you had Parkinson's Disease."

"It's all the fuckin' speed I had to eat."

Shay turns, uses the time filling a water glass with Southern Comfort to collect herself, to clear out the strangled feeling she is back in the trunk of that car speeding toward the border.

Dee drinks. Slow, thick swallows. Her mouth so dry it soaks up the alcohol like raw wood does varnish.

"Where is the girl now?"

Dee puts down the glass. "I can't talk to Burgess about this. He might go clit on me, and then what?"

"Where is the girl?"

"If someone has connected Pettyjohn and Englund—"

"Where is the girl?"

"We got to find out why. If it leads to us—"

"Fuckin' answer me!"

"*I am* answering you."

Yeah . . . a holocaust of delivered feelings. Full bore. One look. One taut virulent, neck-deep stare, and Shay's down a black stairwell, with black candles. Outside, people pass. A girl's electric laughter. Can I be that girl now? Can I? That's all she thinks with her whole insides going liquid on her, can I?

Shay grabs her purse, glasses, her cellular phone, starts around the bar. Dee follows. "Where are you going?" Shay doesn't answer. Dee's arm moves like a bagging hook and locks onto Shay's wrist.

"Let go of me."

"I got rid of the girl's car. I took all her ID."

Shay keeps pulling backward toward the kitchen. "Let fucking go."

"There was nothing in the car. So we have to get into her motel room."

Shay curls down, bends her back. "Then you do it."

"We've got to find out who hired the girl, and why."

Shay comes straight up with all her strength, makes a rigid fist, and hits her mother square in the chest.

Gaffed breath. The grasp of her daughter's wrist lost. Before she can gather up, Shay is gone. Out the huge stainless steel kitchen door. It hits the wall, then snaps back to a cutting stop.

TWENTY
TWO

———

Bundled in a poncho, just inside her patio door, Dee watches the rain first start to fall, thin and slant, out of the pre-dawn dark. From there the San Fernando Valley is a vast imprint of damp streets and freeways marked by still lines of dimpled light. That sleeping grovel of lives out there will wake to find another grisly murder with their morning coffee.

Dee's dark and haggard eyes look back across the living room where Magale Huapaya's belongings are spread out on the coffee table. There's nothing in those silly accoutrements that would answer the question seared in her head. Nothing except maybe that cellular phone.

After Dee had dumped the girl's car downtown, she stopped at an all-night coffee shop. Sitting alone, she took out the cellular and pushed SEND. The display showed the last call made from Toluca Street. The last number dialed—805-501-7133. Before the cellular began to ring, she pressed END.

Walking back to Temple-Beaudry for her car, the cellular rang ceaselessly. Someone was out there who wanted, needed, to talk to Magale Huapaya. Was it the someone who hired her?

Dee is crashing on her feet. She crosses the room, sits on the couch, looks down at the cellular. It's time to learn who or what is 805-501-7133.

She takes up the phone. Presses SEND. The ringing starts. She closes her eyes to hold back her crash and concentrate on listening. The ringing continues. Will she get someone's answering machine, a name maybe? Will it be the message center for a law firm, or a detective agency? More ringing. She can feel all the points of her being start to cave in, and she is about to press END, when—

A voice. A man's voice. Sleepy. "Magale?" She hovers above the moment like a vulture, waiting. The voice concerned, urgent, "Magale . . . Magale?"

She presses END. Puts the phone down. Whoever this *He* is, was expecting her to call. Was expecting it to be her. Even at this hour.

The dead girl's cellular begins to ring. It rings and rings and rings. *He* is anxious. Did this *He* hire the girl? She lays on the couch, curls up in a fetal position. The ringing stops, only to start again.

Anxious . . . this *He* is very anxious. Desperate maybe. She can feel herself falling from the rim of the living world. Everything is shutting down. The phone stops, only to start again. It will be a footrace to the end. Will this *He* find out about her first, or will she find him?

THE ESCAPE

TWENTY
THREE

There's only one thought running through Vic's mind as the plane makes its way from Texas to California . . . I am coming back. Not, I am coming home. Not, I might be able to make my life whole. Or some positive closure could be effected out of this horrific depravity. He will not give hope one opening, yet he is coming back for more.

So Vic wasn't entirely in the dark on who or what he was flying back to meet, Landshark overnighted to El Paso excerpts of his weekly "Big Island/L.A." column.

Each assault was a full page of sheer shotgun journalism. The world as seen from the street newsies and disenfranchised Angelenos who called Landshark's hotline with scoops about councilmen and school board officials.

He was hard into government bashing and political smears. Took it to celebrities. Gave kudos to good restaurants trying to make it, ego pounded any wretch who thought they could power their good weight around.

He followed up stories the major press should have in the first place. Kept up a personal war with *The L.A. Times*, which he considered nothing more than "birdcage liner."

And each run was closed by Landshark referring to himself as the "gay Charlemagne of columnists," which he left up to his audience to decide if it was because of his size or his stature.

At Ontario Airport, Vic is met by a hired car service to take him to Landshark. It's rush hour, and rain on the San Bernardino Freeway. A miserably muddy night, and great waterwells spray up from cars in the diamond lane. Flows of overwhelming roadside memory—his stepfather's favorite steak house, a coffee shop he'd hit after high school Friday nights driving back from L.A., a mall parking lot where he made a girl who snagged him from a bar.

He glances out the rear window. Back through miles of slipstreaming headlights, back through ninety minutes of hard driving is the Mojave National Preserve and that shapeless crib of earth he gasped his way out of, to end up here.

He shuts his eyes. The mysterious uncertainty about who he is and how all this would affect him makes itself known. And the tied-down truth has rage written all over it.

Downtown is a nightmare of struggling traffic made worse by a black-out. Sections of Hollywood and Pasadena are without electricity. Stretches of Koreatown and City Terrace are long blocks patched with night. The streetlights around Superior Court stand dark. It's as if some hand had a little random havoc in mind for Vic's homecoming.

The climb up Mount Washington Drive and San Raphael Avenue gives him his first real look at this neighborhood above Highland Park. The streets are a quilt of eccentricities winding higher through miles of heavily wooded state land. Here the downright shabby meet the shamelessly overdone. Here, off-road niches have been turned into al-leged artists' nests and piles of casually dumped debris co-exist with architectural hallucinations glued to the mountain on stilts.

Andalusia Avenue—home to the recent and the rebuilt—comes to an abrupt wall with coiled wire across the top. Beside a heavy flatiron gate is a freestanding intercom where the driver codes in a number.

A voice Vic recognizes as Landshark's hellos.

"It's Damiano with Town Car. I have your guest here."

The gates slowly part. The black Lincoln starts down a paved sliver of a road through badly unkempt trees. Fifty, seventy, ninety yards, and only the slightest touch of houselights through the damp, black overgrowth.

A short turn the driver is obviously familiar with, and everything opens. They are at the edge of the mountain where a house is built four stories down onto a stone ledge, and seems to be looking out over the whole world.

Landshark watches from a darkened window as the Lincoln pulls up. The rear car door opens, and he gets his first look at Victor Trey as he is now. The boy in those 1987 newspaper photos and graduating sheriff department stills is no more. That youth is another life MIA replaced by a nicked and battered face with a high forehead and receding hair-line. The shoulder-length hair is pulled back at the sides and clasped to the crown in a partial ponytail. Vic wears a thick goatee, and that funky suede coat can't hide the fact his arms are dangerously pumped.

As Vic starts for the house Landshark notices the oddly hypnotic saunter that throws off a kind of rough sexuality, and he wonders if it's something in the man or the damage done to the pelvic bone when he was gunned down.

As Vic steps to the door it opens, and there, framed by floodlights around the entranceway, is Landshark. Vic's over six feet tall, yet he finds himself having to stare straight up into the face of the man who brought him here.

"Come in, please." Landshark puts out a hand to shake. He is freak-ishly thin, impeccably dressed in black gabardine pants and black pull-over shirt. "Why don't you get that wet coat off while I take care of my friend here?"

Damiano carefully sets Vic's duffel and battered suitcase off to one side of the vestibule. Landshark has the driver step out under the por-tico where they can talk privately. Vic gets his wet coat off, and watches their silent monologue, using the time to look this Landshark character over. He cuts the mark at about six foot nine. And with that neat buzz cut and beautifully trimmed moustache, he's the perfect upscale ad. The only off tweak might be an air of detached sensitivity that seems to affect each physical gesture. As Landshark hands the driver an en-velope, he slips a dime-sized roll of hundreds into his pocket.

He closes the front door and turns to Vic, certain this little financial exchange was noticed. "I wanted to make sure my friend had dimin-ished recall about who he brought here tonight, as things have taken a much more serious and ugly turn." He steps up to Vic. "May I take your coat please?"

Vic hands him the wet coat. As Landshark hangs it inside the door of the hall closet, Vic asks, "What's happened?"

Landshark's long frame leans into the closet door before he closes it. "I think I made a terrible mistake."

Vic comes up beside him. Landshark stares into the small dark cubicle. The rain comes in hard sheets against the roof, offsetting the silence.

Vic asks again, "What's happened?"

"The girl I told you was working for me. I picked it up first on my police radio. It's been carried on the news since late morning. A girl's nude body was discovered at the construction across the street from where Magale last called. The body had been violated with a bottle." Landshark notices a pack of cigarettes in Vic's shirt pocket. "Are those real cigarettes, or filtered?"

"Filtered."

His pipish fingers flit at the air for one.

Vic gets out the pack, shakes loose a cigarette. "Has the body been ID'd?"

Landshark breaks off the filter, bends toward Vic's lighter. In Landshark's soft, soft blue eyes the flame is like scars. "It's not possible," he says. "The body was too badly burned."

Vic snaps the lighter shut to kill off the suddenly perverse image of the flame.

"I should never have sent Magale out alone, not a twenty-year-old for sure. Let's go down to the war room."

Vic follows Landshark down a central stairwell toward the second floor. "What have you told the police?"

"Nothing."

"Why not?"

Landshark stops, looks back at Vic. For a moment they are eye to eye. "Of all people to ask that. What did the police ever do for you?"

The whole second floor, all two thousand square feet, is office. There is an L-shaped table with two mainframe computers. A table beside that with laptops and printers, and a police radio. Another table with a bank of phones and answering machines constantly kicking in with messages. Another lineup of cellular phones, each tagged with a number. It's closer, thinks Vic, to exactly what Landshark called it—a war room.

Landshark is behind a bar along the back wall, pouring Vic a cup of coffee and himself a mug of Oban Scotch. He starts around the bar, hands Vic his cup, and motions toward a conference table in the center of the room.

There Vic comes face to face with his life, all neatly stacked in piles. Paper entries from his birth, right up to the sordid newspaper photo of 1987. A cut-and-dry bio of grim reminders.

"I accumulate files on crimes that interest me." He draws Vic's attention to Magale's photos. "I hire people to dig up facts, gather leads. I get off on jump-starting these deaders.

"Let me show you how a few months ago I reconnected with the attempt on your life."

Landshark reaches for a file with a large mix of cutouts from assorted newspapers and opens it across the table.

"The Belmont Learning Center. It was christened the Taj Mahal of Schools, but it's been rife with double dealings, union wars, cost overruns, backbitings, starts and stops, simple screw-ups, city council and school board infighting, complaints the site is too goddamn toxic and that no school should have been started there in the first place and why didn't anyone know better, or do better or say better. . . . This sorry construction hole has been the perfect metaphor for how things mess up when there's big money around."

Landshark pulls a front-page newspaper article in *The Daily News* that features the photo of a poorly dressed old couple standing on the steps of a two-story relic Craftsman with the Belmont construction site behind them. He hands the article to Vic. "They had been complaining to everyone that there was a horrible odor of sulphur coming out of the ground the deeper that excavation pit was dug. They made a lot of calls but no one paid any mind. They got desperate enough to try the 800 number at the bottom of my column.

"I sent out an expert who'd been with the gas company for years." Landshark pulls his article. "I let the man's report speak for itself. That site was way more contaminated than the first evaluation claimed, and the first filings with the city ever indicated."

Landshark then begins to lay out article after article from *The Daily News, The L.A. Times,* and other free papers hammering at the deeply faulted groundwork behind the Taj Mahal of Schools, which by now, thanks to Landshark's nasty way with a word, had been nicknamed "Fiasco High."

"This is when," says Landshark, "I brought Magale Huapaya in. I wanted her to walk the neighborhood. Take pictures. Get names. See what she could pick up."

He reaches for Vic's file. Begins to finger his way deep into a clutter of photos. Pulls one of the little yellow house on Toluca. Hands it to Vic.

It's a long lens catch-all of a man walking out the front door unaware he is being had by a camera.

"See, that house is the only one left on the block. And on the block behind it condos are being built. Well, that character bought the house years ago for dirt. He was offered greed money for the place by the company building those condos, if nothing else to get rid of an eyesore. But he's trying to dick them big time."

Vic looks the photo over. Landshark waits to see if this odd character jogs his memory.

"By the way, that's Jon Pettyjohn," says Landshark, "the CalTrans worker who testified against you."

"I would never have recognized him."

"I wouldn't either. He's gone a little sinematic over the years. And I spell that with an 's,' not a 'c.' But, I did recognize the house. At least, I vaguely remembered it."

Vic stares at the photo. "I don't understand."

Landshark hands him another snapshot. This is the one of Foreman trying to crowbar the windshield of a car across the street from the same house. "That was taken by a wannabe reporter not long after you were busted in Hollywood for possession of a concealed weapon and drunken driving."

Vic's face muscles flinch at the memory of it.

"The reporter wanted to interview Foreman. He had found out who his parole officer was. As you might recall, Foreman was on parole for a possession rap when you snagged him in the desert. The reporter followed Foreman to that house to try and interview him about *your* case."

Vic keeps staring at the photo and then asks the one question Landshark was sure he would. "Did Pettyjohn own the house then?"

"When I started to get into this Belmont mess, when I checked the old records and found him to be the same Pettyjohn who was the witness against you, I found out he did own the house then. Yes . . . as early as '88 you can connect them. So it sure looks to me there was a conspiracy of some kind against you."

Vic's eyes close. There *was* one detail. Even back then. One that could have spared him—

"Who was the reporter?"

Landshark reaches for another dossier of photos from his personal file. "Yours truly," Landshark says. He hands Vic the dossier. "There's more yet, Vic."

Vic takes the dossier of photos. Landshark watches silently as he begins that elusive and headlong walk from work print to work print.

Each picture brings an emotional shift to Vic's being. The nicks on his face contort. The arms, which are dangerously pumped, tighten. The scars on his biceps and forearms that look ominously like blade wounds, whiten. When he comes to that run of color shots with Englund and Pettyjohn walking past the Barclay Hotel there is a violent hitch lock of facial muscles.

"That was the first time Magale linked them together in a photo."

Vic's neck muscles look as if they're bracing for a head-on crash.

"Connect them and see how your attempted murder plays. What if Foreman was coming to meet those two the day you busted him? What if they were all part of some drug scam? What if Foreman threatened to turn them over if their case wasn't blown out? You could see the how and why of planted evidence. *Those two* might have hired the people—"

"Who is the man they're arguing with outside the bar?"

"I don't know. But I have someone working on that now."

Vic doesn't so much set the photos down as they slip from his fingers. A face seething and marbled white turns to Landshark. "I need some air."

Vic walks over to the sliding glass doors, opens them, steps out onto the deck. He slumps into a wind that sweeps rain across the building, soaking him.

Landshark asks him in a low voice to come back in. Vic instead walks across the deck to a chair and sits. He leans his head against the railing and begins to cry. Landshark watches through the glass as the drenched shirt jacks and quivers with each flurry of sobs and the hands tighten around the wooden railing as if they need to tear it loose.

·

Landshark slips a black rain slicker with a hood around Vic's shoulders, then pulls a chair in close beside him. Vic's face rises, strings of matted hair across sad blood-stung eyes, "I want my life back . . . desperately. You don't know how desperately."

Landshark hands Vic the mug of scotch. "In '87 I was existing on tranquilizers and antidepressants. I had severe emotional problems that still own me. I wanted to be a reporter, and, mess that I was, I managed to get on a short list of names for a gig at *The L.A. Times*. But, God bless them, they did a background check on me and found out that I had artfully recrafted my past. So I became unhireable."

Landshark wipes the rain from his face, "One night not long after that, I was fucked up in my house sucking down cognac and lighter fluid. I was throat deep into the idea of committing suicide. Then the news hit about you." Landshark's face trembles. "I knew if someone could crawl out of a grave, I could. Sometime, anyway. So, I connected us. It may have been an implausible and churlish idea, but I used it to keep on. I used your case to keep on through the antidepressants and tranquilizers. But I cracked out anyway."

Landshark closes his eyes. "I think I cracked out the day Foreman came at me with a crowbar. Or maybe that's just another excuse." He opens his eyes. "I was so close to helping you. I just didn't have the emotional courage to keep on."

Vic takes a drink and Landshark waits to see what, if anything, he will say. But Vic remains silently fixed on the mug.

Landshark looks out into a Los Angeles cut with blackout. "I have been a voyeur. A sex addict. I was born Catholic and gay. I am consumed by fear and by guilt. I have enough money for lifetimes, and the fights that go with them."

The rain slants hard across their faces and both men have to turn their heads away. Landshark continues, "And, as aberrant as I am, and I am that, I do believe we have led parallel lives in ways that you don't yet see."

Vic looks up. He can't hold back a sarcastic grimace. "Yeah, I'm sure that's what the driver you paid to bring me here was thinking when he dumped my whole life in those two Salvation Army bags on your doorstep. There's two freaks living parallel lives. Come the fuck on."

Vic takes a drink, then hands Landshark back the mug. That brooding androgynous giant huddles in closer. "We both took assumed names. Mine is a byline. Yours is a through line, as in, you threw away your stepfather's name for your birth father's name. A quiet little revolution against the past I think we are both familiar with. And ... I have no intention of ever going to the police, and neither do you. You want to hunt them out and coup their lives. The right people are going into the grave this game and I want the byline. I want my own redemption."

Landshark goes to drink from the cup, but before he does says, "By the way, if you don't want to be found, dump your social security number and stop paying taxes 'cause any half-assed hacker can track you."

"I'll remember that for next time."

"Yes, I'm sure you will."

The men study each other through the rain. Then Vic asks: "Do you have any idea what you are bringing into this house?"

"The violence?" Landshark thinks about a murdered girl in a construction site who could be, and probably is, the young woman he'd befriended. He looks down into the mug of scotch and remarks, more to himself than Vic, "In ceremonies of the horseman, even the pawn must hold a grudge." He empties the cup, braces his face against the rain, and to Vic says, "The violence is already here."

PART
THREE

―――――

NEVER
COUNT
OUT THE
DEAD

TWENTY
FOUR

Shay rents a small, nondescript gray house with blue trim on the V-shaped corner of Swan and West Silverlake Drive. The side yard is a fenceless slope of ice plants that faces West Silverlake. The only defense for a girl living alone there are the barred windows.

You take the rain and access to those windows from the dark side of the house and a shooter's got a pretty good chance of taking Shay down, then escaping unseen.

> *Love has never been easy for me.*
> *Can't you see I have always been lonely?*
> *Faith, it seems like a mystery.*
> *Girls like me, have to hide our hearts away.*

Shay lies on the living room floor mood bathing to the formless sorrow of "My Secret Love." She bleeds with the music, letting it fill in the lost hopes of existence. The stereo display lights throw small stars across the black ceiling making her a bare, fleshy drawn target.

> *People will never understand,*
> *they'll destroy us if they can.*
> *Say we were struck down by the hand of Heaven.*

She's just a ruined womanchild life is piling on. Thank you, Mother. Your American dream strikes again.

Shay's fingertips slide down the small amulet she wears around her neck. It sits just above her breasts and as she listens to the music she begins to rub the charm across her nipples. The amulet is shaped like a coffin with a lid that can be opened. Inside the silver casket she always has a little something tucked away for when the mind tics get to eating at her.

No drugs tonight, though. And no headhunting for a little genitorture to help further rip apart the suffering shreds of yourself. Just formless sorrow and a moody saxophone and Lilly Banquette's controlled suffering as you follow light stars somewhere . . . where . . . anywhere . . . and hope one day the secret life you're stuck with just might die before your eyes while there's a few ounces of soul passion left to bargain with.

If only—

A concussion so loud blows through the guts of that small room it lifts her off the ground. A muzzle of glass explodes past her head.

The first burnt thought . . . it's a fuckin' driveby. Some hot rider on the venge. Just hold up there in the dark and—

The second shot ends that as Lilly Banquette's voice is blown into a sheath of stereo plastic across the wall. Shay starts to crawl the floor. The hand-nailed phrase inside her head now: "Don't go clit." It's got her mother's voice written all over it as she elbows through the dark. "Don't go clit." There's jagged glass on the carpet where she claws along toward the kitchen. Get to the kitchen. No windows in the kitchen. Your gun in the kitchen. In the shoulder bag on the chair in the kitchen.

She tests the cold linoleum on her bare skin. She grabs the chair. It topples and her bag hits her in the face. Footsteps on the brick outside. Quick clicks against the rain. The metal deck chair smacks stone. Something is moving toward the pantry door.

She braces her back against the stove. Gets her feet up against the fridge. Gets a griplock on her palm-sized Guardian. Leans into the doorway just enough, into the dark just enough, just enough to put two fast shots into the pantry door.

A powderline of blue air. Pop . . . pop! The wood splinters out into holes. She leans back. Waits for the judgment on her aim. Frees up an open hand. Blindly feels for her bag. Empties out everything onto the kitchen floor. Gets a hand on her cellular. No light. Speed dials on adrenaline-driven instinct.

The phone rings. She watches. Listens. She hates her mother at this moment more than anything in the world.

Her mother's voice message picks up. Shay whispers back, "You better get over here. Someone tried to kill me. They're outside somewhere. Get over here."

She waits out an hour in the dark, her back against the stove. Forgoes everything but foreign noises that fill in around a slowing rain. Wonders if some neighbor heard or saw, if the police had been called.

The black angles of that possibility make for some bleak minutes. The fuckin' world is coming back to get her. That chop hole in the desert is opening up. Has a face for her. Has a cold little corner with her name—

She jumps when the cellular rings. Her hand scrawls the floor to find it.

It's her mother. "I'm outside. I've been walking the street the last ten minutes. There's no one around the house. I'm coming in the front door, so be careful not to shoot me by accident."

Dee can hear the acid in Shay's answer: "It wouldn't be a fuckin' accident."

TWENTY
FIVE

From the kitchen Dee scans the darkened living room with a flashlight. The beam follows the trail of damage from wall to window. Dee's got her fangs out anyone would try to go after Shay, and she says so.

Shay answers, "This is as much your fault."

"We're not gonna go there tonight, are we?"

Shay's eyebrows rise with animosity. "No, why slow dance with reality, if you're never gonna fuck?"

She grabs her mother's shoulder bag lying on the counter and starts to look inside for a cigarette. Dee spots up the flashlight to help Shay along. The dusky beam falls across the Parabellum's metallic bunting.

"Talk about flashbacks," Shay says, lifting the semiautomatic.

"I wasn't going to let anyone hurt you."

Shay cracks the weapon down on the counter top. "Present company excluded, of course."

Dee runs the light right at Shay's eyes. Right at them, and holds it there. "Why don't you lay down and get some sleep?"

"You know I can't sleep unless I'm loaded on something. That I haven't slept since my little trip . . . in a car trunk."

"Go rest then."

Shay's eyes do not back down from the light, or her mother's face hidden behind it, "You left me in Mexico for two years. You were fuckin' punishing me bad. You know the kind of ravage you opened up in me."

Dee turns away, exhausted. She is one exposed nerve trying to keep their lives together.

"I can't even find one dream inside me, you know that."

Dee stares into the living room. Runs the flashlight beam from wall to window. "Foreman wouldn't do this until he was sure he couldn't get the money."

"Are you listening?"

"But the two screamers might."

Shay grabs the Parabellum and slams it down on the counter again. She begins to bench strip that semiautomatic for cleaning. She has her mother's taut, sure moves. "Ready to go, Mama? Ready to take that little trip out into the desert again? That's what you want, isn't it?"

Dee's features are slack, her eyes bitter. Shay grabs her mother's cigarettes, "This is why I live alone."

She lights one, inhales, then takes the cigarette and uses it as a pointer aimed right at her mother's heart. "Why I take nothing from you or Burgess. Your whole fuckin' crowd. You, him, his father . . . that little social war party, you are all the culmination of what this culture is about. And I'm stuck living in the shadow of your degradations."

"If you're not gonna rest, then get dressed. We need to get into that girl's motel room."

Shocked that all she's said has just blown past her mother, Shay goes completely off, "I pledge allegiance to the flag—"

"Not tonight."

"Of the unleashed state of mind known as my mother—"

"She could have pictures, notes. Something that might connect us to Pettyjohn and Englund."

"And to the republic of barbed-wire ideas on which she stands—"

"This is about our survival!"

"One notion, indivisible and dangerous to all."

"Don't give me any of your book mind bullshit and walk right past what I'm saying. Get dressed."

"Viva Verboten."

"What?"

"Long live the forbidden."

Dee slams the flashlight onto the countertop so hard the glass spring shoots from its casing and cracks against the cabinet face. A quarter moon piece spears Dee's cheek and eyelid.

"Christ." Dee grabs her eye. Feels the blood. While she curses Shay, Shay opens the refrigerator, grabs some ice, wraps it in a towel.

"Let me look at that."

Dee moves her hand away. The blood bubbles out the eyelid, then streams down into the eye causing it to shutter uncontrollably.

"You might need stitches."

"Fuck what I need. Let's talk about what we need."

"What I need is a clean state of mind, and that isn't within reach."

Shay hands her the towel with the ice. The slowly closing refrigerator door lights the two women's emotional standoff. A fading pool of brief seconds, then all is black as they face each other.

The silence that passes feels like it's weighed down with stones. Dee, in a totally ravaged moment, speaks: "Everything you say about me, Shay, is true. Everything you think, no matter how fucked, is true. All that being said, or thought, won't save you." She points the toweled ice toward a living room raked with pistol fire. "That's where we are now, where you are now."

Dee sags against the counter. A sinking, shadowless shadow. Shay has seen her like this before. When the dam of speed and aggression she uses to hold in place the shortcomings of her being starts to give way at the seams and everything she is, and isn't, floods out.

Dee begins to cry, to cry hard. She's a manic shackled presence, a wasted dark angel eroding before Shay's eyes. She's seen all this before too. Knows her mother is at her most dangerous when she's at her most vulnerable.

"I didn't mean for it to be this way. I didn't want you to suffer."

Yeah . . . it's the perfectly appointed rap, straight down the parental party line, even if your particular parent is a devastation disguised as a collection of decent traits.

"Oh, shit." Dee presses her free hand against the base of her skull where the blood feels like it's getting ready to torch through the veins. Her skin goes whitewash, the eyes become dead as paint chips. Her chest begins to body roll. She sinks to the floor.

Shay's lived through this, too. The shivering hole where human anguish meets the final stroke of poisoned nerves. Seeing her mother like this bleeds her. Maybe it's just your basic issue pity, or genetic coding. Maybe it's an attachment to death, or a need to prove you're the stronger. Maybe it's that substantive emptiness we all try to fill even after the heinous years have attrited love.

Shay squeezes down next to her mother, "You want me to take you to the hospital?"

Dee's crying has become pursued, confused sobs. "I've driven myself to some fucked places."

Dee looks like she's about ready to corpse right there. Shay wraps her arms around her. She leans against Shay's chest in the distorted sentiment of a child. "I can't save . . . your life, without your help. And I need . . . you . . . to help save . . . mine."

Shay doesn't want this. She looks into the darkened living room. It's the open grave again, the locked trunk ride on bum shocks down the 405. She closes her eyes. She knows too well, all too well her survival depends on one thing—self-possession.

"I'll do it," she whispers, "but I want you to know after . . . after, I will be gone. And you will never, never be able to hurt me again. I will not exist for you. Do you hear me?"

TWENTY
SIX

Vic is in a third-floor guest bedroom changing his clothes when he hears Landshark lumbering down the stairs and shouting.

Vic opens the bedroom door, shirt half undone. Landshark is talking on a cellular. He quits his conversation for a beat to tell Vic, "A girl showed at the motel looking for Magale. My cousin manages the place, says the girl has been hanging around. Going back and forth between a bar across the street. She's there with someone."

"Wouldn't some of Magale's friends or family be looking for her by—"

"Not there! I'm the only one knew where she was staying. I own that motel. I put her there so she'd be," his voice deadens, "safe."

Vic starts to fast button his shirt. "We better see what this girl is about."

Landshark hits FLASH, motions for Vic to follow as he talks on the cellular: "Rog, did the girl drive there? Did you get her license plate number?" Vic follows Landshark down the stairs, then through a doorway. Two thousand square feet of track lighting automatically turns on. "Rog, have you been taking your medication? Christ!"

The bottom floor is one vast warehouse of open steel shelving. Aisle after aisle. Filled with files. Vic can hardly keep up with Landshark's thin frame as he slinks between and steps over an abatis of cluttered stacks and weathered boxes. "Rog, I got a call coming in. Hold." He flashes to another line. "Terry. You got my message. Where are you? Ten minutes with the car. Right. He'll be ready."

They reach another door with a chrome nameplate that reads: HARPERS FERRY. As the door opens Vic sees it's heavily soundproofed. He follows Landshark into the room and more track lighting automatically floods on.

It's a pistol range. Built to professional specs. Landshark points to a table full of handguns as he flashes back to the first line. "Rog, put

Vic in the room next to Magale's. So he can go through her stuff." Vic studies the dark, silent gospel of those weapons. "Don't have him fill out any paperwork. Why do you think? Take your lithium. So he can't be identified, that's why." He pushes END and turns to Vic, sees him trying to get in tow with the last two minutes.

Landshark comes up beside Vic, runs the root of his hand along the weapons. "I'll meet you out front. Why don't you find something here that makes you comfortable." As he heads out the door he ends with, "None are registered."

Vic looks over that world of weapons. From neat playthings to specialty items. Pieces for show and tell, or conceal and carry. There's any number of choices for a Joe Average to carry out his will upon the world.

Vic can feel it as he hand checks pistol after pistol. The deep undertow of years. The lost generation of life. He can feel the blood shaking in his heart with the threat of possibility.

What was it Karen Englund had said beside the police cruiser the night he was taken down: "Death puts a question mark around all our lives." Well, Landshark was right about one thing—he will never go to the police.

When Vic shows with his luggage, Landshark is just outside the open door talking on his cellular. "I'm buying all your time, Freek. It'll be vintage Landshark. I get the girl's plate number and you start liberating. Credit, bank, birth certificate, family history, criminal record, if any, taxes. I want to know the last time this girl had a pap smear."

Landshark faces Vic. The rain has slowed to a harmless drizzle. "Freek." The flesh across Landshark's cheekbones clinches. . . . "I believe Magale has been killed over this. Hurt is not enough word to honestly convey it. Freek, recall our talks on how the Great Wall of America is the commodification of the human being. And that murder is the ultimate act of commodification. The Great Wall needs to be scaled, Freek. Scaled, then scaled down. And you're the phreaking Tom Paine to help me."

Landshark hits END.

"Freek must be a hacker."

"Yes. He works with a mag called *Blacklisted! 411*. But you can get his blood up by giving him a shot at playing social patriot." Landshark gives Vic the security guard scan, "You find anything downstairs that suits you?"

Vic puts his arms out as if he were modeling, "Who says that what you can't see won't hurt you? Now, tell me about your cousin. Is he gonna be—"

The intercom kicks on. Inside the front door Landshark hits the gate buzzer. "Rog is bipolar and socially handicapped. Imagine Ted Kaczynski without the bomb paraphernalia." Landshark takes another cellular from his pocket and hands it to Vic. "So we can stay in touch. Eight four two speed dials me. In case you forget the number, eight four two spells Vic."

Headlights strike the driveway trees followed by the first chords of a car engine that sounds like it's had a five-liter transplant. Then into the driveway a black primered Fastback takes a hard turn and makes a dime-quick halt beside both men. Vic looks down into this nasty street Pony, circa '66.

A man comes sliding up out of the heavy-duty buckets. He's fortyish and black with clear gray eyes and a battlement face. Carries himself like someone who did a stretch with a side holster.

From their body language Vic can read that the men are tight. The man hands Landshark an envelope and says, "I got Texas plates like you wanted. And the paperwork will track."

Landshark introduces Vic to Terry Hickman, then adds, "You both get going. And Terry, you stay down there, alright? Watch Vic's back."

Terry nods, tosses Vic the keys, "You might as well feel this dragon out."

As they begin to move Vic sees Landshark is hanging back. "Aren't you coming?"

Staring at the car a wave of panic starts through Landshark's body at the thought of leaving the safety of his house. The courage he thought Vic's arrival would magically arouse becomes the fantasy it always was. Only now Landshark is propped up by nothing but a frantic heartbeat and the need to flee.

"I can't."

"William," says Terry, "you talked about this so much, just try."

Humiliated, Landshark turns away.

———

In five minutes the Fastback forges into the loop that takes you from the Pasadena to the Hollywood Freeway. "What's wrong with him?" asks Vic.

"Agoraphobic . . . he gets anxiety attacks. They fuck him up so bad he has to get someplace he thinks is safe to calm down 'cause he feels like he's gonna die or go nuts. A doctor friend gave him some medication, but he won't take it. And he can't, or won't, see a shrink. He used to be able to get around town, but the attacks got so bad the only place he's alright is that house.

"He hasn't left his property in years." Terry shakes his head, then waves a despondent arm across a windshield full city. "You see, for him, all this is unsafe."

With what might pass as sadness, or humor, Vic says, "You mean it isn't?"

The window is open and they are going so fast the wind is being hauled through. Terry glares at Vic. "If anyone ought to know, it's you."

"Amen," whispers Vic.

Vic starts looking for a cigarette to cut the edge when they blow past the spot where he'd been hauled over and busted by LAPD the night he was following Pettyjohn. Talk about your landmarks and life-marks. In the rearview he watches that nothing piece of asphalt shoulder till it's burned out by the oncoming headlights. Then, he's left with the little rips of torment and a sudden fear to keep watching that mirror 'cause there might be a black-and-white somewhere in those headlights with his name on it.

The way up Sunset Boulevard is marked on the night sky by a red neon Aladdin-style pleasure dome complete with minaret and two swooning electric green palm trees.

The Garden of Allah is a well-traveled Hollywood crash pad for grunge and tourists on the south side of Sunset Boulevard, one healthy scream away from La Brea.

Vic and Terry cruise past. The driveway to the courtyard-style motel runs under the second story, where on the roof is that brightly lit oasis of a sign.

Parked under the overhang, opposite the office, is a beat-up Wrangler. Terry is on his cellular to Landshark. "Green . . . tan cloth roof . . . 727XLY3 . . . it's still there."

Vic takes the first right, pulls up beside a liquor store on the corner called Diesel's. Vic looks back at the motel, "It's my war party now, so you better get out."

Terry nods. Gets out. Takes a moment with the engine idling. "Vic, I ... want to say I'm sorry."

Vic glances at Terry, uncertain of what he means.

"I worked the Hollywood Division—Burglary—when your case went down. I thought you should have been indicted. So I'm telling you now, I'm sorry."

Terry closes the door without even waiting for a response. Vic is left there leaning across the seat. How something so simple as an apology from someone he never met before could reach him so. Could make him feel so human and real. It's a good sign. A good sign, he thinks. It means I am not dead.

The office is under the overhang across from the girl's Jeep. Vic enters, carrying his luggage. The office smells of burnt coffee. Behind a sliding glass reception window the back of a head looks up at a television braced with security bars on a shelf near the ceiling. The news is on; an anchor works up his usual commercial tease on possible leads in the horrifying sex crime of the as-yet-unidentified girl at the Belmont School development site.

The head turns, and it's worse than Vic expected. Rog could pass as an escapee from the ZZ Top gene pool. Only his ragged beard is braided at the edges. He stands, steadies up the black Clark Kent glasses. His shirt is a filthy, filthy few sizes too big. "Are you the guy my cousin is trying to help?"

"I am."

They cross the courtyard, pass a small fenced pool beside the office. "I heard Terry brought you here. Terry used to be one of William's lovers, did you know that?"

Vic looks out through the overhang toward the bar across the street. That's where the girl is supposed to have gone.

"William told me Freek is working this too. Freek, Terry. He's got his whole gay Mafia behind you."

Rog leads Vic toward a black stairwell. His loose flip-flops kick spots of water up off the wet pavement.

The motel pretty much explains itself. Sunworn white, orange scarred doors. Each with two reliefed squares. It's the homey motif fallen upon weird times. Vic knows this kind of place well. Here the desperate and the dreamers hole up trying to outlast reality, till their moment comes.

"Did William tell you I'm bipolar? I was a full professor of organic chemistry at UCLA when I was twenty-six. That's like being an astronaut. But I couldn't handle it. The depression. . . ."

Rog stops at the bottom of an open stairwell. "I'm gay, too. Did William tell you? Everyone in our family is gay. You're not gay, are you?"

"Not so I've noticed." Vic points up the stairwell. "Can I go to the room, please?"

Vic follows Rog along the second floor veranda. He scans the open courtyard.

"Did my cousin tell you how he got all his money?"

The lights reflecting off the pool turn the courtyard into a crisscross of shadows. Framing opaque alcoves and dismembered angles of darkness. Rog stops at the last room. The door to twenty-two faces the veranda. It looks as if it's withstood quite a few beatings over the years.

Before Rog unlocks the door he says to Vic, "Did William tell you he killed his parents?"

Vic's face comes around. There's a pig grunt look to Rog's eyes. Something mischievous and off that seems to enjoy saying such a thing.

"Open the door, please," is all Vic says.

Rog continues on. His tone is provocative, even poisonous. "He was never indicted. They tried though. Eighty million, that's what he inherited."

Vic can't tell if this is just so much brainfreak or—"Open the door, please."

"His parents had a small plane. A wing got damaged. William's father and he did all the repairs. He was fifteen. His parents were swingers. That seventies group-grope bullshit."

"Open the door, please."

"They let their friends make him. He hated them. The police said he didn't put some cotter pins back in the wing like he was supposed to, so the plane went up . . ." Rog's hand rises like Icarus . . . "The plane went down."

On the downswing Vic grabs Rog's forearm and starts to ratchet up a little pain. Rog bends and recoils under his grip. "Open the door or I will unscrew your arm at the wrist."

In. A lamp on the bureau by the bed goes on. Vic puts down his luggage and scans the room. Dead air. A lifeless smell. Wall heater. It's the Sunshine Hotel in El Paso except for the orange bedspread. He points to a door on the far wall. "That go to the girl's room?" Rog nods. "Open it."

Vic pulls back the drapes, and peers through the blinds. He gets out the cellular, speed dials Landshark. As the phone rings he scans the courtyard. Landshark answers. "I'm in," says Vic. "Your cousin?" He glances at Rog. He's unlocked both doors between the rooms. "He's been chatting up your family history." A long silence. Vic gets back to peering through the blinds.

"I was going to tell you," says Landshark. "Everything."

Up through the driveway comes a shadow that climbs the wall. "It's just, I felt the time . . . I never did anything, Vic—" The shadow connects to the girl.

Vic cuts Landshark off. He snaps his fingers for Rog to come to the window fast. "Is that her?"

Rog looks out. He has to hold his glasses in place. His voice flutters, "That's her. That's her."

Into the cellular Vic says, "The girl's back."

Vic grabs Rog by the shirt and shoves him against the wall. He puts a hand to Rog's mouth for silence and so there's no mistaking it, presses a thumb against Rog's throat.

Vic flips off the light. Peeks out the blinds. The girl is gone. He whispers into the cellular, "I don't see her." Urgently, "Get Terry on the line and make sure he's watching." He leans across the bureau to get a hard angle on below. She's not by the Jeep. He scans the office, the pool, a frock of darkness at the bottom of the stairwell. She's nowhere to be found.

He glances down the length of the veranda. The whole open cavity is cloaked in odd wrinkles of pitch and light. He waits, he watches. Street noise only, Rog's hushed breathing. Vic's caught up in some moment that he has no idea what, if anything, it means. Then—

An outline in the deep pall at the top of the stairs. Shoring the darkness along the veranda the girl approaches with upturned collar. With hands tucked into a black hip-length coat.

Vic tries to read her body language for fear, for uncertainty. For something that he can gleam just a hint of guilt from.

She passes under a single light and he catches the edge of her profile. The deep white of her neck, the black hair, the purple-colored trim along the temples.

She knocks on the door. The echo carries into his room. He has to lean back to try and see her. She knocks again and waits. Knocks again and calls, "Magale."

Vic whispers to Landshark, "Damn, if she doesn't act like she expects someone to be there. Are you sure no one knew she was here? The girl seems to know her."

She steps back and the light owns her for the first time. He can see the deeply set dark eyes. She's young, very young. She's tall and there is nothing tame about the face. But there is something he sees, something stronger than naked beauty. Something bare and impossible to conceal. It is sadness. That is what he sees.

TWENTY
SEVEN

As the girl starts back through the skewed light toward the stairwell, Vic tells Landshark, "She's leaving."

Landshark can't understand. "Why didn't she just break in. Fuck the lock. She'd come this far, and gone back."

Vic turns to Rog. He is still beside the nightstand where Vic shoved him. "Is there any other way up to these rooms without passing the office?"

Rog's hand moves nervously, his head shakes no, "William had Terry secure the place because of all the crime in this neighborhood."

"You watch the girl from here." Vic starts across the darkness.

Landshark asks him, "Do you think she's feeling the place out? Rog said she was with someone who went into the bar across the street."

Vic reaches the open doors to Magale's room. He stops. "We're blowing past a road sign here." On Landshark's quick silence Vic follows, "Someone's got Magale's cellular, right? Which means they took her personals. That's why, at least in part, the body has yet to be identified. Now how is the one way that someone would know where she was staying if they didn't follow her here, or force her to tell them?"

A long moment to a realization. "The motel key."

"And if the girl had it, why didn't she just unlock the door and walk right in?"

"Yes, Vic. Why didn't she? Maybe the girl is exactly what you—"

"What she is, or isn't, I'll find out. Right after I look the room over I intend to go downstairs, and if she's still there, lock on."

Before Landshark can voice concern, the line cuts out and Vic slips through the open doors into a dead girl's room.

Terry's got the Garden of Allah under surveillance from a supermarket parking lot on the north side of Sunset, when Landshark calls. He is anxious and talking way too fast about the last few minutes. He's ada-mantly against Vic's idea about locking onto a girl they know nothing about. Better they pick those fuckers to death with details than—

Terry spots a girl coming up through the off light of the driveway. "William," he says, "you're gonna have to take one hard fact to heart if you mean to see this through. If you mean to ever get well. Playing control freak won't work. This is the free fuckin' world out here. And Vic—"

Landshark slams the phone down. There is nothing that infuriates him more than a truth he can't handle.

Shay climbs into her Jeep. In the left pocket of her coat a hand is still around Magale's room key. She looks through the windshield toward the bar across the street. It's a flat one-story brick wall with two eyelet windows set thirty feet in from the sidewalk. Behind one of those mir-rored windows Shay knows Dee is watching.

The dark ride down through Shay's insides has begun. A little taste of morgue stain as she walks through an explanation of why she didn't go into the room right off.

Her eyes catch the image of the motel roof sign reflected on the wet asphalt. A crimson palace braced by two palms momentarily cast apart in the hissing wake of tires. She doesn't want to move yet. Falls into a hypnotic rhythm as that watery mirage is spun outward with each passing car only to be reincarnated seconds later on the streaming pavement.

She closes her eyes, puts her head back against the seat. If only she can be that strong, or at least that elusive, to survive what this world's gonna run past her. If only she can have that much control.

Dee can't understand why Shay is just sitting there in the driveway. It was either get into the room, or come back to the bar. Waiting . . . is bullshit. The Southern Comfort doesn't help her cotton mouth. A slow death by throat cancer would be better than this.

Huddled in the corner booth, she tries to avoid the body-hungry male traffic that floats her an eye. Ghastly recriminations are adrift in her imagination for firing down on her own daughter. Point-blank in the rain on the unsuspecting is a god-ugly play, but she knows that no matter how much she had begged Shay for help, Shay just would have blown her off. So she baited her into a frightful compromise.

Her brain works to convince Dee that the accomplishment of sheer necessity Corleones the momentary dark moods of some bitch, brat child. That the greater good can only be cashed in by a heartbeat juiced for control.

She's about to try and drink away some cotton mouth when she sees a man walking oddly through the off light of the driveway toward Shay's Jeep.

A piece of that secret will be known as her mother still owns Shay. She tracks its ragged fear. Tries to work through the blood-pale struggle when a voice she barely hears says, "It won't stay that bad."

She opens her eyes. Just back of his own shadow stands a man with shoulder-length hair. The driveway by the Jeep is so dark only the voice tells whether it's a man or a woman who approaches.

As Vic comes forward light from the courtyard catches the far right of his features. He works a cigarette loose from its pack. He runs his hand in the imaginary oval of a face, then points to Shay's face. "Whatever is working the drill on you won't stay that way. It never does."

Shay barely looks his way. "Of course it won't. This is Hollywood, right? The birthplace of transformation, and where gutter rain is holy water."

There's no mistaking the bitter shapes around her language. Vic takes a step closer. "I've been to the Hollywood Wax Museum."

That didn't even register a smile. He wants to work his way right up to the Jeep. To get an eyeful of all he can. He notices the dashboard is strewn with worked over matchbooks.

"I'll trade you a cigarette for a match."

She glances at the dashboard, then passes him a matchbook. "No trade necessary."

As he takes the matchbook Shay watches a bus blow through that sea image of a roof sign and waits to see if it will pool together again in the wet midnight street.

Vic strikes a match. "You a friend of Magale's?" Shay's large eyes seem to draw in all the key light from the flame. Her mouth tightens imperceptibly. Vic inhales, then blows out the match, and Shay's face comes around toward his.

"I'm in twenty-three. That's next to Magale's. When I heard a noise, I peeked out the blinds."

So, it was him she half sensed, half saw.

"I thought it might be her coming back."

Shay slowly climbs out of the Jeep.

"I hadn't seen Magale in a couple of days and was—"

Shay passes around him. "Excuse me."

Terry is on his cellular to Landshark. "The girl's crossing the street and Vic's hanging back in the driveway."

Terry works his way west from the supermarket lot. Gives Vic a subtle nod. To Landshark: "The girl's going into the bar. Call Vic. Have him sit this out. I'll see if she's hooking up with someone."

Shay's not even grounded in the bar booth seat before Dee has at her. "Did you get inside the room?"

"No."

"Then you were supposed to come right back."

"I needed time to think."

"To think? Then what was the stop-and-chat about with that motel trash. You fucked up somehow, just say it."

Shay looks out into the crowded wall of human flesh along the bar nighthawking to a little Natalie Merchant.

"You fucked up?"

. . . *Ophelia was the rebel girl* . . .

"You're just plain self-destructive, Shay."

. . . *who remedied society . . . between her cigarettes* . . .

Shay goes cheekline to cheekline with Dee. "There's nothing plain about my self-destruction. Though I can't imagine it's anywhere in your league."

Even cloaked in bar light there's no misreading Dee's insidious call to will. No misreading the grim sweep of the face.

"Yeah, the look still frightens me," says Shay. "But you know what is more obscenely terrifying? You want to know?"

The garish arrowline cut down the eyelid highlights an intractable stare.

"I think I'm as afraid of you as I am of . . . whoever fired into my house."

Dee wants to seem hurt in some heinous way over what Shay has said so not even a hint of guilt might seep through her features. But her face can't switch from one fraud to another fast enough, and she wonders what her daughter might glean from her silence.

"Now," continues Shay, "shut your mind down long enough to listen. I got to the girl's door. I saw, or felt I saw the blinds next door move. How the fuck could I explain having the girl's key." She points out the window toward Vic. "That man talking to me lives next to the girl. He did see me through the blinds. He was asking *me* about her. I told you I'd go in as long as I was sure I wasn't spotted. But I can't now, and I won't take that risk."

"You're fuckin' with me."

Shay reaches into her left coat pocket. "I won't take that risk."

The younger girl's hand comes up from beneath the table. The two women horn through a few more ugly moments. The younger girl's got something clenched up in her palm and Terry tries to squeeze past the body clinches and the exaggerations to see what's being force-fed from one's fist into the other's.

Vic is sitting on the office steps smoking when Shay walks up. "How 'bout that cigarette?"

He stands slowly, awkwardly. He works one up from the pack.

She lights the cigarette. "You vacationing here?"

"I needed to get my life back in order. I thought I'd see how the town feels."

She quietly nods, then starts walking toward the street. She works up just enough interest in what he said to bait him into following her. He does.

"What about you?"

"I'm homegrown," she says, "but I got in an early application for getting out."

She reaches the sidewalk, sees her mother slip out the black bar door and wait. Vic walks up beside Shay. They are both awash in colors coming off the roof sign. "You a friend of Magale's?"

To avoid an answer she stares down at their shadows stretching on into the street. They are framed by the reflection of the neon palm trees on the wet, slaggish asphalt. It's a moody moment better suited to some photographer's whim than—

A photographer. The girl. Shay is shot through with the truth about why she's there.

She looks up, smokes. She crooks her head toward Diesel's Liquor. "I promised some friends I'd pick up beer. Come on and I'll buy you one for letting me bum a cigarette."

"Sure."

They start for the corner. Vic begins to work his way back to that unanswered question. "My name's Vic."

"Hello, Vic . . . I'm Shannine."

Past the motel, the lit strip mall windows burn up the dark around them. Human details become easy pickings. The scars on Vic's arms; Shay's delicate and arched high eyebrows, which make her walnut-shaped eyes all the larger and more wistful.

"You a friend of Magale's?" he asks again.

He got right back fuckin' to it. She takes a hit off her cigarette. "Not a friend," Shay says. "She and this guy come into the bar where I work. She always has camera equipment with her. I had a camera I wanted to sell and she said she would if I give her a few bucks from the deal. It's been a week since I heard from her and I was suddenly feeling very fucked. So I came over here to find out what is . . . but she isn't around."

Shay waits to see what kind of response she gets from Vic, but he acts like it's just so much small talk.

They reach the corner. The light is green and the traffic on Sunset is still running pretty hard so they have to wait it out. Not ten feet back from where they stand, in the doorway to a cleaners, is a shirtless and shoeless street freak. He couldn't be more than twenty but he's got a couple of good years' filth on him. He's playing a stringless guitar and howling out nonsense as if he were possessed by the ghost of Johnny Rotten or some other hard-core rocker.

He's a few years younger than Shay with way too many bites taken out of him. She turns away, presses the crosswalk button, and catches a glimpse of her mother slipping illegally between headlights and car horns toward the motel.

Shay turns, looks back at Vic. His eyes are still locked on that wasted down youth in the doorway. She glances again at the scars on his arms. "Those are pretty nasty scars you have there."

He keeps staring at the boy as he says, "I worked as a bouncer at a bar in El Paso. It was a heavy place for knife fights."

"Couldn't you have saved yourself a few scars by getting another job?"

"Yeah, sure, but I was into self-inflicted wounds at the time."

He suddenly comes around to face her. He didn't mean to be quite so honest. But it just came out and it leaves him with a drawn, uncomfortable feeling. Maybe it was the boy there in the doorway. That wreckage of a human being. That puzzle of pieces who reminds him what lies in wait if you are not careful, nor watchful.

He steps back from Shay and smokes, trying to let the last few moments just ease away. For the first time she really looks at him. And the hard evidence is there. It's there past the graying and thinning widow's peak, past the battered chinks along the nosebone. It's all summed up in one phrase that's stronger than naked beauty could ever be. It's something bare and impossible to conceal. Human suffering, that is what she sees.

TWENTY EIGHT

Landshark is at the bar in his office. A lattice band of light falls across the phone that waits there beside him. There's torture in its silence. His inability to control events, which translates into an inability to control his own emotions, leaves him anxious and depressed. The anxiety and depression feed his anger. Or maybe the hell-whole process really works in reverse, as he remembers being angry long before he recalls ever being anxious.

He drinks down his scotch and stares up at the one possession that has any meaning to him. It is a beautifully mounted black and white photograph, four feet high and five feet across, hung behind the bar.

An unclad child angel from the waist up, with spread wings, is superimposed over a street scene of downtown Los Angeles. It's a wide angle of Broadway, looking up from Seventh into a world of deco movie houses and finely architectured buildings. But it is not from that era of prophetic memory, but a more recent pathetic reality when the movie houses became trash-'n'-carry discount holes where the run-down meet the run out. Where the exhausted and filthy move through the exhaust and filth. Where the senses are inundated by islands of gaudy street vendors and garish signs and a sweeping crosswalk of humanity making its way through the noxious summer carbons.

The centerpiece of the photograph is the child's face. It is weeping. That edge of unqualified sorrow is what touched him into wanting it. From the first he felt the naked, heavenly creature was weeping over the state of the earth, and the black and white celestial moment was a living part of everyone which matched that part of him.

Then he thinks of his parents and what he will tell Vic. The book of his life has carelessly dropped open. It is only the ringing phone that saves him from its torment and wrath.

Terry has time to tell William just this: The younger girl was arguing with a woman in the bar across from the Garden of Allah. The younger girl left, then got Vic to walk down to a liquor store. It was during that play the other woman, whose eye was cut open, left the bar, went to the motel and, using a key, entered Magale's room.

As he hangs up the phone Landshark whispers to the child angel, "We've got them."

Shay's Jeep turns hard up into Dee's driveway. A short, fast climb of asphalt and the Valley lights unfold around a 560SL parked by the front door.

"No fuckin' way Burgess is here."

Shay brakes. Her high-beams drench the house windows. Dee suddenly remembers she left Magale's things out on the coffee table. "Christ." Dee looks at Shay, "Get the license plates. Bag 'em. Put 'em in my trunk. I'll trash them in the morning."

Shay goes to shut the engine off when Dee grabs her hand, "About tonight, about everything. Let me walk Burgess through this, alright?"

"You mean let you lie as you see fit."

"You know, Shay, I may shock you and hit him with the truth. Now get the plates off your car."

As Dee comes through the front door Burgess gravely rises from a burgundy leather couch. An end table lamp is a fixed mark beside him, creating a fixed mark of light on Magale's belongings spread across the coffee table before him.

"I brought the money," he says, "and I thought I'd wait for you."

Dee crosses the darkened hallway. Her boots click out seconds on the Italian tile. "That's good."

He points to the coffee table, his moves are crepe-paper uncertain. "Who does all this belong to?"

Another step and the lamp lights that wounded eye. "What happened?"

Burgess was born to be lied to. The hard tests of manhood don't suit him. Can't be supported by him. But it's too late to matter-of-factly manufacture some through line that will track, especially with the dead cunt's personals staring them in the face. So Dee says, "We could be in trouble, Burgess."

He finds himself needing to sit. Dee walks to the kitchen. Burgess hears a drawer open, then the ice machine starts to grind. She returns with a towel of ice pressed against her eye and sits on the couch near him. She is colored with exhaustion, her loose hand slumps across her thigh. "Burgess, I need you now. I need all your strength and will to see this through."

"You'll have it."

His voice is just degrees of gray, but Dee does not invent conversation. She begins with the truth, the whole truth, and nothing but the truth. Then she hopes to Christ it's worth it.

Shay enters the kitchen, muffles her steps through the laundry room so she can hang back, work the dark, see how much truth her mother is capable of. That last ugly mile from the murder to the motel has Dee in full possession of all her calm, but what runs through Shay's mind, what she focuses on there amidst all the clutter and the acrid smell of disinfectant, is the man at the motel saying, "I could have had another job, but I was into self-inflicted wounds at the time."

When Dee is done, Burgess finds he has stopped breathing and his chest is constricted by the silence of the living room. He's so still it's as if he'd been dead for days until he notices a figure in the kitchen doorway and jerks upright.

"It's Shay," Dee says.

"Shay?"

Shay moves into the living room, her face in full shadow. As she passes Burgess he sucks in a breath for want of something to say, then comes out with, "Well, we're all here. I'm glad."

"Yeah." Shay goes over to the white marble fireplace and sits on its low step. "No need for roll call. It looks like all the open wounds have gathered to share their misfortune."

Burgess smokes, which he does not do often. There's no murderous screaming, no whining argument about why him. But to Shay it looks like a bag full of God has cracked him across the skull.

"You sure there was no one at the motel who saw you?"

"Went in . . . went out. We even had fake plates on the Jeep."

"And you got all the film?"

"There was none in the room. I took what was in the camera. From her car. From her purse. It's Foreman we have to deal with now. He's got to see that the fags are a threat."

Burgess tries not to look at the coffee table, at this new turn of reality. "You sure no one at the motel saw you?"

Dee slips the ice away from her eye. "Ask Shay."

Burgess turns to Shay. She is sitting forward, holding the amulet's chain high up so the coffin charm swings back and forth. "Shay?"

She won't lie for her mother to save face with Burgess. She won't. She leans back against the marble. Feels the cold stone along her neck, hears that voice again, "I was into self-inflicted wounds at the time."

"You're not just gonna sit there and say nothing."

Shay mumbles under her breath, "What's a little poison anyway. No difference if it's in your head or your body, or the ground for that matter. Right?"

Burgess is almost shouting now, "Shay. Goddamn you, answer me."

For that caricature of a man to give her orders like she's a deckhand working on the ship of his life, she will not have it. A headstrong outrage has Shay up and fast. She's in his face before he can blink her into focus.

"When the fuck are you gonna zip up your own pants? You've gone from backbone to backbone all your life. You'll rent one. Steal one. You'd hang on one till it came apart on you." Shay grabs some of the dead girl's possessions off the coffee table and shoves them into Burgess' arms. "Here . . . here! You better get a feel for this, 'cause this is part of who you are . . . now . . . either break with my mother or be with her. But be something 'cause I'm trying to stay alive and I need to find out how."

Seeing Shay like this, with eyes so intense as to seem almost blind, with cheeks and neck an anarchy of purple veins, it's as if Dee had burned up through her daughter's flesh for those few seconds.

Completely humiliated, a compact and lip gloss slip through his arms. He tries as best he can to maintain some dignity and get the dead girl's things back on the table. He then sits next to Dee. She does not move. She shows him neither affection, nor mercy, nor anger. He puts his arm on hers. She looks down at his arm, as if trying to judge why it might be there. He then, with all the tenderness he can manufacture says, to both women first, "You've been right about me." Then to Dee, "But not this time. I won't let you down. Believe it or not, I have enough backbone for that."

An hour later mother and daughter are alone. Shay is out by her Jeep, smoking a joint, looking down the dark bluff hills toward the serene flow of lights along the Valley floor. She's trying to get the poison of tonight from her system.

Dee walks up behind her. "Thanks for handling Burgess."

Shay's eyebrows rise in contempt. She skirts around her mother toward the driver's door.

"You think he'll be alright?"

Shay gets in one long inhale, lets it really fire up the lungs, then after breathing out says to Dee, "You'd better find some new dreams, 'cause I think you're being sized up for very black times."

"Are you talking about him now . . . or you?"

Shay stops, licks her tongue across her lips while she thinks of the nastiest comment she can. "I'm talking about me. Which should give you one more thing to worry about."

As Shay climbs up into the driver's seat, Dee says, "After what happened at your house, you sure it wouldn't be better to stay here? Keep close to me? We need to watch out for each other now."

"I was close to you once, and look what it got me."

Dee holds the door to keep Shay from closing it. "In the end," Dee says, "you'll need me more than anybody else. You'll want to be with me more than anybody. And you know why? I saw it tonight. Burgess saw it too, and that's what scared him. It's because you're more like me than anybody."

The statement holds Shay frozen. She looks at the lights below, but doesn't see them. A breath of wind deeply frightens her. She does not look at Dee when she says, "If that's my horrible truth, then be very, very careful. Now let go of the fuckin' door."

TWENTY NINE

In Landshark's office, he, Vic, and Terry are hard down the path of possibilities. Cigarette smoke hangs like filth around the recessed ceiling lights. The long table by the bar is strewn with abandoned coffee mugs and ashtrays. Three classroom-height bulletin boards on rollers flank the table.

Each has been halved into panels. The first four panels are headered by a photograph; the first is Pettyjohn, second is Englund, then the unknown man at the bar, next a newspaper photo of Foreman outside the courthouse after the debacle that finished John Victor Sully. The last two panels have index cards as headers that read: THE OLDER WOMAN, THE YOUNGER WOMAN.

While Landshark and Terry are writing down whatever facts they know about each on index cards and pinning them in the appropriate column, Vic is staring into the unfinished country symbolized by the face of Charlie Foreman. "Where is he now?"

Landshark looks up, finds a few note pages and a photo of a house clipped together on the table, hands them to Vic. "This will tell you. He's got a small house in Chatsworth. Simi Valley." As Vic pins the information up, Landshark turns to Terry. "The two women tonight. How old were they? What did they look like?"

"So, the fuck's got himself a nice little life."

Landshark again looks up at Vic, sees the resentment and bitterness in his eyes.

"You should get your tenses right, Vic. Had . . . he *had* a nice little life."

Terry tries to cut into the moment. "Both are white. The older one is a hard late thirties. But you can see she really had the look. She can still throw out the vibe."

As Landshark writes, Vic looks through the notes on Foreman. "It says a woman is living with him. Could it be one of the two tonight?"

"No," says Terry, "that woman's name is Alvarez. She's Hispanic. Forty. A little too much around the hips."

With a little nasty flourish Landshark adds, "And she looks like Connie Stevens handles her makeup and wardrobe. Magale got a shot of her coming out of the house about a week ago." His long arm dance points toward the bar, "It should be in that last stack."

"What else do you know about her?"

"Freek's working on that now. He ripped off some of her mail. A credit card bill. He's backtracking. We do know she worked in some capacity for the Department of Education."

"What about back in '87? And was she going with Foreman then?"

"Freek's looking into your first question. To the second we're searching records to see if she visited him in jail, paid any of his legal bills, etc., etc., etc."

Landshark swings his attention back to Terry, who is trying to pace away the deep fatigue. "Tell me about the younger one."

"Early twenties. Very tall. Has the look. And there's a vibe coming off her I used to see in crackups and suicide cases. You know, too much kink and soul for them to get an emotional handle on, so they nose-dive."

Vic holds up the photo of a woman, "Is this the one living with Foreman?"

Landshark nods. "Did what Terry say sound right to you, Vic?"

"To me she looked sad. And when she talked she came across very, very smart."

"There was bad blood between those two women," Terry adds. "You could read it in their body language."

Vic pins the photo of Alicia up next to Foreman. There's no trace there of the sinister nor the forbidden. Just plain, plain, plain. She's sure not the type he'd imagine Foreman getting hard for, but maybe that's the attraction.

Of course he knows what these quick life sketches are worth. He was buried by their cold and brutal work. She could be anyone under all that makeup. Maybe even the woman coming out of a black night and skillet air to end his life.

He starts to turn ugly inside. He glances at Landshark. And what about Rog's little monologue at the motel. That's a question and answer he and Landshark have got to get to, and soon.

He comes around the table. Studies that wall of panels. No one looks exactly like they really are. That's the secret of the human race. How the honest and the dishonest get by in the harsh climate of everyday life. How both beautiful and barbarous motives go unnoticed until it's too late.

"You know what else?" Terry says. "These two women, they looked like they could be related. Their faces were as close as me and my brother."

"Vic?"

He turns to Landshark. "When the girl and I walked back from the liquor store she got in the car and drove away. I didn't even know about the other woman till I saw Terry." He shakes his head. "The girl worked me."

"If they are related they knew each other in '87," says Terry. "If not, that's something else. But in '87 one was in her mid-twenties, the other her early teens. They fit a general description."

"They had the fuckin' key," says Landshark, standing. "We're past general descriptions."

"Vic, what do you think?"

"I didn't recognize the girl, Terry, if that's what you're asking. I don't think I could recognize the woman. All I really remember was black hair. I thought, felt, they were Hispanic."

Landshark slams a fist against the bulletin board. "They got the key by killing Magale or being handed the damn thing from whoever killed her. They went into that room for something."

Terry talks right past Landshark. "The girl didn't recognize you either?"

"She sure didn't act it."

"Recognize him?" Landshark's arms bird through a file on the table. He finds Vic's Academy graduating picture. He's the classic crop-haired clean-cut boy in a khaki sheriff suit. Landshark holds the photo up next to Vic as he is now. "I wouldn't recognize him. And I've been looking at this picture for nearly a decade."

"We're rolling the dice with this. And he should hear the risk out loud. If those two were the ones, then just brushing up against them could—"

A ringing phone ends Terry's sentence.

"It's Freek." Landshark leans down and reaches across the table for a cellular. Terry and Vic are still. "Freek . . ." Landshark listens. Vic sips at his coffee. It's stood long enough to get cold. He's barely gotten through one sour swallow when Landshark grunts out loud, *"Fuck!"* then flings the phone against the wall.

He is like some breathing rabid horror as he goes over and pounds his foot down on the plastic casing. Terry yells to him, "What? What?" but Landshark just keeps boot-heeling the damn box like he's some mad Ichabod Crane, and if that weren't enough, he picks up the phone and flings it against the far wall where it bursts in small plastic bits.

"The plates are dead." The words come out of his mouth with spittle he's so mad. "They were stolen off a vehicle in Tehachapi. We lost 'em! We lost 'em!"

"Those slick bastards," says Terry.

Landshark turns on Terry as if this were his fault. "What did I say all along?! What?! Bring another car, right?! Right?!"

"Who knew?"

Landshark cuts him off and keeps repeating, "I said, bring another car! Bring another car!" It's a frustrated and recriminatory chant.

Terry's had enough. He shouts back, "Sometimes you are an arrogant and fucked-up control freak!"

"Bring another car!"

"Then why didn't you get that phobic ass of yours out of this house so you could be there?"

Landshark stays on that nasty mantra long after a smart man would have stopped, or at least read the signs in that other man's eyes he'd passed some safety point. Terry starts for him. He's gonna blanket that son of a bitch's face with an open hand until Vic slams his coffee cup down on the table. A thin line of cold black fluid spits upwards.

"I hope you haven't forgotten . . . I'm still here."

Both men settle back into their angry corners. Terry apologizes. Landshark prefers to slip his hands into the pockets of his gabardine pants and brood.

Vic won't have it. "You better learn to bolt down that ego of yours, brother. Or start buffing up."

No argument, just a glimpse of humiliation on the long smooth face, and then a nod.

Vic reaches for his cigarettes and stands, "We may be able to find them without the plates anyway." The climate of the room takes a radical turn. Vic breaks a filter off a cigarette, walks up to Landshark, "The girl said she worked in a bar." He slips the cigarette into Landshark's mouth, "Now try listening. The girl had a dozen matchbooks, used matchbooks, on the dashboard of her car." He takes a black used matchbook from his shirt pocket and lights Landshark's cigarette. After he's done he holds the matchbook squarely up before Landshark's eyes. "The matchbooks were just like this one. As a matter of fact, this is one, and what does it say?"

Landshark squints. The matchbook reads: NIGHTLAND ... 1703 SIL-VERLAKE BLVD.

Vic turns and tosses the pack to Terry.

"Maybe she was lying," says Landshark.

"But somebody spends a lot of time there."

Landshark comes back, "Maybe the Jeep was stolen?"

"I was thinking about that while I was sitting here. But the girl ..." He looks at Terry, "Remember when you pulled someone over, or you were checking out a driver to see if it was their vehicle? It's the little things. Most people move, reach for stuff almost blindly if it's their car. That's how it was with her."

Terry nods, looks the matches over. "Yeah ... yeah."

"I don't feel the car was stolen."

Terry tosses back the matches. Vic goes to light himself a cigarette but stops when he notices Landshark staring at him as if he had just stumbled on some odd discovery.

Vic pushes the hair back from across his face. "I *was* trained as a policeman. Now, you got a camera. A good camera? And one of those equipment bags. Something that would belong to a girl."

"Sure." Landshark orders Terry, "In the hall closet, there's a 35mm. Get it."

"How about something that resembles the word 'please' added to that sentence?"

"I see this is open night on putting me in my place. You're absolutely correct. Please."

Terry goes out, but he's leaving behind a five-second stare that would make a sensible man reflect on how he acts.

Landshark comes around the table to where Vic has begun to sift through a stack of Magale's photos. "That's Terry's celebrated look." Then louder so Terry will hear, "The one that made all the boys' assholes become pâté á choux."

"One day, William," Terry shouts back in an ordinary and precise manner, "you will learn the difference between being well-spoken and well-spoken-of is far more than one small word."

Landshark turns his attention back to Vic. His tall frame practically bending over Vic's shoulder. Vic has put aside a shot of Pettyjohn, of Englund, of the argument outside the Scorecard with the unknown man. "What are you doing?"

"I'm putting together a little greeting card, and then . . . then, I'm going to Nightland to see about meeting a girl."

Terry comes back with the camera. He glances at Landshark.

Both men seem to want to speak, but there is a sober reticence to do so. When done, Vic lights that cigarette for himself. He plays with the black matchbook, then slips it back into his shirt pocket. The match itself still burns between the thumb and middle finger of his other hand.

"We'll find out what's happened here. We'll find out who killed Magale. You'll have your story, and maybe whatever else it is you need from this. But if it turns out those two are the ones who shot me—"

Vic stops there. His eyes squarely on the match as he blows it out. He doesn't move after that. He does not finish his thought. But there are layers to the silence that no palette could ever catch. And the speechless message is enough for both men to understand.

Then Terry asks Vic, "But what if they discover who you are first?"

Vic's head comes around. "I'll end up back in the grave I crawled out of. What happens after that, I will to whoever wants it."

THIRTY

Shay does not go home. That insignificant asylum is now just so much violated space. A bullet saw to that.

Shay drives to Echo Park. Finds a spot near the house on Laguna Avenue she and her mother lived in all those years ago. It is still chipped, pink stucco; still a box with rusty barred windows.

She can remember seeing her mother's moonlit face in the misty kitchen glass looking down towards the street crawling headlights on Glendale Boulevard. She can remember her mother telling her that when Shay was not near two, and Dee was getting ready to break with her own mother because she would no longer be a "street hump supporting the bitch's habits"—how she'd no longer put up with the milk-and-memory bullshit of some needy, mute, fucked-up drunk mother—one night, while she slept, shots were fired through Dee's bedroom window, putting a pair of scarred eyes into the headboard.

Gasping and confused Dee crawled across the shag carpet and swept her screaming, crying daughter up into her arms. Stumbling at tilted angles through the blackened hallway, she found the kitchen. Her free hand, wild and haphazard, ravaged the drawer for a butcher knife. With back against the wall, and child against her chest, she waited out the minutes for a bloodletting.

She swayed and sweated and sssshh'd her baby and listened to a house that creaked with breathing death. It was hours later a drunk and disoriented matriarch returned home.

Dee kicked and beat that fat monster to the floor. She held the knife against the throat of that choking sow. The air between their faces reeked of putrid sour breath and Dee warned her mother, warned her that nothing, nothing, nothing in the world would keep her from leaving. And, that if she ever did anything again like this she would wake to find her throat slit.

Even with a glistening blade pressed into the soft, fleshy mass of her neck, Dee's mother defiantly said, in sign, only: "Don't be stupid."

Don't be stupid.

Burgess calls his father's office, is told he can be found at the Belmont School site. That today is dedicated to putting the best PR face on what has become a poisoned well.

Burgess has decided, after sitting up through the pit of a terrifying night, to come clean about the situation and throw himself on the mercy of his father's self-centered ambition.

When Burgess pulls up, the site is a developer's nightmare. The large pit dedicated as a football field is cordoned off by police investigators searching for evidence in the rape/murder.

Along First Street, the lookie-loos and the flash-happys are working for that camera-ready postcard moment: the upfront family album stare, the backdrop site of a horrific slaying, and chain-link fence in between.

Walking the construction site, under an autumn sky much too beautiful and cloud-ridden to have to bear witness to such travesties, Burgess is anything but sure of what he is about to do.

Something intangible gnaws at his conviction to go through with this. Is it a primal instinct offering caution, a sixth-sense warning, or just plain cowardice? He is a jerryrig of conflicts as he approaches a small cadre of reporters grilling his father and the others who have brought this project into being.

When the lead reporters run aground struggling for some slick new piece of hearsay about the murder to lead with on the six o'clock news, they quickly disperse across that dusty site to hustle up a quote from the homicide detectives.

This leaves Harold Ridden and the others to face off against the second team of staff reporters. The Section Two gang that works up fill—otherwise known as important civic news that lacks the salacious page-one punch readers demand.

Harold Ridden is a case study of professional boldness as he walks through questions about the cost overruns that have plagued Belmont since its inception a decade ago, the political snares and civic infighting the controversial project has had to endure, the recent discovery of gas and oil contamination that contradicts all earlier reports.

He handles with grace and good humor the hard fact that a project once christened the "Taj Mahal of Schools" is now nicknamed "Fiasco High."

But when a reporter for *The Daily News* gets a chance to ask about "unnamed sources" claiming there might be notes proving good ground soil was brought in and dumped with contaminated soil to lower ecological sample results, the Q and A is brought to a polite close with assurance that such claims are ridiculous.

For Burgess that question is a statement of sweeping dread. What if Foreman or Pettyjohn made a call and let this out anonymously as a warning?

Burgess now wishes he were not here. That he had not picked this day, this spot, to tell his father. As Harold approaches his son the same reporter for *The Daily News* slips in one more jab of a question, "Mr. Ridden, would you approve of an independent investigation into allegations of possible misrepresentation of environmental data?"

Harold, his face a reflective scowl, answers, "It is not ours to approve or disapprove. We're builders. But I will tell you one thing for sure." The scowl softens into a smile. "We won't pay for it."

Once father and son are alone, the real Harold Ridden surfaces. "I'd like to put a welding torch up the ass of whoever made up that 'Fiasco High' comment."

"Dad, can we go someplace and talk?"

"And those page-three wannabes. Chicken Littles out for their own careers. Christ, writers, they break wind and call it an insight. Even the public lets their rantings go in one ear and out—"

"Listen to me. I'm in bad trouble."

Harold Ridden's Cadillac is parked on Edgeware, half a block from the north gate of the construction site. Burgess sits and stares blankly into the sun. He has made sure all the windows are closed so no one who passes can hear.

"You remember Emmanuel Tills?"

"Look at me when you're talking, Burgess."

Burgess turns his head, but he can't look his father in the eye. "Who is Tills?"

"We hired him to do the initial soil reports on the 56th Street School and on Belmont."

Harold's jaw clenches up. "Why are we going there?"

"His reports were forged after his death and dated back."

A huge truck carrying dirt trundles past. The street quakes so hard the steering wheel that Harold is holding onto for support tremors in his hands.

"His initial paperwork, his notes, hit us bad. He'd even discovered . . ." Burgess wipes his mouth. It's dry, but he wipes it as if it were wet. ". . . a map. In some archive. Of oil wells back in 1901 or 1902 that were between Beverly and First. Exactly where they were."

"I thought the money I gave you was for him, that's what you said, to change those reports."

Burgess' voice ebbs, then wallows in his mouth. "He wouldn't change them. I thought he would. His wife had cancer. He had no health insurance. The money was staring him right in the face and he told me to 'go fuck myself!' "

Harold remembers his son telling him the old man died drunk, that he was drunk and hit his head on a bedstand and bled to death. He bled to death while his wife was lying in a coma.

"Who got the money, Burgess? Who kept him from going public?"

"Dee got it."

The Daily News reporter is unlocking the door to her beat-up white Corolla when she notices Harold Ridden walking down Edgeware with a young man in dire pursuit. There is a jarring rhythm to the scene; the old man using his palm almost like a barrier to keep the boy away. The reporter walks up to a hardhat, "Excuse me." She points down Edgeware. "Do you know who that is walking behind Harold Ridden?"

Fingers hawked onto a chain-link fence. A forehead hot and sweating against those aging slats of flesh. Harold, in a ceaseless silent monologue about betrayals until Burgess' shadow falls across his face.

The father speaks without moving, "All your life you've felt some antagonism against me because I confronted you about your shortcomings. And now this is the end result of some desire on your part to get back at me."

"Alicia Alvarez has Tills' original notes. Even the archival maps. And—"

"Your mother let you go to that Oakes School, where you called your teachers by their first name. Where you're pampered and praised and made to feel smart and that success is your due. And a fool like you actually believed you were owed something. You actually thought you are what those teachers we paid for . . . *we paid for* . . . told you."

"Try to put aside what I am. Help me clean this up."

"Clean this up?!" The continents of their past and all those blocks of construction merge in Harold's mind. "Clean this up! Do you know how much it is already on this monstrosity? How much more to go? You can spread that disaster around if you know what you're doing. But forged documents!"

"I'm so lost."

Harold rails his palms against the chain-link fence. Another huge truck rumbles up the street, and the ground quakes beneath them.

"Dad?"

"Who do you think all those city and county and federal attorneys will go after when they discover fraud?! Not you."

"You have to listen to me because it's much, much worse. I need to get away from Dee. I want to. But. . . ." He looks back at the site, back to where police investigators work the ground. "There's more I have to tell you."

Caught by a 300mm lens. A father with hands covering his face. A son in the perfect physical measure of pain. A chain-link fence behind them. The huge rising girders of that tainted school beyond that. A battery line of welding torch light along the steel railings. Men with their yellow construction hats in motion. Cranes lifting great shanks of steel. A bulldozer moving tanklike along the dusty incline.

All caught by the camera of a woman behind a beat-up white Corolla. She already sees the copy to complement the photo: THE PRICE TAG ON FIASCO HIGH IS RISING.

THIRTY
ONE

———

Landshark is at his desk working on his column when Vic enters. Landshark's been up since yesterday, and looks it. A little of the night before still hangs over both men, and there is a brittle silence as Vic goes to the bar and pours coffee. Landshark is the first to speak. "You haven't asked me about what Rog said. I wanted to tell you. I mean—"

"Not today," is the answer. As Vic approaches the desk Landshark notices a half-torn piece of notepaper with writing on it in Vic's hand.

"I woke up one morning in El Paso," says Vic, "not long after I'd run from this world. And I was hit by a thought that left me ill and disoriented for some days. Everything in that room was exactly as I had left it the night before. Shoes and shirt were on the fire escape where I'd flung them. A pint bottle of vodka lay on the floor where I'd kicked it. Everything was where it was. But what if that order were gone? What would I be left with? How badly did I need that order to survive? How badly did I need it to change?" He hands the note to Landshark. "I felt that this morning."

Landshark looks at the note. Vic has written: SHAY STOREY.

"I called Nightland. Some of the kitchen help was in. I talk a pretty mean Spanish. A girl who fits our description bartends there."

"I'll have Freek check her out."

Nightland. It's snot-rocking music for the hard core. No khaki crowd tonight. No yuppie podheads worrying about their 401Ks. This bunch is straight out of Bar Sinister and the Pink Panther Tattoo Parlor.

A big part of Shay is still back with the last two nights so she's just making it through her gig by rote, she's hanging by a thread no stronger than tinsel, taking orders from a mob two deep at the bar when she sees that rock and creosote face half smiling at her through a thin chute of light.

Loud, so she can hear, Vic says, "Remember me?"

Grappling with her voice, Shay answers, "The guy from last night at the motel." A pause to catch up to herself, then, "What'll you have?"

"Tecate."

He passes the carryall with the camera in it from one hand to the other so he can get to his money.

Vic drinks his way through a vignette of guitar grinders that leapfrog from Social Chaos to Murphy's Law. From Face to Face to DOA. He looks down through that barside ritual to watch Shay. He tries to picture that long, sleek creature in the white body stocking and inkblack jeans as a twelve-year-old in the front seat of a police cruiser leading him to the brink of violence.

The blue light from beneath the bar fills out the dark sensuality to that oval face he studies minute after minute trying to find a way to let it invade him, to possess him in some way, hoping that will crack the stranglehold around his memory.

How did he find me? Why did he find me? Shay feels like she is tied up in leather straps. She needs to focus on every order now for support. A clammy ring starts to form around her neck. While she waits her turn at the register she peeks into the bar mirror. Even in that packed atmosphere he stands out like a roadhouse slammer with his hair pulled back in a Toshiro Mifune knot.

And what about the carryall? Who comes into a bar to sit all night and nursemaid a carryall? What is that about?

He catches her eye and flags her by holding up an empty beer bottle. This'll give her a chance to run a few questions at him.

Shay slips another Tecate in front of Vic. "What made you swing across town to hit this place?"

"I came here to see you."

"I don't recall telling you I work here."

He holds up a Nightland matchbook.

"Am I supposed to know what that means?"

"Last night I bummed a match from you. You had about a dozen of these matchbooks lying all over the dashboard. So, I figured, you either worked here, or hung here."

She gives him an intense appraisal. From his pocket comes a wrinkled ten spot. She takes the bill, then snaps it. "Are you here to meet me . . . hit on me . . . or stalk me?"

He points to the carryall squeezed up by his feet. "I might have your camera, I don't know. But the manager of the motel has been holding onto some of the girl's valuables, the one you came there to see. He's been holding her stuff 'cause she's behind in what she owes for the room, and she hasn't even come back to get her things. I told him about you and—"

Shay doesn't bother to let him finish. She goes over to the register to make change. Talk about the lies that come back to lean on you with their fierce imposing will.

Fuck, she thinks. Fuck.

But what to do right now. She sure as shit cannot have him sitting at the bar and going through the carryall of a dead girl with her playing out that phony drama to a packed house. No way.

Vic watches. It's taking a long time to make change. A bit of light catches her hand. He tries to see if it is shaking. It is not. Yes, she just hangs over the register. She'll have to come back to him. He'll know something eventually. Something will be said even if it's done silently.

He notices her reach for a Nightland napkin. She writes something on it. She comes back with his change. As she puts it on the bar she leans toward him so she can speak without everyone else hearing. "This place may seem hip on your side of the bar, but on my side the managers wouldn't find it too cool me using their time to solve my problems." She holds up a napkin. "There's an all-night coffee shop about a mile up the street. I wrote down the name and address. I go there after work to gear down. Get some food." She slips the napkin in his shirt pocket. "Save me a table."

Vic takes his time with the beer. The girl is steady, and coolly straight as if she had no sense there was a fire licking at her future. He tries to imagine she is a stone innocent; he can and he can't. He tries to imagine she is guilty. That she exists in some sublime and barren state yet can come across as simply human; he can and he can't.

———————

Shay does not see Vic leave. He is just suddenly gone and the space is filled by the next social freak show that wants to get a good buzz on.

During a bathroom break Shay sneaks out through the kitchen. On the street back of Nightland there's a cleaners. Shay slips into the doorway alcove and smokes.

She stares at the pack of Nightland matches. Just another little weight to help sink her. She tosses the matchbook into the street. She reaches for her cellular in a back pocket. She dials up her mother's number. She may fuckin' sink, but she intends to have company when she does.

THIRTY
TWO

DIS is easy to find. On the corner of Fletcher Avenue and Glendale Boulevard is one of those early sixties coffee shops with a wildly angled green sign highlighted by white letters on a thirty-foot stanchion. DIS used to be known as Don-Irene-and-Sis' Coffee Shop, but in the early nineties the new owners took verbal advantage of the coincidence in the lead letters and renamed it DIS.

The hexagonal building is framed by a parking lot, and inside there's interconnected dining rooms around a lunch counter and a grill. The booths are a homage to atrocious green leather.

Vic finds the most aloof booth he can to wait. From there he watches the sleepless wonders and late-night partyers come and go. He steals a look at the hand-holders that linger. Within him some ultimate loneliness that makes the flesh what it is cuts at the core of his soul. He felt it at Nightland, he feels it now. The slow burning of one who hasn't drunk from the source for a long time.

He listens as R.E.M. is sent out through speakers hung from the ceiling. Nothing overdone. Just the right pitch to be socially acceptable for those who don't want their tastes violated too much.

In that fluorescent-lit doorway Shay spots up. With pug hat and sleeveless coat, a fugitive dream if ever there was one.

Crossing the room, she splits a moment of small talk with the hostess. There's a wave from a waitress by the kitchen door. Christ, when she moves it's as if the space around her is being pulled along.

She glides down into the booth and a large Coke mysteriously appears before her. She sets her pug hat down on the table. Her perfume, it smells of twilight. Her eyes, they seem to hold all kinds of night-shapes and a current inside him frightens and lures.

She could be the one, remember that. She could be—

"What did you think of Nightland?" Shay asks.

"It's a great place if you like your meat red and on the bone."

"And do you like your meat red and on the bone?"

"Is there any other way?"

He lifts the carryall and places it on the window side of the table. Her eyes sidestep it as she takes up a menu.

"The food here doesn't do the word 'average' justice. And it isn't even cheap." She slaps the green upholstery. "After all, somebody's always got to pay for all the retrofitting."

"I'm not hungry, thanks."

She flags down the waitress. Orders a hamburger and mashed potatoes. Only then does she turn her attention to the carryall which she has no intention of touching. "Should I be afraid of you, Vic?"

"I hope not."

"I'm not comfortable going through her things."

"I can understand that." So, he opens the carryall instead. He takes out the photos to get to the camera. He places them on the table. As he lifts out the camera he watches Shay to see what, if anything, might her reaction be. But all he gets is the faceless stare you see on gamblers.

As he holds out the camera, she says, "It's not mine. But thanks."

He puts the camera back, he lets the photos sit. "You told me your name was Shannine. But I heard people in the bar call you Shay. What do you prefer?"

"I was born Shannine." She spells it for him. "My mother made it up. But along the way she got hooked on Shay. I'd prefer something simpler . . . like Anonymous."

He can pick up the disdain in her voice. "I know that feeling," he says.

"Do you?"

Having gotten nothing with the photos, he puts them away. She moves and the smell of twilight moves with her.

"If the manager of the motel had the carryall 'cause he was owed money for her room, he wouldn't hand it over to you, would he? So how 'bout the truth?"

Vic zips the carryall closed. "He's a fuck-up, alright. And he likes his pot. So I slipped him a joint, and when he went off to Moodland, I lifted it."

"All that for a girl you don't even know?"

"I thought it was better than bringing flowers."

She doesn't want him to see her smile so she bends around to take off her coat. She then gets her feet up on the booth seat. "Did you steal this thing 'cause you wanted to meet me . . . hit on me . . . or stalk me? I hope you're not stalking me, 'cause you could end up with a very bad surprise slipped into your lap."

His graying goatee holds steadfast around his jaw as it tightens into a serious pose. "My life in El Paso was twenty-four hours a day of straight-up emptiness. I'd gotten lost and didn't know how to find myself. I was down to one dimension and living on fumes. So it was the Percodan Road or get away and get it on. I came here to try and kick the engines over.

"At the motel you came across as . . . genuine. Yeah, 'genuine' is the right word. I thought I'd take a chance, so I took the carryall. That way we at least had something to talk about. You lose the ability to talk when you're alone as much as I am."

She watches his eyes. Like slag, they shift. They find the window as if this conversation were a source of embarrassment. And that word "genuine." He said it so goddamn straight and honestly. As if somehow he'd helped shape the word.

"I was into self-inflicted wounds at the time," she says.

Vic's face comes around. She'd remembered that. "It just came out," he says. "Probably 'cause it's true. And the truth won't stay down no matter how you try to avoid it."

Something about him makes her feel bad. Maybe he's no different than she would be in another town, in some midnight coffee shop sitting across from an agreeable stranger. Of course, she'd have to watch even the slightest conversation because of what might surface. That holds some ugly promise.

He smiles at her as he lifts the coffee cup to his mouth. He's probably nothing more than what he says he is. But still.

THIRTY
THREE

From the parking lot, the windows of the coffee shop are a depthless map of stiffs. Dee has eaten a thumbscrew's worth of speed today and it brings out a contemptible paranoia. She's sure that whole world of useless breathers from table to table is praying for her imminent downfall. Probably all whoring up around that secret premise.

Crossing the lot she can see Shay working Vic. As for Vic, he's a crescent moon of hair obscured by the carryall. Before Dee goes into DIS she dials Foreman one more time on her cellular. When she gets that gruff answer-machine voice she leaves a "fuck you both, call me we got shit to solve, now" message.

Vic is in the head and Shay is staring into what that carryall means, when Dee says, "Slide over."

Shay looks up. There's a small Band-Aid covering her mother's cut eyelid. The eyes, though, are blood-webbed and Shay knows Dee is well into the manic hours.

"Talk to me."

"Inside the carryall there's pictures of your 'soulmates' arguing downtown. The one of Burgess is particularly well framed."

"So at least one round of film got developed." Dee notices a cellular on the table. "Is that yours?"

"It's Vic's."

"Watch for him."

Shay twists around in her seat. Guns N' Roses is working through their rendition of "Knockin' on Heaven's Door." Dee looks to see if the cellular is on. It is. She powers off, then powers on again. Waits to see if the number that appears on the screen will match the number the dead girl dialed last night. It doesn't.

"He's coming."

Dee sits back. Vic makes a wide turn as he approaches the table to see who this other woman is with Shay. Shay makes the introductions. "Vic, this is Dee . . . my mother. Mom . . . Vic."

A prescient moment comes over her as Vic nods cordially.

Ma, take this badge off of me. I don't need it anymore.

A neural wave of claustrophobia as her gun-metal stare follows him down into his seat.

"You look too young to be her mother."

It's getting dark, too dark to see.

She tries to lay the discomfort of just being near him off to all the pulse-tripping meth that feeds her paranoia.

I feel I'm knocking on heaven's door.

"Dorian Gray," says Shay. "Remember, the painting of Dorian Gray got older while he stayed the same age? That's my mother."

Vic nods, throwing his attention to Shay to try and avoid that stare. It's like trying to face down some ghastly fucking shrike. From the cut over Dee's eye and the resemblance to Shay, this has got to be the woman Terry saw in the bar. Now, at least, he knows how they link up.

"Shay tells me you're from El Paso."

"Yes. Except for a few years I spent here."

"Got any friends in L.A.?"

Vic looks at Shay. "Hopefully one."

"My mother comes by sometimes 'cause she knows I hang here after work."

"You two must be tight. That's good."

"Yeah." Dee swings her arm up on the booth behind Shay's shoulder. "We're tight. Aren't we, Shay?"

"There's barely breathing room between us, we're so tight."

The table falls into silence.

Ma put my guns in the ground. I can't use them anymore.

He could believe Dee being the one. He could believe it was her charging at him out of a scored desert benchland.

That long black cloud is coming down. Feel I'm knocking on heaven's door.

He tells himself, "I could believe I am this close to the gunhand."

"How do you make your living, Vic?"

"I was a bar doorman. A bouncer. A bodyguard. I even handled collections for a while."

"Imposing work."

"I know what I am, if that's what you mean." He turns to Shay. "No apologies. No excuses."

"Forget it."

Vic reaches into his pocket. "Let's call it a night." He drops some money on the table.

"I'll pay for mine," says Shay.

"What do you want to do about the camera?"

Shay looks at Dee. "It's not my camera."

Dee stands so she is right over Vic. He can feel the pulse coming off her. Knows she triggered up on something. "The girl ripped you off, Shay. Keep it so you can get yours back."

Walking the lot, the two women, side by side.

"What was all that back in there? You were just plain fucking with him."

"He's not some transient rube, that's my hot tip. And I was fuckin' with him." Dee smacks the carryall.

"If he's no rube then he's probably got the negatives."

Dee looks back, sees Vic easing down into his Mustang. "He's not with the police."

"Do you think he hired the girl?"

Dee, to Shay, "Does he look like the type that would waste the energy?"

"Then what is he about?"

Dee won't say it, not till she's sure. Not till the lightwire terror that's got her going round and round can be turned off long enough for her to think this out.

Her cellular rings. She flips it open. "It's about time you called me back. I'm coming to your place tomorrow. I got money and some very interesting photos. Somebody has been following Hugh and Pettyjohn. Yeah, now try to sleep, you fuck."

Dee flips the cellular closed. Headlights roll up behind them followed by the short burst of a car horn. Both women turn. Vic doffs his fingers along the side of his forehead and tells Shay, "Good night."

"He's not with the police. Whoever hired the girl hasn't gone to the police. Or they would be on us."

She takes out the cellular that belongs to Magale. "Whoever is at the other end wants something. Give me a cigarette."

Shay reaches into her shoulder bag for a pack.

"I always said you were stronger than I am. That you could make it without me better than I could without you. I couldn't without you."

Shay hands Dee a cigarette. "Don't go deep end on me, 'cause when you talk like this, I start looking for cover."

Dee lights the cigarette. Her hands are shaking as she inhales. She watches Vic's Mustang fold into the darkness that Fletcher Avenue becomes going south.

"You wouldn't do anything to fuck me over, would you, Shay?"

"Don't go there."

"I know the others would."

"You got to lay off the speed. Look at you, you're a junkie paranoid."

"Yeah, we'll see."

"The Shave Queen. How much speed do you knock down in a day? Your hands never stop shaking."

"We'll get through this if you don't fail me or fuck me over."

"Your veins are just gonna blow one night."

"That's all we need. That's all we ever needed."

It's a clear night across Los Feliz. The roads above Ferndell Park are a threading band of light from the homes behind walls and gates. Terry is following Dee blind, using only her taillights as tracers, from DIS to Valley Oak Drive where she slows into the abrupt turn.

A garage door rises silently. A thin spew of exhaust slips forward and she disappears into the long, sleek, white concrete structure.

Terry parks. He walks down the long sloping incline holding fast to the far side of the street. From a stand of dipping trees he can make out the address painted on the curb . . . 3399.

Another small bite has been taken out of their anonymity.

THIRTY
FOUR

Vic sits alone in Landshark's office. He stares at the two index cards on the bulletin board that read: SHANNINE STOREY. DEE STOREY. He is trying to reason out the mysterious obliquity between mother and daughter and the why behind the war they may have upon his existence when he hears Landshark yelling to him from the terrace of the floor above.

Vic hurries outside. He leans into the terrace railing and looks up. A morning copy of *The Daily News* is flagged up in Landshark's outstretched hand. "The other man . . . he's got a name, Vic. And he's heir apparent to a middle-class throne. The San Fernando Land Development Company."

One frankly eyes the other, the other frankly will not make eye contact. What Alicia Alvarez despises most about having Dee Storey in the Chatsworth house she shares with Charlie Foreman is the unconscionable fact this craven piece of sewage is staring down her possessions one by one. Down the hall a toilet flushes. Another personal humiliation; thank you, shoddy construction.

A door opens. A belt buckle clacks shut. Foreman grimaces at Alicia as he enters the room, "You and that fuckin' Thai food."

Heavily mascaraed eyes wince.

He turns his attention to Dee. There is a gym bag at her feet. "You look as bad as I feel."

She shrugs.

"Okay," says Foreman, "make me a believer."

Dee carries the gym bag to the dining area. As she pulls open the zipper small pads of money spill out onto the table. From a side vent she takes a manila envelope. "Once the 'boys' set that fag bar for the meeting I knew you meant to ride Burgess hard, so I went downtown on my own. When I was outside I spotted this cholla in an alcove working a camera."

Dee opens the envelope, takes out a small parcel of photos. She spreads them across the table as if they were a flush hand of cards. "Somebody hired the girl to photograph Pettyjohn and Englund. Somebody is tracking them."

"Who is the photographer?"

Dee has no answer for Alvarez.

Foreman's pulpy eyes go from photograph to photograph, "How did you get these?"

"The same way I helped you beat a seven-year jail sentence."

Alicia again, "You expect us to believe this?"

"Charlie. We've got to cut them out."

"Do you know why they were being followed?"

"No."

"This is a rip, Charlie."

Foreman runs his hand through the pads of money, "How much is here?"

"Sixty thousand dollars."

"What for?"

"It's a down payment on your survival."

"You hear what she's asking."

"Yeah, Alicia. I'm asking just what you asked me eleven years ago. To keep his ass out of jail."

Foreman takes up one of those photographs in his mechanic's hand. "It could be nothing, okay, Jon and Hugh are into so many crackpot deals."

Dee grabs the photo of the two of them coming out of the Barclay Hotel. "They should never have gone public. Not even after eleven years."

"I told them that myself, okay."

Alicia stares stony-eyed, "You're not taking her seriously."

"There's only one thing missing from this plot . . . you. This picture lands on a prosecutor's desk, Charlie, it's 1987. Except the boys have gone fag."

Dee can see a thought scurry down into Foreman's skull. He walks around the table to a hutch, searches through his personal rubble in the top drawer. He finds a tightly rolled joint. To Dee, "Let's you and me talk."

As they leave Alicia makes a sound like the faint hissing of sand.

Foreman leads Dee across the patio, through a slat gate, and up the rocky hillside toward the remains of a corrugated cistern. They come to a spot in the high weeds where he has left two old lawn chairs. From there you get the two-dollar view of Chatsworth, where all earthly shades of brown are the bargain basement rip of the real thing.

When they sit, Dee is looking bad. "What's wrong, you didn't eat at the same Thai place, did you?"

"Trying to keep us all from going into a death spiral has caused me a few long nights."

He lights the joint. After he takes a hit he holds it out for her, "It won't kill the down, okay, but—"

"No." She leans forward. It feels like all the connections are breaking down. "How are we gonna deal with this? 'Cause they're a threat to you, you know that."

The bitch is trying to work her witchcraft. He knows. He shakes it off. "Look down Topanga and across Santa Susana. All that used to be the Iverson Movie Ranch, okay. See that hill, on the other side of the 118 Freeway. The one with the small house on top. That's what's left of it, maybe thirty acres. It's got three houses on the property. Fenced. Gated. They still rent it out for movie locations. Back in '87, okay. After I beat that possession charge and you all closed on the 56th Street School. I could have got that place for dick. My cousin, okay, he was dealing. I could have put him in one of the houses, okay. And the place was gated. No cops. We had the mortgage cold.

"And the main house. It had this one room like a museum. The original owner had been an African hunter, okay, so he had this room with all the animals he'd killed. They were all endangered species now. It was awesome. A hundred heads all along the walls. And long trays of butterflies. We used to get ripped on acid and trip out in that room with nothing but flashlights. And those heads would talk to you, okay."

He takes another hit. Dee wonders where in Christ this is going.

That burnt blue-collar frame hauls itself forward in the chair. "All this has been my way of saying, I don't listen to Selena no more when it comes to our financial planning, okay. And you should have just given her the ethics report."

"I told Burgess to. But don't bullshit me. It was your old lady who called *The Daily News* reporter, right. The fuckin' 'unnamed source' was her. She's trying to put a little pressure on us."

He skips right past the question, "We should have gone straight to Burgess' father. We don't need to make a TV series out of this. That's what I told her. But you cunts, okay, you go mental when it comes to money." He gets in another hit. The eyes fire up, the voice chokes on itself coming out. "You hate us, don't you."

"I got no time for that now," says Dee.

"I'll bet you think this is all my fault 'cause I made you take down that prick cop in—"

She does not want to go there. Not with last night so fresh in her mind. Especially if it turns out Vic is who she feels he is. She rebuffs Charlie's questions with, "Let's deal with today."

They sit there in the high weeds, with cars buzzing past below on the 118 and crows along the caved-in roof of the cistern waiting on roadkill. Foreman glances at Dee. Her skin is tombstone white, the face nervous ticking from exhaustion. But he doesn't count on that for much when it comes to dealing with Ms. Witchcraft.

"I'll help you, but it won't be easy."

She rises up in her seat. "Where are the fags now?"

"Nevada."

"What's in Nevada, besides dust."

"They're meeting with some of their geek friends out in Laughlin, okay, about a motel or something."

"They're already spending the money."

"I want the two million."

"I don't give a shit who gets it."

"I hope not." His bullish face clenches up and he spits into the packed brush. "I told you this won't be easy, okay. Now let me give you the bad news why."

Alicia watches them through the window. For one hour they talk, the sky above the hillside browns with exhaust.

Finally they start down, their two long shadows dragging behind them.

Dee goes to her car. As Foreman comes in Alicia assaults him with questions. He silently zips up the gym bag. Her large frame is moving around nervously to the brink of panic. He brings the gym bag to Dee.

Upon his return Alicia sits at the dining area table. Her arm outstretched, her hand where the money was, as if feeling for where it has gone. He says only, "I told you this could get ugly."

THIRTY
FIVE

Dates on microfilm sweep by. First months, then weeks. Finally the slow crawl of days. The past is closing in. Dee remembers the story being in Section Two of *The L.A. Times*. The Metro Section. She scrolls the pages, the motion makes her sick. Maybe it isn't the motion, but who she expects to see.

The hard res of a headline catches her: POLICEMAN LEFT IN SHALLOW GRAVE TO DIE. And beneath the headline is a yearbook grin. Twenty-three-year-old John Victor Sully, in all his spartan simplicity.

Something shuttles through her, like a lost messenger. Something replete with voice and silence. The dead grow less so, the past lives close to the surface of all things. Like poison in the ground, it rises to leave its mark. All that brought her here she can feel in her fingers propped against her stomach and cursing wildly. From those fingers she can feel him slumping into the grave. She can feel that grainy smile looking back at her. John Victor . . . Vic.

But is it him? It's like trying to touch a gap in the wind. Scraps of that boyish face could be his. Refracted by years, yes. By batterings, yes. But time has made the rest of it missing pieces that could belong to anyone. Even the name. Victor . . . Vic—that *could* be coincidence. She is moving fiendishly between possibilities. If it is him, if it is, how could he have breathed his way back into their lives?

She goes to the bathroom and puts cold water on the base of her neck. She is deathly ill and down. The muscles up her spine and into her skull are bundled need. She looks in the mirror. Finds the scraps of the face that were her youth. Refracted by years, yes. By batterings, yes. It's all come back to one more round with certainty.

And Foreman, she knows he means to have at her sometime. She can read that hillbilly doper. He didn't believe the photos. Funny, pathetic. Maybe he's just too deep in with the fags. And Burgess, going to Daddy Dearest. What will the price of that be? She is the simple demographic—the lowest common denominator—they will point to when they want to clean up their lives. And this isn't paranoia talking. She ain't going clit, either. This is the soldier cunt whose insides are sending out storm warnings.

She'll face-to-face them, and finish. And finish. She'll go bruise to bruise with God if that's what it takes, but they won't ever have her.

The painful picture of Burgess Ridden and his father in *The Daily News* has replaced the index card on the bulletin board that read THE OTHER MAN? Beneath that are cards with questions posed: Is Burgess Ridden gay? What happened at the Scorecard? Why the fight?

E-mail from Freek. It says: The Masked Hacker Strikes Again. Faxes to follow!

And follow they do. Pages of them. Copies of Dee and Shannine Storey's driver's licenses, credit histories, tax returns. The paper trail they lay out of the two women is at best a story of fringe life. Neither has credit cards, neither ever has. Shannine's tax records are exactly what you'd expect from a twenty-four-year-old bartendress. But her mother, she doesn't, just doesn't plain exist on a cash basis as far as the IRS is concerned.

That afternoon becomes chilled and overcast. From Mount Washington, downtown is a gray perimeter of shadow buildings. Hints of rain. Terry shows with lunch from a Peruvian restaurant about a block from his condo on Rossmore and Clinton. They fill him in on the news so far. Halfway through lunch, as if he had just remembered, Terry adds to the deepening perplex with information he got from an old lover who still works the Hollywood Division. "Oh, that house on 3399 Valley Oaks Drive, it belongs to the heir apparent of the San Fernando Development Company."

"It seems," says Landshark, "the woman without a tax return is tight with some real money."

Burgess Ridden is now added to the list of targets. Landshark e-mails Freek: Bio the prince back through '87. I'll get corporate promo for overview.

Vic listens as Landshark calls the San Fernando Land Development Company. They've been at the same address on Ventura Boulevard in Encino for twenty-four years. Landshark strikes up a conversation with the office manager. He uses a false name, comes on as the VP for a shell company he set up years ago to work these little scams. He tells her his company is looking at sites in Burbank for a clothes and antique mart. "Something Cecil Beaton would be proud of, you know, bring a little style and wit to Burbank. If that isn't an oxymoron in itself."

He needs a serious promo packet, with corporate history, citations for excellence, bios, etc. Everything she can "in good faith" give out so a decision can be made. Half an hour in you'd think these two were gonna be married. Landshark bets her he can have a runner over there with flowers before she can put the packet together. She takes the bet.

When he hangs up Landshark winks at Vic, "I should have been a scam artist, not a columnist."

Terry slips in behind Landshark and whispers, "William, you are a scam artist."

Landshark breaks a filter off one of Vic's cigarettes, "I'll bet I could have sold her the Princess Di Death Plate."

It begins to drizzle. A rain that is, then isn't. The men work with the intensity of ministers trying to build a groundwork of questions that will guide their hunt forward.

Rog calls from the Garden of Allah. He's on a manic hype. Needs Vic. Says a woman left a message. Terry passes him the phone.

As he listens, Vic pulls a yellow notepad toward his pen hand. He jots down a number. Hangs up.

"Shannine Storey?" asks Landshark.

Vic tears off the page with the number on it, and by way of a cold pronouncement tacks it up on the bulletin board under Dee Storey.

"She wants me to call her at five-thirty."

The men glance at the clock on the bar. It will be a long and troubling two-and-a-half-hour wait.

The sky is the color of gravel as a runner shows with fifty pages' worth of promo material and a swooning note from the office manager at the San Fernando Land Development Company. Most of the promo material is your typical shake-and-bake self-aggrandizement with appropriate color plates and testaments of quality craftsmanship and cost-effective pricing.

There are the usual battery of endorsements: the late mayor, the present mayor, councilmen and women, a lock-step of congratulatory self-serving boards, organizations, and entrepreneurs. There're pages dedicated to the high-profile jobs. An addenda on developing projects.

But this small triangle of men is adrift in detail without direction. They can't unlock from that covert menagerie of bulletin-board faces and names some organic link, some reasoned purpose between one attempted and one achieved murder. Maybe they are just disparate events in the sweep of time.

Rain fed hours. No real progress. Landshark is at the bar on his second Oban. He begins a detailed pass through all that promotional demagoguery. Vic checks the time—five-thirty is closing in.

Landshark speaks to the room, "You know, it would be poetic justice if Los Angeles were ultimately known for only one thing and you know what that would be . . . as the birthplace of Tokyo Rose. She was born here, you know. I'm gonna put that in my column."

Terry grinds out his cigarette butt, "You're losing it, boy."

"Am I?" Landshark holds up in his prayer-clasped hands one page of promo. He comes around the bar to the table and passes it to Terry. "What do you see?"

Terry makes a close inspection. It's a full-page glossy of the opening of the 56th Street School in South Central L.A. And in the corner is an inserted cameo shot of a small crowd at the groundbreaking ceremony.

"What am I looking for?"

"A badly dressed Hispanic woman two rows back of Burgess Ridden."

Terry squints, "Goddamn," he says, "it's Alvarez."

They go to pass the photo to Vic but he has walked out of the room. They see him sitting on the stairwell. He has dialed Dee's number and said, "Hello. This is Vic." They wait and talk among themselves in whispers.

Landshark: "The Department of Education handles all kinds of approvals when they build schools, right."

Terry: "Have Freek run it down. And look, the groundbreaking dates back to '87."

"If she was with Foreman then—"

Vic snaps the phone shut. Comes back into the room. "She wants me to be at her place at nine tonight."

"Did she say why?"

Vic glances at the copy of Dee's driver's license. "The address she gave up in Hollywood is the same as the one on her driver's license. You got to find out how she pays for the place."

"What does she want?"

"She wants to talk to me about a job."

THIRTY
SIX

———

Vic is down on the fourth floor in HARPERS FERRY, giving his semi-automatic a body ride. He's also trying to burn off the anxiety he's feeling about tonight when Landshark enters the room.

Soundproofed concussion. Vents drawing out the acrid afterburn of gunfire. The scent of violence, without its awful import. Landshark takes a seat and watches Vic put a small circle of black holes around the heart of the target. Then his eyes are led on a slow tour of Vic's body. The taut bend of shoulders and back barely flexing with each shot. The tracery of arm scars. The black leather belt across the lip of his faded jeans. The genitals bulked up against the thigh. He puts these thoughts down.

"Are you okay with tonight?" he asks.

Vic palms in another clip.

"No one would fault you for not going on with this. I could get *The New Weekly* to give me a full blow of lead space. I could cover everything. Use the pictures. Facts we know. It would, at least, draw serious reporters like sharks. Blood always does that."

Yes, thinks Vic, blood always does that. He has been the camera's darling once already. And he could let it go. He could sidestep what's in, around, and before him. But he knows this is the most meaningful, the most ugly, the most serious, preposterous, beautiful, just and hideous experience since he fought clear of that womb. Its very tactility will not be taken from him and left to others. He is now powerfully part of that arrant existence called life and he'll be damned if he leaves it to the Landsharks and law enforcements of Los Angeles to declaim what's true, what's real, what is.

"Let's take a walk," says Vic.

The rain has stopped in time for darkness. The driveway where Vic and Landshark walk is shiny and slick. When the wind kicks, it throws down wet from the overhanging branches.

"I want to know now about what Rog said."

Landshark stops. He nods. He reaches for Vic's cigarettes. Begins the ritual of breaking off a filter.

"My mother was an investment counselor. She specialized in pharmaceuticals. My father was a stock broker. They both made serious money. When Roche was first developing librium and valium my mother had him invest. They became millionaires. My father bought property. They kept getting richer. But that was their avocation. Their true vocation was sex. In that respect they were quintessentially American."

He lights the cigarette. Vic starts for the main gate. "Group sex. Wife swapping. Bondage. Gay sex. Aversion sex. I knew about sex before I knew how to spell. A friend of my mother's took me to see *True Grit* when I was nine. She spent the whole time in the theater fondling my cock. Six months later she and her husband were giving me baths and jerking me off. It wasn't long before my dick was a regular on the circuit."

"Open the gate," says Vic. Landshark goes over and pushes the automatic opener. The gears squeak and Andalusia Avenue opens out before them.

"How far down that road can you go?"

"Before I have an anxiety attack?"

"Yes."

"I don't know. Not far."

Vic starts out into the street. Landshark does not.

"If I can get on a fuckin' plane after two calls from some . . . head-job I never heard of, the least you can do is try."

Landshark takes his first steps into the plush quiet. The heels of his Italian loafers scrape along the indifferent road that ends at his house. He can feel the wings of his throat begin to tighten, the mouth starch.

"My mother had a repugnant voice. She was richly repugnant in many ways. Of course, I might be prejudiced being her son. She loved Lloyd Thaxton and would lip-sync with him and she wore Capezio pants that did not gracefully hold in her ass. The only thing I liked about her were the Capezio pants."

Somewhere in the delicate loomwork of that darkness is the fear of a fear that will overtake him. Not there yet, but there. Breathing a half beat beside and behind his own breath. Ready to make itself manifest when it recognizes the slightest provocation there is intent to overcome it.

"I was afraid of everything as a boy. And my father made me pay for that fear regularly. He rubbed my nose in it. He took me on a Ferris wheel once. I was small and when it stopped at the top he made the chair rock violently till I threw up. And then he rocked it again till I hid at the bottom of the seat in my own puke. This was not done so I'd become a man, but so I'd never become one."

Vic picks up the unsure cadence Landshark's voice has started to strike. "I threw a hammer at his head when I was thirteen. I tried to run him over when I was fourteen, and was sent to a psychiatrist."

They're thirty feet out from the gate. Ten poor yards and it's far enough for Landshark to feel that apparition called panic begin to constrict his chest.

This procession of two begins to slow dramatically.

"We lived in Fresno, but kept a small beach house in Santa Monica. In the seventies, L.A. was the perfect 'hot zone' for the kind of sport-fucking my folks were into. My father would fly us down here in a Navion he'd bought. We kept it at Whiteman Airport in the North Valley."

Landshark stops. His breathing has gone shallow. The panic has come. He looks into the windy space around him. The deep well-to-do lawns, the heavily grottoed front yards. What should be just tranquil space is now threatening distance from the safe zone of his house.

"I was fifteen. We'd been doing our best all that year to hack each other's emotions to death. That weekend was no different. We were getting the plane back in the hangar when the left aileron was damaged by hitting a temporary hoist we'd set up."

Landshark starts to hyperventilate to compensate for that gasping out-of-breath feeling. The death spiral has begun.

"My father was a fine mechanic. I was good too. I loved planes, not flying them, just planes. Maintaining the Navion, that was one of the few things we could sometimes do together without . . ." He throws his cigarette down. "But not that day. Not that day."

Landshark goes and sits on the curb as if being closer to the earth will somehow ground him against the dizziness. "A therapist once told me that if you brutalize the psyche long enough it will more than reward the effort. I am the reward of all that effort." He pulls his legs up, wraps his arms around his knees. "There are these cotter pins that go into the cable nuts along the length of the ailerons. Those are the small flaps that raise and lower and give the wings control."

Landshark looks at the wet asphalt, at the streaks of light cast from the streetlamp overhead, as if the past could be augured up out of the vaporous black.

"He . . . we . . . I . . . forgot to put back the cotter pins." Landshark looks up at Vic. "Talk about fate. I just wanted to be rid of them for a few days. I guess you could say it was hate that saved me."

He closes his eyes. "They went down just north of the Grapevine. Near Gorman. The goddamn cotter pins were on a table inside that hangar not ten feet from where the wing had been."

He opens his eyes. "There was so much money and no will and with my history of violence against my father. You wouldn't know to look at me, Vic, that I am completely flipped out with stress at this moment, would you. That I want to run back to my house."

"I wouldn't know that looking at you."

"I was told by a therapist I learned to cope with all the craziness by creating some safe world. That's how I survived. Only I didn't need that to survive anymore, I was free. My body just won't buy the explanation."

He looks back toward his house. The city lights beyond are like stark embers against the darkness. Distance and mood. Enticing and repellant. Beauty and threat. Los Angeles as it is, inside him.

"Remember I told you back in '87 I was on a shortlist at *The L.A. Times* for a job. And that they discovered I had 'artfully recreated' my life. Well, they found out what I just told you."

Landshark sighs, "I hope you can forgive me."

"For what?"

Landshark's face sinks into his hands. "For not having the courage that first time to continue. For not being—"

"William, I gave up too back then. And I wasn't *your* responsibility. Now . . . get the fuck up."

Landshark stands willingly. He wants to go back now. Vic's hair blows across his face. "I knew a hard-case judge in El Paso," says Vic. "A real booze and pill hound who'd hole up in the Sunshine when he'd go on a couple of days' high. He told me, 'Justice is served just as well by the selfish as the selfless.' "

"What I said downstairs, don't think I'd quit on—"

Vic grabs Landshark by the shirt and drags him further down the street. Now well past the lamplight Landshark becomes a stricken assemblage of arms and legs struggling to get loose. But once Vic oxes down a grip on Landshark's arm, he is helpless.

"What are you doing?"

"Do you feel fear? Are you afraid?"

"Fucking right I am."

Vic stops but doesn't let go. "You think I don't feel that? That it doesn't have at me right now knowing what may be ahead. But I won't give it up and you know why?"

Landshark wants to be told.

" 'Cause I am alive for the first time. Not just since '87. But ever. Fear or not, I am alive. I owe you that. I won't let you take it from me and maybe, maybe I won't let you take it from both of us."

THIRTY
SEVEN

———

She gives him a long, calculated going-over as the front door opens, "You're not late," Dee says, "by much."

"I didn't know I was on the clock."

"We're all on the clock, or haven't you heard."

He follows her across the living room. His first thought, it's dark enough in here for trouble.

"A drink?"

"Beer."

"No beer. How 'bout something from a real bottle?"

"Sure."

His eyes make a subtle pilgrimage of the room to make sure they are alone. A door slams shut behind him and he snaps around.

"Sorry," says Dee.

They drink facing each other. She on the couch, he taking a chair with only the wall behind him. He listens for something unexpected. She is edgy but even.

"Why don't you tell me what you're really about."

He puts down his glass, reaches for his cigarette in the ashtray on the glass table between them.

"Don't think so hard. I don't expect the truth."

"Why doesn't that surprise me."

"The camera . . . was that teaser just so much bullshit so you could leave a few cum stains inside my daughter?"

"You don't have an ounce of class, do you?"

"Not unless I snorted it."

———

"You said you might be able to put a few bucks in my pocket."

"Have you ever been to the desert?"

She is smooth as smoke. "Some," he says.

"Barstow? Baker?"

There was no bluff to that face. It was come and get me. "Some," he says.

"You know Laughlin, Nevada, then?"

"Some."

"Handy word. You went into that girl's room at the motel and ripped her off, didn't you?"

"Anything to leave a few cum stains."

A fatted envelope has been lying conspicuously on the table. She leans in and slides it his way. "Shay has to leave tomorrow to make a delivery in Laughlin. I can't be there. So I want her—"

"—chaperoned?"

"Why not."

"I don't run drugs."

"Neither do I."

Dee's eyes are caves tonight. He opens the envelope, seven bound packets. All hundreds. If she was the one, and knows it's him, then this is raw assurance, a pin-him-to-the-mat confidence in something already played out in her head. Of course, she might be just some mid-level skim bitch taking fire for someone else. He pushes the envelope back her way.

Her fingers walk the envelope back across to Vic's side of the table.

"I thought I said no."

"That's right. You thought you said no."

"What makes you think you can trust me. You don't even know me."

"If people were hired by trust the unemployment line would run all the way to the San Andreas fault. I need a bodyguard. You look like you can take care of yourself. I want somebody to be a quiet backdrop. But a dead ringer for someone who can kick ass."

A car can be heard gearing down as it rides the incline up into the driveway.

"I don't think you get it, Vic. We're after the same thing."

"And what's that?"

"My daughter's safety, of course. What else would there be?"

———

Shay doesn't recognize the Mustang. Her mother got urgent, she came. Even squeezed the last drops out of it. Shay thought it was to be some one on one and let's have all this over with. But the Mustang . . . then she gets a hit of these Texas plates.

Dee crosses toward the bar. "I'm sure you have a weapon tucked away somewhere."

"Yeah."

"Be carrying it tomorrow."

Vic stands as Shay enters the house. A round of cautious hellos. Vic picks up the dark reproval in Shay's eyes for her mother, who swings past her.

Dee hands Vic his refill, "My daughter and I need a few minutes. You might as well sit this out."

The women's voices go church light as they cross into the den.

"Why is he here?"

"He's going with you."

"And where the fuck am I going?"

Vic checks out the body english Shay puts into closing that door. Those two are like high tension wires set to cross, a life argument that will not take loose ends for an answer. He does a little of his drink, then . . . Talk about ferrying into the unknown.

"You'll take the sixty thousand dollars to Laughlin. There'll be a contact named Crocker. He will set the meeting between you and the fags. They will show you the papers, you will give them the money. You call me, tell me it's cool. Your part is complete. I finish up. You're back in forty-eight hours and I'm out of your life, like you said."

"The spoken word strikes again."

"I shit you not."

Shay points toward the other room, "Why'd you bring him into this? Has he managed to make it onto your hate list too?"

That look of sheer iniquity comes at Shay like a fast-moving train, then passes. "A little male presence in case the screamers go nasty. I don't think it'll happen but that sperm cowboy looks willing to handle it. Besides, I think he's got the hots for you. So he's the perfect door-mat."

"The bullshit comes free with the flogging, right?"

Vic's eyes prowl. Listens for sounds. The disused cop drill kicks in. Details: the "look at me" furniture. All cardboard flash and impersonal, but worth plenty. The only real touch is all those beautiful photos in the bar alcove.

Let's just go get another refill and see what memory holds dear.

"Don't rag me, alright, Shay. My insides are pure fuckin' jumble. And I can barely parachute through today."

"Asking for the truth is not ragging you. Why don't you bring the money to them in one blow. What's this one step, two step shit. Something—"

"We have to know they got the papers, right. I won't hold my ass up in the air so it can be trimmed like some fuckin' sail."

Scan the photos while you touch up your drink. Eyes narrow. Anxious. Get it done. Mostly old life moments. Pocket-sized time capsules. Dee the looker and her six-year-old in Mexico. Dee and Shay at a barbecue with some freaked outs. A lot of white-trash-on-the-climb snapshots. Real Winslow Homer as seen through the eyes of *Savage* Mag.

Then the real eye turner. Shay Storey sitting on the hood of an Alfa, shirt skinned down over one shoulder. A little too much Baby Doll in the pose. And look who's beside her—Burgess Ridden.

The door opens at a clip. Light falls in a streak from the den to the bar.

"I was refilling my drink."

The women come toward him quietly. Shay takes up the photo of her that he was looking at. She holds it out to her mother, "I was almost a functioning human being then, remember."

Dee passes without notice. "Walk Vic out. Get him organized. Come back so we can finish."

Shay leans against the hood of the Mustang. She writes down her address on the inside of a Nightland matchbook. She hands it to Vic as he comes up beside her, "Since you like to collect matchbooks so much."

"You don't want me coming along, do you?"

"I'll see you at nine."

She starts back for the house. He takes her by the arm, "You didn't answer me. Please?"

She shifts slightly, "I don't know you. What you're really about. I probably never will. But my mother bringing you into this ... she knows how to work people's heads. You could get very fucked up."

There's sincerity and desolation in her voice. Equal drifts. She takes his hand from her arm but holds it one moment longer. Her eyes lift from his ruined arm to his weary face.

"Haven't you paid enough already for whoever you are? Go away. Don't feed the lion."

THIRTY
EIGHT

———

Dee is at the bar when Shay returns. Light from the den leaks past her shoulder and onto the photograph she's holding of Shay on the hood of Burgess' car outside the Franklin Canyon house. "I was almost a functioning human being then." There is deep hurt in Dee's eyes, and a tongue pressed against the inside of her cheek, but all that is soon replaced by more pressing realities. Dee puts the photo down, she pours herself some Southern Comfort.

"Why did you bring him into this?" Shay asks.

"Whatever he is, or isn't, once he gets into the car, he belongs to us. He is compromised. It will be too late. Remember that."

"You just won't tell me the truth."

"There's what I know. There's what I think. Then, there's what I do. All that counts is what I do." Dee leans against the bar for support. She does not look at Shay. "I am sorry I have exploited you. I have done it selfishly. And with the full knowledge of who I am and how . . . how it would hurt you."

"Viva Verboten."

"I'll take the slits girl, okay. Just don't fell me." Dee reaches into her back jeans pocket. "Get it all out. All that hateful Tinkerbell shit. Give me the whole bloodthirsty package you ripped off from the few books you read. 'Cause this is the last of it."

"There is no imperfection you won't use to move me, is there? You think I'll stand here and let you get self-incriminating. This is just another version of the wine and dine. You're working me. Say it, you're working me."

"That's right," comes the vehement response, "for your own good. For my own good. For our own good! Yours . . . mine . . . ours. Get it!" Dee holds out a key ring. On it are two safe-deposit-box keys. "You'll need these later."

Shay grabs the ring and flings it into the living room where it caroms off a lamp shade and pings against the glass patio door. Dee's mouth closes, she breathes heavily through her nose. She walks into the living room. Shay follows at a distance. Dee scoops up the ring, from her back pocket comes a folded-up, handwritten note. Dee wraps the keys in the squared-down paper.

"I have a name here and a number. This character is fuckin' A-one when it comes to getting you a new identity. I mean government approval shit. I've taken care of everything. Paid the freight. He'll be expecting a call from you in a few days."

The moment as visitation. Glimpsed through the barwork of a lifetime. Off-kilter and odd, shaped by unbelievability. Shay can only stare at that small packet of identity.

"Oh, yes," Dee whispers, "we are here. The moment," she says with disdainful trepidation, "we have all been waiting for." She turns away. Leaves her daughter with a handful of futures. Dee opens the patio doors and steps out into the night. Shay follows her. Dee marshals up a cigarette. Behind gray night clouds a moon tries to break through. The city, as always, is luminous. Even when the heavens are against it.

"If you sense anything is off in Laughlin," Dee warns, "anything, turn around. Call me, if you want. Otherwise if you're too far in, lay down the money. Lay it down. Don't spar with the screamers. Let their cocks get hard, but ride. And keep riding. Alone. Straight to that name I gave you. Pick up your traveling papers and the money. And don't ever . . . not ever, daughter, as long as you live, come back."

There is in that face brutal frankness, and chilling finality.

"Is this all you're gonna tell me?"

The head drops a bit. The eyes slide along to avoid any issue with pain.

"Is it Foreman? Do you think he might—"

"I intend to get you out of this alive. Now don't ask any more questions."

Shay tries to get close to her mother, to make her look go face-to-face, but Dee avoids it. And so mother and daughter become just a sparring dance of the unspoken.

"At this moment," says Shay, "I don't even know how much I should hate you. Do you know that?"

"Well, given your grandmother's longevity, you've got a good fifty or sixty years to think about it."

Dee walks inside.

She is pouring another drink as Shay comes in and leans against the archway wall leading to the bar.

"If you had ever used all that will for something, for anything, for the least—"

"Maybe I could have become one of those clits walking through Wal-Marts with a dumptruck ass. Or maybe some white yuppie hostess climbing the corporate ladder."

"Anything would have been better."

"Too bad you weren't making those decisions."

There is a moment of such embittered pain inside Shay, and it's not that she can't understand why it's there, but that it has such a deep hold on her. So absolutely primal and incalculable in the sorrow and anger it arouses. She is being torn apart by the dream of pity and the desire to punish.

"If only it were all . . . right."

That sentence falls long and hard into silence. Dee finishes her drink then sets the glass down. She rests both arms on the ledge of the bar sink.

"I would have done anything for you," says Shay. "Of course, I have." Her voice falls away. "Even now. Am I a born fool, or just so well practiced I don't know the difference?"

Dee watches the water drip slightly against the stainless steel and leave small tear marks.

"You said the other night, 'We'd be alright if only *I* don't fail you or fuck you over.'"

"You never failed me, Shay. I allow you to think that, so I can manipulate you. Even the other night. I am not beyond destructive manipulation. Now . . . get out, okay."

Shay reaches out, touches her mother's arm. Can feel a faint trembling move up that arm and through the exhaustion and into a voice that finishes with, "Ain't we a pair, raggedy girl."

THIRTY
NINE

———

The dark snaps at him. He wakes sweating. It's like being in stir. Fore-man sits in the kitchen with the lights off, facing down a half-drunk can of beer. Thinking about a kill is a lot different than living it. All the diseases of a distrusting mind are prone to eat at the sorry insides of his head.

He knows he's got to kill Storey and her daughter. To leave either is a guarantee of lifelong torture at the hands of the unknown.

Then he hears a voice, "Charlie, what are you doing?" And feels Alicia's warm breasts under a nightshirt against his back. "Charlie, are we alright?"

Pools of pinkish light break on the horizon. They edge upward, out-ward. Around the worktable Vic and Terry are like birds of prey watch-ing Vic check his semiautomatic one more time.

"She sends you out into the desert to bodyguard a money delivery made by her own daughter. What the fuck is all that about? Is she scamming you?"

When the gun check answers clean, Vic goes into his grip to make sure he's packed extra clips and ammo. "If she thinks I'm not who I am, I'll bet she assumes I'm not in it alone. And in that way she's like us. So . . ." He reaches into one of his grip's side vents, "she plays it straight with one hand. The upscale carrier looking for a little protec-tion." He removes an eight-inch stiletto, "But in the other hand," he springs the blade and the glistening length of metal cuts apart the air, "yeah, she's the same as us, I'll bet."

Shay is waiting on the stoop in front of her house when that thirty-year-old Fastback shows. She approaches with duffel bag and cloth backpack. She's wearing black wraparound sunglasses, a white sleeveless undershirt, and jeans. She leans into the shotgun-seat window. Sees the guts of the Mustang are roll barred and the dash is straight-on hot street cruiser.

She tosses the duffel in the back, "I thought we were going to Laughlin, not the Ontario Speedway."

"At least I'm on time," says Vic.

He sees she keeps the backpack with her. "Yeah," she says, "but I was hoping you wouldn't show at all."

The 10 outbound is a nasty lick of traffic, but not a whiff compared to what's incoming. That's a clear strip of chrome and metal miles moving full tilt out of the sun, a megaroad of clock punchers. A frightening wave of alleged honest and uprights trying to hump an existence out of the obscenities around them. And where is she? Sitting with sixty thousand in a backpack between her feet so trash can be reconciled.

Behind her black lenses she steals a look at Vic. Face stoic and jaw firmly set. She recites in her head what her mother said the night before, "If he gets in the car, he's compromised."

She looks out upon a freeway bombarded with roadside sales pitches, hitting you with those life come-ons you got to have. If he's so compromised, she thinks, then what the hell am I?

Approaching Barstow the land begins to dry and crack. As they cross through town on the freeway Vic can almost see the hospital where he fought death to a standstill. The odors of that time return like some sickening artifact, he can feel a ratchet pain where the tubes were pushed through his chest to sump out the fluid and blood.

A long white flash of anger floods up through his body as he glances at Shay and asks, "Anything about what's coming I need to know?"

She flicks ash out into the Indian summer air, "We go to this casino on the river, the Colorado Belle, which ought to be a surreal treat." She pulls a leg up and presses her boot against the dash. "We do some drinks. We sightsurf the natives and wait for some human slug named Crocker to page us."

The ghastly screaming flesh of that night is back, his insides a vault so deep with pain he cannot hear the end of its echo. "What exactly do you want from me?"

Shay puts her back against the headrest and closes her eyes, "Wish for everything to be fast and painless."

Fast and painless, it won't be. That, Vic is sure of. Where 40 starts making its way east toward Nevada the country grows yellow and harsh. The ground erupts into violent peaks and carved-out gullies that give the California desert its visual infamy.

To the north the first traces of Devil's Playground mark the western border of the Mojave National Preserve. Home of that night eleven years ago. Shay's heart starts to feel like a waterskin being squeezed dry.

She scans the dial for music. Not the usual dial-up shit, but something with living mood flavor. But those stations this far out are all crackly until she lands on a Palm Springs FM doing a run of Lou Reed . . . from "Berlin" to "A Bus Load of Faith to Get By."

She looks past the hood cutting up the desert air and out into Devil's Playground. Through the haze she can imagine that gray and iron wall of weathered rock being carved in the ashen twilight of ancient gods, where all things are known.

Just pretend, she told herself that night, it was a petty concealment. Yeah, but, lies are straw men waiting to fall.

They blow past the exit for Kelbaker Road. Not ten minutes north is Baker, California. The Davenport Motel. Indian Springs Trail and that makeshift grave.

They are that close again. Child, and stranger. Stranger, and woman.

Her nipples rise and fall against her T-shirt with each conflicted breath. Vic can see. Beyond that cornrow braid on the side of her face a disillusioned and distressed expression. Vic can see.

"Have you ever done anything," she asks, "that you are truly ashamed of? I mean . . . that leaves you haunted."

He stares at her for a moment. Her hair is being wind whipped. Her long beautiful neck holds her head slightly and sadly to one side.

"I've done things I'm ashamed of."

In the world there is no expression for what is inside her head.

"The way you say it, that's not near what I mean. I am talking the black hole of self-inflicted wounds. The black hole."

FORTY

———

Laughlin, Nevada, is a small strip of hell on the Colorado River where Nevada and Arizona meet. This stretch of battered escarpment and bare desert was absolutely nothing until 1969, when a blue-collar entrepreneur named Don Laughlin started the town with a tiny motel. His idea: Make a fortune by giving people river recreation and crap tables. Twenty years later, Laughlin was a 240-batting-average Las Vegas. Strictly B-team, but a class up from Searchlight, Stateline, or Tonopoh.

The Colorado Belle Casino is a rip of a slave-era paddlewheeler. A Mark Twain riverboat for the blackjack, video poker, and karaoke crowd. Done in colors befitting retirees who travel in those RV prairie schooners and the tanned young Arizona crowd who favor SUVs and water skis. It's where the atrocious possibility that Edgar Winter might play in a room side by side with Charo comes true, and where there really could be a crowd for things like Boot Scootin and Spice on Ice.

Vic and Shay are on the clock. They wait in a bar booth on the upper deck of the Colorado Belle for a page. Just outside the open doors a band is holding up in the sun and easy-miking sixties tunes . . . "I'm a Believer," "The In Crowd," "Down in the Boondocks."

"Pretty radical stuff they got here on the river," says Vic, poking more than slight fun at the band.

Shay nods, but she's not listening. Twice in the last hour she tried to call Dee, to let her know they're in Laughlin. There was no response. No call back. No message left on Shay's cellular. It's not like her mother to go dead quiet.

"Look out across the river," he says, pointing to a thin mirage of colors along the southeast horizon, "those are the Black Mountains of Arizona. Elephant's Tooth . . . that was big mining at the turn of the century. They took about thirty-five million in gold out of those hills before they bellied up." He looks around. "But it looks like another generation is giving it back, hey."

Shay listens quietly. She looks onto the Colorado where water taxis work their way up and down the river in the heat, and sightseeing boats do that slow Instamatic crawl. Across the river, though, the land is as it was for millennia, a raw and untamed habitat.

The discrepancy lived out on those two sides of the Colorado is obvious and blatant. She thinks about what Burgess and her mother and the rest have really done. And the part she played and is now playing with sixty thousand at her feet in a backpack. She wishes she never had come back from Mexico after her mother left her there. She wishes—

And wonders. If America had ever really been discovered. Maybe it had only been unearthed. That it was some huge cavern left in hiding with everything bad that ever happened or is waiting to happen, if only you will just dig a little to find it.

"How'd you get to be a tour guide for," she waves a hand taking in everything around her, "Temptation Gardens."

He grins, "Zzyzx."

"Excuse fuckin' me?"

He spells it out. Pronounces it. "Dr. Curtis Howard Springer, no relation to Jerry Springer that I know of. He was a radio host back in the late forties. A health-food junkie. Built Zzyzx out in the desert as a mineral resort. My family followed him out there. Worked for him a long time. He preached that if you eat good, think good thoughts, lead the good life, don't argue about God, or the law, or politics, or religion, or society you will be alright."

"Will you?"

"No." He takes down some scotch. "He designed and built these steel-reinforced concrete structures out in the desert. They were air conditioned. There was a mineral pool shaped like a cross. His place was called 'The Castle.' He got winos from L.A. to help build the place. The Boulevard of Dreams. He envisioned it all. There was only one flaw. He was squatting on government land. He was making millions but paying no taxes. The AMA went after him, the Bureau of Land Management went after him. The state Food and Drug Commission went after him. They took him off the property on Good Friday in the mid-seventies."

Shay reaches for her bourbon and rocks. "Ain't it the way." She drinks. "Your folks sound like full-time geeks."

Vic's voice grows bitter. "They were decent, simple folks who taught me to fear everything but them. The world was too big. Too hostile. Too complicated. Too violent. Too immoral. Too, too, too."

"Just stay on the Boulevard of Dreams and you'll eat good, live well, and be happy."

"Dr. Springer couldn't have said it better himself."

The band breaks into a white loafer rendition of Jewel Aikens' "The Birds and the Bees."

As if remarking on Vic's first comment Shay says, "Radical band. It's got to be the shoes." She takes another drink, glances at her cellular. "My mother taught me to fear nothing . . . except her."

With that desert light coming through the window beside her, Shay's skin is almost translucent. "The truth is probably somewhere in between," he says.

She nods. He starts to work his questions in. "You don't want to be here, do you?"

"Ask my handlers."

"How come you are here?"

"Friends in low places."

She's maneuvering around him.

"When we were driving in, you asked me if I had ever done anything I was ashamed of. What was that?"

"I got my own self-inflicted wounds, alright."

"Alright."

She stands. "I got to make a call." She takes her cellular and the backpack and heads out onto the deck.

Shay's got the cellular up to one ear, her hand cupped over the other, so she can listen through the metallic ching-ching-ching of the slots and the machine gun of the roulette wheel and writers shouting "Keno" as they move through the crowd. For a third time Shay ends up at her mother's voice mail. "You haven't answered my calls," she says hushed, "I'm not Burgess, for Christ's sake. We're here. Is everything alright?"

At the bar door Shay is met head-on by Vic, who is holding her unfinished drink. "I was coming to look for you. You just got paged. Concierge desk, Level D." He hands her the drink. "In case you want to finish it."

She does not; she sets the glass down and catches her breath. "Let's put the skin to work."

FORTY
ONE

_____

They press through the foot traffic Indian file and under a huge banner that reads: PLAY ROLLIN' ON THE RIVER'S 10,000 GIVEAWAY. Her mother's silence has Shay seeing outcomes one uglier than the other.

They hit a freewheeling human wall watching handpicked guests fling monster dice down the grand stairwell. Shay tells herself everything will be okay. It's nothing but the fear factory working overtime on her head. That in a few detached hours—

She tries to struggle past the blue hairs and the halter tops and polyesters and the J. C. Penney moms with their Beanie-Baby-faced kids and the blue-collar dads all cheering mindlessly that their number will be rolled.

Vic watches Shay's frustration fighting to negotiate this frenzied mob and find a way to Level D now that the grand stairwell has been turned into a long descending crap table. As she swings past him he spots a hitch holster tucked up neatly inside the back of her jeans just above the crack in her ass and below the backpack.

Being a little taller he's got the edge in spotting an elevator sign and he takes her by the arm. He guides and muscles their way through that rabid maze of excitement. They reach the elevator and she gives the button a short clop with her fist and says "Christ" just under her breath. As they wait, a young married couple throws the dice down those showcase stairs where they bound and carom and spring through a fanatic call of numbers and a final roar.

Vic and Shay glance at each other. The perverse comparison between what they're watching and what they're getting ready to do is lost on neither.

"Yeah," says Shay, as if agreeing with Vic's thoughts.

He watches that screaming couple then nods and leans down and whispers to Shay, "Do us a favor and pull the shirt out of your pants."

Off her mute look of uncertainty, "So no one can see the pistol warming up against your ass."

They cross the crowded lobby and find only one person by the concierge desk beside the captain in his eye-killing red vest.

Crocker looks like a collection of side effects. He's a big kid amped by steroids in a tank top and shorts. His head is oddly shaped, his face so droopy you might think there was a leak in his mother's womb. He also has a shaved head, but the closer they get they see it's not just shaved, it's been waxed or peeled. He's got no hair on his eyebrows either, nor on his arms or legs.

Shay, to be certain, asks, "You Crocker?"

Crocker: "Yes, but it's not my name really."

He has an odd kind of central European accent and it sounds as if he learned English phonetically. "It's more like, my essence."

Then as if to explain he holds up his rippled arms and crosses them. Vic and Shay scan the back of each. From wrist to shoulder, crocodiles have been tattooed with jaws primed and tails in the prepared question mark of who's for dinner.

"Pettyjohn said you'd be here alone."

Vic logs it . . . Pettyjohn.

"I don't know where he got that," says Shay.

Crocker labors through his alternatives, then without speaking motions for them to get in tow as he starts out of the hotel.

They hit sunlight. They move through a sea of asphalt and car hoods. Their eyes pin down except for Shay who is holding up behind black sunglasses. They have no idea where Crocker is leading them.

As they walk Vic faces the idea: If Pettyjohn is delivery, will Hugh be there? If he recognizes Vic, then this could be a fast meltdown. He glances at Shay. There is sweat at the edge of her temples.

Crocker stops at one of those overpainted "fuck" vans with the sheepskin seats and dashboard. A scene from the Everglades has been hot touched on the side. And lurking in that calm acrylic swamp, a set of atavistic eyes. Crocker opens the driver's door. Maybe he's reaching in for a cellular, maybe not.

Vic takes no chances. He extends an arm and unnoticed moves Shay and then himself a few feet back and away from the van door should Crocker reappear with anything other than a phone. In that moment of concentration he recognizes within himself a genuine concern for the girl's safety. Not some petty indulgence nor a chess piece move to board her with either. Even being armed with the thought of what that partial revelation back around the Kelbaker exit could mean.

Crocker points his cellular at Vic, "What's your name?"

Of course she could be just some walking tragedy. She's got all the credentials for it. Maybe it was Dee Storey. Maybe Shay knew and has kept silent. Maybe—

"What the hell do you need his name for?"

Christ, it's not hard to master the art of getting lost. Just not now. Not with her.

"So I won't look stupid if Pettyjohn—"

Vic slaps out an answer, "Charles Manson."

The flesh where Crocker's eyebrows were rises and his jaw looms down against his chest. "That's not your name."

"Right. It's not my name. But it's my essence where you and that shitass call are concerned."

The boy's pale green eyes glare against the white. He walks toward Vic. His thighs are so thick the flesh rasps where they touch. Before speaking he lets Vic see a frontline of teeth that have been filed. Every one, top and bottom, into hideous dagger points.

"You know how many people have photographed me," he says. "How many people are blown away by how I am. I have been in magazines in Germany and England." His hands move as if he were taking in his whole being. "This is my calling card. My body armor for dealing. The crocodile is the devourer, the necessity of passing through death to life. If you can. The descent into hell through its open mouth."

Vic gives him a visual shakedown. The slow eye cruise that tells Crocker you are a peep show with a crack in your brainstem trying to mythos yourself out of some fantasy you read, or saw, or were told while you had your head in a glue bag.

Then, without warning, Vic drives a hand right into Crocker's throat. He gets a grip lock on that thin trail of cartilage you have to breathe through and with all his strength backslams the boy into the van. The raw thud is so loud a couple of passing seniors are shocked into a standstill.

"You're fucking bullshit," Vic tells him.

Crocker is an open-mouthed grimace afraid to chance a crushed windpipe and Vic can see into that gaping cavity of a mouth the boy's tongue has been surgically splayed. It is ridiculous and frightening at the same time.

"Be careful, Vic, people are watching."

"You gonna make the call, or do I tear the essence right out of you?"

FORTY
TWO

They follow the van up Casino Drive and across the Colorado. It sweeps onto 95, riding southwest into Arizona. Crocker is going at a nasty clip but nothing the Fastback can't handle.

The road begins to move away from the river. Away from the wave runners and jet skis with their snowy whitewater tails. Away from the long box shadows the hotels cast across the landscape. The van kicks it up another notch but Vic rides him so close you could almost touch the bumper stickers Crocker's got slapped along the glittery chrome ... NIGHT OF 1000 SCARS ... EROTICA AUTOMAT ... Take a vacation from reality with BIZARRE ... THE JIM ROSE CIRCUS SIDESHOW ...

Shay reads them one by one, then looks deep into the windshield to feel out her own reflection. She finds that parhelion of lightwire silver around her neck. The Gothic charm resting on the chestbone. Yeah, take a little vacation from reality.

Crocker's got the windows rolled up. He screams out in sick bursts. The sound is jaw wrenching as he vents his rage at being humiliated. And every time he burns out of air he slams a fist down on the steering wheel so it hurts. But he knows he's got to keep in check, at least till Pettyjohn does the lock and load.

They pick up the road to Oatman. It begins to rise with the earth. Through her reflection in the windshield, long stretches of tan dust and copper hills. A sculpted ferocity that swims past. In her throat a taut sorrow. This is the kind of country where a small girl was brought into a larger obscenity. And now the ghost of that girl is about to make a down payment on her escape.

As Shay silently watches the road Vic asks, "You okay?"

She turns to him. His jaw clicks toward her lap. "You were moving your hands like you were talking to someone in sign language . . . like the deaf use."

She stares at her hands as if they were strangers. She wonders what they might have been saying. Talk about how badly the brain coding can be tampered with. "My grandmother was deaf. My mother taught me to sign. I guess I picked up this little habit from her."

They ride on. No more is said until Shay adds, "I'm okay."

Vic nods. "I got to tell you. I don't like this. I don't like the way it's all shapin' out."

"Me neither . . . me neither."

Shay balls her hands into small fists and closes her eyes. She can feel the heat of the earth climbing into the engine block then rising up through her legs into the pelvic bone, the lungs, the heart. The night of a thousand scars. She thinks, I know that night.

She listens for the rocker arm's cadence. It lulls her into deep memory. From that shadowland comes a suppressed presence. A faint breath that says to burn their sorry asses. Every last one of them. With uncertainty and disregard she lets the notion climb out of the raw hole it came from just long enough to see how frightening it is.

"We're here."

Her eyes open as the van pulls into the remote landmark of a gas station and sheds. It's nothing now but a hull for rabbits and brush, broken bottles and graffiti. A little further on is a roadside stand, locked and recently painted. It says: CASSIE'S CERAMICS—MAY THRU SEPTEM- BER. Beyond that, tall iron stanchions support a weathered rust-brown metal sign inscribed in white that says: BLACK MOUNTAIN TRAILER COURT—INDIVIDUAL SHOWERS AND STORAGE.

The van makes a slow turn through the lot and comes back to the Mustang idling on the cracked cement. The window rolls down and Crocker points toward a dirt road next to the sign, "Blue Fleetwood trailer with the flowers around it. Pettyjohn's there."

They scan the roadbed. It traces about a half mile in from the highway, along a dry wash, to a square of palm trees framing a handful of shiny trailers.

Vic slips the horse into first and as he does Crocker says, "I'm gonna have you one day." The pineal eyes narrow. "I am."

Vic gives him an arrogant nod. "I'll bring the wine."

The van window rolls up and it starts back from where it came. Vic and Shay now face the silence. The dead air hangs around their necks like a stone. Not a car goes east, not a car goes west. A bird of some kind, with deep gray wings, rides the thermals high up on the flats to the west. And that, aside from them, is all.

They start down the road. Rocks crinkle under the wheels. Vic sees there is little tire wear in the caking dust. "This is gonna be a bitch if we got to get out of here fast."

They pass another dirt road that leads off to a gorge awash in red rock and curious shades of sand. Strips of barbed wire hold together naked, rotting posts. On one a sign: DOLMENN QUARRY. On another: NO TRESPASSING—PROHIBIDO EL PASO.

The falling sun leaves that small oasis in a deepening haze. All opaque and still as topiary.

"If you lift the back seat, there's a rack with two shotguns. They're loaded. If we need to."

She sits forward. "You shouldn't have come," she says. "But I'm glad I'm not alone."

They are close enough now to see what is ahead. Through the ochered light that dreamy stillness takes on form. Shay's skin becomes a shivery bodysuit. Vic can feel the sweat creep across his palm where it rides the gearshift.

Black Mountain is a ghost town of shoe-box trailers. A desolate graffitied hovel of aluminum hulls with their doors and windows boarded up, or falling in on their cracked frames. One is a burned corpse lying on a concrete slab.

"We could turn back."

Shay reaches for her pistol and slides it under the backpack which rests on her lap. "I don't think so."

They approach fieldstone portals that once played the part of an entranceway. There are piles of mangled garbage everywhere and cholla and greasewood grow high and wild around the rotting homes.

Shay points, "There."

Off to one side, about halfway toward the back, a blue Fleetwood trailer and makeshift garden of slumpled couches and roadside trash. Out front, a truck-sized Rott fights against a chain and an old man sits at a picnic table under a sun-dyed green and white Tanqueray umbrella. Vic tries to work in every detail, and know how to react in case the worst comes.

"I'm gonna have the car facing the road. Keep it running."

Shay nods.

The old man sits like a watchman, working apart a peach. The screen door opens and Pettyjohn steps out into the softening day. There's a man with him Vic figures to be about thirty with a lathe-tight weathered frame.

"Do you know all these people?" Vic asks.

"Only the one in the purple pants."

Pettyjohn . . . the grim past is alive and well and walking right back into Vic's life. Vic wonders, where is Hugh? His eyes move slightly scanning odd corners of the trailer court. If he's here. If either puts the past and that face together, this small patch of ground will become the last trace of their lives. The Black Mountain Bone Church . . . in its own way, perfect. And what about the girl?

To get the Mustang lined up right Vic makes a slow turn around one of those cement slabs. He passes the motorless chassis of a VW van up on blocks and a dumpster topped out with trash. They move through air poisoned with gnats and flies and the stink of rotting garbage.

"I'm not leaving this seat," says Shay. "I'll handle everything from here."

"If that's the way."

Vic slows as they pass a pickup and a black Lincoln Town Car. He comes to an idling halt as far out from the Fleetwood as possible. Dust kicks up, rides the dead air, then settles.

Pettyjohn walks over to Shay's side of the car. He's wearing an almost smile with those purple pants. He leans into the window, "Shay."

"Jon . . . some place."

"Yeah. When the quarry was at full tilt you could live here. Unless you had a throbbing gristle, then you needed a lot of drugs or a good car. My Uncle Ed," he points toward the picnic table, "that's him and my cousin Travis . . ."

Shay's free hand comes up and offers a dead wave.

Pettyjohn looks across the inside of the Fastback as he continues, ". . . he's sort of a watchman for the owner."

"Really, I guess trash needs a careful eye."

If Pettyjohn is slick enough to get the cut he isn't showing. Instead he is focused on Vic, who sits there staring scrupulously ahead. "So this must be Charles Manson."

Vic does not answer. He only allows his eyes to shift ever so slightly from the trailer windows to the old man and Travis, to the rearview mirror, to the sideview mirror.

"Sorry to drag you all the way out here, Shay, but you know how your mother is. It's a high-wire act with her. You end up having to always look over your shoulder."

In her head she knows that's the fucking truth, but she answers, "That shouldn't be too tough for a two-faced son of a bitch like you."

His eyes become the dark side of the moon. His attention is now drawn completely on that young cunt sitting there defiantly. His fingers tap on the Mustang roof. He straightens up. He looks toward the Fleetwood and makes a gesture that neither Vic nor Shay see.

Travis begins a slow walk around the front of the Mustang admiring all that wretched excess as he goes. Pettyjohn leans back down. There's white around the dog's mouth. He has not stopped barking. His paws dig in hard against the stake that holds him.

"Money in that backpack?"

Shay taps it.

"Come on inside. We'll have a beer and get this done, okay."

"We can handle everything right here. You just let me see the papers and I hand you the money."

Papers. . . . Vic logs another thread of fact as the trailer screen door opens. Someone watches from behind the mesh.

"Come on, Shay."

"I'm not shitting you, Jon. We do it right here."

Moving out from the shadow of the door . . . Hugh Englund.

The Rott is still going at it. Travis has come so far around the Mustang he's hard left of Vic. And Hugh Englund, even though he's pretty far back, is hard right.

Travis says to Vic, "I'll bet you can turn some RPMs with that boogie mill."

Vic watches Hugh as he answers, "It'll make your head snap back."

Hugh does not move.

"Uncle, can you shut that dog up?"

"Fuck no."

Hugh is holding something small and black.

Travis takes another step closer. His hands ease up onto his belt, "What kind of fuel pump?"

"Bosch. Two hundred liters per hour."

"Let's go inside, Shay, and do this right. I'm not at war with you. We know you're just filling in."

"Hey, my asshole is not up for grabs, okay. So do me a favor. Show me the papers, I give you the money. We do it here. Then I go home and fumigate myself."

The space beside Shay fills with that pockmarked stare and those overly manicured nails and the smell of way, way too much musk. And she has decided, man, that if Pettyjohn does anything she thinks will have at her she is gonna put a shot right into his face. Just do it and hope.

Travis takes another step closer and looks down at the gearbox Vic's got a hand resting on: "Tremec?"

"Very good," says Vic.

It's all a little too close for Vic. He eases his foot down on the clutch. Behind all that barking there's the light ring of a cellular. Hugh's hand comes up. So that's what he was holding.

"Alright, Shay," says Pettyjohn, "I'll get the papers. We're not here to freak you out or fuck with you."

As he turns for the house Vic sees Hugh look up the road. A second later the old man has put his peach down and looks up the road. The odd conformation of that moment hangs suspended. Vic feels a coldline moving back of his skull and over the bone behind his ears. His eyes come hard left and look out into the pale landscape to see what has drawn the men's attention. He catches a quick sight of Travis' hands. They're hidden now behind the edge of his hips. But beyond that, where the highway meets the road a plume of dust begins to rise out of the earth like a flame of gray wind rushing right for them.

It's a takedown—

FORTY
THREE

———

Vic pops the clutch and hand drives the gear box and that length of hood lunges forward. The back tires grind up ground. Travis reels away from the charging Pony iron so he won't be killed. It's a chaotic scramble and there's gunfire and Shay flings the backpack to the floor.

Vic screams, "Belt in!"

Crocker can see pinwheels of chalk and dust stretching out from that row of palm trees and hauling at him through the slatted light. He brings the van to a dead halt and the torque sucks his guts right into the steering wheel.

Shay's arm arrows across the dashboard, "Vic!"

As they make that long turn out of the trailer court, Vic sees Crocker tripping out into the dusk with a rifle. There's no getting past him to the highway now. Not unless you want to chance a face full of factory load.

The Mustang flies up that rutted alleyway negotiating the rocks and holes, then Vic cuts the wheel hard to the right and the Fastback kicks up over the ledge and through barbed wire and bone-dead postings that wrap around the grill like the tail of a kite.

Vic shoots down the quarry road hoping to Christ there's another out or he can just plain rum 'em till it's dark.

Shay tries to get around in her seat with a hand gripped to the roll bar for support. Coming out the distance hard, skull-colored whorls. The pickup and the black Lincoln. But the van? Where the hell is the van?

She tries to locate it through the wall of dirt the tires kick out as they charge like blind fugitives into that gorge of red rock and quicksand-colored earth.

"I don't see Crocker! Vic, I don't see—"

The front end rams over a wash of crusted rock and detritus. The chassis lands with neck-snapping cruelty. Shay thuds against the door and the rotted fence posts are dragged and snapped and kicked and spit against the grill and side panels and one boots up and over the hood and Vic and Shay throw out an arm to try and cover each other as the post impales itself into the windshield.

Pettyjohn leans out the open window of the pickup and aims a 9mm Marlin at the specter of smoking ground. He fights every hitch and jar the shocks absorb. His chest racks against the frame but he gets off his shots and the sky around the Mustang closes in with rifle fire.

The gorge is a tunnel of scorched air and reeking exhaust. Vic is putting ground between them until those limestone walls open up into a huge womb a half mile across and a hundred and fifty feet high.

He boots the brake and clutch. Downshifts hard. The Fastback swims sideways in the sand and the right half rises and he's got to counter the wheel to keep from going over. In the swirling dust they try to see.

"How do we get out of here?" Shay shouts.

"I don't know."

Their heads move frantically from spot to spot. Their sweat-streaked faces a tale of desperation. Possessed by inevitable death. Shay looks back to see patches of gray and black eating up the distance between them.

"Where is Crocker?"

"There's got to be some way."

Shay yells again, "Where is the van? Why isn't it back there?"

Vic fires that idling monster into first and runs a huge arc across the canyon searching the twilight for any shift in the rock that might look like a roadway up.

The moments fall away with furious speed. They're a naked agony hurtling past blackening walls that bear out nothing. Desperation moves through their systems like a G force. White dust streaks through the open windows. The engine is burning hot. Their eyes are bound up with every shadow.

Shay yells, "Come around . . . come around!!"

Vic follows the compass of her hand jabbing at the air. "Look . . . look . . . look!!!"

On the far side of sunset, against a bleak piece of landfall. An odd crease. A two-dimensional rift that might widen out into a road.

They got to hump back over the same ground only this time they're not alone as the pickup and the Lincoln pile through that shapeless pocket of roadway.

The Mustang is tire blind dust covering that half mile but Shay can see the men in their cars. They're no longer featureless outlines but the flesh-and-blood nightmare of Pettyjohn's twisted shoulder and head over the stock of a rifle that snaps with each shot, and Hugh and the old man leaning out the windows of that black Lincoln, their arms a picture of straining rage as they pour rounds of pistol fire at the Fastback.

The dino whine is running through the Mustang's stainless-steel hard lines and the double mufflers are throwing out exhaust. They can see it. Scrawled out of the hillface what was once probably a utility road is now a bleached concourse of loose rubble and sand rising to the top and no wider than a truck.

Vic yells to Shay, "Lock down. If we hit this wrong we could come apart."

She pulls back in against the seat. The dust is burning her eyes. Her head is telling her, "Don't go clit," but she hears her voice in short hard huffs saying, "We're gonna make it, we're gonna make it!"

They hit the backsliding trail at eighty and the first jolt up they can hear the leaf springs and the custom shocks become a screaming fury of collapsing metal.

It feels like Shay's upper teeth pile-drive down into her jaw. For a second Vic momentarily blacks out from the concussion on his neck. Sheer velocity is carrying them up. He wills the light back into his skull and clamps down on the wheel and sucks air in hard through his nose. That piece of wretched excess is climbing and if the underbelly isn't torn senseless or a tire doesn't blow—

The pickup is the first to launch up that roadbed cranked out at sixty. The Lincoln is right on its ass. But when they hit that first slick rising wale it's over. The truck's not going near fast enough, it's not geared near low enough to hold, and the bed rafts out and the back tires hammer into a stone mooring and a tire is torn loose from the axle.

Hugh slams his loafer into the brake pedal. The Lincoln's front end eats about thirty yards of dirt and it slows the sedan enough to keep them from all being killed but not enough to stop the Town Car from outright folding the trunk bed in half.

The Mustang is halfway up when it hits a patch of scrabble and the wheels begin to snake spine and kick out scalloped walls of dust.

Hugh staggers from the Lincoln. He can hear Jon inside the pickup groaning. Ed is on his knees puking out bile. Hugh tries to yank the truck door open and reach his friend. He can see the Mustang has stalled and yells to Travis, "Get the rifle and go after them."

"Make it . . . make it . . . make it . . ." Shay tries to will those wheels to do as she says. . . . "Make it . . . make it!" Vic is forced to downshift and she looks back. "Make it!" She sees one of the men sprinting up through the canyoned darkness with a rifle, "One's coming. . . . He's got a rifle."

Hugh muscles the jammed door open and Jon collapses in his lap. His narrow forehead is raw pink flesh and his nose a shattered mass with prongs of white cartilage sticking out in hideous angles. There is blood all over the dashboard and Hugh rips off his coat, "You'll be alright, babe," then he saddles his lover's head in the bundled cloth.

"The wheels just ain't gripping, we might have to get out!"

Shay almost screams in Vic's face, "We'll make it up."

There's still a little soft dusk around the Fastback for Travis to line up a shot.

Vic takes one last try. He drops the gearbox into neutral. The ass end slides back while he revs the RPMs well over six thousand. The air smells like poisoned black carbon. The rocker arms sound as if they will rip through the hood. And when Vic senses the tires hit a spot that's solid enough, he lets the clutch spring back.

The friction disc hits just as Travis fires. And that primeval bow makes one raw lunge upward and they can hear something rip through the trunk metal and explode a piece of the back seat inward. But it's too late.

The Mustang climbs toward that windless jagged crest. The engine is burning up yards till it's at the top of the barren escarpment where it disappears into the blue light.

FORTY
FOUR

——————

They begin their descent at full throttle. The road down to the valley floor is ragged sand through a throat of rock that arcs out and rides the edge.

Vic and Shay get their first real breaths. Have their first real feel of the cold, coming desert air. The windows fill with smells of night. They wind past a craggy outcrop. But in that slippery moment between darkness and dusk and eye-cheating shadows their escape runs straight into . . . the van.

It's parked at a hard angle. The engine slightly ahead and toward the rim of that sandy incline. Crocker is using the hood angle as a palisade to shoot from.

"I told you I would fuckin' have you!!"

There's no braking this one. Crocker begins to fire. The Mustang sears the van's front end. There are blistering white sparks. The van comes off the ground. Slams backwards. Catapults Crocker into the rockface.

Vic tries to keep the Fastback under control but the hit has them skimming the edge of the incline at speeds five times too fast. He tries to ride a catwalk between the road and the crumbly marl. He's using all that streetcar's ground savvy to hold on till they catch a break of turf the wheels can live with. But the underbelly is getting savaged. That fuel-injected machine is a tripwire waiting for the wrong turn of nature. The ground ahead becomes a bed of stone. Needlerock. Double ugly shanks of it. It rips apart the tires and shocks and the left side of the Mustang goes upright.

It's a slow motion snapshot of sixty-mile-an-hour snippets. One side looking at the sky, the other at decaying sand. The only thing saving that car body from going accordion and killing both are the roll bars.

Sheer speed and turning weight pulleys the Mustang over on its roof. A furious skid of metal and dust going downhill. A racked slalom over raw landscape that turns the open-windowed cab into a shovel scoop, the interior into an hourglass of onrushing dirt. Strapped in and eating a storm of earth they're left to gag and gasp.

Shay's face bends against the violent affray that is burying them. She claws at her seatbelt trying to get it loose before she is drowned by a tide of gravel rising over her eyes and nose. A claustrophobic bedlam of hands tries to fend off the powdered waves of earth, to free herself from the white hell of that burial drum.

All sound becomes sourceless and distant. Eyes close from dizziness and lack of air. Shay's insides are going blind, then blinder. She is shutting down, her upturned face in a last strain for freedom. Her hands searching for one last way to save her life. The will and tenacity of screaming flesh not to die finds the door handle. Pulls. Tries to get the door open. Squeezes up a foot. Kicks. Kicks through the dirt. Kicks. Then again. The door jumps out inches and again a landfill of dirt rides up into the chassis socket and over her and jams the door outward where it clips a patch of stone and the Mustang tops around and caterwauls sideways and comes to a jarring, rattled stop.

She slips through raddled dusky moments before she realizes the car has stopped moving. She grits through dirt for air. Sucks in open-mouthed the chilly night. Pieces of her mind begin to put in place the self. Confused, cautious. Groggy watchful to see where, if, she might have broken apart. Cracks in the consciousness fill in. I'm alive.

In the far blackness an outcast voice from where they came. Who is it? Vic?

Travis reaches the ridge and sees the van. The front end is bludgeoned away. He is breathing hard, his legs ache. All light from the far horizon is gone and he comes forward cautiously behind his rifle trying to make sense of the scene before him. What happened to the Mustang? To Crocker?

He shouts, "Croc!"

That voice drives Shay to move. Her head comes around. Vic hangs upside down in the shoulder harness. He is unconscious or dead. Sluggish and shaking, Shay reaches for her seatbelt. Struggles loose the clip. Falls onto the backpack and a bed of dirt.

She twists over to Vic. Touches his face along the mouth. He is breathing, anyway.

Travis slips around the back of the van. Squints when he sees what looks like a human form headboarded against the rock twenty feet away. He approaches as if this specter might do him harm.

Then he sees it is Crocker. He sits with arms draped down onto his lap, one crocodile lying across the other. His head and shoulders are bent in the manner more of a marionette ready to be stood up and played than that of a man. There is no blood.

"Croc?"

Another step tells it. His eyes are open in a way that only death allows.

Shay digs through the debris inside the cab looking for the gun she'd hitched inside the back of her jeans.

Travis steps away from the body. He looks down the mile-long road to see if the Mustang has reached the highway. There are no signs of lights against the darkness.

He starts back to tell the others, moving up along the incline side of the road, when he notices a single headlight burning through a blanket of gray dust drifting along the bottom of the ravine.

Shay can hear Travis yell, "Hugh, Ed! They went over the side!"

Shay bellies out of the Mustang. Slips her eyes up over the bottom of the chassis. Scans the ridgetop. Sees Travis paralleling the road, searching for the best way down.

The part of Shay her mother has by the throat tells her to "fuckin' go." Take the backpack. Empty the safe deposit boxes. Call that number in the desert and pick up your new name. Leave Vic, whatever he is or isn't, for that hunting party. Let 'em all burn their lives to the ground.

————

Running up that road, chasing Travis' call, Hugh is huffing wide-mouthed for air. His loafers slip on the gravel trying to negotiate all that extra weight. You shouldn't suit up for this kind of shit carrying twenty-five extra pounds of broadside.

Two quick shots bring him to a stop. So quick as to feel almost connected. When he reaches the crest he sees the van posed against moonless black. He gets down on his knees and crawls toward the edge of the incline where he guesses the Mustang went over. He scans the ravine. He can make out the wreck by a single headlight buoyed in the dark.

Two shots. Now it's so quiet you could hear the sand move. He waits, then calls out, "Travis?"

Only the acute shifting of his voice down through black stones. Well, he hasn't any intention of working his way to that ravine alone so he can strike some academy pose. He didn't want this, but Charlie and Jon—

He wasn't so fast to believe Storey had been lying about the photographs. Now, he's here with his face pressed to the rock, marble heavy and barely daring to breathe.

"You need to get your ballsack squeezed more to cut the edge," that was Foreman's vicious wisdom when he tried to veto their plan.

He crawls back from the ledge. He'd gotten Jon into the Lincoln before he started up the hill. The Town Car was still running and Ed was together enough to make the hospital. So he'll wait it out. Face what's down in that ravine come morning. If the daughter gets away, so be it. He only hopes the worst has already happened to the mother, because if it hasn't the world will never be dark enough to hide in.

FORTY
FIVE

A brown sedan pulls up to the Garden of Allah office. Rog is behind the desk, his face dunked down in a softback where he's scribbling notes like some wonk, when two terminal-looking suits enter. Rog is so tripped out by what he's reading before either man can get a word in, he's motioning them toward the glass and holding up the book like they were his own private posse: "You got to hear this. It is total clarity." He begins to accentuate every word as he reads, " 'Reason craps out in an instant, when it's out of its safe, narrow bounds.' Don Juan said that. Take a few mushrooms and I'll bet that quote will spin your head."

He puts the book down. As he reaches for a registration form one of the men leans in toward the glass to get a look at the title: PSYCHE-DELIC CHEMISTRY.

Rog slips a registration form through the opening in the glass partition, "You boys need one bed, or two?"

The second man takes out a pocket wallet and opens it. He lets Rog's eyes swim over a badge and ID. "No bed thanks. Just a few questions, if we may."

Freek collects waves of documents from the relevant city and state departments and agencies right on through to the contracts between private firms that co-financed and developed "Fiasco High" and the 56th Street School.

The one disappointing aspect for Freek: Since the documents are all part of the public record his job is time-consuming but, unfortunately, legal.

As Landshark and Terry cull through miles of detailed legal and corporate documentation, they begin to put together a pyramiding paper trail that proves Alicia Alvarez and Burgess Ridden had either cc'd each other or written directly to each other on numerous issues regarding each project as far back as '85.

The extensive files show Alicia Alvarez was an instrumental pathway for all relevant documentation, and that any hope of getting the two schools beyond the inception stage with state regulatories and the EPA had to pass her tight security.

"They all connect to that night in the desert," Terry says. "All seven of them."

Landshark glances at the phone beside him on the work table as he reaches for a cold piece of takeout pizza. "We have nothing yet that proves Foreman knew Alvarez in '87. That's a hole we have to fill."

"We have Pettyjohn. He buys a house across from Belmont in '88. That nothing punk is no speculator. Maybe the house was a payoff, or a way of getting them some cash."

Nervous that Vic hasn't yet called, Landshark bites into that greasy undercooked mass and halfway through stops. "With all the money I'm worth we're eating takeout that was rotten hot, rotten nuked, and rotten—" He tosses the slice back into the box and pushes it away. "Alvarez to Foreman to Pettyjohn is what you're saying."

"Freek's working on her bank recs from the late eighties, right? Did she hire Foreman's lawyer and pay by check? Did she ever see him in jail? Was there anything in both their names? A car maybe?"

Landshark grabs his notepad, scripts out a few thoughts for Freek to make a run at. He pushes the notepad aside and glances at the phone again. Then he looks up at that odd consortium of faces and names across the bulletin board. That crosscurrent of social well-to-do's and misfits, fringers and closet criminals. A sense of prophetic irony that's always had play in Landshark's mind makes him wonder how different is that mad sampling of Angelenos from the ones trying to run them down.

He stands, takes one of Terry's cigarettes and plucks off the filter. He can't help himself from looking at the phone again.

"He'll call," says Terry.

Landshark nods, but it doesn't help. Before he lights the cigarette he asks, "We're in deep shit, aren't we?"

Terry chews on a strip of pizza crust. He doesn't answer right off. He swallows, then says, "It was a rotten pizza." He tosses the last bit of crust back into the box. "Conducting an entirely illegal investigation. Withholding information from the police on the girl's murder. We could end up being the teeth or the tail of this thing."

Landshark lights up nervously, "Or both."

Terry nods. Landshark begins to pace. To Terry, William has always resembled this androgynous George Armstrong Custer. Too intense for his own flesh. Driven hard by sad, desperate needs that might bring about his own destruction. And angry to a point he doesn't recognize.

Landshark walks out onto the terrace. The night sky holds out a city so clear the lights seem almost to breathe with life. He sits on a bench with his back to the railing so he can see into his office, "I can't tell you how much it means to me, all you're doing."

Terry gets up. Takes his cigarette and beer and walks out to be with William. He sits beside him on the bench. Their shoulders touch. This pair of bewildering differences and blunt similarities share a silent closeness.

"I don't know why God made me agoraphobic. I don't know why."

"Maybe God thought you needed to be. That you'd learn, and take from this something valuable. Maybe all this *is* your test."

Landshark puts his head back against the railing and closes his eyes. He tries to take in, to embrace what Terry has said.

"You know, William, I'm a little jealous of Vic. Of all you're trying to do for him. And the feelings behind what you're trying to do."

Landshark's head comes slowly forward. His eyes open and he hikes up his shoulders, "Vic is inside me. He was inside me before I heard of him. Before I failed him. Before I failed myself.

"And I'm hoping," Landshark adds, "that by helping him now, by this febrile quest, which you could call it, I can find a pathway through the crisis of failure that has been my history. That has so shaped and scarred and shamed me. Then, maybe, I'll be a better man. And maybe . . . maybe even *you* will feel that."

Terry listens quietly as one does who is predisposed to willingly accept what is told to him. He rubs the tip of his cigarette along the inside rim of an ashtray then seamlessly shifts the subject.

"To greenlight anything as difficult as a school sometimes takes funny money to juice the paperwork, or the players. Sometimes it's kickbacks to blow down opposition. You got to buy approvals. A well-disguised contribution to a political campaign and you got a councilman's crucial vote. Or a school board member. It's all pretty much the usual plight of the greedy.

"Everyone thought the old Ambassador Hotel was a better site for a school. The unions were against Belmont. There was the whole issue of whether the ground was contaminated, which it turns out it was.

"What if there were payoffs to make the deal fly? Or to trick out the paperwork. What if they knew the ground was more contaminated than the reports indicated. What if someone . . . Ridden, maybe, re-routed the truth along the way."

Landshark considers where Terry is going, "On point. The EPA didn't always go into the properties back then and do ground checks. And the city didn't either. Especially if they didn't own the land. And it was considered . . ." He raises his fingers and flits them as if he were making invisible quotes, ". . . 'too costly' to check and see if there was a toxic time bomb under the kiddies' rumps. They relied on outside reports."

"I say Ridden did something very heavy and Alvarez knew it or had been a conduit to seeing it done."

Landshark looks through the open glass doors to the ceiling-lit vignette of the bar and his prized photo. That small unpolluted presence, staring down into the intangible well of the city and crying, could be anyone.

"Los Angeles was built on nothing and stolen from everything."

Terry takes a deep breath, a drink of beer. He knows these are the veiled cynicisms of an easily and often wounded man.

"Sometimes I think the whole country is a liquidation sale in progress. That the American Dream should be re-minted as: I think . . . therefore I must have. What am I saying, it was always that.

"*The L.A. Times* isn't interested in this except when there's a body around. *The Daily News*, the throwaways, they're the ones that have been digging up the hard facts of life. But I give *The L.A. Times* credit. They know the pulse of the city and exploit it. They know people don't want to hear about the crisis details of everyday living unless it is appropriately buried in a Metro Section between Sports and Business. They know people want to avoid and conquer serious ideas by using TV talk show sincerity and supermarket tabloid digressions. Hell, *The Enquirer* is closer to the heart of the American psyche than all the blood that has been bled out by dedicated unknowns who keep that goddamn heart pumping."

"William—"

"What?"

"Give the Liberty Bell a rest."

"I'm a lunatic, alright. Avoid me at all costs."

"A few people who care have proven often enough they can exact damage against the ones who 'rework' the truth."

"Ridden even got the ethics report for the Metrorail," says Landshark. "Half a million dollars. We haven't added that to our list."

"The others, the ones in the middle, the ones working away their lives to make ends meet, who barely have enough time for their kids, let alone a newspaper, and the ones who can't afford a newspaper or can't read. And the others who are just plain stupid, selfish, disinterested, who are too busy getting rich to bother, or who are plugged into television talk show news bullshit, whatever—"

"Who are not the blood of it, as you say. They need someone, something, some living accident that thinks and acts and offers them a reason. Alright."

Terry stands up, finishes his beer, "Come on." He starts back inside. "Foreman was set to do seven, right?"

Following him in, Landshark agrees, "Right."

"I say Alvarez ran her mouth about Ridden, and Chuckie da Man was willing to rat that snob moneyboy to the DA unless a play was put into action to take Vic out."

Terry goes round the bar and grabs a Corona from the refrigerator beneath a sink.

"Why didn't Foreman go to the DA about Englund and Pettyjohn?"

Terry gets the cap off the Corona, "He could have, except that's punk shit compared to Ridden. A white-collar boy with lots of money. Good press. With the buff boys he'd only have gotten a reduced sentence." Terry takes a long drink, then another drag on his cigarette. The smoke comes out of his nostrils in thick gray lines. "I say Charlie couldn't hack the idea of stir. It happens. Even hard cases. Especially if they're scoring cash and pussy. Some of them would set their own mother on fire on Hollywood Boulevard then dance around her naked with a crowd watching if it would keep them out of stir."

Terry uses the long-necked bottle as a pointer. "Look at that photo outside the Scorecard. Ridden is compromised, otherwise why would he meet the buff boys at some sleaze bar? And I can tell you if they knew Magale was out there shooting film they never, never would have met in public at all. He wouldn't have anything to do with this shit. That's why I say Ridden was compromised, is—"

Landshark's private cellular on the work table starts to ring and he is all over it. "Vic. . . . Rog? What? Slow down, Rog."

Terry sees Landshark go from being annoyed to visibly shaken. "You're talking too fast." Landshark moves the bottom half of the cellular away from his mouth so he can listen and talk to Terry at the same time. "Homicide detectives are at the motel asking about a girl who was murdered downtown."

"Jesus Christ. How?"

He waves Terry quiet then starts out of the office in a bolt with Terry right behind him. "Rog, did you tell them Terry was security? As soon as you get off the phone, you tell them."

Landshark bounds up the stairwell four steps at a time, Terry practically running to keep up. Homicide detectives at the Garden delivers a hellish punch to Terry's solar plexus. "Tell Rog I can be there in twenty minutes."

"Terry will be there in twenty minutes."

"Ask him if they brought search warrants."

"Did they bring search warrants?"

Landshark bellyflops on the stairs. Knees and elbows, wrist and palm slap down hard. He holds out the phone like some priceless artifact. Terry lifts him up, cursing and kicking at the clay tiles.

"No search warrants."

"We got to get in there and get rid of the prints."

"Rog . . . listen now. Listen. Terry will take care of everything. Take your time going through the registration slips."

Perspiring crazily both men cross the darkened living room and make for the front door. "Do the zombie walk, Rog. Rog . . . I'm counting on you. Get the registration sheets for the last few weeks, take your time. Rog . . . I'm counting on you, cousin!"

Landshark clicks off the phone. He swings the front door open so hard it chips the wall plaster where it hits. Crossing the driveway to Terry's car, Landshark says, "Homicide got a call from some hooker who was at the motel. Says she heard a guy in the next room crying he'd killed a girl at a construction site downtown who was staying at the motel and burned her body."

"Storey."

"It's got to be her or Alvarez."

Terry swings around to his side of the car.

"When I had Rog do the paperwork I had him use different names. Make it look like two-day layovers or hooker-and-john shit were in those rooms. All of it trumped. I even had different people write them up so the handwriting wouldn't match. Vic and Magale's names are on nothing."

"But his prints are. I got to get in there first and clean it down."

"I fucked this up, didn't I?"

"William—"

"I've ruined my life and when I was done with that I worked my way out into the world—"

"William, get hold of Vic!"

"If I wasn't a fuckin' agoraphobic I wouldn't have had to send a girl—"

"William, stop thinking about yourself!"

Landshark draws up into shameful silence.

"Storey is trying to lay something on Vic's back, or put him on his back. Now get on the phone and warn him!"

FORTY
SIX

———

They walk the shoulder of the highway trying to get back to Bullhead City. As headlights seep out of the distance, Shay and Vic move with urgent exhaustion off into a sweeping robe of boulders and ravines. They huddle against the moon-frosted ground. High-beams flush out the night around them then satellite on in a long sleek swoooosh of tires. When they see it is neither the pickup nor the black Lincoln Town Car hunting them out, they rise and start again.

At the margins of a ditch Vic asks for the first time, "You could have left me?"

The violent reality of the last hours have left Shay emotionally spent to the point of being almost mournful. She hands him the backpack with the money so as to rest her arm and says, "I almost did."

In the deep reaches of that blind black road with only a cracked opening of sky for the moon Vic tries to fathom the girl-woman walking before him. How do you extract just revenge, if you have to, against someone who has saved your life?

On the bluffs above Bullhead City they can see the Colorado and Laughlin on its west bank. The neon from the casinos turns that trace of purple-black water into an enameled alter-image of colors and shapes. The rippled lettering and sheeny designs are being constantly cut apart by water taxis taking bettors from wheel to wheel or lovers up into the romantic silence of the Nevada night, only to be reformed again out of the settling waketide.

Shay thinks back to that night outside the Garden of Allah when she watched that crimson oasis reflected in the running pools of street water be swished away by a world of tires only to be reincarnated seconds later in the streaming pavement.

Something begins to move through her. A liquid witchcraft, maybe.

Or a wraithlike vibration as old as the earth. Was the unfinished dream of this night foreshown by a neon oasis reflected in the running street water out front of a Hollywood motel and a man moving up through a darkened causeway toward her?

"I'm getting ready to megadive," she tells Vic. "We need a crash pad and soon."

Bullhead City is flat black asphalt streets stretching out across a lunar landscape on the Arizona side of the Colorado. The town got created 'cause the labor that built and worked the casinos needed homes. You can still see T-shirts that say: "Where the Hell is Bullhead City?"

Not far from the Laughlin Bridge is a motel. Gogo's is one story, barracks style. It only survives now 'cause of the cheap price it costs you to enjoy your plain-wrapped secrets.

Vic and Shay get side-by-side rooms. Behind the motel, across a cinderpath alley, is a bar. You can hear the live music through the paltry wall slats.

Vic knocks on the door that connects his room to Shay's. Her voice, thin and tired, says, "It's not locked."

She is sitting on the bed wrapped in a towel. The bathroom door is open and the faded yellow room has just begun to fill with steam.

"I was gonna dig up some food, liquor. Any requests?"

Her hand wearily flattens the waves in the frayed bedspread. "Whatever will help put me out. I don't care." Vic begins to go. "Wait." It takes all her energy to lean across the bed toward the backpack. She pulls it to her, takes out money. "You might as well use this, seeing as how we couldn't even give it away."

Once outside Vic's first stop is a pay phone so he can call Landshark, as his cellular is somewhere back in the Black Mountains.

Shay showers in the dark. She sits on the stall floor. Her knees are pulled up against her chest. She lets the water just beat down on her. The last hours keep coming back in convulsive fragments. She is too blown out to resist.

There are telling moments of human frailty throughout her body. Something akin to seasickness at some unbearable height. The music from the bar is a moody presence under the hard-running shower. A

gritty woman's voice, audible but not understandable. The tone speaks
of hurt.

She sees Pettyjohn's cousin tear at the smoking holes she put in his
back. She has now tasted of what her survival really means.

Vic lies on his bed in the dark. A second glass of scotch rests on his
chest. He is locked into Landshark's panicked replay of what is going
down at the Garden of Allah.

Landshark may not understand why Dee Storey would risk her
own safety exposing Vic to the police, but he does. From the moment
the two sat across from each other at DIS she was as vulnerable as he,
and knew it. Vulnerability has been known to lead to drastic measures.
And to him, Dee Storey could be the trademark for drastic measures.

But there's always one more missing piece to fill. He wonders,
while he sips his drink and stares into the soft dark pond of the ceiling,
would Dee Storey be angry at her own daughter for bringing the two
of them together, would she send both out into the desert to die.

It would be a horrible drastic measure, but one he could see coming
out of the inner discord of that woman. Or maybe there's part of him
that sees it because it would free him to forgive the girl. To find in her
the victim he was. Yes, there's always one more missing piece to fill.

A hand comes knocking. Vic answers, "It's not locked."

A portal of lamplight opens to his room. Just enough to map the
figure of a girl wearing only a T-shirt. Enough to put just a serif of
luster across her wet brushed-back hair and the lit joint between her
fingers.

"There's food on the table, and I even got you some bourbon and
a bowl of rocas."

"Mind if I leave the light like this?" Her voice has smoothed out
from the pot.

"I'd prefer it," he says.

Her shadow climbs the far wall across from the bed. She pulls out
a chair, sets her joint carefully on the edge of the table and begins to
give those convenience store sandwiches the once over. She pours bourbon into a glass, "You got a good memory."

"Too good, I think."

She can make out the woman singing now. Her voice has the rough soul of a Joplin or a Sass Jordan and the song she riffs through seems a little too right-on hip for that white-boy, desert-rowdy bar.

Here I am again, in this old rotten jail . . .

Here I am again, in this old rotten jail . . .

"Thanks for not leaving me in the desert," he says.

Her movements have that slow dusky stone to them as he watches her long white fingers ease ice cubes, one by one, into the glass.

I wish somebody would help me, help me find some peace of mind . . .

Won't somebody help me, please help me find some peace of mind . . .

Shay asks, "Can a person be honest, or decent at least, and still be selfish? I mean . . . selfish."

There's a question that's dragged him through more than a few miles of thought time. "Maybe we're lying to ourselves," he says, "if we say there is any other way, if life is anything but that way."

He watches her shaded breaths up the arc line of her back and the long white finger she uses to slowly stir her drink. When she's done she begins to lick the finger dry, listening to that gritty Big Mama Thornton dirge drifting through the pores of the wall, and Vic can feel a slight quickening of his heart against the scotch glass resting on his chest.

Mr. Warden, won't you please set me free . . .

Mr. Warden, won't you please just turn the key . . .

"So many miseries," she says in a husky defeated whisper, "and so little time to enjoy them all."

Vic sits up slightly. "They meant to kill us today. Right from the opening."

"From earlier than that."

"Your mother—"

"I think she's dead."

Vic sets his glass down on the bedstand and reaches for a cigarette.

"I've left messages since noon. I even left one about what went down tonight. She's too much of a control freak for silence. If she had one last rip in her the phone would ring."

Shay looks across the room and follows the slim beach of light that runs up the length of Vic's body and when the match flame is struck she follows it across the darkness to where she finds his eyes staring at her. They speak with the rough trade of unadorned feelings and her senses fill with some moody black heaven that frightens her and excites her at the same time.

She reaches for her joint. "I lived in Mexico twice. The second time

I should never have come back. I should have packed up my life and kept driving south till I found a nothing bar where the people don't speak English."

"Maybe someplace," Vic says in clean street Spanish, "where they've never heard of English."

She runs the joint under her nose, snorts in the dry smoke. "That would be better," she answers back in Spanish, "Muy preferable."

The band has slid into an instrumental riff of straight-on low-rent pathos.

Shay finishes up part of her sandwich. Then, as if she had some destination in mind all marked out, she begins to talk, "The one at the trailer park, who did all the talking, is Pettyjohn, and the man behind the screen door, his name is Englund. They have paperwork that shows two schools in L.A. got their approvals from the city with forged paperwork."

Vic comes slowly up off the bed not wanting to distract, and not believing what Shay has begun to lay out in detail.

"They hang with a nothing named Foreman and his Latina girl-friend. Her name is Alvarez. Alice or something."

Shay turns to Vic. Her back straightens and she is like one well-tailored scar with a controlled voice, "Get all this down in your memory bank 'cause I won't be repeating it. I was to give them good-faith money when I saw the papers. I call my mother, tell her it's cool. She would meet with Foreman carrying the balance due. They would trade. There's a limp-dick named Burgess Ridden who my mother fucked and fucked over for years. He forged the documents."

She turns back to her drink. A deep silence follows, but for the music next door. The bedsprings squeak as Vic edges his way forward, "Why tell me?"

"I don't know where you are in all this, if you are at all. And I don't want to know, alright. My mother thinks . . . thought . . . you were connected in some way to the dead girl."

The way she says "dead girl" it sounds like there is not one single illusion in Shay that he shouldn't know what that means. He's been caught so off-guard the last few minutes he doesn't know whether to quite touch at the truth or let things go along in a lie a little longer, so that all he says is, "What dead girl?"

"I'm not out to fuck you down," says Shay. "If I wanted to do that I could have back there on Witch Mountain. And this isn't some hit-or-miss social gesture. I'm just trying to—"

She moves against the vagary of the dark. Finds her drink, the joint. She stands. Her white skin is caught by inches of delicate light, "Have you ever been truly honest with someone?"

The silent movement around his mouth turns melancholy. And that he should feel this in front of her who asks the question confounds him. But he does. He moves toward the edge of the bed to get his feet on the floor. "I met a nurse at a gas station where I worked for a while in El Paso. Midnight to six. Spontaneous combustion is how I would describe what we had. We were married in three weeks. She divorced me in four months. When she left she said, 'You are always somewhere else. You won't tell me where that is, so I can't meet you there. And I can't find the place alone.' "

"Do you know where you were?"

He knows. He can see the heraldic green roadsign in the hot desert sun flash by that cranked out Mustang: KELBAKER RD. And only a slow song's drive from that grave and all that came with it. He answers her with a sad venom, "I was miles ago and years away. Leave it at that."

She moves past him. Her steps cat quiet on the bare floorboards till she is at the door, where she stops, "Translated, no one will find you here. I know that story."

Shay can hear the band make a slow turn toward the next number and with those first chords she knows where the music is going. She looks toward the curtained window. A bass line drills in on a silvery ether of alley light and she wishes it would not be so. It makes her feel too much. It touches upon her own pain too much, and then the singer's gravelly voice turns the words into a haunting purgatorial.

Love has never been easy for me
Can't you see, I have always been lonely

Vic looks at Shay. A short sweep of wet hair has fallen across her face and the threads of her white T-shirt coin up around the skinpink nipples and there are shoots of pain along the creased edges of her eyes and that full heartshaped mouth moves to the invisible pull of her breathing. In that moment he senses her vulnerability so he asks, "Who killed the girl?"

"You have to throw that question to my mother."

"Why did she send me with you?"

Her eyes slip down toward Vic. He sits there leaning forward. No, coiled would be closer to correct. He sits there coiled forward. To her, he is the carpenter's vision of manhood. Planed from the vein of life where souls are broken and rebuilt, broken and rebuilt until they become the chiseled culmination of what some tragic machinery could not crush under its merciless drive to take.

If only, we could live one day
Without the need to hide away

"She said once you got in the car you'd belong to us. That you'd be compromised." Shay cups the joint in her hand and holds it up to her nose. She breathes in. Then: "And you are, aren't you?"

Her voice is a soothing ellipsis that makes of that short phrase both question and statement of fact.

"Do you think your mother knew how bad it was gonna be out there in the desert?"

The stark iniquity of her mother's face that last night standing at the bar and staring down at a picture of Shay carries its own truth. "I'm not into the violent overthrow of my own mind," says Shay.

"Is that your way of saying she'd throw you to the wolves?"

Shay knows it was her mother who fired those shots at her. She was lying on the floor of her house, listening to this very song, staring up at a ceiling full of stars created by lights from the stereo. "I've learned to live with all kinds of possibilities."

He can hear she's on the verge of crying. "Not another question now," comes her plea. " 'Cause there isn't much left of me to burn down and I have to have something later to build around."

She walks into her room and turns off the lights. She puts down her drink, the joint. She sits on the bed. Her body is trembling from all that has had at her. Across the alley a hurt guitar begins to stand in for a woman's voice. Shay can hear the bed creak as Vic stands. His boots track the floorboards to her room and she looks up. It is too dark to see his face as she says, "Are you here to meet me . . . hit on me . . . or stalk me?"

He comes into the room and squats down by the bed before her. He is so close she can feel his warm breath on the flesh just above her knee.

"I'm here," he whispers, "to save my own life. That's the cruel honesty of it."

Her voice subdued, but not hesitant, "There is nothing more cruel than survival, and certainly nothing more honest."

The singer's shrouded, hungry voice visions up through a slow progression of chord and counterchord and Shay reaches for the elastic that holds Vic's ponytail and works it loose and his hair flows out across her palm like some blooming fan that brushes the outside of her leg.

No, don't say a single word

Can't be sure, can't be sure that we won't be heard

His calloused fingers move up the milk-pure softness of her thigh and he can feel her muscles relax and open slightly to let in his hand and she is naked beneath that white shirt and the flesh is wet out into the black kinks of her hair.

Like Romeo and Juliet, they will chase us to our death

And voice their false regrets

The liars

The breath through her nose gets heavier as her face comes to his and he can taste her mouth on the stubble up his neck and her heart-shaped lips and skin talk into his ear with the gospel of existence as her hand moves down the length of his muscled shirt in a wavy stroke, soft as if the flesh were wet clay where she finds the leather strapping of his belt and tears at the clasp.

Since the day that we first met . . .

He strips the T-shirt up over her breasts.

Until I take my dying breath . . .

Her fingers fight to be down inside his jeans.

I'll be tangled in your net . . .

Mouths dripping, they become a turbulent physical mural that finds the bed. Their lungs collapse and fill in desperation and need. Their muscles wire through the last of their clothing. In the black architecture of that room they claw and hold as if the dissipation of time itself were at hand.

Their moon-touched shadows move like possessed witches in some nightstarved dream and she cannot pull him in fast enough. She cannot get her white naked legs around him fast enough.

They are beyond eyes and thought. They are a raw symmetry where there is no above, no below. She is real and transparent. She is liquid and the strength of sinew and bone. The world is all and nothing and his shoulder smells of white salt flats. And what his mind knows and what his body feels cannot be reconciled. Her gasps are violent and velvet and he wants to possess her and destroy her and save her and be some weighted part of her.

Her face pressed into the cup of his shoulder and his teeth along her neck and the smell of the earth overwhelming on his skin. The musk of desert and night and as he lifts her by the thighs her fingertips dig into his back until they leave pearled red welts.

Her mouth opens and his throat chokelocks with the sheer pleasure of it and his unshaven face shudders against her soaked chest as his stomach slaps hard into hers and when they orgasm it is like some hemorrhage of blood.

It is as if some huge gash in the ground has opened them up into a world more intense than pleasure. More incalculable than lust or love. The ghost of years, now unloosed.

They begin to ease back into the folds of the frayed bedclothes soaked with sweat and saliva and semen. The violent physical emotionality subsiding in short pauses and shudders until all that is left are two drowsing hearts talking to each other through the weight and duration of life.

FORTY
SEVEN

———

He aims through the silence. His Uncle Mikes taut around the black Santroprene grips. The barrel of that 454 Taurus sits on the still air for a moment before the kill. And then the Raging Bull explodes.

One shot. One shocking kick from the muzzle of that four-pound powerhouse and somewhere inside Landshark's head the enemy falls.

He steps back from the smoke. He's trying to burn off stress by taking his aggression out on a target fifteen yards away with a cannon of a handgun better suited for knocking two props out of the sky.

He removes the Pro-Ears and puts them down on the table beside his other weapons, the only sound now the ceiling vents whirring out the smoke. At least he knows Vic is alive.

He looks down through the quiet shell of that target range. From birth to death he will always be surrounded by walls unless he can bear down on the severe inertia born of his own fear. Unless he can find peace in giving control over to the dark passages of uncertainty.

He looks through the iron gates out into the night of Andalusia Avenue. With its inscription of windows and streetlamps to light his way toward the world. He presses the remote and the gate begins its creaky slide.

How the minutes have become years. And the years, they suddenly weigh no more than minutes on the scale of memories. That is how little of him there has been beyond those gates for the last decade. He has never felt so utterly landlocked as he does now, stepping into the spaceless sea of the world alone.

He takes slow deep breaths and long strides as if getting somewhere quicker he could outsmart the panic he knows is lurking inside him. In short order he is staring at the spot of curb where he and Vic talked. What was it he said? "For the first time in my life, I am truly alive. And you're not taking that from me."

He's got to find that part of Vic inside him. He will use this spot as his benchmark. He will pretend that he'd lost the use of his legs for a time and this is as far as his strength could carry him. But each night he will press on a little further until he is no longer afraid of the fear.

The eerie pattern of chest constrictions and lightheadedness smokes out his insides by the time he reaches Mayfair. He's a meager sixty yards from a gate he can no longer see for protection. He demands of himself to keep on, even though the voices of his head are telling him he will go mad or die if he does not turn back to safety. He works to face down the deathreek of that powerless victim within him. To have one part of him, the part that knows this is all nothing, play Vic and promise the other part, the William Worth part, that he will be alright. He can climb out of the grave of his past and survive. And for the first time in years he finds a way, without being medicated, to lean on himself and make a demand, even the slight demand of a few hundred yards, and meet it.

Feelings begin to jump his thought process as he turns on San Raphael. Snapshots of his parents on the last day, as he makes his way up the long incline of that sidewalkless street. Dread at the sight of his father pulling the Navion from the hangar and the nose touching the sun where his mother's arms wave monstrously. Anger as his family tries to hack each other emotionally to death.

A car horn somewhere behind him is hit.

He is sweating through his shirt and his strides can't get long enough as he tries to run from the rage at a life that led him here.

The car horn again.

And just inside the shadow of that hangar door, on a plain pine table, the cotter pins.

A wave of remorse through that cold hall where the heart resides. He finds he can go no further. The cotter pins. He clings to a street sign for support. He can see them there. He can—

A flood of brightness around him. He squints and follows the trail of light back to a set of halogen eyes and a car door opening. "William?"

Terry walks up to Landshark. They are at the corner of San Raphael and Mount Washington Drive, a good half mile from the house. Terry can see William's shirt is soaked and that he must have been giving his gun hand a good warming up 'cause he's still wearing his Uncle Mikes.

"You walk this far?"

Landshark nods, but he is at this moment a fifteen-year-old inside a hangar looking down at a plain pine table. "Could I . . . have a cigarette?"

"Good for you going this far," Terry says as he snaps off a filter and hands the rest to his friend.

"This far tonight, tomorrow a little further." He puts the torn end to the flame and inhales.

"I got the room wiped clean."

"They getting a search warrant?"

"Yes. I told them we would cooperate in any way we can."

"Good."

"Good and not so good. A Channel Five news truck showed as I was leaving."

Landshark looks across the rooftops and into the dark shore of the heavens. "Death and fear, when it's all said and done, might be the most reliable friends we have. They never let us down, they never disappoint or fail to deliver. They can be counted on in good times and bad and in some cases, they are all we have to look forward to."

"I will repeat what my instructor at the police academy told us," answers Terry, "and maybe this time, you will be ready to hear it. 'There are two important moments in every policeman's life. The first is when you learn what fear is. The second, when you learn what fear does not have to be.' "

A flickering look in Landshark's eyes. Counting time from star to star. And taking a long drag on a cigarette. He wonders if God is waiting somewhere with a little handout called forgiveness.

He glances across San Raphael, where a white wall runs the length of a long, long block, to a gate with a gold sign that reads: SELF-REALIZATION FELLOWSHIP HEADQUARTERS.

He points. "The followers of Gunga Din are trying to petition the city to see if they can have his remains buried there."

"Don't get nasty now, you know very well he wasn't called Gunga Din."

"I don't know why they bother asking. I've been buried up here all these years, and I never had to petition the city."

Terry rides out his friend's little riff. "Have you heard from Vic?"

"Yes. Pettyjohn and Englund tried to kill the girl and him out in the desert."

"Christ! Where is he?"

"In Bullhead City with the girl. She thinks her mother is dead."

Terry leans back against the car. "They might be starting to un-ravel." Landshark keeps staring at the white wall and the gate with the gold sign. He can see beyond and into the property. Into a landscape of tall pines and deep lawns and old arched rooftops, serene and opaque against a night border. It is, to Landshark, an obscenely peace-ful sight.

"We still have the girl's things in the office," says Terry. "When they walk in with that search warrant we better have reached a decision on what, if anything, we tell them."

"Vic will be back tomorrow. We'll decide together." He flips the cigarette away. "There's only one thing." He moves Terry aside so he can get in the car. "If there are any legal problems, they belong to me. You know nothing."

"What?"

Landshark looks back over the seat at the white wall and the tall pines that drape over them and the dark shore of the sky above that. He could understand why Gunga Din's followers would want him bur-ied there.

"William, what the fuck do you mean if there's any—"

"I need to go back now. I've come as far as I can tonight."

FORTY
EIGHT

———

The sky is pinkish cream. New pools of light on the horizon edging upward, edging outward, to reveal the contorted outline of a body lying by the overturned Mustang.

Hugh begins his descent over loose rock toward the ravine bottom. His collar is up against the cold. He slips clumsily time and time again until his pants tear at the hip and his thigh is cut open.

He stares at the face-down shape. On the back of Travis' shirt are sticky red blotches where bugs and flies have begun to feast. Misty huffs come from Hugh's mouth as he bends down sluggardly and looks inside the Mustang.

Empty. The glove box open and cleaned out. No sign of blood. He looks in the back. The rear seat has been pulled down to expose a rack built into the substructure for two shotguns. One is gone.

He spent a whole night sitting through the naked cold to find this. He goes and sits on a rock to gather himself. In the back of his mouth the taste of sand. He'll play grave digger this morning and then he'll have the rest of the day to think about how much worse things will get.

Vic wakes to sounds across the alleyway. The clatter of dishes and glassware. Latino talk radio. Water hosed onto a concrete floor.

As he lies there wrapped in the sheets there is a deep calm inside him. The curtains keep the room dark. His hand moves to find Shay, but the bed beside him is empty.

When he opens the rooms to light it is a pleasant and sunny day, until he finds the money and her note.

He walks out into the hot eye of sunlight. A dreadful and despondent feeling overtakes him as he stares down into a piece of paper telling him she is gone.

Shay sits alone in a rear seat of the Greyhound as it makes its way over Christmas Tree Pass. She takes from her pocket the folded paper her mother gave her with the name and number of the man working up her new ID.

Shay could close it all today. She could recuse herself from the landslide that is heaping down on them. She glances at the backpack on the seat next to her. With that money and what's in the safe deposit boxes she could call this Ferryman, as he is named, pick up her walking papers, and become a simple ghost somewhere in the southern latitudes.

In the window she finds herself. The threadbare art of facts speak for themselves. How do you recreate yourself from ruins. And will a different name alone be enough to keep a child whore of providence from ending up another defeat in progress?

Through a thin reflection of her tired eyes the desert mountains run. A hard, austere country of high walls formed from upheaval and transformation, where a thousand years since men and women painted out their dreams on stone. They drew upon the strength of the rock to help them through a world vaster than understanding. It was a simple beseechment born of the desire to be connected to that delicate structure we know as humanity.

She looks up the aisle and eyes one by one an underclass, for whom the bus is all they have. The pathetic and the off. Those vandalized by darkness, those who cling to a lifeboat of dregs as they pray to God. The hand-me-downs and the rootless moments to moments. The ones you avoid in common daylight.

And who are you, she asks herself. Another time puncher in a savaged land. Another unaddressed package heading to Valhalla carrying a six-pack, a roach clip, and a cache of ripped money.

She knows she is a borderland soul who's had to endure too many secrets, partake of too many illicit disgraces to ever be afforded true north.

She stares down at the paper her mother gave her. At the erratically wild handwriting. She needs the concrete truth of her mother's death and then—

Shay tries to sleep. She tries to put the feel and touch of Vic from her mind. She accomplishes neither. She looks across the aisle and watches a blanket-wrinkled face the shade and fiber of many years help her grandchild with open vowels while the plain ground of time fleets past the windows. That brown and buff firmament crossed by migrants with nothing but their souls, an ox, and a little water. An allegory of silence that has seen all our yesterdays, todays, and tomorrows in endless repetition.

Dee always said Shay was the stronger one. But Shay senses that was only meant to make her more compliant, to buy her allegiance. Not with praise, but with promise.

"I can't survive without you, Shay. But you could survive without me. You're the stronger one. You'll know that in time."

Yes, not with praise, but with promise. Because by saying it, by reenforcing it, Dee only made Shay weaker, as she made her more susceptible to her mother's words. For if it were true, if Shay were stronger, and Shay wanted desperately to believe she was strong, would she not be more likely to believe everything else her mother said was true? Who wants a truth we need to cut in half to find the lie at its heart?

She closes her eyes and tries to just ride out the miles, but her thoughts have begun to fall prey to a question: Did her mother send her into the desert with the full knowledge that she would die?

The wrestling match of the last hours is brought to an end when the driver announces, "We'll be entering the downtown Los Angeles terminal in about thirty minutes."

Shay opens her eyes and looks up the aisle. The window frames a sunset of unrelenting extremes. Colors heap upon colors and lights begin to fill the purple landscape.

She looks again at the name and number her mother wrote down, but she already knows. The road offers no escape. Distance alone won't do it. There are too many lives between her and that far-off point defined as anonymity. Those living signposts she's known most all her existence . . . Burgess . . . Foreman . . . Pettyjohn . . . Englund . . . They need to be taken down. They need to fall to insure her freedom. Even if such a word as freedom exists.

Maybe freedom, in truth, is little more than a temporary reprieve from what was, or what is. Maybe freedom is achieved only by death. The death of a previous life, the demise of past ideas. The exculpation of living regrets and failures. Yes, failures of conscience and character. The exorcism of everything that has exercised hatred or had hold over your being. Maybe it is as much the positive as the negative and maybe that is all well and good. And fair.

And maybe she can cut one lie in half and find the truth hidden at its heart.

FORTY
NINE

Vic knows that no matter how he feels, he better stay in the present tense. He gets a cab to drive him from Gogo's Motel to the Laughlin Bullhead City Airport. He walks the hangars till he finds some pilot with a two-prop who'll cash and carry him back to L.A.

Just after four o'clock Terry picks Vic up at Whiteman Airport in Pacoima. Before they leave he says to Vic, "Since we're here, I want to show you something."

He drives Vic down a double row of corrugated hangars at the rear of the airport. He stops at a rusting hangar door protected by two huge silver padlocks.

"That hangar," Terry uses his sunglasses to point, "with the DD40 painted just above the lock, that was where the Worths kept their plane."

"The one they died in?"

"Yes. William had the wreckage brought back. It's in there now."

A grotesque and macabre feeling comes over Vic.

"I had to go in there once to collect some papers. It's 1974 inside that metal shell. Everything is just like it was the morning of their deaths. Dishes are still in a sink to be washed. An *L.A. Times* is open to the sports page on a table right beside where the cotter pins were."

Heart needles at the very image and feel of what it must be like inside that red-gray metal door. "Why'd you show me this?"

"Well, for one, you landed here. Second, I love William. But his emotional life is as locked away as that hangar. Living in the past sees to that."

Terry slides his sunglasses up over the bridge of his nose then stares at Vic, "My mother was a deaconess at her church down on Crenshaw. She was a very religious woman and she used to say, 'Our lives are made up exclusively of what we are wise enough to keep in our hearts, and of what we are brave enough to throw away.' "

That grotesque and macabre feeling turns to cautionary remorse as Vic realizes what Terry is saying. "I hope William appreciates what a good friend you are," says Vic.

Terry looks up from his coffee and over to the office bar where Vic is pouring another shot of tequila. "I say we turn her things over. People always skip out of these motels leaving stuff behind, with unpaid bills. We cleaned the room, she owed money, we would keep her stuff for thirty days and then sell it. We have no idea if it belonged to a murdered girl or not. We wipe our hands, and see how it all settles."

Landshark rises from his desk and turns to Vic, "What do you say?"

"I thought about this coming back on the plane. Terry is right. Even if they connect me, I'll just say I hired the girl myself. I wanted her to scope out Foreman and Pettyjohn. I hadn't heard from her so I flew in from El Paso. I went to the motel and she was gone. I'll say who I really am and that's it. That leaves both of you clean."

Terry and Landshark glance at each other. Then Terry asks, "Why didn't you go to the police after the girl disappeared?"

"I figured she was just a flake."

"When they announce her name on television, what then?"

"I'm not there yet. And anyway, I was supposed to be dead." He tosses down the tequila. "That's why Dee Storey sent me out into the desert. I'm sure, so sure of it. I'll bet she thought if I'm alone she's finished it. If I'm with someone else maybe she could scare them off with my death. If not, what difference does it make. What difference. I thought about all that on the way back too. From the moment she sat across from me in that coffee shop. From that moment she knew she was . . ." He remembers how Shay voiced what her mother had said about Vic getting in the car and he uses the same word, ". . . 'compromised.' She knew it cold."

He places the glass neatly down on the bar, "I think she was doing the best she could at damage control. She knew about the photos. She knew Pettyjohn and Englund going public could be fucked. She got to handle a payoff for Ridden. She got me out there. I say inside her head she was thinking her last best hope was getting that money and instead of making the payoff she does a quick goodbye. 'Cause she knows the futures are not good on this. Not for anyone."

"Not for her daughter, that much is sure."

Vic's eyes narrow as he turns to Landshark, "No, not for her either." He crosses the room and walks out onto the terrace. He breathes in the dusk. The sunset is an extremity of colors. Something befitting the robe of an emperor. From the Elysian Hills past the skyline of high-rises as far as the eye could see. As far as the eye could imagine. And in that vast expanse his thoughts are with a single human being.

Terry stands. He passes round Landshark who is looking out toward the terrace. Vic has his back to both men. He is framed by the dusk, and his head is slightly bowed.

"The papers are out there somewhere," says Terry. "We need to know where they are. We need to get them. They are the indictment. They prove what we know. They are all that really does."

Landshark walks to the patio door and says, "The daughter is our best chance for that."

Vic turns, "Yes, she was our best chance. As strange as it now seems."

Landshark can see Vic is holding Shay's note.

"I wouldn't be classless enough to ask what the note says."

"That's right," says Terry, "but you would be classless enough to want to know what it says."

"Very true, but I would have said that much more elegantly."

Vic folds the note and slips it into his shirt pocket.

"I understand," says Landshark.

Terry comes up beside Landshark. The two men fill in the doorway. "The daughter," says Terry, "must have been the one who took you into the Preserve that night."

"I'm certain you're right, without being certain."

"But she didn't abandon you back there in the desert."

"No, she didn't."

"Do you think she knows who you are and is just trying to—"

"Trying to lie her way past me?"

"Yes."

"I don't want to think it's possible, but it's possible."

"If that's true, then what are you going to do to her?"

"If I see her again. And I knew—"

"Yes."

Vic is the picture of a man sparring with himself over the uncertain reality named Shay Storey. "I'm not sure." He looks at Terry. "We can't live in the past. No matter how much the past keeps changing as we add to it."

Vic starts into the room and both men give way. He crosses to the bar. He pours another shot of tequila. He looks up at the black and white photo behind the bar Landshark so prizes, and hopes this does not all turn out to be a case of tragic clarity.

Terry goes back to his mug of coffee, Landshark to smoking and pacing. But in short order the men converge on one thought.

"If the papers are still with Foreman and his," says Terry, "we could try to hunt them out."

"If they're with Foreman," answers Vic, "Ridden is still vulnerable. And after what happened in the desert think how vulnerable he must feel. If he doesn't have the papers he'll try and get them back. It's just a matter of time. How do we manage to find out when and where that little transaction will take place?"

Silence. Terry has no immediate answer, but Landshark goes over to the worktable. He sits. Takes the San Fernando Land Development Company promo pack and turns to the inside page. "There are ways, and there are ways." He begins to dial. "First we need to find out if he's got the papers or not." Into the phone: "Burgess Ridden, please."

Both men's attention now falls squarely on Landshark's shoulders.

"Who am I talking to please? Annette . . . and you are Mr. Ridden's secretary? I'm a columnist with *The New Weekly. The New Weekly.* . . . Yes, we have columnists and people who cover hard news and serious subjects . . ." His tone dances with the borderline nasties. "We aren't only personals and ads for people interested in breast augmentation. . . . My column is called 'Big Island/L.A.' . . . My name is Landshark and . . . yes, Landshark. And—"

He stops abruptly. He stares at the phone like some man in pain. His body rises up to its full height. His neck twists around the phone. He starts to dial again. "I have the urge to call Freek and turn him loose on this young lady's Experian and bank records." Into the phone: "Annette, please . . ." Waiting, his mouth rounds angrily, "Annette, this is Landshark again and I want you to think before you hang up. . . . Would Mr. Ridden appreciate you not giving him the opportunity to comment on what was soon to be put in my column and then sent on to the wire services . . . there's no need to suck your gums . . . I am always nasty and I have no friends. . . . And the sooner I'm away from nice people like yourself, the better off I'll be."

Landshark looks at both men and gloats over getting in even one little cut. "Now, Annette, you tell Mr. Ridden a source has come to me with information that certain documents needed for approvals on both the 56th Street School and the Belmont School might well have been forged and that executives with the San Fernando Land Development Company were behind that forgery. I would love to give Mr. Ridden every opportunity to confirm or deny. I will gladly leave you my number."

That done, Landshark hangs up. He sits back and his face takes on a reserved stoniness. He glances at the cellular phone Magale used to call him on. It is sitting silent where Landshark left it since those first nights after the murder.

"William, what are you going to ask Ridden?"

The flesh along the upper part of Landshark's face pulls back and the lines across his forehead deepen. "If he calls back, and I'm not sure he will, I'm going to ask him about his relationship with Alicia Alvarez. Then we'll see if I can stir up a little panic in the boy we can take advantage of."

FIFTY

Shay slows past the driveway that leads to her mother's house. The gate is closed, the lights are off. From what she can see of the driveway her mother's red Le Baron isn't there.

She continues past, then on past the house after that. She shuts her lights, and parks against the railing that looks out over the Valley. The road has curved enough so from where she's parked the second floor of her mother's house is visible. The lights are all out there, too.

Shay is not taking any chances. She reaches into her shoulder bag. When she's checked the Guardian she slips it into the pocket of her leather coat. She rummages under the front seat for a flashlight. She aims it at the floor to find out if the batteries are good. Once assured the street is quiet, she gets out and slips over the railing and starts down the hillface.

She starts along a ruined pathway between rampant vines and paddle-shaped opuntia. Dee's house and the house next to it were once one property, and during the twenties the owners had turned that chaparraled hillside into a garden of walking trails even though most of the land was owned by the city. Now it is a strangled mass of branches with crumbling stone terraces and grottos framed by rotting arbor post beams where once benches looked out over the tranquil warmth of a San Fernando night. A dead eucalyptus had been cut to make steps, and these Shay follows in their forgotten cracked and clumsy rise to Dee's patio.

Close to the ground Shay peers through spiny and strong-smelling plants. She takes in the back of the house. Nothing seems out of order and that alone gives her cause for alarm.

She eases along the patio wall. She reaches the house and tilts her head slightly so she can see through the glass doors.

There is only moonlight to guide her. Where the shadows are cut away she searches with her eyes, till she makes out an odd shape on the floor. It is another moment before she can piece together the image from that obscure mosaic.

The lamp that had always been on the end table now lies on the floor. The shade is at a mad-hatter's angle and just beyond it a table drawer sits upside down with its contents strewn on the carpet.

A wave of sickness works its way up through the fetal reaches of Shay's life knowing what she is probably about to face. She enters through the laundry room. The Guardian in one hand, the flashlight in the other. She can hear, from somewhere in that dark mix of rooms, running water.

She crosses the kitchen. On a counter she notices the message light on her mother's answer machine blinking furiously.

Her feet leave barely a sound on the rose and gray linoleum as Shay steps through the doorway to face a badly wrecked house backlit by the moon. And that running water? It sounds like a tap. But where is it coming from? Not the kitchen or laundry room. The bar sink, maybe . . . the bathroom at the end of the hall . . . upstairs? This all has to be some kind of monstrous hoax.

Her jaws are a tense mass as she turns on the flashlight and scans the floor for her mother's body.

She tries to keep her emotions on a tight leash. The tapered beam cuts the room. Strobes the stairway railing and the wall beyond it. Reshapes into a small round sphere against the empty darkness until it plucks out a twinkling of light on the steps up to the bar alcove.

Shay approaches the spot cautiously. The prismatic starfield turns out to be shards of glass from one of the framed photos that had been on the wall next to the bar sink.

She tiptoes up through the broken pieces. She bends down. She finds the photo. It was the one of her sitting on the hood of Burgess Ridden's car. The one Vic had been looking at. She can hear herself saying, "I was almost a functioning human being then."

Shay stands. The running water is not coming from the bar sink but she can now tell it is from a bathroom at the end of that narrow hallway. A bathroom beside a door that leads to the garage.

Shay does the last thirty feet hunched over behind a thread of light. She opens the bathroom door with her gun. A white cycloptic flash stabs at her eyes. She shunts back and away from the bathroom door. The light disappears as her gun hand comes up and then, in that heart-racing haze, she realizes it was her reflection in the bathroom mirror burning back through the darkness.

Shay steps back into the bathroom. Her light keys on the sink. The tap is running full bore as if drawing attention to itself. Droplets spittle up and outward in all directions and there, she sees something has dried in burgundy streaks down the outer skin of that porcelain sink.

She lets the light drop through black space to where bullet-sized discolorations have fallen onto the white tile.

She knows what this spells out. She can see her mother's blueflame stare as she said, "Don't come back, Shay. Don't ever come back."

She follows the bloodtrail past her boots where fobs of browning cinnabar on the plush powderwhite carpet stop at the door to the garage.

The reality grows more unreal. What the child never suspects, the adult knows better. Death's existence . . . Shay is staring down at its leavings.

She pushes the door to the garage open. She aims that beam of light into the cool, concrete darkness where it illuminates the shiny red hood of her mother's Le Baron.

Contraband emotions. The legacy of painful years will be answered soon enough by the silvery light that swims along the gray concrete floor where blood fell in matchbook-sized splotches toward the driver's door. No one had ever driven Dee's car, except Dee. No one.

Shay has forgotten to turn off the bathroom faucet and the sound runs cold and echoey through the stillness. From fingertip to palm her hands clam up trying to hold the flashlight steady, trying to hold the gun starkly forward.

She wants to be rid of the consumptive presence of her mother, the hatred and angers. It is a painful and frightful fact. A terrifying truth glimpsed at in dark seconds moving forward. Like the Sisyphian ancient, she doesn't want to push the stone of her mother up that hill night after night to find the daylight screaming . . . again.

Shay fights the consanguine emotions that tie us one to another. She tells herself they are the inventions of a childhood river she has drowned in many times, only to rise like a weightless fetus into an air of lonesome and hopeless incomprehensibility.

Whatever pity her mother deserves, whatever prayers, whatever leniency human souls warrant in their walk to a next world, if there is a next world, Shay is willing to advance, as long as she does not have to pay for it now by finding Dee alive.

She pushes the flashlight into the open driver's window. She hears a gasp caught in the noose of her own tongue. Her eyes lose direction and focus. The deep calamity of her life issues forth in a deathless cry as she sees that the leather seat of the Le Baron is streaked with blood.

FIFTY ONE

———

Burgess Ridden does not return Landshark's call, but the following day, Harold Ridden does. Landshark bridges the shock by limiting his rhetoric to silence until Mr. Ridden says: "So you're the one who named Belmont 'Fiasco High.' I should be very upset with you."

"Mr. Ridden, I only coined the phrase. Everyone who's had a hand in that disaster helped name it Fiasco High. And that is the criminal truth of it."

Landshark puts particular emphasis on the word "criminal," and Mr. Ridden then says, "When your column wrote about the family on Toluca who'd been smelling noxious gas coming up from the ground and you brought it to our attention we got someone right out. We had a report written. Action was taken.

"This project has been a template for how not to build a school. We know that. We are trying to climb out of the hole we've dug as best we can."

"You'd think having dropped all the excess baggage they call ethics would make that climb all the easier."

"This school, which is essential to our children's education, has survived one hostile inaccuracy after another. And what you have just said is a hostile inaccuracy."

"You're right about this school being essential to our children's education. Especially in teaching them the meaning of accountability right on through an alphabet of other essential character-driven words and phrases."

"I hope to turn your statement into a compliment and not the condemnation you mean."

Then with quiet certitude he adds, "In response to your message. No documents, that I know of, were altered. If you have information to the contrary, I would appreciate hearing it, or seeing it, so I may take active measures. If you have proof of what you claim, publish it. If my son were involved, all the more reason. And you can quote me.

The Ridden name is a lifeline of achievement and purpose. Prove otherwise. But if this is just the usual negligent gossip or Enquirish slander that you print as a fact, I will come at you hard and you will know how much baggage the world of accountability carries with it."

"To quote you, then . . . your son in no way altered documents that help get the Belmont site to meet all the necessary city, state, or federal requirements."

"To quote me," says Ridden.

Landshark lets Harold Ridden ride the moment to wherever he thinks it's gonna take him. He listens as the older man's lungs fill with air. He's got to give Ridden credit, he handles the gloss and conceal as good as anybody.

"One last question, Mr. Ridden. Could you, at least, outline for me your son's relationship with a woman named Alicia Alvarez and whether or not he knew she has certain criminal ties?"

Having sidestepped the minefield of Landshark's final question, for now, his confidence shaken, Harold Ridden stares out the office window, toward Los Encinos Park.

How many times had he taken Burgess to that park when there were dreams to be had. When Encino was still a quaint reminder of the forties and fifties. How many of these dreams have fallen upon barren ground to become the blighted landscape of a son.

Harold Ridden understands that whether the truth becomes part of the public confessional or not, he must position his own life for afterward. He knows he's done nothing wrong, yet he realizes in the language of human relations people will hear his words, even as their thoughts slant toward the untrusting denominator of parenthood. That he or she who somehow will have failed. It is the convenient intellectual criticism that keeps people from taking measure of their own lives. After all, the child will always be a blank tablet the parent has inscribed their will upon, whether it is the Ten Commandments or the ten thousand unaccountables of man.

No matter how you frame the Garden of Allah with sunlight, it is still a poster child for how far the dream of Hollywood has fallen upon hard times.

Shay pulls up in her Jeep and parks out front. Walking up the driveway she notices a transient cross section of types at a table by the pool answering a reporter's questions while they stare into a news camcorder and try to hype themselves onto a few seconds of air time.

At the office counter Rog is wrapped around a copy of *The L.A. Times*, where a feature story has put name and face to the girl murdered at the Belmont School site. The last two days have dropped Rog into a bad manic state where every five minutes he imagines some new reason why the corpse grinders in their black-and-whites are gonna come and put the clamps on him.

He's looking through a drawer for his medication and trying to remember how much valium he's sucked down this morning when the office door opens.

He recognizes Shay right off. She picks up on the nervous trip his eyes make from her to the reporter and that miscreant tribe around the pool, then back to her. She walks up to the bulletproof glass that separates them and asks, "Is Vic here?"

She says it like he's supposed to know. He scratches his chest. The coffee-stained Hawaiian shirt is open to his waist and Shay can see the skin needs a scrub brush and bad.

"Vic who?" asks Rog.

"Vic in room twenty-three."

He looks through the registration files while his brain tries to a-priori an answer on how best to handle this. "Room twenty-three . . ." His voice is no better than a mumble. "In twenty-three we have a couple from Belize . . . no Vic, though . . . twenty-four, no Vic . . . in twenty-five, no . . ."

Shay slams her fist into the glass partition and Rog's head and neck jostle back from the fleshy imprint that was crosshaired on the center of his skull.

"Listen, screwhead. Do you know how to take a message?"

Rog rights his battered glasses on the bridge of his nose. He continues for a few seconds with some indeterminate inner dialogue she can hear out loud then says, "With both hands. And in three languages. No, four if you include English as a language."

A lonely window table of the coffee shop after dark but between hours, with Shay staring despondently at a hamburger and mashed potatoes barely touched. While she tries to figure out how to reinvent herself in the face of the world, Vic slides into the booth without a warning. She looks across the table and up. The silence of exposed and unspoken emotions is broken only by a waitress who stops to ask if he wants coffee.

Once they are alone, Vic says, "We seem to have been in this booth before."

"They say déjà vu has a mind of its own."

He scans a room practically empty, but hosted by the solitude of Neil Young coming from the wallside speakers.

Afraid of what is behind what he feels, he fiddles with his napkin, knife, and fork. And she, this undefined secret across the table, just watches him order and reorder the simple placement of the silverware.

"I didn't think I'd see you again," he says looking down at the table.

"I never said you wouldn't."

"No." His eyes rise tentatively, "Your note was just short and painful."

"I feel like I've escaped into the world."

"Why am I here?"

"You stole my question," she says; "that isn't fair."

The waitress comes back with the coffee. A makeshift silence until she is gone then Shay continues, "I'm sorry the note was short and painful. I'd written another, but it . . . it was long and painful and it made me feel too much so I—"

He can hear her voice is breaking up and when he tries to look inside her and find where the wounds are he can see how pale she is, and how the eyes swim in a moat of exhaustion.

"My mother is dead," she whispers.

He regards the moment like some silent executioner. He finds himself staring at Shay's coffin necklace on a stretch of black T-shirt and he's only sorry God cheated him out of that particular exercise.

"I went to her house," says Shay, as she leans into the table so only Vic can hear, "It looked like somebody had used the place for a mosh pit and in the garage I found her car. There was blood on the driver's seat. A lot of blood and on the concrete floor. A box of lawn bags and some were cut in parts and there was rope and what was left of a roll of electrician's tape. Whoever it was, Vic, they came prepared."

Shay looks out the coffee shop window. The thought of Dee Storey in some shallow grave and all it implies freezes Shay's throat.

It's better to burn out, than it is to rust . . .

A hand drained of energy points to a wallspeaker and Shay, her voice buckling, says, "Maybe it is better to burn out, than it is to—"

Tears and rage commingle just beneath the surface of Shay's face and Vic quietly gets out money for the bill and stands. He takes Shay by the arm and gently, very gently lifts her and she rises at his will, all in one almost smooth motion and they walk into the cool night air of the parking lot as the music fades behind the swoosh of a closing door.

FIFTY
TWO

———

Shay's Jeep is parked on the Glendale Boulevard side of the lot. She
sits on the front bumper and rests her head in the basket of her hands.

"Do you think this . . . Foreman, killed her?"

"Maybe," says Shay. "She was to bring the money and meet him
after I cleared it. But back at the house, my mother's machine had a
number of messages. I played them back. Two were from Foreman. He
didn't leave his name but I know the voice. 'Why haven't you called,'
he said. And 'How do we get this on.' "

Vic leans against the Jeep. He makes a finger line through a coating
of fine dirt on the hood. "Maybe they met after, and he killed her.
Maybe he already has the money and—"

She shakes her head vehemently, "No, I talked to Burgess. When I
called to tell him what happened to my mother, he was already
freaked. She never showed to pick up the money."

He attempts to systematically walk this through, but can't. He looks
out into the street where the cars try to out-hustle the light at Glendale
and Fletcher. "Why would Foreman kill her before he got the money?"

"You have to know Burgess Ridden. He's negotiated his whole life
with a white flag in one hand and his eyes covered with the other. If
my mother took a breath it was his chest that expanded. She was the
only thing that kept Foreman and the others from blowing him out."

"That only leaves Burgess."

"Or his father," she says. "Burgess told him about everything a few
days ago. I knew the boy was about ready to jump ship."

"The father didn't know?"

"His father knew there were payoffs. But that is how they always
did business. It being Burgess' gig the old man stayed more low-key,
more corporate. He sure didn't know there were papers that could
prove his boy was a forger. Or that they had killed the girl. Or—"

She stops. She rubs her hands. There's things she just doesn't want to see or say. "Harold Ridden hated my mother and she hated him. If you could only tape the verbal parade of insults when they got together."

"Well, someone is lying."

Yes, she knows someone is. Practically everyone is.

"For the last two days," says Shay, "I've been walking around Echo Park trying to deal with all this soul banging. I spent a lot of time around Echo Park growing up. Suddenly I found myself for hours staring at this alley behind a Mexican seafood place. I dumpster dived for food there when I was twelve 'cause my mother made me live on the street for a week. It was the banishment trip 'cause her little Cinderella wasn't quite—

"Fuck it, anyway. I wondered why I was there. Was I reliving all those times so I wouldn't succumb to an attack of sympathy or remorse because she was dead, or maybe 'cause I was hurt that she never really existed except as the toxic wasteland I learned to love and cherish and follow.

"For those two days I lived on cigarettes and coffee, on roscones and buñuelos. I even copped some speed from her medicine chest." Shay reaches into her coat pocket and takes out a vial. "My mother was a speed freak." She looks at the vial. "I took one and then this hostile revelation just hit. Right on the corner of Sunset and Echo Park with all that human traffic around me.

"Was I trying to keep her alive? Did I need the connection that bad. Did I need to imitate her particularly diseased vibe 'cause that's all I knew or understood or was comfortable with in my own horrified uncomfortable way? Was I that much some unfinished painting of my mother? I—"

She takes the vial and flings it into the street.

What Vic can see in her face is what had once been his own. That point where the human being is beyond all telling and belongs to those realms where they are ready to enact some crime against themselves, if not others.

He sits on the bumper beside her and says very quietly, "Why did you ask me here?"

"You want the papers, right?"

He rides as close to honesty as he can, "Yes. That is part of what I want."

"You want them exposed, right."

"Yes, again."

"I'm to see Burgess tonight. Foreman still wants the money, and Burgess and my mother want the papers."

While she waits on his answer, she adds, "I know you're not in this alone. When I saw the *Times* this morning, there was nothing about the girl taking pictures. Nothing about a carryall or a camera or all those photos. You sure didn't go to the police. Neither did the people who hired her otherwise someone would want to ask questions about why I was at her motel room. And when you showed up at Nightland, I told you before I don't want to know what all this is about. And I'm not sure you'd tell me all of the truth anyway. I don't really expect it.

"But I don't think Foreman will let you just walk away. I don't think Pettyjohn or Englund can either."

The shadows around Shay's eyes clear when the flare of oncoming headlights fills the space around them. "Requiescat in pace," she says.

Yes, he thinks, he feels very well what he sees in her face. "Let's walk," he says.

Up Glendale and into a cascade of oncoming headlights that give everything around them a glossy sheen.

Neither had noticed the coffee shop sign high above the parking lot. The neon I in DIS had gone out leaving only the presence of Dee Storey's initials branded in green on the night sky behind them.

They pass a bar called the Red Lions Tavern. It's a European-style beer garden accented in red trim. In the back there is a walled garden where they sit. Vic makes Shay eat. While the tables around them are marked by small talk and laughter he asks, "If you could do this and just walk, what then?"

She uses her fork as if she were inscribing a headstone, "Shay Storey ... born 1974 ... got a new name for her luggage tags 1998. ... Thank you, ladies and gentlemen, but the girl has left the house."

Watching her movements across the candleflame, and under those rhenish lights he can hear himself in her, on Landshark's rainswept terrace that first night crying, "I want my life back desperately."

There are complete bodies of reason why he should not do this, but her unchartered stare and the puzzle of his insides will have him do differently, and he tells her so in a gesture when his hand finds her bare forearm and holds it tightly.

She looks down at his hand and arm crossed to hers. The knife scars are like welding lines on a sheet of iron and she says, "I was into self-inflicted wounds at the time." Then, with a warning tone to her voice adds, "I hope this is not one of those times."

FIFTY
THREE

While Shay presses the buzzer Vic stands back in the street and stares at the white Mayan edifice altered into the hillside and considers how much of his own suffering helped pay for this elegant landmark Burgess Ridden gets to call home.

A voice on the intercom asks, "Who is it?"

"It's Shay."

A flat buzz and they are in. They climb a white and tan stairwell to where Burgess appears in subdued light. He sees Shay isn't alone and nervously takes her aside when she reaches the top of the stairs.

"Who is that?"

"This is Vic. He's gonna do me a little favor and make sure what happened to my mother doesn't happen to me."

Burgess looks over the gruff unshaven face, "Why don't you have him wait in the reading room while we talk?"

Shay leads Vic to a room off the atrium done in Chinese silk wallpaper and lit by deco sconces.

Vic looks back through the doorway at Burgess, "He's even less than I expected."

"Give him time, he'll get smaller."

Once they're alone in a room that opens to an artfully appointed garden Burgess turns and holds Shay tightly. His movement is sudden as a child's and just as awkward. With the sheer weight of events in his voice he says to her ear, "I can't believe Dee's dead. I can't believe your mother is—"

She is metered silence, and as human and hurt as Burgess sounds, so many handfuls of Shay's life have been spilled in his service it is all she can do to ease the grip of his arms without him noticing she is repelled.

"In a lot of ways," he pleads, "it's you and me now."

She can count the ways on one finger but resists the image and instead softhands him with, "We've got to be there for each other."

The room once had a pool table in it and a slot machine Dee had stolen from a Tahoe club, now it was a hiply austere home office befitting a climber.

Burgess goes to his desk. He hard searches through a drawer. "Foreman called me right after Dee didn't show and he was ranting she split with the money and fucked us all."

Whatever he's looking for he can't find and grows more upset by the second, "He swears he didn't kill her." He slams the drawer shut and goes to the next. "Where is he coming from?"

"Did he tell you he tried to kill me?"

"I've been on valium for three days and I don't know where I put them."

"Did he tell you?"

"Yeah, and he's freaked. He and Alicia blew out of their dump in Chatsworth so you won't find 'em."

She opens her coffin charm, "I won't have to go looking to find them."

Burgess is making the rounds of drawer after drawer so he doesn't catch her drift.

"Will this cut the edge?"

He looks up. Between her fingers a well-packed joint of no little substance.

"I just need to flatline," he says coming around the desk.

She gets the joint lit and slips it cleanly into his mouth. "We're not gonna freak and we're not gonna flatline. Foreman still wants the money, right?"

Burgess holds the smoke down till his reflexes force a breath. "Foreman said to be ready for it to happen tomorrow or the next day. He'll call with a time and place. And you know who's to make the delivery? Yours fuckin' truly.

"And that's not all. Take a look at the article I cut out on my desk from *The New Weekly*. Go on."

She crosses the room.

"They might as well just build the colosseum around me 'cause I am food for the lions."

On top of a stack of half worked up contracts is a full-page column. At first glance the header reads: BIG ISLAND/L.A. And beside it, instead of the usual author photo, is a child angel looking down at the city and crying.

"The guy calls to talk to me, but my father handled it. He said he had information I forged some of the Belmont paperwork. He asked about my relationship with Alicia Alvarez and did I know she had criminal ties. We're unraveling, Shay."

Burgess stands at the open garden door and rides the first wave of a good stone. He closes his eyes, the night air is washed in scents. "I had the landscaper duplicate here what she'd planted around Dee's patio. That's how much of me she owned."

Shay folds the page down and down until it is easily slipped into her pocket.

"And my father." He turns and opens his eyes, "He's making me put together a paper trail for the money like I've had some deal in the works for a year."

Shay walks over and takes Burgess by the arm. "They know how to work us for what they want, don't they?"

His gauzy red eyes flicker a bit with understanding as she sits him down in a Shaker chair. "Yeah . . . yeah. Only you can take a hit better than I can."

She kneels before him. She rests her hands on his legs. "You and I need each other more than ever."

He runs his open hand palm across her hair and down the soft texture of cheek. He finds the cusp of her neck and shoulder and she can feel the pulse of blood inside his fingers on the bone above her breast. He's no different now than when she was fifteen and he'd get her loaded so he could try a little quiet groping when Dee wasn't around.

"I feel like the whole world has to die, or I do."

She stands. She's all face staring down at him. "You're not gonna play the downer mouthhole with me, alright. We'll get this taken care of. You tell Foreman you'll deliver the money but I'll be there first to see the papers just like last time. And that this whole exercise better be as boring as a trip to the supermarket."

Burgess looks like he was just wheeled out of a coma and into some violent confrontation. "He won't have it."

"He . . . he! Burgess, get your dick strapped on. Tell him. Convince him. Order him. You go in alone he could take the money and keep the papers, then what! He could try and do to you—"

Even that deer in the headlights they all talk about looks like it could put up a more interesting fight than Burgess Ridden. Then, this partly stoned piece of inertia says, "I'm just a clit, okay. Like Dee used to say, I'm just a clit."

"I saw your father's car parked downstairs. He's in the house somewhere, isn't he?"

"The video room."

She turns hard on her boot heels.

"Don't burn the energy, Shay. He won't talk to you."

When Shay enters the video room, Harold Ridden stands. "I need to talk with you," she says.

He slights her silently by walking out just as his son steps into view. Up that long white hall, past rooms with their subtle changes of hue, Shay chases after the older man and shouts across the house, "Vic . . . Vic!"

The four converge in the atrium. Floor lights behind plants cast a jungle of shadows across the ceiling. For a moment things are museum quiet as Harold Ridden tries to understand what this rough-looking outcast is doing in his son's house.

"Vic, Mr. Ridden thinks he's not going to talk with me."

Disregarding the obvious, Harold Ridden starts for the stairs only to have Vic block his path, "You can start a problem or solve one. Those are your only two choices." Then, even before Burgess can create some makeshift reaction Vic tells him, "And you, for the least reason I will drop you on your wallet."

The moon floats across the surface of the pool, which catches light from the video room where Harold Ridden emerges with Shay right behind him.

"I know how much you hate my mother."

"If I could send the devil a thank-you note, I would."

"I'm sure there's been a run at all the card shops."

Harold Ridden folds his hands behind his back and just settles down into a sober and unattractive silence to make Shay speak her piece and be done with her.

"When Charlie Foreman calls you to set time and place you will tell him I'm coming to see the papers first and clear the way for Burgess to deliver the money."

Harold Ridden turns away from Shay and starts walking down one side of the pool.

"Charlie will say no. He will come on like a real headhunter but you will tell him it's your way, or no way."

Harold Ridden moves through a light blue off the pool and his figure waves and ripples as he walks on.

"You will tell him that after what's happened you are not going to jeopardize your son and that you are paying me to see this through. That you want no trouble, and there'll be none from me."

He continues on, every now and then running his fingers along the bougainvillea that hangs like pastel garnish from the courtyard walls. It's the black patrician vibe he's throwing off. That bored but listening so get on with it.

"No matter where you walk, Mr. Ridden, you are going to have to come back my way."

He just keeps on.

"I hear Charlie keeps saying he didn't kill my mother. Now, either he's a ranting liar or someone else had their little run of luck. You wouldn't have played devil in this now, would you, Mr. Ridden?"

On that, he stops. But his face returns a marble weathered stare unfit for reading.

"I'm not out to hotwire your pacemaker, okay. My war chest is filled with all the revenge I can handle."

She takes a few steps toward his side of the pool, if only so he can see her face through the narrow lattice of shadows. Close enough so the cold ferocity to carry out what she is going to say is as clear as the face of that moon on the surface of the water.

"If you don't do what I'm asking . . . If you fail to get done what I'm asking for any reason . . . If you say you will get it done just so you can blow me off . . . well. Some night, when you've settled back into that Love Boat life you built for yourself out there in Studio City, you will wake from a nice deep sleep 'cause you heard a sound. You will try to turn your head to listen for what it is, only to discover your throat has been cut."

The small black of his pupils star momentarily and Shay knows the part inside that has to hear what she said . . . has heard.

"Oh yeah, Mr. Ridden. I'm a Storey. Only next year's model."

FIFTY
FOUR

Father and son. Framed in a window. Watching Vic and Shay leave and soon thereafter only the damp cool darkness of a black street remains to tend their features.

"She asked if I killed her mother," says Harold Ridden.

Suspended in the glass, Burgess poses no threat by question or look. But Harold Ridden sees the black art of life—not time, not lineage—is making the two men look more and more alike.

"Burgess, if this doesn't work, you better leave one hell of a suicide note."

Landshark walks off another quarter mile of anxiety. He gets far enough out Mount Washington Drive to look across the open canyon and see his four-story safehold backdropped by skyline. Another first in a sludge of years. He sits on the guardrail at the canyon's edge, his Italian loafers way out of place scuffing at the weeds and broken glass.

The bitter curse that are his insides feel like a balloon held to earth by a thin thread that at any moment might work itself loose and be lost or . . . a feeling emerges ephemerally and his whole body straightens . . . or, be freed. Yes, be freed. And that suddenly is just as frightening a thought as being trapped. How would he live then?

After an hour he's ridden the fear to a hard standstill. This adumbrate figure, no longer who he was, is yet not honest enough to entrust the Adam inside him with who he should be.

He sits there frozen in time facing the fearful symmetry of this conflict when he hears remote footsteps. He turns and out of the sloping dark comes Vic.

"Terry told me I'd find you on the road somewhere."

"Somewhere . . . how did it shake out?"

Vic swings his legs one at a time over the railing and sits beside Landshark. "It could happen as early as tomorrow."

"That fast? Do we know where?"

"That's the worst of it." Vic leans down and begins to pluck up a small handful of stones. "Foreman said he would call tomorrow afternoon. He'll give us the time this is gonna happen. Burgess is to be ready with the money. Shay is to be ready to see the papers. I'll be with her. Foreman's next call after that is a go. Shay and I will be in one car, Burgess in a second car following us. Foreman said he's gonna run us around some. He's being very cautious and said so, in case there's a little retribution on anybody's mind. When we get to the drop point, we go in first. We see everything. Then we call Burgess on."

Vic takes one of the small stones and tosses it into the breathing dark. The air is chilly around both men.

"How do we prepare?" asks Landshark. "The idea was if we knew where, Terry and Freek could work something out to take Burgess after he gets the papers."

Vic angrily tosses another stone down into the coalblack mouth of the canyon, "I don't have a fuckin' answer to that."

Vic has taken to rattling the stones like dice. Landshark asks him, "Can the girl help?"

"Shay's going back to her mother's house tonight. Since the mother was to meet Foreman we thought maybe she wrote something down about where they were to meet. An address maybe. A phone number."

"What are the odds of Foreman picking the same place?"

Vic's only answer is a frustrated huff as he tosses another stone out into the canyon. He then reaches into his shirt pocket. Landshark watches as he opens out a folded page from *The New Weekly*. "Given to me by Shay Storey. As taken from the desk of Burgess Ridden."

Landshark sees where Burgess Ridden has circled his lengthy diatribe that stops just short of being slanderous.

"She gave this to you?"

"And said, 'Maybe you already know about this.' "

"What did you tell her?"

"From the way she asked the question she was not expecting an answer."

Vic stands and begins to pace. Under his boots the crink of broken glass. In his hand the stones are rattled more viciously. "I don't like the way this is all shaking out."

"What will happen to the girl?"

"What will happen to me? To Terry? To you? To Burgess Ridden? What am I suddenly the prophet of Mount Washington? This is not some preplanned exercise. If this goes south it will be at close range. It will be terrifying. And white faced. It will be fuckin' madness in real time. And the only paper trail you may end up with is a nice neat stack of morgue slips with your friends' names getting no more prominence than your enemies'." On that, Vic half turns and flings the stones to where they cut the dark like scattershot.

Small blips of sweat register across his forehead. His underarms are blooming stains. He looks down Mount Washington where headlights slow cruise the curves up through a stretch of wooded roadway. Could it be just a few weeks since he first was driven up that hill in the rain to Landshark's?

"I used to think the safest place in the world was inside the steel shell of a police cruiser." Vic points across the canyon to Landshark's monstrosity of a home. "If nothing else gives you pause, that should."

"I've been sitting on this filthy guardrail for the last hour letting my nice shoes be ruined by the wet California weeds and staring over at Master William's mausoleum and realizing—"

Landshark stops. He knows Vic is waiting for him to finish but he can't get the courage up. Can't go real to real. He can't be honest to the degree necessary if he ever expects to get well. So he tactics the moment away from himself and asks, "It's about the girl, isn't it?"

Vic squats down.

"Just say it."

"It's about Shay Storey."

"In the end you're going to have to know who she is. Which means she is going to have to know who you are. Then you are confronted with what you are going to do and who you are going to be after that."

Vic scratches at the ground with the edge of his fingers as if the answer might be buried under a skin of dirt. The headlights Vic had seen down below make the turn and approach. Both men have to squint against the light.

Vic asks Landshark, "Have you ever been completely honest with someone?"

"Do you mean when I actually could see the unenviable cost staring me in the face?"

"Yes."

"William Worth was never that honest," says Landshark. "But

Landshark, he's trying to, dare I use the phrase, come out of the closet on that one.

"Of course I am a phobic. A maestro of the lie. The lie created to survive. The lie to keep you alive. The lie so you do not have to confront the lie. The lie so you can be comfortable, even in the limited sphere you tell yourself is some form of truth. The phobic learns to mine the lie to their advantage. To relish and exploit it, even when they are most ashamed. It is, as a matter of fact, in their moments of shame, when they are the best liars. They get so good most people around them never even know they are lying. The phobic creates a willing soulless force that rails against them, with an abusive horror. That old bum rap from on high known as 'why me.' Another lie, but perfect for an afternoon of tears and then forgotten. These, of course, are lies a phobic like myself shares with the common, ordinary everyday, garden variety rinky-dink with a Bart Simpson smile and a lunch box as they try to slip past the teeth of the world. The lie as tuxedo, as I like to call it. So you are dressed for any life circumstance that comes along from Cole Porter to cold storage." Landshark opens his huge hands. They are wide and delicate and look to be so gentle you'd believe every feeling that was ever entrusted to them would be safe there.

"Do you know how the poison gets into the ground, Vic? It starts in our hearts and works its way up into our throats where we give voice to it through our actions or lack thereof."

Landshark folds his hands together and they form an arrowhead he points right at Vic's chest, "If you find out she's the one, do you turn her in? Do you kill her? Will you? If she finds out, can she kill you? Will she have to? Does it matter either way . . . to either one?

"If you're asking me what to do, William Worth wouldn't be honest enough to answer, and Landshark, he isn't quite ready to take on the responsibility."

Landshark brings the edge of his folded hands up against the bridge of his nose and forehead. He closes his eyes. For a minute he rides out the sighs and steeps of his emotions.

Vic stands. "I told Terry earlier, if we get a shot at those papers you've got to be in the car with him when we go."

Landshark's head snaps up. His mouth is gaping uncertainty.

"You're coming off the mountain with us, or it's a no show. Burgess goes his way."

Landshark stands to his full, drooping, angry, frightened height. "You wouldn't do that."

Vic swings one leg over the guardrail and then the other. He starts back to the house.

"You wouldn't do that," repeats Landshark.

"Just vision it's you living in the Sunshine Hotel and this is the call."

FIFTY
FIVE

———

Using the night shadows as cover, Shay returns to Dee's house by way of the old garden path along the hillside. When almost through the overrun thistle something black and implicit moves past a second-story window. The ghostlike figure of a man in a motorcycle jacket with short-short white hair.

Staying close to the ground, beneath the milk-blue moonlight Shay searches each dark space of glass. It couldn't be Pettyjohn or Englund. The old man in the desert, Travis' uncle, did he have white hair? Nothing stirs inside the glass except for clouds being curried by the wind out to the desert. Foreman? When was the last time you saw that piece of dirty laundry? He had short-short gray hair back then. Yes.

Shay gets out her Guardian. She lizards her way through a stretch of wild overgrown dark that takes her around the house to the garage. She will enter from there, that way she doesn't have to cross a moonlit living room to reach the stairwell.

A door edges inward so quietly the night sounds around Shay are not disturbed. The beetle rustling of weeds is not once disrupted by a hinge or loose door handle. The closing door blackens in her outline and she is alone with the garage. Alone with the scene of her mother's murder.

She crosses the cool concrete floor trying to avoid the blood trail left by her mother. Footsteps light as snowfall around the front end of the Chrysler. It is too dark to see the front seat through the windshield, but she can see it all the same. She is manacled to it by right of birth.

She stops. Her eyes blink like slow-dropping blood. The door from the garage to the house is not as she left it. There is now maybe two feet of black space between it and the wall.

She presses the silence with squinted eyes, with each careful, careful step toward that piece of black space she will have to pass through.

The one concrete step up to the door her foot negotiates like it was reading braille. Her head hour hands past the doorframe. The long funnel of the hallway ends with the living room. Anyone crossing into that moonlit composition she will see first.

But why did they come back? What is it they want? What is here to hurt them?

Shay moves past the door without touching it. She starts down that catwalk of a hallway with gun hand at arm's length. Pressed to the wall tight as sashwork and her Guardian chest level and ready.

A thought flashpoints as she passes the bar. Her dumping the dead girl's possessions into Burgess' hand on that last night they were all together in the living room. Giving him a dose of vicious reality. Well, it's all being dumped into her hands now. One death after anothe—

The center of her back is clubbed. The single braid down the side of her face is torn backward and her head ropes around. Grasping panic as the leather coat sleeve mousetraps across her throat.

"Shay—"

Her feet stumble backward as she is pulled around.

"Put the fuckin' gun—"

Shay hits the bar. Bottles rattle.

"Shay—"

Shay catches a glimpse of face above her shoulder. Her mother's furious burnt-match eyes. Shay stumbles back into the wall. Her tailbone spikes the floor hard. The dark and imminent figure she saw in the window grabs her.

Dee's hair has been marine chopped. It has been peroxided down till it's Red Cross white. The speedfreak skin looks like it was painted with acrylic glossy yellow.

Dee grabs her daughter's faint pale face. This perversion of the woman she was says, "I knew it would fuckin' work this good."

With no hair to soften her cheeklines, jaw, and neck Dee is all face. And there the personal heap of her appetites cannot be hidden. What she has memorialized in word and deed is now measurably defined.

"The blood in the car—"

"I'm gonna teach them all a fuckin' lesson. It's one I just learned." She twists the gun out of her daughter's hand. "And since you were fuckin' stupid enough to come back after I told you not to, you will learn it too."

She pushes through the darkness closer to her only born and with those protruding bones caught on the cutting edge of half shadows Dee Storey looks to be a hand-painted diablerie sprung from the book of hours.

"And you know what that lesson is, raggedy girl?" There's the viper in her voice. "Never count out the dead."

PART
FOUR

THE
ULTIMATUM

FIFTY
SIX

―――――――

"Get off your goddamn ass and don't touch the lights." Dee turns and works the dark along the bar. The first liquor bottle she finds, she pours from. "You wanted to be rid of all this, I arranged it. I gave you money. I set you up with new identification. And what do you do?" She hisses through lipless bleached teeth, "You fuckin' come back."

Shay's buckled shadow rises using the wall. She points to the garage. "The blood." Her voice is a contradiction of moments, "Whose blood is—?"

Dee holds up her left arm awkwardly. "B negative. And straight from the main vein." She eases the arm back down. "Getting all those little shots of xylocaine right wasn't easy. Most of the spots were dead, but others . . ."

She offers Shay the glass: "Have a drink."

Shay looks past the glass to her mother's left arm. Talk about your self-inflicted wounds.

"Shay, remember that night on Laguna Avenue. When we were preparing to go out into the desert. And I told you that killing someone isn't all there is. It isn't even the hardest part. The cleaning up afterward. The details. That's what counts most. That's the difference between escape and discovery."

This little rant disguised as wisdom Shay cuts with, "I remember. I wear the crap you spew like concentration camp victims wear their numbers."

"Well, this is part of afterward. This is me trying to clean up the mess as best I can. And you came back, so you're part of it now."

"Should I be afraid of you, is that what you're telling me?"

"I think you're somewhere between dying and drivin' on. Now, have a drink. 'Cause you look pretty ripped up."

Shay reaches for the glass and sips. "I hate gin."

"Why, Shay? Why did you come back?"

"Maybe I don't like your friends trying to have their way with me."

"My friends. Are we gonna start trading punches? I don't have any friends. I never did. I only had you, remember."

Dee tries to take another drink but her bad arm jerks slightly.

"Is this another one of your manipulations, like you warned me about?" asks Shay. "Is that what is happening? Is this another part of your manic dance?"

"What manipulation? I told you not to come back. You kill yourself, don't blame me."

Dee holds her left arm and starts up the hall. She wants her daughter to smother for a little while in what she's said. She tries to point toward the bathroom beside the door to the garage. "I thought leaving the water running was a nice touch. Like somebody tried to clean up in a panic and just forgot." Dee slides down the floor. Gets her back against the wall, "You've seen Burgess?"

"Yes."

"Did he say he was here?"

"He said he wasn't."

Dee shakes her head. "Your name and fool have the same amount of letters. He was here right after I didn't show for Foreman. I only wish Burgess did a head on with the mailman right there in the driveway. I think some of my sutures popped. Help me off with my coat."

Shay does not come forward to help. "I don't understand why you're doing all this."

Dee opens her coat and shoulder eases the sleeve down far enough to slip it off. "I've had Burgess' phone tapped for a long time. His office phone too. Even dear Harold's phone. And getting that one tapped was no easy trick."

She cradles the arm in her lap. "That last night, when you told me I better get some new dreams 'cause I was being sized up for some very black times. I heard you. And you were right."

Dee's arm is bandaged from the wrist to the elbow. New plots of blood wet the white gauze. "Burgess went to Daddy the next day. Dear Harold was into sizing us up for some very black times. Not just me. But me and you. He even suggested Burgess talk to Charlie about their 'mutual problem.' "

Shay starts up the far wall toward her mother.

"It was unraveling, Shay. Ever since the screamers and idiot boy got photographed downtown. I did my best to hold it together, but we were unraveling."

"Talk about selective memory. You're an altered state, do you know that. We've been unraveling since you took your first breath."

Dee jabs a foot at Shay. It catches bone. Makes a hammer on clapboard sound. But Shay doesn't cave. She comes right back and her boot strikes kraitlike at Dee's bad arm. The blow is clean on and Dee screams out. She slings in the bad arm and her bony skull slumps in a grimace. Her throat gets small as a pipette, trying to grab breaths and speak at the same time.

"Stitchin' . . . your own . . . arm . . . is no easy . . . gig. 'Cause you . . . got one hand . . . to . . . do it. That part I . . . didn't think . . . through. I should have . . . cut my leg." Her strychnine-thin body angles up. A cord of slow, slow, slow breaths. The top of that burned white head shakes off the pain. "I couldn't be too straight or . . . too juked out on . . . speed. One way I had the tremors and the other . . . way it might look like some amped Dr. Frankenstein had operated on me."

Her long neck dips toward the wound. She takes the next few moments to work the wrapping loose. As the white gauze thins blood streams out onto Dee's fingers.

"You've got to be with the real. You've got to know you can do a vein, but not an artery. The how deep and where."

Shay steps back, tries to buy a little more dark. She does not want to see. 'Cause this is some kind of masochistic freefall. Dee could have just as easily put a needle into her arm and vampired a liter's worth of blood and spilled the living shit out of it without this inverted bloodletting.

An incarnate anger is set off within Shay. A sense that the whole experience she's viewing she lived too much once already and here it's around for a second try at her being.

"I won't listen to your weirded out, half warning shit."

"You'll listen if you want to come out of this alive. Now get me a towel for my arm."

Shay holds close to the wall and nothing more. Dee struggles to her feet letting the wound bleed on the carpet. Her coat hangs from her other shoulder. As she passes her daughter she says, "Don't fill your mouth up with my blood so fast, you may choke on it when you find out what I have to tell you."

"I don't want to hear that carny talk anymore."

Dee moves around the bar in the dark, "When this falls apart, as we know it will, who's gonna eat most of the blame. Ridden . . . Foreman . . . they will try to cut a deal on my back, this time. If I'm to die, it's better I did it by my own hand. Don't you think? Let them work it out then when the DA is up their ass."

Under the bar Dee finds a towel. Standing she presses it against the wound. "This whole thing is on the verge of being ratted out and we both know it. Right . . . right?"

"That's right," Shay whispers.

Dee comes around so she is right beside her daughter. She wants to be close enough to literally control her personal space.

Dee's voice drops down to a bare flame. "It was the only way I could see, for me, alright . . . to maybe . . . maybe get out of this. I couldn't keep it together with the Riddens and Foreman. Call me fuckin' desperate if you want, but that's how it is."

This is the old carpet ride. The quiet reasoning before the dead reckon.

"Reach into the upper left coat pocket for my speed, will you?"

Shay can see it just beneath Dee's face. She never learned to hide that ferocious mean to will. Shay only hopes she won't be that easily read. The jacket leather rustles like dried skin until Shay finds the speed.

"Open them, will you?"

Shay opens the vial. It is rimmed with amphetamines.

"I told you I tapped their phones. I know what Ridden said to Foreman about you being there to see the papers before Burgess delivers the money."

Shay does all she can to hold onto her calm. To keep it so her face muscles don't quiver or flex because inside she is trembling. It is as if the ground that makes Shay up is moving with her mother. This story, she knows by heart. There is a trap being set for her.

"You want all fifty or what?"

"One will do nicely."

Dee holds the towel in the crease of her folded arm. Shay drops a single amp into Dee's slightly bloody palm.

"I hear two people were killed in the desert."

Quietly, very quietly, Shay answers, "Yes."

Dee pops the speed then sends it down with a little gin. "I hate gin myself. So you frightened Harold Ridden. Alright. But what are you about?"

Shay closes the vial and slips it back in the coat pocket just above Dee's heart. She then zips the pocket closed. "I am going to burn them."

Dee flexes her bad arm. "Tell me about Vic."

"He lived, if that's what you're asking."

Dee's tongue strains against the inside of her lower lip. "That's what I was asking. And what have we learned about Vic?"

"Vic wants the papers."

Dee draws out the words, "And that's all?"

Shay takes the glass from her mother's hand and steps around her. She fills the glass with water from the bar sink. She drinks.

"And how was this to be accomplished?"

"After Burgess left with the papers," says Shay, "he'd be taken."

"And you were going to help Vic?"

"I am going to help him."

"Whose idea was this?"

"Mine."

"Welcome to Camelot," says Dee.

Shay takes another drink of water.

"You are desperate, aren't you?"

Shay puts the glass down. From question mark to question mark Dee is closing in. "Yes," says Shay, "I am. I am desperate to earn a little self-respect."

"Ohhhhhhhh, that!"

"I've been down so many alleys with you I got lost. But I'm not some cardboard figure without an existence. And not something to be shaped into the approximation of a human being. I won't quietly stand by while you handcuff my future to yours. I won't allow the utter annihilation of myself for the future of Dee Storey." Then Shay gets right in her mother's face and begins to say in sign: "I read you, even when you're not speaking, and I won't end up another hole you fill."

Her mother returns the favor. Her wire-thin fingers work in harsh time to tell Shay, "You'll find out soon enough what a good choice of words that was." Then she speaks, "Good thing I'm already dead. This way I can look out for you. Now, what is it you want here?"

"We know Foreman may try to kill us when we come to see the papers. We want to find out where all this is to take place, if we can. That way, we'll be prepared. That way, it won't be like it was in the desert."

"Not like the desert. No, not like the desert."

There is an altogether oblique tone to Dee's words.

"And I thought," says Shay, "that since you were to meet him somewhere—"

"I might have left a map stuck to a wall with huge neon arrows pointing the way? You're a fuckin' joke."

"And you're a vulture in the middle of a manipulation. You're circling me in the dark. If you want to exploit me, land so we can get on with it."

"A joke with a saddle on her back."

"Viva Verboten."

"Alright. When Foreman was out on bail back in '87 he used to meet Alicia at a house in San Frasquito Canyon. They split their place in Chatsworth, which you probably already know. Vulture that I am, I've been doing a little circling. The house where I was supposed to meet them is the same house. It's where they are now."

"I want the address."

"Who is asking? My daughter . . . my ally . . . or my enemy?"

"Your daughter would be too afraid to ask. Your ally wouldn't need to ask. And your enemy just plain wouldn't ask at all."

"How did I get to deserve my own little declaration of independence?"

As the bleeding has almost stopped Dee tightens then ties the towel around her arm. She lets the arm stretch out and begins to coil and uncoil the fingers. "Talk about going exile. You want me, to help crime them. You need me, to help cut their throats publicly."

"The only crime I intend to commit is the one that sets me free," says Shay.

Dee's fingers keep coiling and uncoiling. "In that we are a pair, raggedy girl."

"What do you want?"

"I want the money. I have nothing. I gave it all to my daughter, ally, enemy. My—" The speed is starting to move Dee's blood around and the muscles along her nostrils and eyes pulse as if they were slightly possessed. "If Foreman lets you walk out of there, go. I'll throw a surprise party for him later. If it isn't that simple, you'll see what it means to fuckin' need me."

"What else do you want? Do I run you a bath? Gas your car up along the way?"

Dee answers as if what she had to say was purely an afterthought, "One of us has to kill Vic."

Shay's body flexes.

Dee reaches for her motorcycle jacket on the bar, "One of us has to fill that hole with Vic."

"Where are you going with this?"

Dee gets one sleeve on. "Things will be happening so fast I probably won't have the chance so—"

Shay tears at the coat. "Where are you going with this?"

"One of us has to—this time."

Shay's mind does a hard stop. "What do you mean, 'this time?' "

The merciless current known as her mother takes all the time she wants getting on her jacket. But Shay isn't going to wait out the hand-sounds of the leather, "What did you mean, 'this time?!' "

"Because eventually Vic will find out, if he doesn't know already, that it was you and me who dumped him into that grave in the Mojave."

The statement is a lightning blow from the horizon line right into Shay's heart.

Dee now, her head cocked to one side on that scarecrowed neck, before her daughter: "He's John Victor Sully."

Shay tries to clear the disbelief. To clear the body snatched shock. To understand—

"Do you want to be hammered into the ground like a fuckin' nail? Understand now what he's here for!"

"Are you lying?"

"Ask him! Go on! Then see if you can get out of the way of the first shot!"

Shay is a short circuit trying to merge man and memory.

"You're not some cardboard figure without an existence," Dee snaps. "No!"

Was the man inside me the boy fighting death in short gasps?

"You won't stand there quietly while I handcuff your life to mine! No, you'll let Vic do it!"

A despair hits that only complete obliteration could ease.

"You won't end up another hole I fill!"

For seconds Shay is deaf to her mother's screams.

"I told you not to come back. I gave you money. I gave you a chance. I was trying to save your life."

When did she know? Why didn't she tell me? Why—

"You failed the first time, that's why we're here!"

Shay slips to the floor. She pulls her knees up to her chest. Dee is down at her fast, her hands crimping Shay's face like some instrument that measures weakness.

"There's nowhere to fall after this."

Everything within Shay is becoming needlehole small. Her eyes close. There's not even space for a bubble of air. She is back in the trunk of that Granada where she belongs. Speeding away from any chance of connection. She starts to cry. Tears that reek with failure. She breaks through the sobs with, "It must be good to know that you've destroyed me again. That you've left something toxic and ruined in your wake."

Dee pulls Shay's face to hers. Flushed hot skin against an only child's tears. The moment is empathic and surreal as Dee practically pleads, "Would I tell you the truth to destroy you? Would I give you the money and let you go if I meant to dirt you? There's only here and now . . . or I can't help you. Please, don't be stupid."

THE TRAP

FIFTY
SEVEN

In short time, when Shay becomes subdued, she says, "You sent me out into the desert with him to die."

"I didn't know it was him until later."

"But if you even suspected?"

"No answer necessary."

"Not even a word to me for my own protection."

"No answer necessary."

They both hole up in their small stretch of darkness.

"I know it was you who fired into my house."

Dee Storey is insidiously quiet, so it's left to Shay, "No answer necessary?"

"At least," says Dee, "we each know now who we are."

Come morning Vic and Shay meet at DIS. The sky is a gray damp California fall before the burnoff. The air thick with mist and mildew. Shay waits in her Jeep with steaming coffee and a cigarette. Vic crosses the lot where the few cars and trucks are like small arks docked in a runny cloud. He gets in the Jeep carrying a faded blue jean coat.

"You don't look well," he says.

"I got my period and no sleep. So let's just say I'm not fit for human consumption."

"Did you find out anything?"

Her whitish face in the rearview mirror, the pale undertow of her eyes. A look that at its core is labored and lost.

"Yes, I did."

Vic is on a payphone to Landshark by the coffee shop door. "San Frasquito Canyon. Do you know it?"

Landshark swings around his worktable to a shelf piled deep with maps. "It's up by Newhall. Where the aqueduct comes over the mountains."

Shay watches Vic from the idling Jeep by the payphone. Does he know? Could he map out his emotions that well through a manipulation? She tries not to feel the sex of his tongue inside her. She lingers on his graying profile to find the face of that boy she obliterated from her mind to survive.

"Shay tells me the Department of Water and Power keeps property up there. Work sheds and a few old houses they rent to employees. Pettyjohn's sister is only a part-time blackjack dealer in Vegas and Laughlin. She's been with DWP for years. She rents one of the houses. And that's where Alvarez and Foreman used to meet secretly when he was out on bail back in '87."

As they talk Shay reaches nonchalantly for Vic's coat. Her fingers trace out the frame of a gun within its folds. She slides the semiautomatic from the pocket.

"How did the girl find all this out?"

Vic glances at Shay, "She didn't tell me."

Her middle finger presses the clip release and it springs into her palm.

"Vic, your voice sounds off. Is something wrong?"

One by one she removes the bullets and reinserts the clip. And not once does her appearance give anything away.

"I can't be sure," he says.

As Vic climbs back into the Jeep he asks, "Do we need to talk?"

Shay's eyes swing past him as she shifts into gear, "We need to drive."

They ride Route 15, striking east for the desert.

Vic ventures one question, "What happened last night?"

Shay looks as if she has surrendered to some unspoken direction when she says, "The violent overthrow of my mind."

Vic huddles back in his seat and prays to the silence—please don't let this be what it feels like.

———

Through the windshield, light falls like an echo across the black garden of that night in the kitchen on Laguna Avenue when Dee prepared to murder John Victor Sully. Shay can see her mother's fingers work the weapon with taut sure moves. In her hand the blue-black monster of a weapon seemed almost childlike. Not something to be feared, but a benign trinket of certain construction and design. Not a creation of terror, but something to be tamed and controlled. Something one could use to hold sway over the tales that feed on her.

But now she realizes, riding back to the grave what she felt facing her mother was true. She was the gun. She was that benign trinket of certain construction and design. That something to be tamed and controlled. That something one could use to hold sway over the tales that feed on her. Last night was no different. She was being taken apart and wiped clean for the next killing.

Landshark is at his computer talking to Rog through a headset. Terry is sitting on the desk behind him laying out for Freek over the phone what he's got to get done. "San Frasquito Canyon is about a fifteen-mile run from Copper Hill Drive in Saugus north to Lake Hughes. It's mostly national forest. A few isolated farms, homes." Terry glances at Landshark. "He's getting ready to fax you a couple of maps."

Landshark gives him a thumbs-up sign, then to Rog: "You got the camcorder. And enough tape? Get fifty hours' worth." Back to Terry: "He'll be on his way in five minutes."

"Freek, Rog ought to be rolling up to your place in about half an hour. Now first, I want you to video the road. Slow up one side, south to north. Down the other side . . . what do you mean can Rog drive? He's bipolar not blind."

Landshark gives Terry a handsignal Rog is at best, a so-so driver. "He's a great driver," says Terry. "Does he have a license?"

Landshark runs a hand across his throat. No license. "Of course, he's got a fucking license," says Terry.

Vic counts off town after town toward Barstow. Through waves of heat the specter of a flashing ambulance light coming toward them. As it rushes past, the chilling whine of its siren sends Vic back through the tunnel of his life. "Where are we going?"

She looks at him hard, "Baker."

The inside of that windblown Jeep has gotten small as a cupboard in a prison cell. And when he can, Vic moves his hand across the bundled insides of his coat to find the gun.

The day is flat-out beautiful. The sand's color true to the light it is given. To the north and east mountains rise to snowbroken peaks, but Shay's stare points toward one spot.

Baker, California. Down Below, as it is in this case, aptly named. The Jeep glides into the exit, like an endless wheel of cars before it, and cars to come.

The Davenport is still there, though now it's painted blue. And the dirt lot where he sat in his police cruiser has since been paved. Shay turns onto Kelbaker and begins the long winding drive south into the Mojave National Preserve.

Vic's heart is filling with black blood. He holds his gun where she can't see it. Once again child and stranger, stranger and child are moving into the far reaches. And all those scotch and Percodan newsprint moments begin to drown his mind with poison.

Each mile leaves Vic more doubled up than the last. He is ready this time, but to what end? Shay slows to find her way. Her breathing is erratic, awful. Her face sweaty and white finds a sign: INDIAN SPRINGS TRAIL. She leans into the turn and the Jeep skids slightly but continues.

Long silent, running down that alluvial fan with the ground cracking under the tires. Down they go, where there is nothing but silence. Silence and a world working its way out flat and rutted where no one will hear a scream or a cry. Where graves weather forgotten. Where people fall to time.

Shay is hunched into the wheel. Great boulders, the dark outcroppings of that night, own pieces of the roadside. Her hands are griplocked as she guides the Jeep's rise and fall over dry wash gravel. Everything inside the cab clatters or slides across the dash.

She drives and drives. Even with all that sun and sky Vic feels like he is moving through a black wave. A slow rise and the Jeep descends on game shocks into an open wash and stops.

The wind takes the tires' dust and spreads it like dry filthy rain across the skyline where it veils and falls across the hood and black canvas top. They are now again as they were.

Shay rests her head on the steering wheel. "Have you ever been entirely honest with someone?" she whispers.

Before he answers he slides the gun from his pocket. She steps out of the car. She moves along her side of the engine. It is hot from the long drive.

"Is this the spot?" she says.

He moves up his side of the hood, using it as cover.

"Is this the goddamn spot?!" Her voice is frantic.

Without taking his eyes off her he does his best to see. Shadows move like dark water across the landscape, depths of light and dark that deceive the eye of shape and symmetry. The earth is working at the tricks of its trade to bring about tomorrow.

His voice barely carries, "Yes."

She flings the bullets from his gun across the engine. They ping and scatter. As he catches one in his free hand she slams her Guardian down on the hood.

He stares at the weapon in her hand. She is holding the gun so tightly her skin is white and bloodless.

"Are you here to meet me . . . hit on me . . . or stalk me?"

"Both of us," he says, "know better than that now, don't we?"

She bangs the gun down on the hood a second time. The sound moves up hollow through her arm.

"Are you going to kill me, again?" Vic asks.

Her heartshaped mouth squeezes down into a bloodspot of pain. Her head drops to the engine. She can feel its heat against the crown of her skull. "I can't stay in here." Her chest constricts, "I can't." Her mouth wires out into a gasp, "I can't stay in here." Her face comes up crying and ashamed, flooded in defeat and recognition. "I can't stay in here. Do you understand?" She hits her hand against her chest and her voice breaks down. "I can't."

She slings the gun across the hood and it sleighs right into Vic's hand. She stands back. "It was me that night."

To hear those words.

"It was me who . . . who led you here so my mother could kill you."

The spare cadence of her steps. Her face looking over the broken edges of that ravine.

The sheer anger that he is being used somehow overtakes him. That he is being tempted to decide between pathos and pure hatred.

She slumps to the sand like some acolyte at the altar of her own death.

He drops her Guardian. He starts the slow descent into the pale cave where the worst he is and could be waits. He takes the bullet he caught and slips it between his teeth. All those years gone and he has never really left this place. Have you ever been truly honest with anyone?

He springs the semiautomatic clip into his fist. He can hear the question in the cracks of his breathing. He hasn't. Not even with himself. He sets the bullet right and home. He isn't like Landshark; no . . . he is Landshark, a boundary walker trapped inside the self of past. He locks the clip back where it belongs.

Pathos or pure hatred. Selfish need or the need for something more. He starts across the wash. Karen Englund was right. He is afraid. He is a man willed to himself from the cast-off ideals and wars of others. A fraud of black-and-whites trapped in a black and white cruiser shell collecting license plates.

His shadow moves across Shay's huddled back, the weight of all things bears down on him. The inner mountains of pain and understanding. He is afraid of the demands of a world that strips you down and wants you bare and vulnerable to every wound and every hope. That preaches you must forgive a universe held together by faults. That the road to innocence is paved with one's own blood. What he knows, he will not acknowledge.

The sobbing face beneath the black metallic barrel is not a fuckin' child angel crying in some photograph. He will not let that idea poison the rage. His long arm is about to bring testimony and revenge. To bring justice, that is what his will tells him, bring justice.

He snaps the bullet into the chamber. He knows that to be something more, a part of John Victor Sully must be laid to rest. The devastated human being he was, was everything he needed to birth a man. The horror he survived was the true womb that bore him. He knows it is the faults of the world that teach us about the faults within ourselves. But he can't face that now. It is an accumulated warning of ministries he will close his ears to, because he knows what it will ultimately ask of him. So, he tries to stare past the self-inflicted wounds that muscle the grip of his gun. His aim is on the easy end.

Not once does she ask forgiveness. Not once does she plead for pity. Is it some fuckin' ruse that words like "I'm sorry" do not rise from her lips? Even as a cheap con. Isn't she slick enough to work those good old-fashioned whorish excesses for her own survival? Or is this her version of the turn on the turn?

There is a truth before him he doesn't want to see. He clenches his mind against it. But it speaks to him in a language he understands too well. It is in the geography of a face drenched with gruesome lost hope, a face that shows a trapped human being who has tried to eat through the bones of itself to be free. Yeah, child and stranger belong here. Child and stranger are the perfect set piece of how one moral wound is born and lives and kills.

He grabs her by the hair.

Every wound and hope is waiting.

He pulls her head back.

They sit on the lip of the ravine like spectators in the Colosseum of life with their fingers poised up or down. Up or down.

He sets the gun beside her skull.

In the glare and silence of sunlight he must now decide on what he needs, in order to be.

A tearing wind makes him blink. Then, he fires.

FIFTY
EIGHT

———

An explosion. A jet stream avalanche of sound against her ear, against her skull. The world lifts. She grabs at the side of her head and screams through a long deafening hole of sheer pain that burns the nerve endings and shatters the eardrum.

Her whole body turtles in on itself as she tries to survive a thousand small cyclones that knife blade across the inside of her brain.

Terry is pressing a thumb into his temple and talking on the phone to a friend who owns a little company called Sidewinder and Son, which specializes in surveillance goodies.

"I'm running a gig up in San Frasquito Canyon. Know it? Good. I need to keep three cars in contact. A key. And two watchers. The watchers minute-to-minute the road. Yeah, I'm a little concerned about cellulars up there."

Landshark enters his office. Reads that thumb imprint just behind Terry's eye socket and heads for the bar.

"Shortwave . . . yeah. I'd have to give it a test run. When? . . . now. Yeah . . . now, as in fifteen minutes ago. Drain the snake and let's get it on."

He hangs up. Landshark holds up a bottle of Excedrin. "Freek says he's got plenty of good video on that DWP cul-de-sac." Terry nods. "He even snagged somebody coming out of the Pettyjohn place."

He flips Terry the Excedrin. "He also wants me to update you on the fact that Rog has no license and he already sideswiped one guard-rail and Freek's seriously thinking of beige boxing your ass for fuckin' with him."

Terry pours out four Excedrin and downs them with a beer chaser. "You want to explain to me why most people who are really good at what they do, I mean really good, turn out to be such whining fucks?"

"Are you asking me because of my Thomas Mann knowledge of human subtleties or because I am a whining fuck?"

" 'Cause you're a Thomas Mann whining fuck. And who is Thomas Mann anyway?"

The pain inside Terry's head is a rip, so he decides to just finish off the beer in one prolonged swallow.

"Don't you know," says Landshark, "with your background in illicit drug taking, that could be a stroke coming on and not a headache."

"If a stroke is what it takes to shut out all your chatter, bring it on. But until then," Terry uses a pencil to draw Landshark's attention to a map of San Frasquito Canyon he's been marking up. "There, almost in the middle of the canyon is that DWP cul-de-sac. You heard me talking about getting shortwave radios. Here's my idea."

He runs the pencil south along the thin stretch of road to where San Frasquito ties into Copper Hill Drive. "Most of the canyon traffic, what little there is, will be coming from Copper Hill north. We put Rog in one car with a shortwave radio. Then . . ."

The pencil cuts across the canyon to a curve of road north of the cul-de-sac. "Somewhere here we station Freek. He's not in his car. It'll be nearby, but he'll have a shortwave radio. His job is to be able to watch any traffic coming from the north and to watch whoever goes in and out of the cul-de-sac.

"Now. You and I will be in a third car. Understand. You and I." Terry stares at Landshark who seems a little pale at the reality that is closing in on him, but he nods weakly.

"I hear you."

"You and I will be in a third car somewhere just north or south of the cul-de-sac where we can hide and wait. We'll have shortwaves in the car and be able to hear everything from Rog and Freek.

"We'll know what Ridden is driving. We'll know when they go into that cul-de-sac and we'll know when he comes out. And which way he's driving. But since south is closer to his home, my guess is he'll head south."

"And hopefully he'll have the papers," says Landshark.

"He better have them. 'Cause when Freek cues us, we move."

"How do we take them from him?"

Terry's voice wavers a bit. "I'm not sure yet. It better be fast and it better be clean. That's why I want Rog and Freek watching for traffic."

Terry glances up at Landshark. His face looks particularly strained. "If this doesn't go right things could get very, very ugly."

Landshark starts rubbing his fingers together and seems particularly uncomfortable in his own skin. "What if this isn't the place? What if they have somewhere else set? And we're making a plan that—"

"Why do you think it feels like somebody planted a soldering iron in the middle of my skull?"

Shay lays in the sand for an hour rocked by pain, a floodgate siren burning inside her left ear.

Vic sits against a large rock with the sun to his face, letting the fall heat put a faint burn of color back into his cheeks.

Shay silently sits up and looks around. Dazed and woozy she struggles to her feet and Vic watches her cross the dry wash to where he sits. She climbs the few feet of rubbled earth and slips down beside him.

Across that short space of light each stares into the face of the other. With all that brought them there, disasters unfit for any age of life, they're badly spent and sorry gestured. She leans down and rests her head upon his thigh. He does not push her away.

They remain just so, with the desert quiet holding all about them. With a landscape of tortured extremes that is itself a manifestation of beauty.

Vic finds he needs to talk, wants to talk but what comes into his head is either fragmented or rudimentary until: "I need an answer to something."

She does not move. He looks down at her.

"You never even asked me to forgive you."

"I can't hear out of my left ear. Will I be deaf?"

"I wasn't strong enough to forgive you without hurting you in some way."

She closes her eyes, "I can accept all that as long as you come with it."

His voice wanders back to, "You didn't even ask me to forgive you."

"I didn't feel worthy of asking."

He puts his hand out and holds her shoulder. In time her arm reaches up and her long fingers tie themselves around his forearm. He looks down to where the arms cross. A union of milky white flesh and scars. Then to her eyes, those deep black motionless pools, tired but set somewhere on the distance.

He turns his head. He feels the warmth of the rock along his neck. The wind sends small ghosts of dust across the flats. Beyond that are the hills. This is a country that is burying itself in the sand and decay of millennia. He can see it in the slides of earth along the gouged slopes, in the scarred hillfaces where rain and wind have eaten out bone lines. Where sleeks of rock have cracked from moving faults and fallen down upon each other in disordered heaps. Yes, it is a country burying itself in the sand and decay of millennia. But it is also a country that is being reformed, a country being reborn by the fateful will of nature.

He can see that now through the vermillion colors of late afternoon that tint the landscape with a fire. It is something he can hold on to, something that will remain true when life slips out of focus, or when it wrestles free of his grasp. The country of his youth and disgrace, of his past and pain, can be the country of his strength, and of his soul.

He closes his eyes and silently says "thank you" to whatever grace is listening.

Shay grasps Vic's forearm more tightly and says, "My mother is alive."

She can feel his muscles wrestle with the news. She sits. A wave of dizziness takes her, but she holds. Against the fading light his face a wall of distress.

"She was at the house last night. She is a complete burndown. Chopped her hair off, changed its color. She'd even cut her own arm open to leave the blood. I mean from elbow to wrist. She did a slice job on herself."

Vic sits there letting this new reality settle in. "Why?"

"Everything is unraveling and she knows it. She's always had this hyper-sense to stay one step ahead. She knows who you are. She told me last night."

He starts to piece together reasons with actions. He looks across the ravine. A grave once dug, less the man. "Yeah . . . there are advantages to being thought dead." He leans toward Shay, "She told you about me last night."

"Yes."

"That's why you brought me out—"

Shay puts her hand against her chest and repeats what she said before. "I couldn't stay in here, that's why I brought you."

He understands about those holes inside you, holes you just can't close. She presses her head against his chest. "Give me a chance to find you, Vic, and I will work my way there."

He goes to run his hand along her slumping shoulder but hesitates. She remains as she is, betrayed by the human need inside her.

"I swear, I will carry all the pain it takes to get there. But you'll see it's worth it."

Honesty suddenly becomes a simple but frightening web. "If your mother knew who I was, then she must have been willing to send you out into the desert to die."

Shay closes her eyes and can hear her mother's voice across the dark hallway of the night before.

"No answer necessary."

"What does she want?"

"The money." Shay looks up, "That's why she gave me the information about San Frasquito Canyon."

"But that's not all . . . is it?"

"She wants you dead. If she can't do it herself she expects me to do it."

They leave the Preserve after nightfall. They stop in Baker for gas. Shay walks across the street to the Davenport to buy coffee and food for the ride back. Her left ear is a tidal vacuum.

Vic watches her cross the lot where she walked up to his police car eleven years ago. He cannot describe to himself the feelings of looking back at that moment from the perspective he now is. It's as if his lives have begun to merge but have not yet settled in.

The lot is packed with cars. People have set up tables and chairs. Bundled up they watch the heavens with binoculars and video cameras.

When Shay returns, Vic asks, "What is all that about?"

"There's supposed to be a meteor shower tonight that can be seen from here to China."

Shay gets into the car, but Vic keeps staring at the lot. She can well imagine what little memory might be tinkering with his feelings.

"I never really left this place," he says, "not till tonight. Now, I can leave it. Now it's just a part of me, not the one part that owns me."

Soon after they are on the road meteors begin to cut the sky. Vic drives.
They have the blowers on, the top off. They're in a swirl of cold and
heat as great swaths of electric rain jet stream from horizon to horizon.

"Do you think your mother is lying to us about San Frasquito
Canyon?"

"She is capable of anything."

"If you don't see this through as she wants, you know what she
will probably try to do."

Shay keeps staring up at the night white streaks that suppurate the
heavens for seconds. She watches as red and blue star trains cross the
blanket black sea. Vic glances at her.

"Did you hear me?"

"Yes, I heard you. I heard you even before you said it."

Vic has the sudden need to touch Shay. To have contact. His hand
comes across the gearbox and finds her.

FIFTY
NINE

————

Landshark and Terry are locked tight around a monitor running through stacks of video Freek shot of San Frasquito Canyon.

Long, slow, wide POVs through the windshield of a badly driven van. There are few landmarks in the canyon. It's mostly just straights and swerves of road with the occasional ramshackle dwelling or classless overblown two-story box painted California pink. There's a ranch called the Home Stretch. And miles of tall trees with cuts of wide-open brush. The canyon is that rural free-form California of poverty, cash, and isolation. From wall to wall San Frasquito is maybe three-quarters of a mile wide.

The camera rocks a bit into a slow wooded turn. At the high arc of the road a concrete structure back amidst the trees. Freek's voice on the soundtrack: "This is the DWP power plant the ranger down at the fire station told me about. The cul-de-sac should be just up ahead."

The road veers left. The camera pans across the dash, picks up a nervous chain-smoking Rog behind the wheel. The road floats back. Ripples of light through the high trees flood the windshield.

"There . . . there. Slow it down, Rog."

On the west side. A gravel driveway that moves up into the trees. "This must be it." There is an isolated and wild feel. "Alright, William, I'm gonna go up there and make sure it's the right place. If it is, we'll doc it out."

The screen is black. Fade in on Freek's voice: "I got to show you guys something." The van is parked off the road in a dirt field. Rog sits on the bumper smoking. Freek is way back videotaping a hill beyond the van. It cuts across three-fourths of the canyon west to east. It is maybe seven stories high. "You guys notice anything weird about that hill?"

He pans left. He pans right. It is mostly just short grass and brush. Terry and Landshark glance at each other without a clue. The camera begins to zoom toward the hilltop. "What do you guys notice up there?" asks Freek.

Close enough now. The long lens picking what seems to be rubble then runs the length of the ridgetop. It looks to be concrete with iron lathe rods protruding at insane angles, and oddly broken concrete stanchions. What looks like the collapsed hull of a bridgetower. "Remember your history, William . . . 1927 . . . The St. Francis Dam Disaster . . . San Frasquito Canyon."

Cut to black. Slow fade-in. We are at the top of the hill looking down at Rog and the van. Rog gives the camera the finger. The camera lifts and pans. We look out the length of that hill.

Freek's POV of the remains of a concrete parapet. A cement roadway ten feet wide that looks to have been torn asunder by catastrophe and time.

"This was Mulholland's last earthen dam," says Freek. "The completion ceremony was held on New Year's Eve day in '27. Remember any of this shit, William? Then everyone went home and that night the dam collapsed. This is the earth part of that dam."

Terry is counting clock. Frustrated at sitting through some fucking history lesson he goes to fast forward when Landshark stops him.

Cut to black. Slow fade at the edge of the hill looking straight down at San Frasquito Canyon Drive, which cuts its north-south line at the bottom of the precipice. Just east of the road is a stream that sidles the canyon wall. The wind whips hard this high up and the camera manages only a shaky zoom down toward cracked white concrete mounds the size of large homes the stream has to slip around as it courses south.

"I'd like to put a boot down Freek's throat for wasting our time," says Terry.

"This is where the concrete part of the dam was," says Freek. "This is where it gave way. The roadbed is built right where it collapsed. This is where five miles' worth of backed-up water blew through and killed four hundred people in Newhall. Talk about your faulty construction, William. Talk about your forgotten disasters."

The camera widens to capture the open expanse of canyon where once seven stories' worth of reinforced cement a hundred yards across was blown outward.

"I'm sure," says Freek, "Terry is ragging my ass for this little sidebar, but I have my reasons."

The camera swings south. Frames up the road. "Alright, Terry, get your hands off your padded cock and watch this." Freek works a slow zoom and pan following the roadway up past the DWP station. He walks across the matrix of that rubbled dam ridgetop and picks up San Frasquito again as it arcs west and passes the cul-de-sac. Then he zooms in tighter till the untouched light picks up a few rooftops and a long white row of sheds. "That's where Pettyjohn's place is. Get it now, Terry. You put me up here with a shortwave radio I can track every car moving up and down the canyon."

"So that's San Frasquito," says Vic. Both men turn suddenly as Vic walks into the office. "It looks like Freek did a good job."

Landshark eyes Terry. "That's just what Terry was saying."

Terry's eyes slide past that comment to Vic, "Where have you been?"

"The Mojave National Preserve."

Landshark hits the mute button on the remote. Vic goes to the bar, pours coffee then spikes it with scotch. He walks to the worktable and slumps down into a seat.

For a few seconds he watches the video play on as the camera begins a slow crawl up the cul-de-sac, then he turns his attention to Landshark. "The other night. Out there on the road when we talked and you said in the end I'm going to have to know who she is and then I'd be confronted with what I'm going to do and who I'm going to be after that."

"Yes?"

"We know the truth now."

A silence follows that seems to distill Vic's emotions down to a calm exhaustion.

"What happened?" asks Terry.

"She drove me out into the Preserve. She told me who she was, and she handed me her gun."

Vic looks down into his coffee. He drinks. Landshark and Terry wait on Vic to continue but he goes back to watching the screen. The van makes the first turn up the cul-de-sac and there on the right, the camera picks out a small house and just past it a long row of white sheds. While he watches the screen Vic says, "It's like we talked about the other day, Terry. The past just keeps changing on us."

As the van comes around a man walks out the screen door of that old sagging craftsman cottage. The camera pulls back in the van so as not to be seen then, is carried to the back windows where it peeks out. "That old man on the porch," says Vic. "It's Pettyjohn's uncle. He was one of the men who tried to do us out in the desert."

"She gave you her gun," says Landshark. "What did you do?"

"In my own cruel way, I forgave her."

The shock of that word hits both men hard.

"Where is she now?"

"In a motel off Western waiting for Burgess' call." Vic looks from man to man. "If I need a car. Something clean to be put up in the canyon somewhere. Could it be arranged. Even if things happen tonight."

Landshark glances at Terry, he nods.

"There's something else you both need to know which could turn all this on its head. . . ." He puts his coffee cup down as he speaks. "Dee Storey is alive."

SIXTY

Hugh Englund hates San Frasquito Canyon. He hates that creaking dump of a house. Just being there puts a fleshy lump in his stomach, as it was here he first met Charlie Foreman.

"I don't think we should do it. I think the timing is wrong."

Around that underlit room Alicia Alvarez, Foreman, Jon, his uncle, not a look among them in Hugh's favor.

He stands. "Right here in my gut . . . disaster." Foreman goes to say something but Hugh cuts him with, "Charlie, if you tell me I need to get my ballsack squeezed, I swear to Christ—"

Charlie throws up a hand and answers cynically with, "No más. No más."

Pettyjohn walks over to Hugh, who stands alone in the middle of that small living room. Pettyjohn is having a hard time breathing through all the gauze and padding used to hold his shattered nose and cheek in place. "What do you think we should do?"

"We got the papers. Let it sit a few weeks."

Alicia won't hear of it. "One newspaper already threw my name out there. I get a call from *The Daily News*. It's now. I don't want to start answering questions till we're done."

"The paper's getting on it, could maybe be to our favor. We're in control here."

"No . . . no! Charlie! I won't do it!"

"We won't wait," says Charlie.

Pettyjohn asks Hugh, "Give me a better reason not to go."

"I don't like letting the girl walk in here. Or that fuck with her. And what about Storey. What happened? Did she just get sucked off the planet right before she comes to see us?"

"I think Harold Ridden did her," Charlie says. "He practically asked me to."

"Right here," says Hugh, hitting at his guts. "Right here . . . disaster."

He walks out onto the porch. Pettyjohn waves for the others to hold a minute then follows Hugh out.

Under a single spare light are both men. The night cool around them. At the end of the porch a glass mobile twinks with the wind.

"It must be an old cop thing."

"Maybe," says Hugh. "And your uncle. I didn't say it in there but he wants a piece of that girl for what happened to Travis."

"I'll handle him."

Alicia passes the screen door. "We got to make the call."

Pettyjohn comes around fast and slaps at the wire mesh with an open hand right where her face is and she jumps back.

"Just keep it tucked in, honey, alright."

She mouths him down in Spanish then moves on. Pettyjohn turns to Hugh. "We can't stop this show. But maybe we could move things from here. Take it further out. I know this place has a lot of bad vibes. Maybe we just take the close further out."

The silence of the dark, the safety of a cool concrete garage. Burgess sits behind the wheel of his car with his stocking feet pulled up on the seat. Upstairs god the father waits by the phone.

That night in Franklin Canyon, lying in bed while Dee drove Shay to Mexico, he prayed for them all to die. The slow march of wishes has started to come true, a nightmare present from the world to a man who is just cowerings and bluffs on a set of legs.

He looks down at the revolver Dee had given him. Spreading through the fabric of himself, a thought takes hold. There is a second chance somewhere with your name on it. Not just a trading of dependencies but meaningful change.

Staring out the slashed white of his eyes into the shadowed glass of the rearview mirror he makes that definite pronouncement.

Then, from the pitch black flue of the stairwell he can hear the phone ring. And he can feel the test of it begin all the way down in his bloodstream.

"You took him to Baker? To the very spot? And did his whole fuckin' soul crawl?"

"I did," says Shay.

Profiled by darkness Dee's eyelids drag heavily through each blink as she makes frustrated stabs at why Shay had done what she had. "And he just took it up the ass?"

Shay remains as she intends, back against the bureau, standing, arms folded and the edge of her fingers moving the coffin charm. In the motel room next door, canned, heckling laughter from a television.

"Did you do this because you gambled on it insuring his trust, or to keep me in check?"

"As of now," says Shay, "I am the only thing between you and him."

"I see."

Shay sticks with the raw part of the truth but holds a little back: "If he knew you were alive—which he doesn't—you'd be done."

"No. You have it wrong. I'm the only thing between him and you. That's the difference. He needs you to get Foreman and all the rest. But after that—"

"Will be answer enough." Shay reaches for her cigarette burning in an ashtray on the bureau.

Dee tries to fathom this black exchange of moments: "Why didn't you tell him I was alive?"

A reedy gray line of smoke then the slow shaping of words, "I didn't need to lie. You're not alive."

Dee stands. "You want something. That's what we're getting to here." Her face breaks with light as she fingerpicks the blinds. From their window on the second floor balcony of the Harvard House Motel, Dee can see east down Hollywood Boulevard. The neighborhood shops and storefronts now bear Thai names and lettering. And that odd juke of color and cultural iconography is a fuckin' eyesore upon the staid architecture.

"We're back where we belong, aren't we?"

Dee turns, faces Shay.

"In a shabby motel room where you can hear the humpers and the toilets next door. Even Laguna Avenue was better than this. But I'm glad. It's a good place to finish from."

"If it wasn't for you—"

"Don't," orders Shay, using that cigarette like a police baton. "Don't try to turn your life into one of those sixties puke ballads so you can run the table. 'Cause my hearing ain't too—"

The phone rings. It cuts across the silence of dead seconds. Shay answers. "Yeah? Jesus, Burgess, you're choking on your own words. Slow down. We'll be there."

She hangs up.

"Let's hope," warns Dee, "they don't change the location on you. Then you'll see who your survival depends upon."

Shay points to her own heart. "My only hope for survival is right here. And you aren't getting near it this time." Shay stubs out her cigarette. "And I do want something. There's no death card with Vic's name on it, not this time."

It takes all Dee's strength to ride out the rage and get through this narrow exchange. Shay walks around the bed and gets right in front of her mother. "I know for you I have been some kind of deformed security to get you through life. I also know that if something happens to me—"

"Why do you think I brought the police to the Garden of Allah?"

"—you couldn't hold it together. There'd be no one to confess to. To break down in front of. No one to try to intimidate. To dominate. And in your own fucked-up way to love."

"I have been planting evidence against your friend."

"There would be Burgess, yes. But no one who came out of your stomach and was the lucky part of you that got away."

"By the time tonight is over the door will be shut on him."

"Have you heard me?"

Dee's face is that frozen stare used to hold back any cracks.

"I understand the war inside Dee Storey. There's a part of you that fired into my house. That sent me into the desert to die. And there's another part that gave me the money to run. That warned me about who you are. I am your battlefield. I know that."

"I won't give you what you want."

Shay grabs Dee so violently she almost stumbles. She drags her to the mirror. "Look at you. You're coming apart. You're a toxic wasteland looking to hold on. Look!"

The mirror waits upon her stare. Side by side now, mother and child in the fierce turn of memory.

"I'm counting on one thing," says Shay. "That you will remember I came out of your stomach and was lucky enough to get away. And that a part of you needs me to get away so there's some purpose to your wasted life. I'm counting on that, otherwise—"

Dee can't pull away from their image in the mirror. It is as though this memory had taken hold of her and now possessed her. It is as real as anything she has ever felt made of flesh and blood.

Yes, the memory is there to see. To take her back to that moment on Laguna Avenue when they prepared to kill John Victor Sully. Only now she has the chopped down hair and the raggedy clothes and some dark horrible purpose finds its home in the pit of Dee Storey. Her voice, almost shaking, says, "I can't."

"You know," whispers Shay, "there's a part of me that wants to kill you. So I understand. But I also know I might need you tonight. We might need you tonight."

Shay takes her mother's hand and using sign across the palm pleads out the word, "Please ... please ..." Then she bends her mother's hand around her fingers and holds it there.

SIXTY
ONE

Terry's getting the shortwave radios set up in the back seat of the car he's driving when Vic comes out of the house carrying snapshots of San Frasquito Canyon.

"The call just came," says Vic.

Terry slides out of the car, looks at his watch. "Freek and Rog should be up there by now. And the car you wanted is on the way."

"I want to show you something before I go," says Vic, laying the snapshots printed from the video out on the hood. Terry squeezes in where he can see. They start at the road leading up the cul-de-sac then proceed shot by shot north along the west side of San Frasquito. They panorama a stretch of woods from the cul-de-sac to what might be the remains of a fire road or a turnout.

"It's maybe three hundred yards of wood from the DWP inlet to that dirt area there. Hide the car in the brush. That's gonna be my escape route if everything goes terminal."

Vic hands him the photos. Terry squares them up like playing cards. "I have something for you," he says.

Vic follows Terry around to the trunk. He opens it and removes a Kevlar vest modified down into the shape of an undershirt.

"A friend of mine did crack patrol on Pacoima. He had these made so he wouldn't look padded, otherwise he'd a been spiked." He hands it to Vic, "Don't wear a shirt. Cut the sleeves up on your jean coat. Button her up. You won't come across padded."

Vic takes the flak jacket. Both men stare at the black-gray bullet-stopper. They have played the last few minutes as pure matter-of-fact, as if this were just some offbeat outing. But they understand what their false dispassion covers. They are skilled enough to feel with honest gravity what is now just a drive away.

Landshark is faced up to a monitor rerunning video on that long section of hill once part of the St. Francis Dam. As Vic returns to the office Landshark is in thought on how the immeasurables of time have altered the landscape. How a point of tragedy has become an anonymous mile of beauty.

"We should pay tribute to our disasters," he says turning to Vic, "so we don't forget them. A dam . . . a school. It's all part of that one chanson we never seem to get right as a culture. As human beings."

"I have to go now," says Vic.

Landshark stands. "I know. I heard you before on the phone." He sees Vic is carrying his blue jean jacket and the Kevlar vest Terry brought.

Vic tosses the coat across the table, "Could you cut the sleeves up to the shoulder?"

Landshark reaches for scissors, "Are you certain about moving on information from a woman who wants you dead?"

Vic pulls off his shirt.

"Who's exacted her own disappearance. Who sent her daughter to be killed. Who—"

"I don't have the answer you really want."

Vic tosses his shirt on the table and Landshark can see the black aureole of flesh along the ribcage from a bullet wound all those years ago. "And what is the answer I really want?"

"Certainty." Vic slips on the Kevlar vest. "I can't give you that." He begins to tighten down the Velcro straps, "I can only tell you uncertainty is what must be accepted. Even embraced." Once the straps are tight Vic tests his arms for the full range of mobility. "And uncertainty includes chaos. It includes the random shot that marks your death."

At that Landshark sits. A ripple of fear moves across the back of his mind that soon he will have to cross twenty miles of city.

Reaching for his cigarettes on the table, Vic's eyes catch the photo of that crying angel. "You know what you are most afraid of?"

Landshark begins to cut at the sleeve and offhandedly asks, "Tell me?"

"Freedom. And the responsibility that belongs with it. Uncertainty is part of that. Chaos is part of that. Death is part of that." Vic taps the Kevlar vest, "And one of these won't stop them all." He lights a cigarette. Looks at the clock on the wall. Knows he's down to minutes. "All those years in El Paso I could have had a life. But I was an enraged moment in the past. And just like I forgave that girl to move on, you need to forgive yourself to move on."

Landshark stops cutting, and just stares at the half-gone sleeve.

"What was it you said that first night I came here? Something about a chessboard and revenge?"

Landshark is still tied up with the phrase "forgive yourself."

"William, do you remember?"

He goes back to cutting the sleeve, "In ceremonies of the horseman, even the pawn must hold a grudge."

"Well tonight, all pawns will settle up their grudges. Maybe even you."

Landshark begins on the next sleeve. Vic smokes. Again he looks at the clock, then at the crying child. He makes his eyes take in everything around the room. "You can end your prison sentence tonight."

Landshark keeps cutting till he is done. He has no answer.

"I won't see you again after I leave here," says Vic.

He keeps cutting until he is done. He takes a long, long breath. He looks up, and pushes the coat across the table, "What do you mean?"

"If I'm standing . . . I'm gone."

"For where?"

Vic slips on his jean coat.

"With the girl?"

He begins to fasten up the buttons.

Landshark wants an answer but he knows he is being asked to just let it go. "I was hoping you'd know me when I was someone . . ." his voice cracks, "you could be proud of saying was your friend."

Vic walks over and sits on the edge of the table beside Landshark. Landshark's elbows rest on the table, and his upturned hands half hold, half hide his face. Vic leans down.

"If it wasn't for you," he says, "I'd still be in El Paso. I'd be angry . . . lost . . . broken. Certain any control of my own life did not exist. But you found me."

He leans down and holds Landshark as if he were his devoted only brother. "Now listen to me. You've served enough time. Even your parents would say so."

Landshark's face comes up shocked at this jump of a statement and what he feels it implies. He goes to speak, but Vic stops him.

"The past is changing all around us. You don't have to let it own you."

SIXTY
TWO

————

Vic and Shay wait in the same small room where Vic sat with Burgess those nights ago. The waiting is dark time. An unbearable quiet Vic uses to try and think through all the unforeseeable disasters.

"A gun," he says to Shay in little more than a whisper. "A gun. Does Burgess have a gun?"

Landshark steps out of his house. He's confronted with Terry beside an idling car. The driveway out to an opening front gate. And an unnaturally warm night waiting beyond.

He wishes all this did not exist. That he could crawl back inside and pull the calendar up over himself like a blanket.

Instead he grimly tosses the shoulder bag he is carrying in the back, stuffs his long frame down into the shotgun seat and tries to feel and believe the words, "The past is changing."

Vic is showing Shay snapshots of the cul-de-sac and the area just north of it where that other car will be hidden if they need it. Burgess walks into the room, is met with cold silence. Vic gathers in the snapshots.

"What is all that? You can talk in front of me."

They don't. Vic pockets the snapshots.

A simple ride down Mount Washington feels like being in the flat open seat of a runaway roller coaster. Landshark is already in the first waves of panic. His mind is ripping off those lies. Setting the cage around throat and lungs that he is trapped. That he'll go mad unless he gets back home. That his only chance for breath, to avoid a heart attack, to kill the cyclonic knot of brain fears is to run, run and get the front door to the world shut behind him.

He titans down on himself. How strong does your will have to be, in a face-off with your own will?

The phone rings. Burgess stares at the black cordless. It rings again. The third time's the charm.

Shay watches as Burgess listens to the voice at the other end. He reaches for a notepad. He writes. Shay watches as he keeps writing. His hand resembles a smallish trembling bird and Shay realizes her life, Vic's life, in no small part rests in the hands of who that man is.

When they swing down and into the business district lights of Figueroa Street Landshark gasps, "I'm freaking out."

Terry pushes through a changing yellow and onto the Pasadena Freeway. "There's no turning back."

The words hit Landshark in the chest. The speedometer finds sixty and fast. This is like the liftoff of the space shuttle. Your whole being carried helpless into the universe on a million tons of thrust.

Burgess hangs up the phone. "We take the Hollywood Freeway south to the 10. We take the 10 west to Robertson. We get off. Just north of the corner is a coffee shop. We wait in the lot. Foreman will call me on my cellular."

Burgess starts out of the room. "I'll get the money." He stops at the door. "Charlie wants this to be simple and clean. He said he's gonna be watching us to make sure we come alone."

Once Burgess walks out of the room Shay turns to Vic, "If we were going to San Frasquito we'd be driving north on the Hollywood, not south, then west on the 10."

Vic's jaw tightens around that little speech he gave Landshark about uncertainty. "It doesn't look like it," he says.

With every mile Landshark's mind comes up with some new unraveling wish. If only a tire would blow. . . . If a semi should jump the divider. . . . If the earth could just stop rotating on its axis—

He fights this phobic lunacy that lashes at him with a caustic reminder his whole life has been a pledge of undying pain, a promise of relentless suffering, and then, if he's lucky, death in the black throes of despair with a life half-lived and time well spent in vain.

He is back in the airplane hangar. At the cutting edge of his life. Staring at the cotter pins as his father wheels the Navion toward the sunlight.

Burgess comes out of the house carrying two briefcases. Vic and Shay wait by his car. Burgess sets both down on the shotgun seat. Vic asks, "Do you have a gun?"

"What?"

"My mother," says Shay, "gave you one when you moved here."

He tries to look in both their eyes to see what they are thinking. "I lost it."

Vic pushes him against the hood.

"What are you doing?"

He begins a hard frisk while Shay checks the glove box, then beneath the car seats.

"I don't understand. You're treating me like the enemy."

With the hood of that car charging through highway night, rushing toward San Frasquito Canyon, Landshark is dragged back through the dangerous downdraft of that plane as it fell from the sky. He stares at the run of white lines in the road and admits to himself his whole phobic life has been a replay of that one moment of war inside himself when he let his parents die.

His hands bundle up against his face. He can hear Vic, "You've served enough time." He knew. He knew.

Out loud, with scorched invective, Landshark says so Terry can hear, "I've lied to everyone."

Vic rides Burgess' taillights from the Hollywood to the 10.

Shay looks down at the cellular in her hand. "If they moved the location she knows by now. She knows."

Vic glances at the phone. At Shay. "No call tells us nothing."

She places the phone on the dashboard as if trying to get the very thought away from her. She takes up staring at the Mercedes' taillights as it halfbacks from lane to lane. She keeps seeing her mother's face tunneling out of the dark those few hours ago.

Killing isn't the hardest part. It's afterward. That's the difference between dying and drivin' on. Shay closes her eyes. "I'm frightened, Vic. Is it alright to say it?"

With eyes wrapped shut, Landshark walks a tightrope state of mind between panic and calm where, for the first time outside the safety of a closed door, those unhinged shadows of fear can be clearly looked at and touched.

He can see how the man created from the war within himself for letting his parents die helped set in motion the phobic ruination of years that fed the need to create events in his own life, some with hideous results, so he might one day earn the freedom of wholeness.

From keeping files on the wronged, like Vic. Sending Magale Huapaya into danger on the promise of a future. Bringing Vic back to feed on his strength and will. Vic and Terry. Vic and the girl. Rog and Freek. The drive to find the truth behind the story of the crime. He used all those struggles as a catwalk of strength to walk a little further. To be prodded a little further.

Mile after mile. Turn upon turn. This convergence of events he helped create, he can see recreating the war within himself so he could wheel the plane of William Worth out into the light of atonement and become one human being with Landshark in a sky of uncertainty.

The shortwave radio in the back seat crackles with Rog's voice: "Is that you guys? William . . . Terry? Is this fucking radio working?"

Landshark opens his eyes. They are turning into the isolated blackness of San Frasquito Canyon.

The coffee shop parking lot is shabland. Lots of freakboys with their black-stocking chickies. Burgess waits in his aquamarine 560SL. Vic and Shay stand outside their car not ten feet away.

She looks down at the radio clock. It's been a nerve-flinching hour not knowing if they are watched, if they've been checked out, or if this wait is a gloved hand around their throat to make them feel how vulnerable they are.

"I'm sorry, Vic. I'm sorry for my part in making any of this come to be."

The light across her face. Music from a car radio sweeping past.

Her absolute honesty and need. This moment should belong to another time, another place. Vic comes around so Burgess cannot see him take her hand.

As they talk Burgess reaches across the seat and uses this chance to open one of the briefcases and remove the revolver Dee had given him. As he conceals it in the glove compartment he thinks, "Fuck you both."

Up from a ranch gate with a sign that reads THE HOME STRETCH is a shield of trees. Hidden there, they watch the road. The night air is parchment dry, more Indian summer than fall. Landshark is numbly quiescent. Internally too exhausted to feel waves of panic, or sea-level calm.

The wait has been so treacherously long Freek takes up singing over the shortwave. When he starts a nasally riff of "Sgt. Pepper's Lonely Hearts Club Band" Terry shuts him down.

A short course in silence, then Landshark asks, "Can they hear us?"

"No."

"Before, when I said I lied to everyone . . ."

"Yes."

His shame-racked frame leans into the dash and after a moment Landshark says, "I killed them."

Terry's eyes keep to that curve in the road, past the ranch gate where they will be coming from. If they come.

"I saw the cotter pins. A part of me wanted to stop them, but the other part. And I knew I could get away with it. If you call my life getting away with it."

Every breath of that dry canyon air sends electric pin burns through the system. "I lied to Vic. But I think he saw right through me."

Landshark reaches for his shoulder bag. Retrieves a bottle. "What is that," Terry asks.

"It's either cognac or acetone. I can only hope it's acetone." Before drinking, Landshark questions Terry, "All these years, did you know I was lying?"

Terry turns to him, "Yes, William, I—"

The shortwave cuts in. Rog's hyped-out voice: "I think this is them. Two cars just turned into San Frasquito. Can you hear me?"

THE
MURDER

SIXTY
THREE

Dee Storey once told Shay she thought San Frasquito Canyon was the perfect hiding spot for covens and corpses. Tonight she will prove to be correct on both accounts.

Pettyjohn, Foreman, and Alicia walk behind a flashlight down the porch steps of the Craftsman Cottage. Dee watches from deep cover as they cross the gravel driveway tailorwise, step up a fieldstone abutment, then continue over damp lawn towards a two-story house the DWP has under renovation.

Burgess follows Vic and Shay into San Frasquito. The canyon road is a turning shore constantly moving away from the headlights. An unreachable illusive hollow.

When they pass a farm gate with a sign saying THE HOME STRETCH, Vic looks for and finds that shield of trees off the road.

"Is that where they are?" Shay asks.

"I hope so."

A smell of sage is thick about the brush-swept darkness where Dee moves from shadow to shadow, trying to close in on that small grouping around the flashlight. By the time she is close enough to hear them talking, a door closes and the light is swallowed.

Terry's eyes follow the headlights until they stream off into a curve. He hits one shortwave toggle switch: "Rog, everything coming up this canyon I got to know about." The next toggle switch: "Freek, we're in it now." He turns to Landshark, who is holding onto the door handle for dear life. "I hope," says Landshark, "we all get a chance to celebrate the first anniversary of my death as a fraud."

The flashlight climbs steps. Moves down a second-story hallway stacked with sheetrock. Enters a bare bedroom of open slatted walls. Frames up a single chair by the window.

Pettyjohn turns to Alicia, hands her a cellular, "You'll watch from here. You see anything that looks off you call us."

She stares nervously at Charlie. "You'll be alright," he says. She glances out the window toward the gravel driveway where the cars will stop. As she says, "Let's go over everything one more—." Charlie whispers, "Wait . . . I think I heard something."

Their faces focus in on the swimmy wheel of light Pettyjohn points through to the hallway.

The sky is moonless above the canyon walls. A black expanse touched by only a few stars and trimmed with jagged ledges and treetops. Shay has seen that gunmetal-colored sky before on a desert night.

"Whatever happens," says Vic, "I'll make sure you're alright."

Shay turns to Vic. Burgess' headlights cut a glary path between them. "What do you mean you'll make sure *I'm* alright?"

The flashlight sweeps an empty living room, a dining room where construction gear is stacked up and waiting for Monday. The light leaves rips of darkness in its wake. Dee sucks in her breath. Holds so motionless she can feel fireburns where the speed has turned the heat up on her system.

"Nothing," says Pettyjohn. "Will Alicia be alright?"

Foreman looks up at the ceiling. "She'll have to be."

Freek on the shortwave: "This is Freek coming to you from the top of the late St. Francis Dam. I see their lights, boys."

Terry is checking his gun, "Asshole."

Freek again starts riffing, "We're Sgt. Pepper's Lonely—"

Landshark, fighting to stay grounded, grabs at the toggle switch, "Shut down that wimp-ass nasal shit, alright."

Freek's answer is to keep on singing, "We-hope-you-will-enjoy-the-show."

Four men are spread across the cottage living room anchored together by a desk lamp near the fireplace. Only a screen door separates them from the night to come.

Hugh looks over this menagerie of acute tensions that have shaped out in the stark phrasing of each physical body. The old man staring at the floor like something just pulled from a crypt. Charlie Foreman trying to balance scissors on the tip of a single blade.

One more time Hugh tries, "We could just let them walk."

Vic can feel the intangible meanings of his life move inside him as he turns up the driveway. In the climbing headlights every thought traces itself back to the beginnings of his existence. In the breathless quiet as they ride a slow turn into the cul-de-sac life becomes about ultimate resolutions. In the tires scratching on gravel, devil sounds he remembers, that score out every inch of his soul. What began in Baker, what had been preordained before that, and before that, and was about to be.

The old man's colorless face, closest to the door, says, "They're here."

As Alicia sees the first hint of lights star the glass, a penny-sized coldness presses into the back of her neck.

A half turn. A gloved hand across a mouth. Eyes that drown in terror at the burnt visage before her.

A voice thought dead whispers, "Welcome me home, cholla."

With binoculars Freek can see headlights ripple through the trees. A patchquilt of lights that stop, then go out set by set. Car doors open. Small islands of domelight in that far black bay. Human forms stand into the night. Car doors close.

On the shortwave Freek relays what he sees then just to play with Terry and Landshark's heads a little more he riffs: "We're Sgt. Pepper's Lonely Hearts Club Band . . . Sit back and let the evening go."

———

Alicia is pulled into the dark, pleading. Across a rubble-strewn floor, into a far room where this tough mouth turned sobbing clit is driven to the floor amidst paint cans.

Burgess looks up into the cul-de-sac. A hundred yards back is a line of trees the road curves behind toward a few isolated lights.

Burgess turns to Shay and Vic. "They wouldn't try anything here," he says; "not here."

Dee wedges a filthy rag in Alicia's mouth. Gagging, she is turtled over to one side. Her hands are bound behind her with more rags. She is then forced onto her stomach as Dee swings around her. Alicia's heavy frame bends back and up to breathe. A sheath knife unseen is pulled from Dee's pocket.

As expected, resistance is pitiful.

Gun cloaked in by his hip, Vic does a slow eye crawl of the cul-de-sac. The jungle of undergrowth by the road, a stretch of long white sheds, the silent face of that two-story house.

Shay points to a shape that bulks against the inside of the screen door, "Vic."

He sees it's Hugh Englund.

"Are you going in," Burgess asks Shay, "or what?"

The wind zithers up branch and weed. Vic orders Burgess to be quiet. The sound carrying on that warm canyon air is ghostly feminine, and all too frighteningly human. Like the song of sirens Ulysses heard when bound to the masthead.

Landshark on the shortwave to Freek, "What is happening?"

Freek: "They're just standing in the driveway."

Landshark looks to Terry, holding behind the wheel, understanding all that cannot be done.

"I want to run," says Landshark. Terry's face corners up a barbed stare. "I want to, but I won't anymore. I swear. Tonight has burned a hole right through me I know I have to fill."

Dee grabs Alicia by the hair. "I'm only sorry I couldn't use the shotgun like I promised I would."

Alicia never sees the knife blade that mines her flesh all the way down to the jugular.

Shay starts for the front door. As she passes Vic she brushes against him. "We'll be alright," she says.

He is staring at the tiny cottage. At dim apparitions moving against the windows.

"Vic, do you hear me?"

He thinks back to what he heard preached once as a boy in a desert chapel on the Boulevard of Dreams: Fate's elaborate framework waits its turn with flawless simplicity.

He looks down into her face, into the blood-warm tensions he wished he did not see there: "Cada diá mejor."

Every day getting better, I can live with that, she thinks; "Cada diá mejor."

Dee watches the travesty of blood on the bare wood floor. The body's frantic entanglement of nerves and physical mismotions. The writhing and belly slaps like a fish trying to pull away from death.

Paint cans are kicked. Some totter. One falls and coughs out its inky cream.

Shay reaches the screen door. Can see small reefs of smoke across the light. Can see Charlie Foreman at a desk by the fireplace. Can see the outstretched legs of a man off to one side. Can see a grim-faced Hugh Englund leaning against a window sill. Can see too much, and too little. Can feel heartsounds and fear. Can feel the faint figure of her mother stalking the darkness.

You never walk into a madhouse and try to handicap the outcome. Her hand reaches for the door.

———

A choking mouth full of cloth. Blood and iced-cream color latex. A disparate and desperate collage swirled up by thick flailing legs.

Dee's ghost face, her suture line eyes. Fed by speed, by hate, by fury, by need, by money, have turned the horror of death's last clawings into a downward cyclone of exhilaration without end.

As Vic watches Shay she opens the screen door. She takes one step, turns, looks back. Framed by a gauzy lit room, facing that fragile opening and where it leads, he knows, she is proving it now, showing herself and him, that she is willing to take his place all those years ago.

SIXTY
FOUR

Dee's breath leaves quick foggy stains on the window as she stares out toward the driveway. Shay is nowhere to be seen, which means it's starting.

Shay crosses toward the desk where Foreman sits. The living and dining room are an open floor plan in that old California style. The low-key light from the desk lamp has left the upper reaches of the room a moody black, has bled most of the light out across the floor casting faces adrift in shadow and leaving them difficult to read.

But she can smell the men over the cigarettes and coffee. That nerve burned sour odor she can almost taste on the warm air.

Foreman puts down the scissors. "First thing, we didn't kill your mother."

"I'm just day labor now," Shay tells him, "so you don't owe me an answer." She points to a thick brown cardboard folder on the desk. "Are those the papers?"

"Harold Ridden practically asked me to—"

"Was he at the goddamn trailer park?! I must have missed him there."

Foreman gears down into a grubby silence. The old man, sitting in a high-back wood chair by the door, leans forward. Underfoot the floorboards creak as he does.

"Why don't we do this civilized," says Shay. She looks at each of those four burned-down bastards imagining what kind of meal they have in mind for Dee Storey's slit. "Alright? I look the papers over—"

"What deity did you ride in on?"

She turns to Pettyjohn. His tarpaper eyes try to stare her down through the heavy bandages.

"I walked in alone. Which should tell you something." She faces Foreman now, "My mother wasn't fucking with you about those photographs. There are people running you down. You don't want any more trouble."

She is met by a stiff silence. "I know what you're thinking, but let it go."

"Relax," says Hugh Englund, as he approaches from the dining room, "we don't want any trouble either." He pushes the file toward Shay for her to look at as he gives the others a quiet glare. "We reached the same conclusion you did." And when his look falls on Foreman he stresses the point. "Let it go."

Dee strikes out through the dark. Grabs up a shotgun she left among the trees. Slithers along a riverstone wall overrun with vines. From there she can see Vic and Burgess waiting by their cars. Talk about the bookends of your life.

A dozen thoughts cross-pump through her mind. They've got the money. It's probably in the Mercedes. If she could cover that sloping grass without Vic seeing, without him getting off a shot she could kill them both where they stand. Her eyes cut toward the cottage.

"What's taking so long in here?"

Burgess looks to Vic for an answer but his attention is on each black fold of darkness that might hide Dee Storey. He knows she is out there somewhere. And that if she wants the money bad enough, if she wants him dead hard enough, it is these few minutes when they are most vulnerable.

The dry California air is playing havoc with the senses. It's like putting a little rawbone under your nose, lighting it, then breathing in until those synapses feel as if they've been torched.

Burgess tries to burn off a bad case of nerves by rocking against the side of the Mercedes, and mumbling to himself acidly, "Come to the colonies . . . Here's a chance to begin again in the golden life of—" He spots Shay. "There she is!"

Dee can see Shay at the cottage door waving Burgess in. He starts for the near side of the Mercedes. He opens the car door, sets the two briefcases down on the hood.

Dee straddles the moment. Vic is still on the far side of his car and it's forty yards of open ground. If he sees her?

The Mercedes door slams shut. Burgess lifts both cases. Vic moves toward him.

Just a few more feet. All the drugs and desires that feed and fuel her blood need just a few more feet. Need him for one moment to cut those brittle head movements that leave her vulnerable to being seen too soon.

Shay disappears back inside the house. The wind blows down the canyon. As Burgess passes Vic, Vic lockarms him. "Change of plans."

Dee sees Vic begin to take the briefcases from Burgess. Something isn't right. A panic moves over her like some huge tarp.

"What are you doing?"

Vic's eyes scan each crimp of possible cover, each night-hidden cranny, each quilted corner of concealment from where a kill could come. It won't be like the desert.

"When Shay comes out with the papers, take them fast and go. Pedal down. No looking back. And don't glitch it."

"I don't understand all this."

Burgess looks upon an impassive stare and Vic uses the truth for all its hateful potential. "You will later."

Freek's voice in a panic over the shortwave says: "Something weird here. Vic is taking the money in, not Ridden!"

Terry's whole body locks. Landshark jumps out of the car as if it were suddenly on fire.

Dee's mind is a mad thoughthole. Who decided this? Vic . . . Shay? Has she turned into a little cum stain for that fuck? Her best, best chance is burning down before her eyes as that odd hitch of a walk presses into long, quick strides toward the cottage.

Burgess slides down into his Mercedes. Starts the engine, reaches for the glove compartment.

Dee takes a hard angle back up toward the trees where she can cross the cul-de-sac unseen and come down behind that row of white sheds.

Landshark pleads to Terry for an answer, "Why is he doing it?"

Terry pulls two fists up toward his face. "You don't know? You of all people!"

Dee phantoms her way down the pine-strewn asphalt. Crabs between a small tractor and the corner of the last shed closest to the cottage. She has a forced angle on the porch. Her stitched up arm throbs. She fights back the insanity that Shay is somehow behind this.

The wind increases across the rim of the canyon and over the ridge-line that was once the St. Francis Dam. On the cottage roof a scraping affray of low hanging branches as Vic looks from window to window.

As Landshark leans against the car window his voice crumbles, "I'm responsible for this."

Terry tells him, "We have to get those papers."

"Please don't let anything happen to him."

"I know, you know, he knows. We came for the papers. And you're no more responsible than any of us. We all own a piece of it."

Vic climbs those sagging steps keeping out of the light as best he can and when he's close enough to the single white bulb burning above the front door he takes one briefcase and, using it as a scythe, cuts right through the bulb.

There is an explosive pop. The shattering of glass. The old man is rocked out of his chair as the porch goes black. Pettyjohn and Foreman are quickly up, but unsure.

Englund calls out. "Burgess?"

Vic eases his way into the shadowy breach of the screen door. Shay cannot believe it's him standing there with the money.

"Well," says Pettyjohn, "it's Charlie Manson."

Vic keeps his face down. "The briefcases were too heavy for Mr. Ridden to carry, so I brought them."

The men in the room stand there like surprised creatures leaning on the others with a look until Foreman orders Vic, "Bring the money in."

"I have a different idea," he says. "I'm gonna let you see the money." He squats down. "From here." And he does. He sets both cases down cautiously. He snaps the clips open on the first. Pushes it to the light. Then closes it back and sets it down. He repeats the process with the second. He stands. "Give the girl the papers. As she walks out, I walk in."

Foreman repeats, "Bring the money here."

"Send the girl out."

"That won't happen," Pettyjohn shouts. Then he points to Shay, "And don't you move."

Shay has not moved. She has not taken her eyes off Vic, who hangs back in the half safety of that dark porch. Never once does he look at her.

The next seconds are at the edge of a catastrophe with Pettyjohn giving Vic rabid orders to "bring that money in." And Foreman glancing at the cellular. Alicia must have seen Vic take Burgess' place. Why hadn't she called? Maybe she thought it was nothing, but why?

The old man starts in like Pettyjohn, and Hugh realizes the room is about to be turned into a foxhole, which is what he does not want, so he takes the folder and presses it into Shay's hands. "Go on!"

It happens too fast for the men to react. Hugh bulls her across the room using the back of her coat as a leash and talking to that dark figure outside the screen door. "As she goes out, you come in." The men are behind Hugh arguing him down but he stays on it. "We're doing this my way. No trouble. None!" He yanks Shay as if she were a dog so Vic can see then says to him, "You, don't be stupid."

Hugh shoves her the last few feet. She hits against the screen door as he stands back. The men frame up in the four corners of the room. Shay, holding the heavy folder in both hands, uses her shoulder to edge the screen door open. As she slips out Vic skirts in around her.

They meet crossing the threshold. That slim piece of space where the profane and the sacred touch. Where all boundaries meet.

Needing to know, she asks him so the others can't hear, "Why . . . chance this?"

What words could fill the few seconds with all he feels? How does he answer, that when faced with the question of going where all the evidence is against survival he would willingly surrender that meager handful of demands which live under his name because he has felt the weight and symmetry of all things as never before.

That the earth he was born of, and buried in, and rose from with all its mistakes and madness, its struggles and sinister designs, its greeds and lack of apparent goodness, its appearance and disappearance of truth holds something breathtaking in its heart through the simple call to forgiveness and sacrifice.

How does he tell her? A silent pause, eyes that try to find hers through disordered shadows. In that moment of passing, he whispers, "I want to be found . . . willing."

Before she can tell him she understands, even with a look, he pushes her away from him, and on into the night.

Freek relays to Terry: "The girl is out and carrying something."

Dee watches Shay run down the porch steps.

Terry's voice comes back: "Where's Vic?" The screen door slams behind him.

Vic starts toward the desk. His thick bare arms carrying those two briefcases like some traveling salesman with a few samples of bad news. The collar is up on his buttoned jean coat. His hair loosely corners in his profile.

That doomed fraternity watches the briefcases be set down on the desk. Vic has noted the room is lit only by the desk lamp and a thin border of illumination coming through the closed swinging kitchen door. He can't get those rooms dark as a casket, but it might be close.

Shay runs toward Burgess' car. He gears in kicking out gravel to get as close to Shay as he can.

Vic glances at Pettyjohn, and then mocks that mental defective they met out in the desert, "Of course Charles Manson isn't my name. It's my essence."

Shay throws the folder into the Mercedes' passenger-side window. "Go on. Go back the way we came. That'll be the fastest."

"Aren't you coming," shouts Burgess.

"No!"

Vic's face turns to Foreman, who stands across from him behind the desk. "Of course, you know my name." Then he turns to Hugh who is in the archway between the dining and living rooms, "And so do you."

There is momentary confusion, followed by a contemptible silence and curious stares that border on the dumb. Vic presses his face toward the light, daring them.

The Mercedes speeds down that gravel road with Freek into the shortwave: "Our boy's moving."

And Dee watching Shay turn back toward the house. What has she done . . . what is she doing?

Hugh steps forward. Time begins to clear away. It is said the same things happen to you again and again until you tire of your failures. Then, a sudden growing black takes hold of Hugh's features. And that phrase from years ago, with all its sinister infamy replays inside his head: "One grave opened, as one grave closed."

"Sully . . . John?"

Vic can see Hugh clearly in that one second. A man's whole face is being deformed by fear and confusion.

"Fuckin' right," says Vic. Then he grabs the lamp, and flings it into Foreman's face.

SIXTY
FIVE

The room becomes a black womb of wordless seconds with Foreman stumbling back over the desk chair as he tries to dodge the desk lamp. Bodies scatter and pull guns. Hugh dogcrawls into the dining room, taking the table down behind him. A figure cuts across a thin fissure of light from the closed kitchen door. Dropping to one knee Vic fires. From Pettyjohn's belly a fierce blood grunt.

Shay leans into their car window to get the engine running for when and if Vic makes it out. As the Mercedes guns past her down the cul-de-sac Shay sees white electric pops inside the darkened windows. On the shortwave Freek calls it: "Burgess is humping for the road."

The living room is a blind of arrant madness. The old man claws past a drink-stained table and a cup of hot coffee topples onto his face, scalding him. A bullet hits Vic square in the back of that Kevlar vest and he body-slams against the desk. Pettyjohn drags across the floor, gasping in the heated air.

Dee rises. She moves toward the screams and flashsparks. Frames up one intent as she pumps a shell home into the shotgun's chamber. Help kill everyone in that cottage.

"Do you hear me, Terry?" shouts Freek. "Ridden is coming to you."

The Mercedes cuts into San Frasquito too soon and the right front satellites through a wall of underbrush and fallen tree limbs. The headlight is smashed in then torn loose before the car swerves back out onto the road.

Foreman fires at Vic through the desk. Needles of wood are blown into his cheekbone and jaw. Rushing to the porch Shay sees the bent outline of her mother against a claw of low-hanging branches. Dee begins to fire at the house. Shay dives to the ground as glass lightnings inward. Teeth-sized shards cut apart the powder-burned air. A collapsing window frame hangs against the night sky like St. Andrew's

Cross. Vic swim-kicks back and away toward the wall with blood streaming out the open tears of his face.

Terry starts to edge their car out from that shield of trees. No lights, the shocks hitching over the ribbon scraped ground. "Get Rog on the line. Tell him it's about to happen. No screw-ups now."

Landshark squeezes between the buckets. He's hanging there, working the shortwave on the back seat, sweating through a dozen panics when Freek hits back on the line: "There's shooting. Jesus Christ, I can see flashpoints." He's starting to lose it, "Cue me up. Can I blow outta here?"

Terry shouts, "Tell him to keep his ass where it is. I got to know if anything comes down the canyon."

Landshark switches gears. His fingers spider nervously at the switches. He's wedged up between the seats like a huge child, laying it on Freek while Terry stares into the black pitch that is San Frasquito.

The cul-de-sac is just minutes away. Vic is just minutes away. Landshark can feel the terrible thing that could happen. It tears right into the promise he made to see this through so he has to sit there and recite every reason why he can't and won't go help him, knowing it will have to be enough to live with, later.

Pettyjohn snakes toward Vic, bleeding, the last few feet exhausted miles of dragging distance for a set of dead legs.

The old man stands. Tries to cross that gray shapeless length of room when a blue shock flashfires through the window and wall beside him. He is scatter hit in the lungs and chest. His body lunge falls toward the screen door as Hugh keeps sliding back and away through the overturned furniture, back and away from that maelstrom in the living room trying to understand how Sully got here, how he hooked up with Shay, who is firing at them, and how he can stay alive now that hell has arrived.

The old man's hide coat has quarter-sized holes where his blood oils out. Pettyjohn fires up from the floor at a possible shape. Vic is hit. The bones in his wrist are shorn loose from the seams. The concussion and pain cause the nerves in his arm to whipsnap and the gun is thrown loose.

Foreman rails his way upright against the wall, firing over the desk as he comes. Vic uses his left hand to get at the knife he keeps hidden up inside his belt.

Shay crabs her way up the porch to try and reach Vic. She holds beneath the top step. Through the wire mesh she can make out reefs of yellow smoke, and funnels of welding fire there and gone with each shot. All this while the world outside goes on without notice.

Vic's knife blade strikes an open stance. Pettyjohn can't hold the gun steady any longer and his shots ride wild into the lightless void. Vic lunges toward the isotropic barrel eye of that gun. He lands on Pettyjohn's back. He finds the mark he means to teeth. The knife digs straight down into the neck at the base of the skull. The spine is pithed. The blade shanks bone and snaps. A rolling wail comes up and out of that gauzed and bloody face as Pettyjohn falls blindly toward death. The years of him now mindless and useless space filled with the last of his horrid, wracked agony, agony that Hugh can hear but cannot answer. Will not answer. He'd warned them. He'd warned them all.

A single headlight snowballs down San Frasquito.

Landshark squints to see better, "Is that a motorcycle?"

"Freek didn't say anything about a motorcycle."

"Maybe he missed—"

They should be moving, but uncertain they wait and then the Mercedes hits it past them flat out.

"Fuck!"

Terry guns the car across those black acres of furrowed ground, leaving a wheel wall of rock and dust behind them. They better make the road fast or lose him. It's a bone-jerking charge until they hit asphalt and then the ass end tops out before Terry can right her.

As Vic twists Pettyjohn's gun loose from his bloody fist Foreman leaps over the desk. Feet sky past Vic, who crossbows his arms, and Foreman half trips but keeps on drag-running across the dark with a chair tumbling over behind him. As Shay reaches the porch Dee sees her and screams, "Get away! Get away, I said!" But Shay keeps on for the screen door, which slaps open in her face as that junkyard dog of an old man staggers right down on her.

Burgess is pushing that 450SL through curves of canyon. Dizzy from all the adrenaline that's pumped through his system, frightened he'll faint where he sits, his mouth hangs open like a scoop shovel trying to drag in air. He hits a long straight of canyon and sky. His eyes wolf in on that single beam of lit road before him. That's all there is. That's all, until something stars in the rearview mirror. He looks back as the speedometer tops seventy and there they are, white cold white and coming fast.

Foreman straight-arms the kitchen door. Vic drags himself up after him. That ruined old man with his tilting face has finally got hold of something he can try and kill before he dies and, using his arm as a club, bludgeons Shay to the porch floor.

As Dee moves toward the cottage a figure crosses a row of kitchen windows and point-blank she fires. Foreman's whole body bends around the scattershot that has scored him from cheekbone to thigh. He stumbles into the laundry room alcove and collapses. His blood smeared face slaps up against the washer. He holds there trying to keep from losing consciousness.

An old woman trembling in the dark calls the police and tells them she hears gunfire somewhere down below near the entrance to the cul-de-sac. Shay kicks her way upright retreating along the porch and away from the old man's almost involuntary clawing as she tries to get at her gun. Vic hits through the swinging door just as a second burst of whitefire tears apart the kitchen. Glass shatters. The phone is blown off its wall mount and up into the ceiling. Stinging rawburns mark Vic's neck and shoulder where the shotgun has put its teeth to him. The old man's eyes roll wildly as he sees the girl arm up a semiautomatic and he stagger-charges her behind a poisoned cry.

Vic drops hard behind the doorjamb as he sees Foreman in the laundry room getting ready to make a fight of it. The Guardian hits the old man clean. A small fleshhole in his throat spurts blood and he falls like so much stone, chop-blocking Shay's legs and sending her back first off the porch and into a mire of thorny hedges and rock.

Closing in on Burgess, Landshark hands Terry a mobile police light. He gets an arm out the window and clips it to the roof.

When Burgess sees that twirling red specter he crumples. Is it some private security? An unmarked sheriff's unit?

"He's not pulling over."

There're mop stains of blood on the floor around Foreman, who fires at the kitchen door as it swings back shut. Threads of light follow through the bullet holes where Vic huddles against the dining room wall. His right hand is practically powerless, but he concretes up all his strength as he takes hold of a dining room chair.

Dee moves across a shank of branches beside the house. Vic kicks in the kitchen door and Foreman fires. The chair is flung at the alcove and he fires again. It caroms off the wall and strikes down at his head. As he flings it off him Vic keels in low under the windows angling across the smoke-filled kitchen, emptying Pettyjohn's gun. One shot bores out the soft flesh of Foreman's stomach with such force the blasted metal pings when it smashes into the washer wall behind him.

Burgess wades through the grim apprehension of who's behind him and why. He sees how far back that turning red still is. Maybe they haven't nailed his plates. Could he outrun them to Copper Hill?

Over the shortwave Rog calls out a minivan has just turned up into San Frasquito. Landshark can feel the fugitive fear that must be having at Ridden. He faced that truth once and lied his way to a clean bill of health. Well, not quite.

But as they keep eating up ground a stark and striking exhilaration suddenly comes over Landshark. A testament to some dark pleasure that he is there chasing down a life.

"Why doesn't he pull over?"

Vic crawls the kitchen floor for Foreman's gun as Dee chambers in a shell. She can hear the cum stain screaming for Vic as a shadow arcs the discolored kitchen ceiling. Hugh rises along a black break of dining room wall with one fucking thought: *survive*. Get out and survive.

Dee moves with manic rhythm toward the laundry room door, her chest heaving, wire fingers ready, jaw curved in like a claw, and fires. The barred opaque Plexiglas implodes at Vic and he reels back. The room around Foreman's body fills with the sickening odor of blue-yellow smoke as the shotgun barrel parts the bars and fires again.

Stop or run. That red light is engraved in his rearview mirror now so he's got to decide. Stop or run. Burgess glances at the folder on the front seat. His mind begins to click up lies for questions he might be asked: What happened to your headlight? Why were you speeding from that cul-de-sac? He then remembers the gun Dee gave him in the glove compartment with his registration.

Shay's at the screen door, pressed to the clapboard siding, flat on the porch. What light there is from the sky diminishes by feet to nothing. She presses to mesh and at the edge of that black garden of space she sees a hand lying on the floor like a crab upturned, and calls out quietly, "Vic?"

The back of Ridden's head is awash in high-beams.

"Why isn't he stopping?"

Terry reaches under the dash. "He'll stop soon enough or we run 'im off the road."

"What about the car coming up the canyon?"

Terry has no answer, and just then the night around Burgess fills with a jerry-rigged siren, a blood sound that sends terror right through him. That says the altar of consequences might be looking for its next Isaac. That has him frantically reaching for the gun in the glove compartment.

"We'll see what that shit does now."

Dee moves through the chest-high weeds behind the house. They are windbent and their brittle tips click together and sound like beetles talking. The shotgun barrel still breathes a little smoke as she walks the length of that sagging gray shingled cottage watching the darkened windows and listening for anyone who might still be alive besides her cum stain of a daughter.

A voice carries to the screen door, "Shay . . . I'm here."

Hugh holds his breath as best he can to try and get a feel for where Vic might be.

"Did you see Englund?" he asks.

"No."

"The old man?"

"He's dead."

Tongue stuck up in his jaw, Hugh now knows he's alone. The dead have seen to it. Then he hears Vic tell Shay, "Your mother's outside somewhere with a shotgun."

The Mercedes begins to slow. Its tires track off onto the earthen shoulder. Burgess looks down at the gun wrapped up in his hand. He is torn between survivals. Maybe all this is nothing but a bum headlight, or a little too much foot and he should ditch the gun while he's still got a wall of dirt kicking out from the tires he can use as cover.

Dee Storey is alive. The words eat into the depths of Hugh's system like a venom. His eyes close. The silent cursings of a speechless fool hellholed, desperate, and all but done. Then he hears Vic whisper, "I need a gun. Do you have your gun?" And a small window of hope opens up inside him.

A sandbox held together by rotted boards, a rusty swing: The lost time of childhood marks Dee's passing as she circles through the ratty brush on the far side of the house. The police will come, someone in the long corners of that cul-de-sac must have heard the shooting. She knows. Battered minutes is all she has, at best, to cash out.

Terry belts his 608. "Once I get him flat on the seat you pull up. I take the papers, his keys, we go . . . right?"

Landshark looks out into a feral landscape. He stares at the taillights as the last dirt snows down on the windshield. I've gone up in the Navion, his mind says, I've gone up after seeing the cotter pins there on the table.

"William, can you handle this?"

Crouched down, Vic's good hand moves across the desk like a divining rod, cautious and slow, soundless, trying to find something of weight. "Slide the gun in from there, then go."

"No."

His fingers nearly tip over a glass ashtray, "Please . . . just do as I ask."

Landshark slides behind the wheel. Waves of leaves tangle up the branches that cover Dee's approach to the porch. Hugh grips a .45 against his chest, double-handed, doing his best police stance at the gritty turn of a hinge. The world is closing in.

The chrome autoloader skates a runner of skylit floor, but stops short. In the sideview mirror Burgess sees a man skiff the darkness pulling out a wallet badge. Numb and frightened, does he use the gun? Dee sees through bristling leaf shadows her daughter edging up the porch wall looking in at something, but what.

Vic crawls across Pettyjohn's body where the blood has formed shallow pools in the folds of his gray-green shirt. The Mercedes door wings out. Ridden is up and around. Vic flings the ashtray. The light from the minivan frames Ridden's back and Landshark is the first to see the shiny metal in his extended hand. He hits the horn, screams "Gun!"

Hugh steps flat-handed into his shot, fires at the stone-skipping sound. Dee wheels toward the eyelet windows that pupil spark with pistol fire. There's inhuman work to be done, so let's get it fuckin' on.

Terry's raven frame hits fast for the asphalt. Vic fires back at gunfire but misses and Hugh finds the hallway and is gone. Burgess tries to shoot over the square corner of car trunk and Landshark's hands move almost autonomically upon a thought. You can't let him hurt Terry. You can't let him—

The screen door swings open and shapes warp in with shadows as Vic grabs Shay and drag-lines her away from a flashlight burst that funnels up the hallway walls.

The dining room windows behind them are blown in and they bend under a cyanic wave of splintered wood and glass. She grabs his face. The short life of seconds. Is he alright? Bits more of time. His bad hand rising in a painful arc, terrifying with blood, touches her.

"Get to the car and get out. I'll see you in—"

Another shot rides the other dining room window and its frame like a pinwheel right across the room.

"Let's both just—"

"Englund can't be left alive. Your mother—"

Another shot. From wall to wall, the inside of that cottage is one gray licking stench.

Terry fires his stopper up through the trunk. Its sheer concussion sends Burgess swimming back into an onrushing chrome and headlight grin. Hugh pulls a blanket off a bed and using it as a shield hurls himself out an oblong window as boots and stark breathing hunt him out.

Ridden is flung into the air and lands on Terry's hood. The minivan's headlights swamp the road then swerve. Vic leaps into the darkness chasing Hugh's path through the chest-high weeds.

Landshark swings the wheel, eyes half closed in terror. The Mercedes is scored. Briars scourge Hugh's legs, his hands, his neck. Burgess batons across the engine in sledgehammer thuds as it charges on. Vic lunges through a black pool of vines after a memory he knows too well.

Glass and skull collide. Screeching tires. Terry scrambles to his feet. The minivan spins out onto sloping sand. A jaw is riven, teeth rent. Bones sever before Landshark's eyes as a face is turned into the crushed imposter of a living thing.

Shay feels her way along the smoke-choked hall. Landshark brakes. The body spills lifeless off the hood as he leaps from the car to make sure Terry is alright. Hugh crosses an ascending crease of open ground. Vic spots him and fires. Terry grabs the folder from the Mercedes. Hugh's side pinches but he keeps running and the woods swallow him whole.

The dark is cut with the sound of the screen door and Shay stops, but too late—Landshark looks back across the well of that canyon as a man steps frightened and clumsy from the minivan. On the shortwave Freek's voice in high thin panic. A car is coming down San Frasquito, there's still shooting, he won't stay any longer— The world is collapsing all around them as Terry shoves Landshark back toward the car.

Stepping out of that coalsmoke frieze is Dee Storey. Mother and daughter stare at each other like strangers. Hugh rams past sabered branches that tear his arms, but the ground is getting harder to climb. The vines strangle his every step. The bullet is taking its share of blood.

Terry fires a warning shot past the rim of that turning police car light to chase the man into the minivan. To keep him from getting close enough to fill a face with details.

The short life of seconds. Bits more of time. The shotgun rising in a painful arc of seconds as Dee demands one answer, "Who are we?!"

The man can't coward back into the driver's seat fast enough. The minivan kicks up sand speeding into the asphalt road with the driver's door slapping wildly at the darkness. Another set of headlights comes pouring out of a curve down San Frasquito as Terry's car tramples over Ridden's legs.

Vic sweeps into a nightshade of tall pines, his body living on the last fumes of adrenaline. He can hear his old friend, his partner, his superior's locomotive breathing slip closer and closer and closer.

Shay looks over the shotgun barrel at the endless and unbending stare that repeats, "Who are we?!" And her answer is filled with threat, "We aren't."

The last view of San Frasquito Landshark has is a rear window, wide-angle nightmare of a body crumpled up on the asphalt and sets of headlights cutting sharply to avoid a crash.

"Do you think we can be identified?"

"Get Freek on the shortwave," Terry orders. "Tell him to get out. Tell him what's happened."

The short life of seconds. The last bits of time. And all the panics Landshark ever felt seem almost unworldly as the road blackens in behind him.

"We're gonna have to dump this car and fast."

"Do you think we can be identified?"

The sheer exhaustion, the bleeding and confusion have Hugh scrambling at the rim of a sloping ridge to make a fight of it. He aims at the juggernaut of sound coming at him through the dark. Fires at the bullrushed thicket, into the green-black wilds. Into the mad hitching wall of bracken and branch. But nothing stays that charge against the held-together dark until it becomes a man and the space between them dissolves in a fury of seconds carrying both down into a ravine.

"Is he dead?"

The shotgun touches Shay's face. She sees her mother's glare momentarily shift to wherever that hall might lead and says, "You don't have much time, if you want to get out with the money."

"Is he dead?"

To keep her from following that look Shay tests the end. She slaps down the barrel, shoves past Dee, starts for the living room, repeats, "You don't have much time if you want to get out with the money."

Dee turns on Shay.

Bodies grunt and fall. Vic won't let go of that swag-assed fraud as they tumble down the hillside. The gravel ballast and snapping limbs tear up their backs until they bottom in an earthstone ravine, feet deep with leaves and rot.

Dee tracks her daughter up the pitched hall and finds her coming about by the desk holding a briefcase.

"Is he dead?!"

Both men staggering and spent try to come up first out of the decay for the kill, bleeding wrecks on the dire side of the darkness only to discover one has a gun, and one doesn't.

"Is he dead?!"

Shay throws the briefcase at Dee. "You don't have much time if you want to get out with the money."

Down Bouquet Canyon sheriffs' cars hit turns, their tires handicapped but holding, the men tight but ready.

Shay crawls the floor. Her hands doing a braille search for the other briefcase, bumping into the bloody remains of that bandage-faced shit.

Dee shouts, "Is he dead?!"

The Guardian, small as it is in Vic's hand, can't be missed. Hugh sinks into the rotting mulch, blood-spent and broken. Vic starts toward him, the leaves bristling about his legs. All that's left for Hugh Englund is the sacrilege of screaming, "Look at you. You're dying. Look at the blood. It's over. You're gonna die just like I am."

"No," warns Vic, "not like you."

Shay flings the other briefcase at Dee. She stands, starts for the door. "Kill me here if you want. 'Cause he ain't dead. And he isn't gonna be."

Vic lifts the Guardian. It is just a kiss out of Hugh's reach. The chrome eyelet with its black pupil marks time.

Dee charges out of the house, both briefcases locked up in one hand, the shotgun in the other. Shay makes for her car. Dee is hard behind, her fifty-caliber eyes locked into Shay's back.

Hugh keeps on with his frantic mantra as the gun steadies. His end will come on his knees, in a narrow ravine at night where no lie, no planted evidence, no conspiracy can save him. And but for the dry-standing pines and brush, not much different from the end he helped prepare for the man about to kill him.

As Shay swings into the driver's seat Dee strikes her down with the shotgun barrel across her neck.

The Guardian fires. A white-tailed moment followed by a black hole exploding out of Hugh's cheekbone. The body lurches backward head first into a bed of soft decay.

Dee flings the briefcases into Shay's car. She pulls the half-conscious girl by the hair into the back seat. Shay's arms swim at the air.

Vic steps away from the body. Full will spent, he collapses. He clings to trancelike moments and tries to gather up what's left of himself. His jaw moves, giving the order to rise.

Shay's face slams against the briefcases. Her stomach swills up into her mouth as the car starts a fast sharp gliding turn out the cul-de-sac.

Vic's legs are reedy at best the first moments he is upright. Weakly his head looks down at his legs and arms and chest. It is as if the wind had blown all the blood squandered to get here across his body.

He can feel somewhere inside that Kevlar vest is a wound, an unseen fragment. Another little story he'll have to carry with him if he expects to leave this canyon, alive.

THE BURIAL

SIXTY
SIX

———

Shay is strung across the back seat and floor trying to fight waves of bloody-headed sickness. The briefcases clop against her face with each curve. The future is being left behind as a black-and-white fever of road shadows speeds past the interior roof. She can hear her mother's verbal slashing through the thin reef of space that separates them.

She has been here before. She has been in this speeding coffin before. She has done her lockdown time when they tried to run from the black sacrament of that night in the Mojave Preserve. She can see her mother's prescient shape against a momentary light. Feels the black air of her words, "You've got to be still, girl!"

She will not cross that border again. Not this time. Her mind begins to twist around one thought . . . get back to Vic. She uses it as a lathe to hold her muscles. Her body feels like marble as she begins to move.

"Stop the car." She can barely sop up enough air so the words sound like what they are. "Stop the car."

As her fingers feel for something to grip and get herself upright the car seems to wing sideways. The raw breaks of an unpaved road hammer at the chassis. Black sky pouring in the windows is cut by huge, weathered concrete boulders with wire rods protruding violently from their surface. The remains of that concrete dam flung a half mile down-site near a century ago.

The car hits a rise then skids down to an ugly halt. Dee jumps out of the car screaming. "You're not going to stand there and let me handcuff your future to mine." She pulls open the back door and half drags Shay upright. "Well, I won't allow the utter annihilation of my life 'cause you've gone cum stain."

Shay sneaks a glance back up the road. They have turned off San Frasquito into what looks like a long, open wash. Dee pulls the shotgun out through the window and wields it around. She is ghost white revenge. She points the gun, "Look over there."

Shay follows the length of that barrel to where a mound of dirt rises against the stony white earth about fifteen feet from the car. It is a grave. Ready made and waiting.

Sheriffs' cars strike up into the cul-de-sac. They form a wide V and stop. Officers step out into the flashing strobe of their lights.

The place is empty and still but for a single mobile on the cottage porch back among the trees. The officers begin to spread out, talking among themselves, to see what, if anything is wrong.

Dee's eyes move from the grave to Shay. "That was for your friend. But maybe now, we should all just crawl into it."

Shay can see all the flaws are just looking for the slightest crack to charge through and finish this. If there's black work to be done Shay intends to meet it in silence.

"Nothing?!"

One side of Shay's head is deaf. Words and night sounds are watery. She wipes at the sweat on her face. But she does not answer.

The silence poisons Dee. The silence she knows points to some primal extinction that has taken place. The extinction of fear. And there is nothing more deadly to control than the loss of fear.

"I hate you," Dee craws, "because I needed you so much and that means nothing. And I still need you and I hate you all the more for not—"

She doesn't want to give up that much more of herself in what she is about to say so she just screams out, "Say something!"

Shay can feel a steadiness moving up through her legs. The groans inside her head have begun to clear enough for her to say, "You're on your own, fry girl."

It's a straight-on scornful rip that puts them right back at the dusky parking lot in Baker when they were watching John Victor Sully and Shay freaked.

Stepping up onto the cottage porch a deputy sees what looks like a human shape lying on the lawn. He puts a searchlight to it. It would seem as if someone had found a perfect spot to sleep off a drunk, except for the blood.

Dee's flameblack eyes go dead. "You killed us both, only you don't know it yet."

The shotgun makes a sudden tilt and Shay jerks back expecting to be murdered, but the motion is just Dee starting toward the car. "Wherever you're fuckin' goin', you can walk."

Dee pulls the door open. Shay doesn't understand. Is this a little slash and burn before Dee shoots her down? Or is she actually letting her go. She can't read that sliding shadow of a face, but Shay can't let her wheel out of here. There's too much uncertainty back up that road. Is Vic alive? Is he lying somewhere too wounded to go on? Did he get away already with the car that's hidden up in the brush?

Dee steps back into the driver's seat bending her head. Maybe she wants Shay to slit her own throat trying for the shotgun.

Under the intense scrutiny of her mother's glare Shay's harrowed poker face watches as the shotgun slips into the dark cab, watches as the door begins to close, watches those few inches where the black-gray barrel hangs in open space between side panel and window frame.

Those few inches, these fewer seconds may be all Shay has. They may mark the difference between dying and driving on. So she lunges, knowing full well the dates on calendars are always a long way off.

The barrel is caught in the vise of her chest shouldering into the door. Her left arm rakes through the window leaving deep marks down the side of her mother's face.

Dee reacts with fiendish speed, throwing herself at the door. She is half out of the car but Shay has gotten a grip-hold of the barrel and pulls Dee hard. Dee's arm is extended and again Shay throws her full weight at the door and it slams in hard on Dee's sewn-up arm.

A blunted hiss. Dee's grip falters. She kicks at the door. The rim clips Shay across the mouth and she staggers back as the gun stock hits the stony ground and totters over.

That slanting bench of sparse terrain becomes a deathbed of screaming mouths and eyes gone electrocuted wide. They tumble to the earth locked in a death grip. Mother and daughter claw and crawl and kick toward that shotgun, a possessed witch and the tail of some great beast turning over and over and over as boots cudgel dust inter-knit with flailing arms. Hands rake chests and throats but that black-gray barrel lies beyond either's grasp.

Wild and desperate. The wind blows sand across the lee side of the grave. The manifest language of human violence in the scarred gasps. The atavistic, contorted faces. The sheer physical anarchy until Dee manages to slip her fingers down inside that coffin chain necklace.

Shay's head is snapped back like a puppet's. Dee pushes a knee up into the girl's spine. Shay thrashes from side to side but the chain won't break. She can't reach back and land a solid blow to free herself. A strangle line of white cords across her throat but the chain won't break. A wire mark of blood takes its place but the chain won't break.

Shay begins to lose consciousness. Black folds in on black from the corner of her eyes. Dee's voice somewhere on the deaf side of her head vengefully, "I begged you. I begged you."

Falling into the deep well of the lost. There in a canyon where the dead have a long history of complaints. Frantic life is slipping off; Shay tries to find strength in the lie her mother used against her.

I am stronger than you are . . . Pitted words . . . I am stronger than you are . . . The neck muscles tighten down to try and twist her neck to relieve the chokehold the chain has on her windpipe.

I am stronger than you are . . . She can see Vic fighting her mother in the dark of the preserve . . . I am stronger than you are . . . His teeth trying to tear into her neck as Dee scoured the ground for a rock to kill him with.

Their bodies at wrenched and tortured angles. Shay's hand scars the cold ashy sand for a stone. Her fingers are going numb.

I am stronger than you are . . . the neck flesh is grotted one link at a time till the windpipe is clear.

I am stronger than you are . . . and with the last few pockets of will she can pull together before all memory is blindly dead, Shay tears loose from her mother's grasp.

The chain snaps. Shay fishswims the ground bellowing in air, looking for something to use as a weapon. Her mother is back at her, just as Shay grabs a handsize pyramid of concrete from the damn rubble.

Shay is rolled but manages one swing. One. The tan bludgeon lands a clean blow to Dee's skull. Everything inside her head lights. Burns. She collapses back against the mound of dirt used to make the gravehole.

Shay crabs away from the agonized cry. She finds the shotgun. Huddled like a beast just escaped from a trap she comes around to face her mother.

Dee lies against that mound on her side. The skull above and behind the left eye is cracked like an eggshell and bleeding badly. Blood streams out both nostrils and into her mouth. She tries to sit but can't. She tries to speak but can't. Her boots move as if they thought they could walk or rise but they leave only a few trickles of dirt in their wake.

Shay approaches the woman who has owned her life. Her breathing is fevered. Even with Dee lying there broken Shay is afraid Dee has some power to will herself past a mortal wound.

Another step closer. Dee's eyes flit then freefall toward where her fingers lie. They begin bit by bit to speak in sign, "Please . . . please."

It is a faltering mimic of the last few moments Shay and Dee had together in that motel room. The flesh cannot perceive what the flesh means. Kill me . . . help me . . . spare me . . . forgive me. Or is it the last cold mock of the acid mind? The carved face of doubt cannot fathom truth from some trick. But each will have its cross to bear.

The barrel moves into position. Dee's fingers stop asking. Shay closes her eyes. She hears her mother's futile breathing, and the wind carving out the shape of hills.

She fires. Time is marked by one single explosion, by the fierce recoil of the stock. The bow of Shay's good ear is rocked with a stinging echo, her deaf ear holds the silence.

Shay opens her eyes. Not to see, but to see what to do next. Her mother taught her killing is not the hardest part. It is afterwards . . . the cleaning up. That is the difference many times between escape and discovery.

Shay buries her mother and the money in a grave of her own making, with a shotgun and a pair of hands as shovels. Her eyes are burning match heads against the dark around her.

She feels deep hatred, and uncontestable pain. But somewhere else inside her, beyond the history of things as they are come the rattling cries of remorse. Of pity. Of hurt for the lost being the rubble slowly covers.

The lasting piece of her birth that defies logic, that longed for a world before it all began, watches the wish being buried, once and for all.

SIXTY
SEVEN

———

Shay slows as she approaches the cul-de-sac. Up that silent glade searchlights move about, huge handheld fireflies that walk the trees.

Sheriffs probably. She keeps driving. Her heart hammers against her breastbone so hard it hurts. She's got to find the inlet where that car was—or still is—hidden. The speedometer barely tops ten miles an hour as she passes cubbyhole after cubbyhole. Nothing. Did she miss it? Maybe he got out? The wind washes down the canyon walls turning each pocket of dark stillness into mirages impossible to decipher.

Make him be gone. Make him be on his way to the desert where they planned to—

Her headlights catch something metallic back in a carbon-colored hollow. She eases off onto the opposite shoulder. She stares toward that long tunnel of trees. It's the car. He didn't get out. A wave of sickening fear overtakes her. Could he be dead? Or lying somewhere in the woods too wounded to move on. How would she find him? How?

She cruises with her foot off the pedal down into a slough of high weeds and comes to a stop behind a roosting line of willows. As she nears the road a siren cuts apart the dark.

She falls to the rocky soil just beneath where the asphalt dips away. A great wall of light fills the turn coming south then bears down on her. She presses herself flat. Her neck burns and she can feel where the blood has made the collar of her shirt wet. A wave of heat and exhaust speeds past taking the siren with it.

She crosses the road low to the ground with a terrible anxious speed. She reaches the trees. Up that long cave of branches she can hear the engine running.

Why is it running and the car just sitting there? Make it anything but what is foremost in her mind. Anything but that.

She moves into that arbor of treelimbs. The leaves talk in drifts

above her, the wind climbing, the night warm and beautiful. She can
see the muffler line of exhaust, and the barrel itself slightly trembling
from the heavy idle. But the car isn't moving. The engine's steady cadence, but the car isn't moving.

She calls into that dim windraked corridor, "Vic?"

Her voice falls away unanswered. She pushes past the sparring
leaves so to get to the driver's door. The dim insides of that car fill her
eyes, then turn her heart to stone as she finds him lying across the seat.

"Vic?!"

He does not answer. His hand still grips the steering wheel, his
fingers curled so tightly around the dark plastic the flesh across his
knuckles is streaked red and white.

He has to be alive. Shay forces the door out against a webbing of
undergrowth so she can squeeze in beside him.

She will not let the dark irrational have its way. Not if it is within
her grasp to stop it.

Landshark is a shivering wreck saddled up to his office television in
the immediate aftermath of this nightmare. Rog was so stressed he had
to be locked down for the night with sleeping pills. When the phone
rings Landshark is certain it's Terry with word the car they drove is
now just so much pressed sandwich metal.

But it's Freek. He blows right into a hyper monologue about how
he got out of the canyon and home. Landshark puts up with about ten
seconds' worth of this endorphin rush then asks the only question he
needs answered right now.

"I don't know if he got out," says Freek. Then he adds with detached honesty, "But by tomorrow morning, either way, the truth will
be self-evident."

Landshark hangs up on him.

By morning the only self-evident fact is the vampyric onslaught of reporters upon San Frasquito Canyon. The news landscape is littered
with phrases like "a grisly multiple homicide" and "gangland-style
shooting."

Burgess Ridden's name is leaked to the press as one of the victims
and there is a rumor a witness is working with authorities on a com-

posite sketch of two men, possibly posing as undercover policemen, who might well have committed at least one of the murders.

Landshark gathers all the information they have collected on Belmont. To that he adds the contents of the folder Terry took from Ridden's car. He types an anonymous note that reads: Information Magale Huapaya was collecting on the fraud behind the Belmont School site.

He mails this package of material to the woman reporter at *The Daily News* who had photographed Burgess and Harold Ridden arguing outside the construction site.

The dead are identified. Vic is not among them. Harold Ridden holds up under the devastating news as best he can; his wife collapses. His only statement, "We have no idea how or why something this terrible could have happened to our son."

Rog, Terry, and Landshark remain bunkered down in the office. Freek is too paranoid even to chance leaving his house. The first composite sketches get plenty of air time.

How close are the composites to the faces they created? Terry's isn't much more accurate than the one of Shay Storey back in '87. But Landshark's is enough to chill a man for years.

There are reports a car is discovered in the woods around three hundred yards north of the cul-de-sac.

Joseph Stinson, a retired attorney recuperating from prostate cancer surgery at Cedars Sinai, is shocked to find Charlie Foreman, Hugh Englund, and Jon Pettyjohn as victims in one homicide.

He remembers that triad of names from a far different case. He asks his son to pull the file. He calls the DA in Barstow and a friend who does freelance crime reporting for *The L.A. Times*.

For the first time since 1987, John Victor Sully's name is resurrected from the list of the dead and forgotten.

The Daily News lays out the case of forgery and corruption against Burgess Ridden and Alicia Alvarez. A paper trail soberly details their reinvention of the truth. Were they not dead, indictments would be handed down against them.

Harold Ridden issues a statement through his attorney: "Neither myself, nor my wife, nor any member of our corporate staff had any knowledge that my son was party to such activities.

"If these accusations prove true, we are deeply ashamed as loving parents and apologize to the community at large, which we have worked so hard to serve."

Lawsuits are filed against the San Fernando Land and Development Company, as Burgess Ridden was a corporate officer.

A news chopper gets its first look at the car being towed from the woods three hundred yards north of the cul-de-sac. It isn't the one Terry had hidden away, but the one driven by Shay and Vic into the canyon.

Burgess Ridden's personal life is good for miles of print and whole segments of show and tell. The monied boy who'd gone bad. The rise and fall of the well-to-do yuppie. It's a whole trash-'n'-carry basket of reality and rumor to pick from.

It is discovered he had a part-time girlfriend whose garage and house seem to be the scene of a homicide. When police go to question the daughter about the mother she is found to have quit her job as a bartendress at Nightland and disappeared just days before the San Frasquito Murders.

There are bullet holes in the wall of the daughter's living room and tiny blips of dried blood on the kitchen floor that end up being a perfect match for the blood in the garage. The blood is her mother's.

Photos of Dee and Shay Storey haunt the news. One is viewed as a victim, the other as a material witness in a murder case.

Homicide detectives work the long-termers at the Garden of Allah through a lineup of photographs to see which face among the dead might register a memory.

With almost incomprehensible innocence, the night manager, Roger Worth, picks out the jail-cell stare of Charlie Foreman as a sure possibility for the man in the motel room overheard by a prostitute, crying about a girl he'd murdered at the Belmont School site.

The ensuing weeks become a dense webwork of disconnected facts. Teams of detectives get no closer to understanding who the shadow players in this drama are, nor to the motive behind their execution of five people in San Frasquito Canyon.

John Victor Sully's graduation photo makes the news. Based upon the relationships between Pettyjohn, Foreman, and Englund that have come to light, the 1987 case against Sully takes on tragic proportions.

People wonder why he doesn't come forward to make his rightful claim of innocence. The usual suspect answers are thrown about.

One answer with the most teeth, but the least probability of truth, is that he did come back to make his claim of rightful innocence, and that San Frasquito Canyon is the living proof.

One of the most underappreciated truths of the human experience is that there will always be another crime to sweep across our consciousness, a new atrocity that will titilate and tantalize our imaginations. Feed our disdainful, prurient interests and pay the mortgage of a select few who get to capitalize on degradation for all it's worth.

A Christmas stocking of new disgraces catches the readers' fancy amidst all those toys they need to have. By New Year's the names of the dead have merged with the names of others murdered, and lost.

The only detail left to the backwater of sometimes-read columns: Is it safe or not to open a school on such contaminated ground?

Could this be a version of some god speaking?

All spring Landshark meets with a psychologist at his house to work through the agoraphobia. By summer he ventures out twice a week to the psychologist's office in Pasadena. By fall he begins facing the ultimate tests of the world on a daily basis.

Freek has nicknamed their little group Sgt. Pepper's Lonely Hearts Club Band. There are no indictments in the San Frasquito Murders. The Belmont School sits unfinished atop a twenty-three-acre bluff just west of downtown L.A. It must be boarded up for the winter against vandals and rain.

By late fall there is an earthquake at Joshua Tree National Monument, which is not far from where the first shot was fired in Baker, California. Memories are stirred across the landscape of one's life. Landshark collects the others and they venture to San Frasquito Canyon for the first time since that night.

Landshark climbs the earthen ridge that was part of the old dam. He walks that cracked and crumbling parapet of a roadway. Terry is there, so is Rog. Freek remains alone in the car.

The canyon stretches for miles in the deep velvet sunlight. From north to south it's alive with a brisk wind, and beautiful beyond comparison. Who would ever suspect all the pasts that have lived and died there.

Landshark looks down that seven story drop to the road, then back up to the cul-de-sac. The cottage sits partly hidden beneath a waving sheet of trees.

The obscure purpose of time is to be history's most privileged grave. It moves across the landscape, this silent unseen, obliterating all that was. Reforming the past again and again and again.

Landshark looks into the tranquil silence of that upland canyon. He has evolved from one murder to another. Where does that leave him, where does that take him?

In *The L.A. Times* "Letters to the Editor" column, kids who ultimately would attend the Belmont School write in. Even with its problematic dangers they are split over whether the facility should be opened or not.

From down below the first chords of a CD on the car stereo. The wind just takes the music right up to the crest of that long ridge.

We're Sgt. Pepper's Lonely Hearts Club Band—

Freek is on his own little ego riff.

Landshark walks to the edge of that green and brush-stroked salient. There alone, he speaks to the silence, "I see you all the time, you know. Whenever I look at that crying angel back of the bar. When I'm out on the terrace. Or when I walk past those two spots of road on Mount Washington where we talked at night."

The clouds are so strikingly white they seem engraved into the sky.

"I know you're alive. I know because you're a part of the living me. And I wanted to come here and tell you, I carry you around in my heart and . . ."

He hesitates. If only the world of words said as much as what he feels all about him.

"There is something of you I will always love. Not a day goes by, not a day, I don't wish. But I know better."

Into the deep reaches of that canyon goes a single car Landshark takes to watching, then he says, "Thank you for being my courage, when I had none. Thank you for being my friend."

EPILOGUE

EPILOGUE

The winter rains did not disturb a shallow grave south of the San Frasquito dam site. Nor did the desert winds that scraped dust from that sculpture of living ground.

Time goes about the slow and rightful task of cleaning Dee Storey's bones. Of returning her, properly attired, into the womb of the human race.

Soon, the only clue left to her demise will be a coffin charm necklace, so prominently featured in newspaper photographs around her daughter's throat, and now still clutched up tight in a broken angry fist.